TWIST OF FAITH

ALSO BY ELLEN J. GREEN

The Book of James

TWIST OF FAITH

ELLEN J. GREEN

THOMAS & MERCER

This is a work of fiction. Names, characters, organizations, places, events, and incidents are either products of the author's imagination or are used fictitiously. Any resemblance to actual persons, living or dead, or actual events is purely coincidental.

Published by Thomas & Mercer, Seattle

www.apub.com

ISBN-13: 9781503949065 (hardcover)
ISBN-10: 1503949060 (hardcover)
ISBN-13: 9781542047807 (paperback)
ISBN-10: 1542047803 (paperback)

Cover design by Rex Bonomelli

Printed in the United States of America

First Edition

For my children, Eva Elizabeth and Ian

CHAPTER 1

The house was a mottled gray color that reminded me of dead fish. Scaly paint peeled from the weathered clapboards. Shutters that looked like they might have been black at one time were now streaked and speckled, hanging at odd angles on rusted hinges. A tall, narrow, ugly house built on top of a steep hill. The wind was blowing hard, and for a moment I imagined the concrete foundation splitting, the house lifting from its resting place and landing on top of me as if it were my due.

My feet were planted on the first of eighteen stone steps leading to the front door. I glanced down, scanning the photograph again. The black-and-white Polaroid was grainy, but the house hadn't changed much. I wanted to go to the door and knock, but hesitated. What would I say if someone appeared? It would be easier if someone opened the front door, noticed me lingering—but the windows were dark, though the sun was just a splash of color in the western horizon.

I gulped the last of the cold coffee in the cardboard cup and climbed the steps. Curtains in a ground-floor window were parted, so I cupped my hands and peered inside; the glass was spotted with grime and offered only a shadowed view of an empty living room.

A voice startled me. "Can I help you?"

A woman stood at the bottom of the steps, her swaddled gray hair peeking out above a scarf, her hands stuffed deep in her coat pockets.

"Oh. I was looking for the owner, but it doesn't look like anyone is home. Do you live here, in this neighborhood?" I walked down the stone steps to meet her.

"I do, yes. And if you're going to wait for the owners, you better bring provisions. No one's living there now." Her thin lips moved upward to a hesitant smile. "What did you need?"

"Has it been empty long?"

"Six months with no tenants. I live next to the eyesore, so I know. Oughta just knock it down, I say. Why? Are you interested in renting it?"

"No. I was doing research . . ."

"What? Is it the anniversary already?" She pulled her scarf down a bit and cocked her head to the side. "That can't be for another couple of months yet."

"Anniversary?"

"The murders. Isn't that what you're researching?"

"No, I—"

"House is owned by a development company now." She shrugged. "I thought they'd tear it down, but they've been holding on to it. Five years I've been dealing with this."

I'd been backing up little by little as she spoke, unaware that the sidewalk dipped behind me. I lost my balance and the Polaroid slipped from my fingers. I leaned down and grabbed it, but not before she got a glimpse.

"Is that the house?" She took the black-and-white image from me and studied it.

I thought about Claire, the woman who'd adopted me, who'd raised me for twenty-two years. She'd always claimed to have no information about how I'd been found wrapped in a yellow blanket in the narthex of the Holy Saviour Catholic Church. Barely six weeks old, she said. Though I'd begged for more details, clues, information, she'd insisted there weren't any.

I suspected this wasn't the truth, because I had memories—unformed fragments punctuated by vivid recollections that didn't jibe with her version. It was the ongoing mystery of my life. A project never finished. I'd stumbled and fallen through my teenage years and young adulthood trying to sort it all out. Who had abandoned me, why, and when? When asking questions didn't help, I resorted to anger, manipulation, and, lately, alcohol to try and forget.

Digging through a crawl space after her death, I'd stumbled upon the photograph tucked away with other mementos from my childhood: school pictures, report cards, my high-school diploma, a yellow baby blanket. The photograph had been inside a blank white envelope, sealed shut.

Since the day I'd disturbed that seal and seen the image, I'd felt a growing sense of urgency—unfinished business, a chapter not complete. In the two weeks and three days since—while signing papers, helping Anais arrange for Claire's body to be flown to France, comforting Aunt Marie—I'd returned to the photograph daily: What had it meant to Claire and why had she kept it? The little lies and secrets she'd clung to during life were about to be wrested from her now that she was dead.

I stared into the woman's watery gray eyes. "Who was killed?" I asked.

She took so long to answer I wasn't sure she'd heard me. "Husband and wife. Both of them in there."

"Did you know them well?" Strands of hair came loose from my ponytail and I tucked them behind my ear. I was listening to her words, but my eyes wandered to the street behind her, waiting for something, though I wasn't sure what.

"Well enough to say good morning, or take in their mail when they were away, I guess. Let me see that picture again?" She held out her hand.

I gave it to her just as a car slowed near where we stood. An older man leaned out the window. "Excuse me. Can you tell me how to get to Flourtown?" He was talking to her, but his eyes were glued to mine. I held his gaze while she pointed him in the right direction, then I watched him pull away.

She turned back from the car, shaking her head. "Now what were you saying?" She held the picture out, studying the words—almost entirely faded—that were printed after the date.

"This date is the same as the date of the murders." Her finger ran along the back of the picture, and then she turned it over. "And it looks like it was taken from the lower part of the stone steps, about there." She pointed a few feet away. "Crappy Polaroid shot, but it's definitely that damned house." When she shoved it into my hand, it was clear she was afraid.

"What? What's wrong?"

"The door was left open. After they were murdered. The door was left open, that's how they found the bodies." She pointed. The front door of the house in the photograph was opened so wide a hint of the darkened foyer inside was visible. "Was that taken after those people were killed?"

Before I could answer, she demanded, "Is this some sort of prank? Because it isn't funny. It was horrible. They were beaten with a hammer. The mailman found them the next day . . . The man was lying on the floor in the living room. Where did you get that picture?"

"Like I said, doing research. Tell me about them, please, and what happened after they were killed."

I thought she was going to walk away from me, because her expression turned rancid, but she didn't. "The family name was Owens. Middle-aged man and woman. Destiny and Loyal Owens. He was a big guy. Might have caught a prowler in the house when they came home—"

"So they think it was robbery?"

She shrugged. "I didn't hear if anything was taken. People around here were scared, though, I can tell you that. To kill people like that. Police never found out who did it."

I glanced up at the house; I'd been here long enough. The eyes of the man in the dark car were dancing behind my eyelids, distracting me.

"All this is giving me the creeps. I should probably go now." I turned away and then back to her. "Thanks."

She gave a slight nod. "If you want the place, I'm sure you could get it for a song."

I smiled. "Sorry, I don't sing."

◆ ◆ ◆

I leaned against my car and studied the house. The sun was gone and the streetlamp blinked on; the stone steps were illuminated. I felt the warmth of my breath collect in front of my face. "What the hell, Claire?" I kicked my heel into the dirt.

I opened the car door and got in, clicking the locks securely into place. *2/15/10. Destiny calls us, bound by Loyalty.* I knew the words printed on the photograph by heart. *All things that spring eternal can never be crushed.* I rubbed at my eyes, blurry from fatigue. Destiny and Loyalty—Destiny and Loyal. *All things that spring eternal can never be crushed.*

"And what springs eternal? Hope," I muttered.

Had Claire known this photograph pointed to me, Ava Hope Saunders? How could she not? She must have known about these murders—that's why the picture had been shoved away, out of sight. Claire's face was there in front of me, angry, tired, the crow's-feet winning the battle at the corners of her eyes, her thin lips twisting with the nasty words flowing from her mouth. Distance and time hadn't improved our relationship. It all seemed to just sit and fester, and had picked up with the same intensity and bitterness the day I returned from college.

Though to be honest, she hadn't exactly been herself these past six months. I could see she was tired, distracted, anxious. Usually meticulous in her grooming, she'd let her salon appointments lapse, allowing gray to peek through along her hairline; her nails were short and unpolished. Days of endless sleeping, or not sleeping enough, had taken a toll. Every second of her forty-six years showed on her face.

In the last few weeks of her life, we'd barely spoken on the rides to her doctor's appointments. He had no answers for her lethargy, sore muscles, lack of appetite, so he'd inject her with vitamins and send her home. After ruling out Epstein-Barr, HIV, allergies, his only suggestion was weekly vitamin B shots and plenty of rest. This would surely pass. But it didn't.

I'd walked into her room to see her in bed again, the white duvet pulled up to her chest. Coffee and a book on her bedside table. I'd reacted with apathy tinged with frustration.

"You wanted me home, Claire, and all you've done is lie in bed. I'm getting a ticket back to Montreal."

When she looked up I saw the deep-purple patches underneath her eyes, the soft, pretty face that had become skeletal. For a moment I thought she was dead, but she wasn't. That took two more days.

"College is over, Ava. It was time to come home." Her voice was stronger than I'd anticipated. I took a step back. "We have things to deal with, you and I. Let the past go."

I slapped my hand against the bedpost. "Let go of the past? Why didn't I think of that? If only it were that easy."

"What's happened to you?" Her eyes were glassy and seemed to have shrunk into her head.

I stared at her, contemplating my next words. *What did happen to me? How did I end up with this family?* "You want to talk, Claire? Have a heart-to-heart? How about answering some questions? Huh?" She reached her hand toward me but I pushed it away. "I didn't think so. I'm late for work, but we'll finish this later."

We never had the chance. Two days later she had a heart attack in the hallway on her way to my room.

I started the engine and scanned the street again. Nothing. The man was gone. I took one last glance at the house before pulling away. It sat, its facade barely illuminated by the streetlamp, on top of the steep little hill, desolate, isolated, alone.

CHAPTER 2

As the dark-brown Chrysler LeBaron pulled up to a stop sign, he squinted into his rearview mirror. They were still there, on the sidewalk, talking. He had been parked at the far corner of Evergreen, had been sitting and watching them until the cold made his fingers stiff and difficult to move. Then he'd started the engine to get the heat circulating, rubbed his hands in front of the vent, and waited.

She'd been there, in front of him. He'd been hoping for this opportunity for as long as he could remember. To find her, lure her away from Claire's protection. Whenever he'd thought he smelled them nearby and started closing in, Claire had the prescience to disappear. And then the hunt would begin again.

Once, nearly fifteen years ago, he'd almost been close enough to grab her. She was at a playground and ran to throw something in the trash can. She'd stopped and stared at him like she knew he'd choke the life out of her if he could. He smiled at her instead. At that moment Claire swooped in and took her hand, pulling her away. Claire never even looked him in the eye. But she'd known who he was—she had to. He was sure of it.

Now Ava was here, all grown up. He hadn't suspected where she was going as he followed her silver Honda Accord across the Ben Franklin Bridge to Philadelphia. He'd taken the exits without a thought.

It was only as she'd started up the slight incline of Germantown Avenue to Chestnut Hill that his pulse climbed. She went right for the house, like she knew what had happened here five years ago. He went around the block and parked farther down so he could watch. Beads of sweat had collected on his upper lip and he wiped at them with his handkerchief, though his feet remained cold and numb.

Just then the old woman had appeared on the sidewalk below and called to her.

Ava, what are you doing? Going to the house wouldn't do her any good. Five years ago, maybe, but not now. There was nothing to find here. And as soon as he could dispose of Ava, the last link between him and the murders would be gone too.

Ava had started down the hill to meet the woman. Not for the first time, he was struck by her looks—those unnerving green eyes. They'd made his skin crawl when she was a child looking up at him, her dress spattered in blood.

Old-soul eyes, they were. All knowing. Clear and intelligent. The thought that they could see inside him made him nervous.

But even if she turned back and saw him now, he doubted she would give him another look. He was so average in every way: five ten, graying hair, pudgy potato-like face, small deep-set brown eyes, middle-aged midsection. He wasn't memorable. He'd met the same people over and over and they never seemed to recall his name, let alone anything else about him.

The woman's head was down now, studying the damned photo, reading the words printed below. She had to have gotten it from Claire. In her things after she died. With enough bits and pieces, and that photograph, Ava would start putting the puzzle together. In one impulsive move, he had gunned the engine and pulled up alongside them. He wanted that picture.

"Excuse me," he'd called out the window to them. "Can you tell me how to get to Flourtown?"

The nosy old woman came to the car, that Polaroid flapping from her fingers. He was about to grab it when she turned to point him in the direction of Bethlehem Pike. His opportunity gone, he glanced at them, nodded, waved, and proceeded down the street.

He continued through the stop sign and turned right onto Germantown Avenue, watching them in his rearview mirror. Another time, in a quiet moment, when the right opportunity presented itself and he was sure he could cover his tracks, he was going to take the photo and end Ava's life.

CHAPTER 3

I turned on the lights and flopped onto the armchair near the front door, grateful that Aunt Marie hadn't yet come to start packing things up. Sorting through Claire's belongings had been too overwhelming a task right after her death. First I'd found reasons to put it off, and then I just let it go. But Marie never could abide a task undone.

I shut my eyes.

They say your life flashes in front of you when you're dying. But I only *felt* like I was dying, and it wasn't my life that was passing in front of me, it was strips of my life, my life in shreds, that I was seeing.

I was young, maybe four. It was barely a memory, more like a flash of an image accompanied by a strong feeling. Fear? We were on the move, bags and suitcases shoved into the trunk. Claire, hurried, abrupt, and angry, pulling the seat belt across me. I heard the snap of the buckle. The image faded.

Another one took its place—Claire hovering over me while I lay on the couch, drowsy, half-asleep. I was around ten. Her breath in my ear roused me. "My life won't be my own. I will never have peace, because of you. Remember that." I'd opened my eyes, startled; she'd looked down on me and then wandered away.

Then I was standing in the bathroom, staring at myself in the mirror. Sixteen years old, long tangled brown hair, puffy eyes. I hated my image at that moment. The red mark from where Claire's palm had smacked my cheek was visible in the mirror. I hated her.

I'd resented our move that year to Haddonfield, New Jersey—a quaint, upscale town a short drive across the border from Philadelphia and close to the church where I'd been told I was abandoned. Claire's sister, Marie—or, I should say, Sister Marie—was here too, having transferred from a convent in California only a month before we arrived. Maybe that's why this move felt different, more permanent than the others. And I despised all of it. This town was expensive, exclusive, pretentious. I didn't fit in. I would never fit in. Always the only girl in the class not invited to the party, always the new girl without a lab partner—a kaleidoscope of towns, schools, upheaval. Adaptation, rejection. But I'd been right: this was the last stop. Claire's death ensured that I would never have to move again.

I opened my eyes and shivered. The house had a cold, stale, closed-up smell to it. I got up and wandered onto the porch. This had always been my favorite place—part of the house, but not quite. I would have moved my bed out here if I'd been allowed. But it wasn't as comfortable a haven as I remembered. Something had changed, shifted.

"Ava, I'm so glad I found you!" The words broke the stillness.

"Aunt Marie?"

She'd exchanged her nun's habit for slacks and a sweater. She climbed the steps slowly and sat next to me. Her dark hair was cut close to her head, her delicate features unadorned with makeup, giving her a gamine look. She was in her forties but her eyes, large and brown, dominated her unlined face, making her look years younger and much more innocent than she was. "I was looking for you earlier, but you didn't answer your phone."

It was hard to see now, but Marie had been the wild sister growing up. Pretty and impulsive, she'd been into boys, drinking, running away, and flunking out of school. She'd been volatile, succumbing to uncontrolled mood swings and outbursts until her mother did what rich people do and shuffled her off to the uberprivate, expensive Calda Clinic on Lake Zurich, Switzerland.

Grand-Mère Anais said Marie'd been given every diagnosis, every medication, intensive therapy for over a year, until she finally just grew up and grew out of it. She emerged from the clinic doors made placid by therapy and decided to join a convent—peace, structure, quiet, and God. What more did anyone need? When you looked Marie in the eye, sometimes you could still see the insanity in there, rolling around, waiting to come out.

Claire was hardly a nun, and the two girls sparred as they grew older but finally settled for civil tolerance. Until Claire's death, they'd made a yearly pilgrimage to France to see their mother, who owned a small cottage in Cherbourg.

I'd spent every summer there when I was little. The small, silver-haired woman was perfect in every way to my young eyes. She strolled into town and bought her bread every morning. Breakfast with Grand-Mère was always the same. Coffee, diluted with lots of cream and sugar, or thick hot chocolate, served in a huge bowl-like mug. There were teeny chips in the handle, and worn colors ringed the bowl. But it was mine, and Anais never let anyone else use it. I had my coffee-cream and warm rolls with butter and lingered with her on the patio, practicing French.

Anais Lavoisier's family had been residing in Hanoi, Vietnam, as rubber traders and diplomats when French colonization was winding down in the '50s. As tensions in the region escalated, some of her family moved south toward Saigon, taking posts in the French embassy, while others returned to France and settled in Cherbourg. Ross Saunders, a millworker's son from Philadelphia, had the misfortune of being drafted by the army and sent to Saigon in the late '60s. Their initial meeting sparked a romance and protests from both families, but they were married and living in the United States within two years.

They settled in a small suburb of Philadelphia. Ross got a job in the paper mills; Anais stayed home, had two children, and pined for the life she'd left behind. The romance of wartime diminished as each day passed and Anais came to the realization that she found Americans uninteresting and uncultured. One morning, she packed her bags, took her two girls, Claire and Marie, and moved to Cherbourg.

Ross, the story went, was devastated but not altogether surprised. He'd found Anais increasingly difficult to live with. Part of him must have felt some measure of relief. He never divorced her. He never remarried. He never traveled to France. He just continued his life in Philadelphia, alone. Even after they returned to the States, Claire and Marie saw their father only sporadically before his death a year ago.

"Why don't you come to Mass tonight? Light a candle for Claire. Pray. I can even get Father Martin to hear confession."

I looked out onto the neighborhood. The familiar houses across the tree-lined street showed no signs of life. "Claire's dead, Marie."

She hesitated. "Are you all right, Ava?"

I glanced up at her. "Who named me? Who gave me the name Ava Hope? Was that my birth name?"

Marie's head was down, and I was sure her lips were moving. Was she trembling or praying? "Claire wanted to name you Simone. She loved the name Simone. I wanted something a little more meaningful. Therese or even Mary. Anais came for the christening, held you, and said, 'No, her name is Ava Hope.'"

My head hurt. My eyes hurt. "But Hope isn't even French. Neither is Ava, really. Grandma Anais would never appreciate a name that wasn't French."

Marie nodded slowly. "Yes, well. There were actresses that she liked so much. Ava Gardner and Hope Lange. So Ava Hope it was. Why these questions?"

"Hope springs eternal."

Marie finally raised her eyes. They were dark and expressionless. "Yes, it does . . ." After a moment, she pushed herself up from the seat. "Should I wait for you at Mass?"

"Do you think Claire really wanted me, Marie? I've wondered that. Now more than ever."

Her face paled and she dropped back down next to me. "I know my sister could be harsh at times. Lord knows she and I had our bad moments growing up. But she did the best she could for you."

"The best she could. Is that something you say about an adopted child? I mean, it was her choice, right? To take me in? I wasn't an accident, an unplanned pregnancy?"

"No. No. She didn't give birth to you." I couldn't help but give her a sideways glance. "And Lord, no. I wasn't pregnant either. Don't even think that."

My hands twisted in my lap. "I found this Polaroid in her things. A picture of a house. I went there today, to that house. I just had this feeling—"

Marie's hand was on my arm now. I was aware of the pressure of her fingers against my skin. "You went to some random house? For what?"

I turned to face her. "It wasn't just any random house. I went because I had a feeling it had something to do with me. The picture had this writing on the bottom. Do you know it turns out people were murdered in that house?"

Marie's gaze skittered away. "Who was killed?"

"Loyal Owens and his wife, Destiny. Have you heard the names before? Did Claire know them?"

Marie stood. "Whatever this is, it has to stop." She moved to the railing, keeping her back to me. The hand that held the railing trembled ever so slightly. "I know being adopted must be hard . . . the not knowing. But you can spend your life looking for answers or you can accept the fact that you're a Lavoisier-Saunders. One of us. Come to Mass and let's light a candle for Claire. Okay?"

"Light a thousand candles, Aunt Marie. Watch them burn. It won't make my questions go away. I promise you that. This photo means something."

"*Ça ne veut rien dire.* Nothing."

With that she hurried to where her car was parked on the street. I crossed my arms and watched. She hesitated just a second before opening her car door. I could only see the outline of her form, but she seemed to be taking in me, the house, everything, before getting into the car and driving away.

It means nothing, she'd said. "Liar," I muttered.

CHAPTER 4

I woke up to filtered light coming through the blinds. My first thought was that my head hurt. The constant pounding hadn't gone away. I sat up, confused and disoriented. My mouth was dry and tasted like dirty socks and vomit. I'd fallen asleep on the living-room couch in my clothes. An empty bottle of Château Lafite Bordeaux from Claire's wine collection lay on the floor near me. A regular drinking glass lay tipped near the bottle. I remembered raiding Claire's stash, then the warm, velvety feeling of the wine going down my throat. The woozy, forgetting happiness that followed. I was only surprised I'd taken the time to pour it into a glass.

After Marie left I'd been so angry, I'd wanted to follow her and squeeze some measure of honesty from her throat. Honesty was what I needed. Marie was quiet and reserved, but underneath all of that she was a fluttering wreck, a stone's throw from a nervous breakdown. She seemed to think the structure of the church would keep her from utter madness, but those walls of piety could only support her for so long.

I forced myself to get up and made coffee, then took the mug onto the porch and sat down. The cold air made my head less foggy. I thought about throwing a few things together and catching a flight to London. It was quicker to fly to London and then cross the channel to Cherbourg than it was to fly into France. Anais still had her little stone cottage. I could sit on her patio and eat baguettes with fresh cheese and tomatoes and sip wine, get away from everything. But I knew I'd spend my time helping her tend to her house and gardens, listening to her lectures and advice. She'd tolerate my presence in her little oasis, but I'd come back with just as many questions as I had now.

I glanced at the clock. Nine thirty. I still had time to make it to Sunday Mass. I looked down at my wrinkled clothing. Then I raked my fingers through my matted hair and grabbed my coat.

When I entered the church, Sister Regina was walking toward the door. Regina was a bubbly, friendly woman in her early sixties. Today, she was deep in thought and didn't see me until I was right in front of her.

"Sister. Good morning."

"Goodness, Ava." She scanned my attire and then pursed her lips. "How have you been?" She reached out and placed her thick hands on my upper arms.

"I'm okay, Sister. Is Marie in the back? I'd really like to see her before the service starts."

"Marie's not here."

"But I saw her last night. She came to Claire's house. She was trying to get me to come to Mass. Where is she?"

"She had things to attend to this morning. That's all I know."

"What kind of things? Church things or personal things?"

"I don't know." Regina took my arm, urging me forward.

"Wait, when's she coming back?"

Regina didn't answer. She had her head bowed as she walked with me to the front of the church. I lit a candle, crossed myself, and knelt before it. I tried to keep a prayer for Claire in my head while I was at the altar, though images of the murder house and then Marie kept flitting through my brain.

I crossed myself again and stood. Regina was to the side, watching me intently. I slid into the nearest pew and settled in for the service.

I'd spent many hours in pews just like this growing up, and I did the same thing every time. Closed my eyes in the silence and said a prayer. It was mostly a single-themed prayer with only slight variations over the years—*Make Claire love me.* Then, *Help me find a way to fit in somewhere in this world.* Then, *Let me find out who I really am. My real family.*

Father Martin's voice droned on in the same intonation; the entire homily sounded like white noise. I studied the ancient woman seated in the pew in front of me methodically rubbing lotion onto her spotted knuckles. Her movements matched the seesaw monotony of the priest's voice, and I felt my lids grow heavy. My eyes drifted to the front of the church. The blessed mother was serene; the little candle I'd lit sent flickers across her delicately folded hands. Then I studied my own fingers. Cuticles raw, fingernails chewed, they were a mess. Like the rest of me.

The service ended and I got in line to exit the church. Father Martin was standing near the entrance, talking with each of the congregants. I let others go ahead of me while I scanned the chapel for Sister Regina, but she was nowhere in sight. When I turned back to the door, Father Martin was gone.

I threw myself into a pew and stared straight ahead at Jesus hanging from the cross. His thorned head was tilted to the side, slightly down, mouth agape. Blood dripped from his wrists, ankles, and wounded ribs. He'd surrendered to his fate willingly. The fate of the Owens couple was suddenly there, almost superimposed upon the man on the cross: Loyal Owens on his side in the living room, wounds soaking the carpet around him. I leaned forward and made a silent vow that I would never come to this church again.

I headed out of the building, contemplating stopping for coffee on the way back home. A grande caramel latte might wake me up and wash the Catholic from my mind. I saw Sister Regina out of the corner of my eye. She was talking to Father Martin—I could hear they were deep in conversation, their expressions intense and fluctuating. I stepped back to avoid being seen.

“She was looking for Marie. And she looks terrible,” Regina said.

“We never know how death will affect us,” he answered.

Regina was shaking her head. “There are other considerations here, Father. This whole thing worries me.”

“Do not worry about tomorrow, for tomorrow will worry about itself.” He patted her arm.

I put my back to the wall and took a deep breath. My heart almost stopped beating.

“Yes, I know Matthew 6. But Marie worries that the child knows more than she should. That this is just the beginning.”

There was silence during which I could only imagine what was happening.

“Claire’s passing has certainly created problems, but this was going to happen anyway. I told them both that. Ava should have been told the truth long ago. Marie and her sister couldn’t go on like this forever.”

“But Father—”

“This is one time I can say I wish I hadn’t heard confession. I could have done without Claire’s sins on my mind. My advice to you, Sister, stay out of it, and pray.”

CHAPTER 5

The sky was filled with clouds, and he was afraid it was going to rain. He hated driving in the rain. Traffic was surprisingly heavy, though Haddonfield was nothing but a sprawl of expensive Victorians spread over a few square miles. Funny Claire had settled here, of all places. But it was probably because she could hide in plain sight. She was one of these people, tucked in her neat house: uppity, arrogant, aloof. A first-class bitch.

It was strange that Ross could have produced the two children he had. Claire, an elitist snob, and Marie, hiding behind religious garb, pretending her cold, flat stare reflected some higher calling to Jesus. Flip sides of the same coin. Ross had been a Philly boy. From the neighborhood; son of a millworker. Blue collar. Long working days. Longer drinking nights. A row-home-filled-with-plastic-covered-furniture kind of guy. Honest, loyal, nice. Which was maybe what started all this.

He looked around at this street, at the town—decorated with lights, the cafés with outdoor seating, the Starbucks on the corner, and a multitude of expensive stores—and he scoffed. *What bullshit.* She'd come to rest, literally, in some New Jersey version of Chestnut Hill, where Owens lived. He'd imagined something more dramatic from her. Maybe Oklahoma on a windswept ranch, or Quebec City in a crumbling-chic townhouse. Or maybe even Portland, Oregon, near an organic market. But boring New Jersey, so close to her father's old stomping ground?

He turned the corner onto West End Avenue and pulled up in front of the house. The porch was empty; no movement through the windows. He waited, feeling the anticipation of ending the nightmare of the past twenty years, right here, right now. It was going to feel so good to walk away from this. And he wasn't going to make any mistakes this time. Clean. No prints. He'd even toss the house, take a few things to make it look good. What better time for Ava to die than on a quiet Sunday morning when all these idiots were either in church or sipping a cup of ten-dollar coffee in one of those shops in the middle of town?

He scanned the street. There was ever-present traffic, but everything else was quiet. He slipped on leather gloves—his breath was labored, making him light-headed as he climbed the stone steps to the front door. A small hunting knife was stuffed in his jacket pocket. No cars in the driveway or out front. No sounds or movements. No one was home.

The knob turned under his hand. She hadn't even bothered to lock the door. *She's oblivious.* For a minute he almost felt bad. He wanted to feel bad. But too many things had happened over too many years to stop now. He slipped through the door, closing it quietly behind him. He scanned the living room. Empty wine bottles were scattered across the floor. He counted six at first glance. He picked one up and smiled. *Drinking the expensive shit. Probably Claire's shit.* A blanket was stuffed at one end of the couch. She'd been sleeping there like a dog. Maybe he'd let her get drunk before he slit her throat. One last bender.

Then it occurred to him. The photograph. Did she have it on her? He saw her purse lying on the floor in the corner. *Where'd she go that she didn't take her purse?* He thought for a moment that she might be sleeping off her liquor upstairs, but her car was gone. The front door was unlocked, no purse. Maybe she went to visit someone, or to the market with cash stuffed in her pocket. He needed to be quick and ready in case she returned. He dumped her purse onto the coffee table.

Old receipts, crumpled papers, sticks of gum, her wallet, and one small empty bottle of vodka. No photograph. He riffled through the papers left on the end tables, tossing them onto the floor as he went. Then he moved into the dining room.

He went from chair to chair, flinging clothing to the side after digging through the pockets. Becoming more frantic and irritated as he went. This girl had the photograph, and he was going to find it. He climbed to the second floor, each step feeding his anger. Her bedroom was half-filled with boxes and bags never unpacked. The night table was strewn with water bottles, empty coffee cups, a wineglass, the sticky red vestiges still in the very bottom.

No sign of the photo.

Back in the living room, he flopped onto the couch in frustration. Then he saw it. On the floor near the heel of his boot, half-hidden beneath the sofa. She must have been looking at it before she slipped off into a Bordeaux coma. He grabbed the Polaroid and stuck it in his pocket as he stood, growing more uneasy as the moments passed. He didn't want to look at the place where Loyal died. The picture taken where he'd been butchered. A calling card for the next intended victim. Sweat trickled down his forehead. Thinking about Loyal's murder only made him realize that whoever'd killed the others was coming for him next.

He took a seat in a wing chair, out of view of the front door, and waited for his prey.

CHAPTER 6

Dark-gray clouds loomed overhead. I got into my car and sat there for a few minutes. I was going to head to Starbucks, then realized I didn't have my purse. No caramel latte for me. Claire's house was only a few blocks away. I contemplated whether it was worth it to go home and get money and come back, but then I just gave up altogether. What I really wanted was a long hot shower, a change of clothes, and some Motrin. I'd been slipping over the past few months. Drinking too much. A glass of wine turning into a bottle. Stopping at the liquor store to grab some small bottles of vodka to mix with my orange or cranberry juice when I was on the go. Something to keep me just a little unfocused. I wasn't sure if I was consuming alcohol or if alcohol was consuming me. A little of both, maybe. But perhaps it was just a the-only-mother-I've-ever-known-just-died-and-I-can't-handle-reality kind of consumption. Our relationship had been difficult, but I hadn't been prepared for it to end so abruptly. Now there'd be no closure, no fixing it.

The streets of Haddonfield were filled with the Sunday crowd. Shops opened their doors, contents spilling out onto the sidewalk despite the chill in the air. People were gathered outdoors, sitting under restaurant heaters, sipping expensive coffees and nibbling on bagels and smoked salmon.

While I'd been contemplating my next move after returning from college, I'd stumbled onto a job that suited me—an internship as a translator at the Camden County Courthouse. So, despite my determination to get as far away from Haddonfield as I could, I'd somehow still been living out of suitcases and bags at Claire's when she collapsed.

I jogged up the steps to the house and went to put the key in. Unlocked. Had I left it unlocked? Sister Regina's words rang through my head. *But Marie worries that the child knows more than she should. That this is just the beginning.* I pushed the door open and stood in the entryway, hesitating, unsure about going in. I'd opened up something by going to the Owenses' house; I'd sensed it would happen before I'd gone. Marie was right, this was just the beginning. I stared inside the darkened living room.

"Avaaaaaaaaa!" I turned to see Joanne, a coworker, charging along the sidewalk and up my steps. She grabbed me, the abundant sweetness of Shalimar wafting from her.

"Come in," I said when she'd released me from her grasp. "I just got back from church."

I took her arm and crossed the threshold. My eyes darted back and forth across the room, scanning for movement. Joanne Watkins was my shield, but she disengaged from me quickly and dropped her enormous canvas purse onto the sofa. She flopped down next to it and looked around.

"Good God, Ava. You need a cleaning woman. Is everything all right with you? You know . . ." She waved her arm around, taking in the entire room. "And you're lookin' a little thin. And a little rough."

"Good to see you too, Joanne." I scanned my mess with a critical eye. It looked like the beginning of a trashy hoarder's nest. Something crunched under my heel. I stared in dismay at the smashed lipstick tube, the pink color now smeared against the hardwood floor.

Her eyes were on it too. "Is that my tube of Lancôme Vintage Rose? You borrowed it like two months ago?"

It was but I didn't answer her. I was surveying the room. Was it this way before and I hadn't noticed? My purse was upside down in the corner, the contents spilled onto the floor. I knelt and started putting my things away. My wallet was there, all my identification and three dollars. I tossed the small empty liquor bottle that had rolled out of my purse back in, hoping that Joanne hadn't seen it. It was as if someone had been in here, rooting through my things. Even the sofa cushions were pulled out a bit. They hadn't been like that when I left—but I couldn't be sure.

"Do you have anything to eat?" Joanne said. "I didn't have breakfast."

Since I'd started at the courthouse, Joanne had become a friend—against her better judgment. She was older than me by fifteen years and a secretary for one of the superior-court judges. She hadn't cared much for me when we'd met. I'd heard she called me "the stuck-up bitch with the green eyes." She'd ignored most of my questions, giving me blank stares instead of answers. Joanne knew everybody and had a lot of pull. She practically ran that floor and could probably pass the bar exam in New Jersey if someone put it in front of her.

I had shied away from her—*civil but detached*, I called it. Then one morning in the courtroom, our relationship changed. I'd followed a fellow translator into court to hear a young man during his central judicial processing. He was Dominican, arrested on drug charges, and couldn't or wouldn't speak English. He screamed at the judge in Spanish and spit on the floor, and they couldn't do anything until a translator arrived.

When Joanne saw me enter the courtroom, she rolled her eyes and muttered something to the secretary next to her.

The other translator, Tomas, began translating the inmate's Spanish word for word: "'This is bullshit. I didn't do it. I'll take this to trial. You're just doing this because I'm Dominican.'" Then suddenly the inmate switched to French. Tomas, confused, just listened.

The judge looked at him and then at Tomas. "Is there a problem?"

"He's switched to a Creole," I jumped in.

The inmate turned to me and began an angry tirade.

"Tell him to speak Spanish," the judge said. "Or we'll send him back to holding until he remembers how."

"I can interpret, Your Honor."

"Go ahead, then. Let's get this over with."

I took a deep breath. "'Fuck all of you white fat asses. You think you're going to put me in jail. I'll kill you first. I do what I want and nobody can stop me. You don't even know my real name or where I come from because you're stupid. And you're a bitch thinking you can speak my language. You need a good ass fucking.'"

I said this all with a straight face. The judge stared back at me, and the courtroom fell completely silent. "I believe he's Haitian, not Dominican," I added. "I would call ICE."

Later that afternoon Joanne pulled me aside. "I can't believe that guy this morning. But you gotta admit it was funny."

I leaned in a little. "Which part? When he called you 'white fat asses' or when he said I needed a good ass fucking? Which I don't, by the way."

Joanne roared at this. "You're all right after all, you know."

Her iciness melted away and it became a running joke. "Hey, Ava, I'm going out, do you need anything?" If I said no, she'd add, "That inmate said you did. But I can't buy you that at the food truck." We started going to lunch together and sometimes came back popping mints to avoid smelling like wine. Once I got to know her, Joanne was open, warm, honest. We were as opposite as any two people could be, but we connected in ways that mattered. We might have been a funny sight walking down the halls of the courthouse. I'd always had a slight frame, but over the past six months a combination of stress and lack of food had rendered me bony. I dressed conservatively, often in black. Joanne was short, a little plump, with brownish-red frosted hair, overdone makeup, garish accessories, tight, sometimes too-tight, clothing, and always high heels.

"So are you going to feed me or what?" she asked again. "Bacon and eggs sounds good."

She followed me into the kitchen, scanning the place. "Ptomaine poisoning comes to mind. Maybe just coffee for me."

She plopped down at the kitchen table while I cleaned the coffeepot. "So, what's going on, Ava? I wanted to go with you, to that house in the photo."

I'd told her about the Polaroid, but I didn't want her coming with me. It really was something I needed to do on my own. I concentrated on the soap and water in front of me. "I was fine going alone."

"Why d'you think Claire kept that picture, anyway? Why didn't she just throw it away?" She studied me. "No offense, but she wasn't exactly all schmoozy and sentimental. Or even nice, according to what you've said."

I felt a heavy pull on my heart, the words speaking a truth I knew but wanted to deny. No childhood drawings ever graced our refrigerator. My Mother's Day mementos were trashed a day later. Any mother-daughter threads connecting us had been ripped apart by constant criticism, anger, and my occasional bouts of drinking. I poured two mugs of coffee and sat across from her at the table. "It wasn't a sentimental picture. It was probably important to her in some other way."

Joanne stared straight ahead. Deep in thought. I knew that look. "She never showed it to you, but keeping it meant risking you finding it. Where was it? Where'd you find it?"

I stood up and waved her on. "Come look."

This Victorian had been gutted and modernized, yet the original fixtures and character remained intact. We climbed the steps to the second floor and entered Claire's room.

The walls were painted a shade somewhere between gray and pale blue; the woodwork was a dark varnished walnut. I stared at the bed, Claire's slippers still sitting neatly on the floor where she'd left them, waiting for her feet. A book was on the nightstand, the tassel of the bookmark visible, marking the last page she'd read. I picked it up. *La Prochaine Fois.* I turned it over and smirked. She was reading Marc Levy. A little trashy for Claire even if it was in French. Joanne stood behind me.

"What is it? What does that mean?" She pointed to the cover.

"*Until Next Time.* Until next time, Claire." I dropped the book onto the table and headed to the closet.

A small dressing room had been made over into a walk-in closet. I buzzed by the clothes—pristine, perfectly organized—and dropped to my knees in the corner. There was a piece of wood, not even what you would call a door, closed and latched only by a hook. I pushed it open and crawled into a storage space behind the closet. The alcove was part of the space underneath the stairs to the third floor. The ceiling was at a sharp angle, and it was impossible to stand.

Joanne followed with some difficulty. "A little creepy." It was stuffy and dark.

I crawled to the corner and pulled the white box to her. "Here." A book of school photographs fell into her lap. Then the envelope. She tipped the box and pulled out the dress, holding it up in the dim light.

She then turned it over. "Someone sewed this dress by hand. Cute hippo," she said.

"What?"

"There's a hippo on the back, didn't you see it?" She turned the dress around to show me the blue embroidery.

I reached out and ran my finger over it, finding the rough spot where the thread had been doubled, without knowing what I was looking for. Then a flash of memory came over me. I was hysterical when I was wearing this dress. I was lost, or alone, maybe. Very young.

Joanne hit my arm. "What else is in there?"

"Just my school stuff and the dress. Her passports too." I tossed them into her lap.

Joanne flipped through the pages, examining the photographs and stamps. "Issued nineteen ninety-two. She traveled a lot. A whole lot."

Every page was filled with the familiar stamps of Immigration from when she'd exited and reentered the United States. "Nineteen ninety-three, nineteen ninety-four, nineteen ninety-five, she was back and forth to Europe. Nineteen ninety-six. A lot of travel with a little kid. Do you remember any of it?"

I was confused for a second. "We went to see my grandmother in France, but I don't remember going anywhere else."

"Here, early nineteen ninety-six, it looks like she spent a month in Spain. And she went to Morocco. You don't remember that? The marketplaces? The desert and the camels? You would have been what, three or four?"

"No. Nothing."

"Hmmm. What's the first thing you do remember?"

"I remember that dress." I reached out and touched the blue checked fabric. Commotion, being grabbed roughly. Running. Chaos and maybe blood. And faces. Claire's face. That was my first memory and I'd been wearing this. But I wasn't going to tell Joanne that.

She tossed the passports into my lap. "This is giving me the heebies. I'm going downstairs."

She turned and crawled back into the closet. I heard feet on the stairs, then the front door opening. I assumed it was Joanne, but when I got to the kitchen it was empty.

"You left the front door wide open," she said, appearing behind me several minutes later.

"I did?" No, I remembered locking it after Joanne and I came in.

"Must have. I stopped to use the bathroom upstairs and it was wide open when I came down. I'd be locking this place up tight, if I were you. This whole thing is creepy."

But I'd heard footsteps going down the stairs. I wasn't going crazy. If it wasn't Joanne, who was it? Had someone else been in here the whole time? I ran to the front door and secured the chain.

Joanne followed me, her arms folded in front of her. "Are you okay?" I gave a slight nod. "So, anyway, how many times have you been in that crawl space in the past, say, coupla years?"

"None. Zero. There would be no reason to. That was Claire's closet."

"Exactly. It was hidden. The picture. The passports. The dress?" She leaned toward me. "It was important enough not to throw away. The date on that picture is enough to call the police. It's connected to those murders. Do it, Ava. Now."

"No, not until I can think this through a little. And figure out why Claire had that in her possession. If she thought it was connected to me somehow."

"So what, then? You can't do this by yourself."

"Do what?"

"Play detective. People were murdered. It might have been a few years ago, but still . . . Why don't we call Russell?" She punched me in the arm.

Russell was a detective assigned to the Prosecutor's Office. He was what Joanne called DDG. Drop-dead gorgeous. She would walk by me and whisper, "DDG is in the building, go put lipstick on." And she never let me forget the one afternoon that she and I were sitting out in front of the courthouse when Russell asked to join us. He bought me a fruit salad and water. We got so involved in a conversation about his time in France when he was in the military—apparently Russell had been stationed in Cherbourg for a year and went back several times after that to visit—we forgot all about Joanne, and Joanne never shut up about it. I told her over and over again that Russell had a girlfriend and that he wasn't really my type.

"This attitude of yours is why I didn't used to like you. Contrary to what you think, Ava, you're really not too good for him," she'd say. "Yeah, I know you're all French and everything, but so what? He's got that curly hair and those big brown eyes."

At first I'd try to defend myself, but after a while I figured out that was exactly what Joanne wanted me to do. Instead I would egg her on. "I am sort of too good for him, so let's move on."

Yes, I noticed Russell when he was around me. I couldn't help it. There was no denying that he was good looking, but he was more than that. He was smart and funny and interesting. He'd been appointed to the Prosecutor's Office after six years on the Cherry Hill Police Department. He downplayed it like it was just another job. I found out later that it was sort of a political assignment and in those circles it was a big deal.

"So, what do you think? Just get his opinion?" Joanne was on the edge of her seat now.

I was shaking my head before I even realized it. "No. I'd rather not involve anyone in this. I mean it."

"Seriously? You're going to figure this out by yourself?" She glanced at me sideways. "Ummm, no. Russell. And that's final."

I put my head down. "He'll make this an official part of the record. Turn the photograph over to the Philadelphia police. You know he will. And I can't take that. Not now. I need to know why Claire had it in the first place. Then we'll talk about it."

"Ava—"

"No, I mean it. If we tell him, you need to make sure he keeps it to himself."

Joanne rolled her eyes and I shut up.

CHAPTER 7

"Wait, back up." Russell stared at me. His eyes could have shot me dead across the table. "The couple was murdered five years ago? Unsolved? And you never called the police after you left there? To give them your information?" I couldn't help but notice that those irritated eyes were the color of whiskey. Jack Daniel's, maybe.

"Well, we kinda are now," Joanne responded. "We called you."

He rubbed his forehead with his fingertips. "I mean the Philadelphia police. The police who might have investigated it to begin with?" He was straining to control his voice. "And you didn't even bring the photograph with you? So I could see it?"

"Sorry. I swore it was in my bag . . ." Which was a lie. I didn't bring it, because I needed to know he'd help me look into this, keep it to himself, and not just snatch it from me and leave.

"Her mother just died a coupla months ago." Joanne thumbed in my direction. "And on top of that, she finds all this out. She doesn't know if or how her family might be involved. Give us a break."

Us. I suppressed a small smile. Just then a waitress appeared and set our sodas down on the table. "Are you ordering or just drinking?" she asked.

"No, just the drinks," Russell answered for all of us. He wasn't sitting here any longer than necessary.

The waitress shrugged and wandered off.

Russell began to wiggle the straw around inside his glass as we talked, until it was moving so fast some drops flew out and landed on the linoleum tabletop. He pressed the drops with his fingertip. "Okay, I'll look into it. A little. See if I know anyone in Philadelphia. Not draw too much attention to it—"

"How about this? We'll all meet at Ava's house the day after tomorrow to get a game plan together; maybe you'll have found something by then?" Joanne stood and picked up her large purse.

"That's a Saturday. I have plans. How about you give me at least a week."

Joanne's face was a picture of disappointment. She'd hoped that Russell would be so intrigued and excited that he would drop everything, including Saturday plans, for this. I just knew she was wondering what kind of plans he had. She was always repeating the stories she'd heard about his girlfriend. Despite never having met her, Joanne had already decided she didn't like her, even though no one had ever said anything bad about her. She was a surgical resident at Cooper Hospital, and that seemed to irk Joanne even more.

"Big deal. So she's some doctor. It doesn't impress me one bit. I just have to figure out how to get her out of the picture for good. Maybe there's some asshole doctor over there that would love to take her out," she'd say. "What do you think . . ."

She never missed an opportunity to play matchmaker. Once she'd caught Russell looking at me when I was talking to one of the public defenders. She couldn't wait to tell me all about it.

"She's pretty, isn't she?" Joanne had asked him.

Judge Powell had wandered by, and Russell nodded and smiled at her in greeting, then turned back to Joanne. "I think she was probably really something in her day."

Joanne said she'd smacked him and told him she was talking about me. And took the opportunity to offer my selling points. "Ava's not really stuck up, you know, though she seems like it. She's not. She's shy."

With glee and a laugh she'd reported his response: "I never thought she was."

Now here was a situation that would put us together for a reason. It was interesting and mysterious, with a hint of danger. And she wasn't going to let some supposed relationship he was having get in the way.

She looked hard at Russell. "Wednesday night, Ava's house. I'll leave you two alone. I'm sure she'll give you directions. You guys can finish your drinks."

We watched her leave the diner and then started laughing.

"I'm sorry about all this, Russell. She means well."

He rested his chin in his hand. "I'm a little more concerned about this whole thing than I let on. I'm not going to call the police, because you asked me not to, but . . ."

"What?"

"People kill in different ways, and it indicates something different about the person doing the killing. And their relationship to the victim. Shooting someone is a whole lot less intimate, for instance, than strangling them. Touching someone makes it much more personal. The more intimate and personal, really, the more anger is involved. To take a hammer and hit someone repeatedly means that someone was *very* angry. Most likely these people didn't die with the first blow." He hesitated. "Ava, please let me make a few official calls to Philly."

"No, please don't." My eyes were welling up. "I have this awful feeling that Claire"—I hesitated—"my mother has something to do with this, and I've been through enough." I wiped at my eye with my finger. "I can't handle the police crawling all over my family, my personal life. Please?"

There was silence and I was afraid to look at him. Afraid he was going to ignore my pleas and start talking about police procedure, so I studied the melting ice at the bottom of my glass.

"Okay. I'll see what information I can get about the murders without raising any eyebrows over there," he said. "Once I look it over, I want us to take a little ride back to Chestnut Hill and that house."

"Okay."

"What if your mother was involved in this? Can you handle it?"

"Let's just take one day at a time, Russell." I smiled. "Or five days at a time. I'll see you Wednesday."

"Before then if I find out anything."

"Thank you. *Merci*, *gracias*, *danke*, *arigato*, *hvala*, and any other language I can think of. Really."

"Yeah, what language was that last one?"

"Croatian. Bosnian. Slovenian too. They all use the same word."

"You speak Croatian?"

"It's a hobby."

We stood up from the table. "You call that a hobby? How about fly fishing or collecting stamps?" He laughed. "Go." He put his hand on my back and propelled me out of the restaurant.

CHAPTER 8

The news was on. I heard the low murmurs in the background. A male anchor—a rumble—punctuated by higher-pitched female voices. I'd fallen asleep in my bedroom, on top of the pale-blue coverlet. I must have turned the TV on before passing out, but I didn't remember doing so. When I opened my eyes, I realized I'd been crying. It happened sometimes. Emotions seeping out when I couldn't keep them contained.

The picture was at eye level, so when I rolled over, I couldn't help taking it in. Me, at seven years old. I was dressed in denim shorts and a white smock top, smiling, holding a small fish. Claire was next to me, leaning into the shot, her blue hat and sunglasses obscuring her face. I remembered that day so clearly, each detail vivid. The sun had been searing, the boat small and blue. Only one other couple aboard. We had left Long Beach Island on a two-hour fishing trip, but I was the only one who caught anything.

Claire had been in a good mood, laughing, helping me reel my little bass in. She wasn't nervous or angry like she usually was, and those two hours that we were away from the shore were a real vacation. She sat down, had coffee, chatted with the other passengers, smiled. But after we got back, disembarked, snapped the photo, it was like *Boom, fun time over*. Not even ten minutes later she'd pulled one of my ponytails hard enough that my scalp swelled. But those two hours on board were what I'd held on to. It was what my life could have been with a different family. My real family. And so I asked to have the picture framed. Some nights I'd stare at it and pretend the woman next to me wasn't Claire at all. She was my mother. My birth mother. And that every day was just like this.

I looked over at the clock. The green neon numbers were glowing—it was nearly five o'clock. The days were beginning to disappear from my grasp. No routine, no structure. I'd come in earlier to lie down, the last bottle of wine from the living-room cabinet in hand, and now the sun was setting. I was pulling the blanket over my head when my cell phone started rattling on the nightstand. I pushed the button to answer, but before I could say anything—

"Ava. Are you busy?"

"Russell?"

"Yeah. Listen, I'd like to stop by for a few minutes, if that's okay?"

That was maybe the last thing I felt like. "You mean now?"

"I'm near Haddonfield and found a few things you might be interested in."

My pulse rose slightly. "Sure. Give me ten minutes."

I went into the bathroom, confused, not even sure what day it was. Sunday. We weren't supposed to meet until the middle of the week. What could he have found? I stared at my reflection in the mirror. My hair was smashed to my head and tangled. I'd been sleeping in just a tank top and boxer shorts. Russell couldn't come through the door with me looking like this.

I brushed my hair and pulled jeans on over my shorts. No time for much else. I ran a toothbrush across my teeth and was swishing some Listerine to cover any traces of booze when the deep sound of Beethoven's fifth began to play overhead. Claire had installed the doorbell shortly after we moved in. Those four notes were charming when you first heard them—but grating after a while.

I opened the door. "What's going on?"

Russell came in and locked the door behind him. It was then that I saw the gun tucked into a holster at his side.

"Work on a Sunday?" I motioned to it.

"Work doesn't end on weekdays at five p.m. Do you mind if we sit down?"

I pushed some clothes off the sofa and made a spot for him to sit. He was polite, but not so much that I didn't see his nose curl at the mess.

"I read the report on the murders, Ava. I went through four people to get it so it'd be harder to link back to me. Gruesome. I don't know how much of that was leaked to the general population, but whoever killed those people was probably in the house already and caught them by surprise when they came home. The woman was in the kitchen, near the front door; her keys weren't too far from her body. Theory is, she was attacked as soon as she came in through the garage."

I was silent; a dull ache twisted my stomach.

"He was in the living room. Multiple wounds to his head and face, and investigators thought he was the real target. The investigation went on for months, but the leads were sketchy. No one saw anything. No evidence of a forced break-in. The weapon was left behind. A run-of-the-mill claw hammer found near the bodies, apparently belonging to Owens. The only prints found matched family."

"So was this a robbery gone wrong or something else?"

"If someone were robbing the house and were caught in the act, and then things escalated to murder, it would stand to reason that something would have been stolen. But the house wasn't ransacked. The woman still had her rings on. The man had his wallet full of credit cards and cash. And then the killer just walked out of the front door and left it open."

He ticked off options on his fingers. "So either the killer was very eager to get out, not paying attention, arrogant and sure they wouldn't get caught, or familiar with the environment and not afraid. I'd guess the latter." He got up and paced a bit.

"Why?"

"Because they felt comfortable enough to stop and take the picture, that's why. And that's why I don't think it was a robbery gone wrong."

"Unless someone else took the photo? Someone who saw the killer but couldn't snap a photo in time, but still wanted proof or—"

"The bigger question here is, how did your mother get it and how is she connected to all of this? Did she write the words on the photo?"

I reached out and put my hand on his arm to keep him from moving; he was making me nauseous. "It doesn't look like her writing, but I can't be a hundred percent sure."

"When did you go to Chestnut Hill?"

The staccato sound of his voice made me pull my hand back. "Umm, a week ago Tuesday."

"Something is just not right about this, Ava. I'm not sure what, but it's in my gut." He stopped talking, concentrating. "Let me see that photograph."

"What?"

"The photograph that started this whole thing. The one that you didn't bring to our meeting the other day."

I stood up and grabbed my purse. Rummaging through it, then dumping the contents onto the coffee table. Russell peered at me. I felt his judgment at the empty vodka bottle that rolled onto the floor. He picked it up and set it on the table. The photograph wasn't there. I stood up, scanned the living room. I hadn't cleaned it since the morning Joanne was there. Papers, clothes were scattered everywhere.

"You lost it?" He was irritated.

"No." I turned to him. "No. It's here. Just give me a minute." But it wasn't there. Not that I could find.

Hands on hips, he turned in a circle, looking at the room. "Maybe you just imagined this whole thing? The photograph? Is that possible? You saw something about the murders on TV and then twisted it into this story?"

"No. Stay here. Don't go anywhere." I ran up the steps into my room and pulled it apart in a frenzy. I came down empty-handed.

"When is the last time you saw it?"

"The other day. I was looking at it down here. I was lying on the couch."

His eyes went to the couch—piled with clothes and a blanket. He sighed. "All right. Think about the day you went to the house. Does anything stand out?"

I tried to think—I had to come up with something. Russell was beginning to assume I was an idiot. "Okay. A man stopped and asked directions when I was talking to a neighbor. She was looking at the picture. He was weird. Staring."

"What did he look like?"

"Sixties. Graying. Balding, maybe. Fat face. Car was a dark color. He was only there for a minute."

"Okay."

"Do you believe me now?" I said. He had no reason to. I was a disaster. "The other day I came back from church, this place was a mess. My purse was dumped on the floor. I'd forgotten to lock the doors. Do you think someone came in here? And took the photograph?"

"You mean more of a mess than it is now? Was anything else out of order, different?" I could tell his cop wheels were turning. Ramping up. "This is the first it occurred to you that someone might have broken in, gone through your stuff?"

"Yes. Well, no, I wondered." I was starting to panic. "I saw my purse tipped over and the cushions pulled out." I motioned to the couch. "But I didn't notice anything missing and I couldn't be sure—"

"I want a coupla things. One"—he ticked his finger—"I want you back at work. Your bereavement leave is done. Two—"

"Wait, why do I have to go back to work?"

"You'll be safe there. I'll tell the sheriffs to tighten things up a little. Be on the lookout. You go into the courthouse and don't leave for anything until the end of the day. I'd rather have you there than sitting here alone all day drinking. Or out and about."

"And two?"

"Two, you can't stay here alone. Either you get a hotel room or you move in with someone."

"Someone who?"

"You choose. Joanne, your aunt. Someone else. Three, from this moment forward you say nothing, and I mean nothing, about any of this to anyone. Not even family. Not that aunt you mentioned. If she brings it up, act like you were wrong. Act like it's over, no big deal. I don't even want you telling Joanne what we talked about tonight. Give her fluff, no details, and if she presses, just make up something. Understood? The less people know, the better."

"Russell. What if I just leave the country? I need to see my grandmother anyway. Let me just go to France. I'll stay there until you tell me to come back. Really, I will."

He shook his head. "No. Who knows where this goes—"

"You think Grand-Mère Anais might kill me?"

He looked up and his eyes softened a bit. "She wouldn't kill you . . . probably. But I wouldn't be able to keep tabs on you. And four. Take a shower and wash your clothes." He gestured at me. "Get yourself together and give up the booze. I need you with a clear head."

"Anything else?"

"Yes. If you find that picture, call me. And make sure this house is locked up tight, windows and doors, all the time. When you're home and when you leave. Are we clear?"

"Russell. You have no idea how sorry I am I got you involved in this."

The corners of his mouth twitched into a little smirk. "It's okay. I weighed it out: investigate a five-year-old double murder for you or meet some buddies this afternoon for beer and football. Who needs football anyway?"

Just then Beethoven's fifth symphony sounded overhead.

CHAPTER 9

He sat at his desk, staring intently at the two Polaroid images in front of him. He reached into his pocket and pulled out the photograph he'd found on Ava's floor, placing it between the others. Three Polaroids, each of a different house, probably all taken with the same camera. The front door visible and open in all of them. This middle photograph completed a set. Claire must have gotten it from her father, Ross. Had he told her what it meant, or had she simply found it after he died?

Two murders within two years, then one more last year. The killer had made them all wait, holding their collective breaths to see who would be next. Bill had been the first of the three. His throat had closed, leaving him unable to breathe. Apparently caused by a tree-nut allergy. He was found by the front door, trying to get help. Nobody thought it was anything other than a tragedy until Loyal received the photograph in the mail—the front door of the rectory, the door ajar. The date of Bill's death had been printed underneath. The words *The church does not exonerate all Sins* written beside it.

Before Bill's death, the four men hadn't seen each other in over eighteen years. What happened that night ended in a brawl. Bill broke it up and Ross left, running almost, to get away from them. Each feeling apprehensive, angry, and betrayed by the others. Bill had become a priest, a man of the cloth. He'd disappeared into the church, shutting the door on the past. So why kill him?

He remembered Loyal calling him, panicked, the night that picture arrived in the mail. Over a few drinks they'd dragged it all out again, studied the implications. Who knew about their pact and what they'd done to fulfill it? How could anyone? They had no answers. Loyal gave him the Polaroid that night to be rid of it. Neither of them went to Bill's funeral. Neither said another word about his death. But hiding their heads in the sand didn't stop whatever they'd set in motion. Loyal had been next.

No mistaking that one for an accident. He'd been butchered. His wife too. Left to bleed into the carpet. The killer had been bold this time. This time, the Polaroid was mailed to Ross. And it was enough to make him break the silence after all those years. He called one night, his voice shaking as he read the words—*Destiny calls us, bound by Loyalty. All things that spring eternal can never be crushed.* Cryptic yet specific. He told Ross about Bill, the photo Loyal had received. Maybe they should meet. Bury the hatchet. Make a plan. But it never happened, and that was the last time they spoke.

Word of Ross's death came in the form of a sealed legal-sized white envelope. The address was typed. No return address. Postmarked from Philadelphia. This time the Polaroid image was of Ross's apartment, the door open. The date of death was printed neatly at the bottom along with the words *Ave Maria, Joseph too.* He'd felt sick after reading that; actually vomited. Ross had supposedly died after falling in the bathtub and hitting his head. He'd died alone in a crummy apartment near Harrisburg, separated from his two daughters. The daughters he'd entrusted his life to.

He assumed they believed their father's death was just an accident. He'd followed the story closely, talked to people in the area. There was never any hint of an investigation. He did go to the funeral, stayed in the back, but only to see if either of them showed, so he could track them and find Ava. They didn't. Anais wasn't there either. Ross had a total of ten mourners. That's what righteousness got you.

He knew he was next. Not just because there was no one else left, but because each recipient had died shortly after getting the photograph in the mail. Except in his case, the killer had waited. Over a year. To taunt him, keep him looking over his shoulder? What made him any worse than the others? Or maybe it was taking longer to get to him because he'd packed up and moved the day after the photo came in the mail. One crappy apartment after another, sometimes just renting a room. On the run. Maybe the killer just hadn't found him yet.

All the while, he was thinking there had to be a way to figure out who was doing it, shut it down. He just had to put the pieces together. And then take care of Ava. He'd been cautious, but too cautious. For the first time in twenty years, she was wide open. And just when he had the opportunity to deal with her, she brought a cop into it. And not just any cop.

When he first saw Russell Bowers, he'd laughed. Just a pretty boy with political connections. When he saw Russell's military record he'd changed his mind. Bowers had joined the navy out of high school and made the Navy SEALs during his commission. He'd seen combat in Afghanistan. He was a decorated veteran by the age of twenty-two. As soon as he was honorably discharged he went to college at Rutgers, graduated with a degree in philosophy and history in three years. He'd joined the Cherry Hill police force and then was plucked up to work with the Prosecutor's Office. He was high profile.

Of all the people for Ava to start blabbing to, a cop was the most dangerous. The secretary couldn't be eliminated either. She was connected to all the judges. There would be crushing political pressure for the cops to find whoever did her in. It was too risky. If something happened to either one of them now, Ava would never buy that it was an accident, and maybe she'd spill all she knew. Murdering either of her colleagues would draw too much attention to things best left alone.

He sat forward and kneaded his hands. How the hell had she linked the photo to Loyal's house? He stared at the photograph again. What if Claire had told her everything before she died? Claire was a smart bitch. It would be just like her to leave a final bomb to explode after her demise.

He had to defuse it, and there was only one way.

CHAPTER 10

I sat in my cubbyhole of an office at the courthouse. I'd done everything Russell had asked of me. I'd returned to work, showered and ready. For four days now, I hadn't seen Russell once. I didn't even know if he knew I was here. Or cared.

"Hey, hey, roomie. D'ya want me to grab you something to eat when I go out?"

"Hmmm." I crossed my arms and looked at Joanne. All of this was getting to me. Silly as it had seemed, I'd moved into Joanne's house the same night Russell had showed up at my door. Her fourteen-year-old son, Steven, was there too, when he wasn't with his father. Her house was small, crowded, and I'd been relegated to the couch half the time. The worst part was that Joanne followed me around. If I went outside, she was right behind me. If I tried to find peace by going into the bathroom and shutting the door, she'd be knocking within five minutes, wanting to know if everything was okay. Joanne didn't take a hint. And she talked a lot. She talked until the minute she went to bed. Sometimes she even got out of bed and came to the couch to finish a conversation that was already finished.

I loved her. I loved her when we were coworkers living in separate places. I didn't love her so much when we were forced together day and night and I had no place to retreat to. As things were, I was becoming a nasty shrew. And Russell, he'd just blasted into my house that night—made demands on how I was going to spend my time, deposited Joanne beside me as bodyguard—and then disappeared.

"No, thanks, Joanne. I'm good. I have water and vending machines."

"Fine." Her big purse was in her hand. "I'll bring you a treat anyway."

I sat in the office for half an hour, restless, my leg bouncing up and down. Then I grabbed my bag and left the courthouse. The sheriff's officers gave me a sidelong look when I brushed past them and scooted out into the damp Camden air. I started half walking, half running. I knew exactly where I was going but I wanted to pretend, at least for any prying eyes, that I was on my lunch break. The Prosecutor's Office was only a minute away. I just had to keep a sharp eye out for Joanne. If she spotted me, she'd make a ruckus and drag me back to the courthouse for a lecture and a snack. When I got to the corner, I ran the half a block to the Prosecutor's Office and threw open the glass doors. I stood in the little lobby until someone noticed me.

"Yes?" The woman was in her forties, and her messy shoulder-length hair seemed fitting with the rest of the chaos in the office.

"Russell Bowers, please."

She stopped shuffling files and looked at me. "Did he have some sort of appointment with you?"

I shook my head. "No. I work at the courthouse. I need to see him."

The woman smiled. If I had to translate that look into English, it would go something like this: *You and fifty other women. Stand in line, honey.* "He won't be in for a few days. Want to leave a message?" she asked.

"No. Well, maybe. This is really important. It's about a case over there." I pointed across the street. "Look, if he calls or anything . . ."

"Do you want to come in and talk to another detective?"

"Oh." There was something unsettling in her expression. "Did something happen?"

She crossed her arms. "You work in the courthouse, right?" I nodded. "I'm surprised you didn't hear. Hit-and-run—"

"*Run over?* Is he okay?"

"He hit his head. Hurt his shoulder too. Are you sure you don't want to come in and talk to someone else?" Her tone was softening.

"Is he going to be okay?"

She nodded. "From what I heard. He's home, recovering—he might be out of work for a while. Just awful what these people do these days. But look, if they catch the guy that did this, we'll prosecute, believe me."

I raced back to the safety of the courthouse and slammed the office door behind me. It wasn't just my office. Three desks were crammed into this closet, but the other two translators were at lunch right now. I dropped onto my chair and threw my purse on the floor.

Russell had been hit by a car, but he wasn't going to die.

And then my next thought: *Weird timing for a hit-and-run.* If it wasn't random, that meant someone was watching me, following me, knew what Russell was investigating. Probably the same person who'd broken into my house and taken the photo. I grabbed my purse and raced back outside, ignoring everyone as I went.

The wind coming through the car window slapped my face and blew my hair into a troll-doll bush. I was free for a moment, and I really needed to find Marie.

The church was dark and empty. The only signs of life came from the Catholic school across the street. I went around to the convent and knocked at the door. After a short lull, a woman answered. She was young but her face was creased with worry. She wore a pale-blue dress and white nun's cap.

"Please. I'm looking for Sister Marie. Is she here?" I asked.

"She's at the school today. They needed help." The woman pointed to where children were playing in a parking lot.

I found Marie supervising a group of kids playing tag during recess. I watched her for a few minutes without announcing myself. Marie was laughing, egging the children on, working them into a frenzy. Everyone looked happy. The last time I'd seen her, she'd rushed off the porch, seeking refuge from my questions. Questions that were becoming even more urgent.

"Marie?" I cleared my throat.

Marie looked startled for a second. "Ava. Where did you come from? I didn't see you."

I leaned against a tree. "I've been here for just a minute. Did Regina tell you I was in church on Sunday looking for you?"

"Yes." She said nothing more while the children were ushered back into the building. "Did Mass help you?"

We walked across the street to the church and convent. "I lit a candle for Claire. As you asked. But where were you? Regina said you had some business away."

"Why are you here, Ava?"

"Just wanted to let you know I'm fine. I thought three weeks was enough time away from work after Claire died, so I went back—getting back into a routine. Trying to figure out my next move." Marie reached out and hugged me. Her thin fingers dug into my back and made me angry. I smoothed my hair and pushed myself from her grasp.

"Next move?" she asked.

"Yes. I'm not sure where I'm going. If I want to stay here—"

"Ava, you can't up and leave on your own." The always-present nervousness was there in her voice. "Anais wanted you to come to France."

I folded my arms. "I'm almost twenty-three. I don't need anyone to make plans for me anymore. I have a job, I can support myself, go where I want. I don't need anyone's ideas for my life." I didn't try to mask my irritation. How much had Claire shared with her about our fights?

I watched Marie's eyes get bigger. "You can do whatever you want, of course. But for now maybe you could visit Anais? She found a nice flat for you, if you're interested, in the fifth arrondissement, Paris?" I said nothing. "It's beautiful. She said she'll pay for it. You can just rest."

I shook my head. “Is there some reason I should be running away to Paris, to a flat in the fifth arrondissement? To rest? And why is Anais suddenly willing to pay for me to move there now? She’s always refused in the past.”

“No, not running away. We just thought—”

“Ah, it’s ‘we’ now, is it? And this has nothing to do with the photograph I found? The murders? Tell Grand-Mère Anais we really do need to talk, but right now I’m going to go back to Claire’s. I’m going to start packing her things, and I can figure out my own life just fine.” I started to walk away.

“Ava,” she called. “How did you find the house in the photograph?” The words were spoken to my back. “How did you come to assume it had anything to do with you? Your adoption?”

I hesitated, didn’t turn around. “I’ll tell you next time I see you. It’s a long story.”

I could see Marie standing by the convent door, her arms folded in front of her, watching as I climbed into the car. She wasn’t going to be nearly as effective as Claire had been in orchestrating the events of my life, forcing me to move, to come home from college, as if I were a dog and she had a whistle. I might have been grateful for their protectiveness, even absent their love, if I wasn’t so convinced that the secrets Marie and Claire had been hiding were to protect themselves more than me.

CHAPTER 11

Russell rolled over in bed and looked out the window. He had to be careful how he moved, or bolts of pain shot through his head. Juliette was in the shower. Steam filtered through the crack under the door.

He'd been in her house for four days now. His head bandaged, his limbs sore. He kept thinking about the car that had come out of nowhere. His injuries would be much worse if he hadn't leaped out of the way. As it was, the bumper just nicked his hip, throwing him a few feet. Juliette had been patient since his release from the hospital—watching him, checking his pupils, doing a neurological exam every ten minutes, changing his bandages. He could sense Juliette's thrill at having him living in her house—her hope that this was the first step in a permanent change. But he was beginning to feel trapped. Even just sitting at his desk and moving papers would be better than this.

After he'd spilled just a little about the case he was investigating before the accident, Doug, a friend who had been with him in the police academy, had insisted on putting an officer out front to cover the house. It was a smart precaution, but it contributed to making him feel like a prisoner, helpless. And he'd never been comfortable with either of those things.

He had been spending most of his time rolling the facts of the Owens investigation over in his head. His working theory was that the couple was connected to Ava's adoption. It was the only thing that made sense. Who was Ava, exactly? Where had she come from? Why had her parents—or someone else—dumped her at a church like that? He needed more information. He needed to know more about Claire. And Claire's entire family.

He thought of Ava and he smiled. She was probably still living at Joanne's house, and when she saw him again, he knew she was going to tell him off in that clipped, precise voice of hers. When Ava was angry, her eyes were like bullets—they could shoot you dead in seconds. He had once seen her argue with one of the public defenders. They were in the hallway, going back and forth. At one point Ava got so angry and flustered that she mixed her languages. When she realized it, she didn't miss a beat. She looked at him and said, "I don't have time to translate, look it up." And she walked away.

"Why are you smiling like that?" Juliette slid into bed beside him. She moved over next to him and wrapped her arms around him.

He winced. "Watch my shoulder, Jules."

"I have been watching your shoulder. For days now. I've cleaned it, changed your dressing, given you your antibiotic." She moved closer. "Now I want to take care of you."

She kissed him and he winced in discomfort. His face was swollen to nearly twice its normal size, and the pain was only slightly dulled by the medication they were giving him.

"I don't want to, Juliette. Not tonight. I'm in a lot of pain."

"I'll be gentle," she whispered. She touched him slowly. With each movement of her body against his, he tensed up, anticipating agony if she touched him in the wrong spot, but surprisingly, his body responded.

He thought Juliette was the one; he was just waiting for their lives to settle down a little to make it more permanent. Her four-year surgical residency had been demanding; she couldn't take time off to get married and start a family. And he hadn't been ready either. But now that she was finishing up her final year and had been accepted into a fellowship, he knew that the time had come to move things forward.

Still, some force was holding him back. He'd never been a procrastinator, but everything about Juliette seemed so difficult lately, like he was moving against water.

Just at that moment, an image flashed into his head of Joanne seated cross-legged on the end of Ava's bed, eating a bag of Cheetos and talking nonstop while Ava was trying to read a book. A laugh escaped his lips as he climaxed.

Juliette smiled as she slid off of him and lay by his side, holding his arm. "I'm glad I can still make you happy."

CHAPTER 12

I unlocked the door to Claire's house and stood in the entryway. After a few days of being closed up, the place was beginning to smell. I had gotten so irritated at Marie for playing nursemaid in my life, but I wasn't doing a very good job on my own. I resisted the urge to crawl under the covers and sleep the rest of the day away with a bottle of vodka by my side. Instead I climbed the steps and changed into an old T-shirt and shorts from bags I'd never unpacked. Then I set about cleaning up the mess I'd made.

Several hours later things looked better, at least to an uncritical eye. The hardwood floors had been swept and mopped; the collection of coffee cups in the sink had been piled into the dishwasher. I pulled the trash bag from the kitchen can and found one source of the odor. Chicken I'd thrown in the can days ago was there, rotting. I dragged it to the outside garbage can without gagging. The wine and vodka bottles filled the recycling bin.

My last task was to sort through all the papers in the living room and find that photograph before Russell had me committed. But after almost an hour of sorting and searching, I came up empty. It was gone. I'd even pulled the sofa apart and moved it. I'd done the same to my bed. Nothing. Russell would be interrogating me about it again, no doubt. And I needed to have some answers.

Disgusted and tired, I headed to the patio with a cup of coffee. The back of the property line had been planted with trees, which gave the place the illusion of privacy. I needed an hour of peace to clear my head. Just then the phone rang.

"Damn it, I thought I turned that off," I muttered. "Please not Joanne." I turned the phone over and studied the number. I didn't know it.

"Don't be mad at me," the male voice said when I answered.

"I'm not mad, Russell. How are you? How's your head? And your shoulder?"

"You know?"

I picked up the brightly painted coffee cup, one of a set Claire had brought back from Mexico, and took a sip. "Yeah, well. After four days I went looking for you. I admit I was kind of pissed at you for disappearing on me, and then they told me. Russell, I'm so sorry. Really sorry."

"Where are you?"

"Claire's. I had to get away from Joanne and the courthouse. I just left work. They'll probably fire me."

"Nah. I doubt it. Can I come and talk to you? Just for a minute?"

I looked at the swirls of color that ran around the mug. "No. Uh-uh. I think I just want to be alone right now. Just me and my coffee."

He half laughed. "I'll only take a minute of your time."

"The photo is gone. I spent the last couple hours taking this house apart and it's not here. My best guess is that whoever came in here ransacked my mess and took it."

"Listen—"

"And my aunt suddenly wants to bundle me off to Paris. Oh, and you got run over. I forgot to add that. But other than that—"

"Are you finished? Because I'm coming over."

"Jeez. You and Joanne are a pair. All right. But listen, I was cleaning, I'm grimy, and I'm not changing. And secondly, I'm telling you up front I'm irritable."

"Really? Are you done?"

"Yes. Ring the bell. I've got the house locked up tight."

I did as promised and didn't so much as glance in the mirror before he arrived. My hair was pulled back in a ponytail and I could feel loose pieces flying around my face when I moved.

I opened the door and stood there for a second. Russell's head was partially shaved and bandaged and swollen. The bruising went all the way down the side of his face; he looked pale and drawn.

"Come." I motioned him in. "Follow me." I padded across the living room into the kitchen. "Coffee?" He nodded. I handed him another cup that matched mine. We sat on the patio, saying nothing. Finally I looked him in the eye. "You look terrible."

"So do you," he responded.

Well, maybe I should have at least combed my hair. I glanced down at the shirt I was wearing. It was streaked with dirt. "It's better to have a clean house and dirty clothes than the other way around." I hesitated.

"I'm furious." Russell jumped into the lull.

My eyebrows went up. "Because someone ran you over in the street like a dog?" I laughed. Then I realized that was horrible. "Sorry. A sad attempt at humor."

"Thanks."

"So, any leads on who hit you?"

"Good question. The only real witness, the one that called the ambulance, said it was a dark-colored car. They have next to nothing. But I can't shake the feeling that it has something to do with your missing photograph and the fact that I've been looking into the Owenses' murder. Though I have no proof."

I raised my cup to him. "Great. Add that to my plate, right next to dead Mommy and the murder house. Why not?"

"Ava, I'm serious. It's just a hunch. But I think this thing's a hornet's nest."

My stomach twisted a little. "I believe it's filled with something worse than hornets. What now, Russell?"

"When is the last time you actually sat down and ate a meal?" he asked.

I pushed out of my chair and headed back to the kitchen for more coffee. Russell followed me. "I eat. Maybe not a lot, but I eat." I poured coffee into my cup.

He was looking at the refrigerator. Pictures were held in place by magnets. There was one of Claire, Marie, and Anais outside of Anais's house in Cherbourg, taken three years ago. I hadn't come home from college that summer. Russell picked it up and leaned against the counter. He kept looking at the picture, then me.

"What?" I asked after a minute.

"I'm just looking at your mother. Both her parents are French?"

"Her mother is. Why?" I asked.

"Her father too?"

"He was American. Irish, I think. He had black hair—turned gray later. Anais's is dark too—well, was. Now mostly gray."

"Did Claire's father live in France? Is that how they met?"

I sat down. "No. From what I know, they met in Vietnam, of all places. Anais's father was a diplomat in the French embassy. My grandfather was drafted and sent to Saigon. They fell madly in love. Got married; Marie and Claire were born here. But neither family was happy, from what I know."

"Why?"

I shrugged. "Grandma Anais's family was well-to-do. My grandfather was just a working-class schlub from Philadelphia. I'm not sure what they saw in one another. Maybe they weren't sure either. One day Anais just packed up Claire and Marie and went to Cherbourg. Some of her family was back in France by then."

"Is he still alive? Your grandfather."

I shook my head slowly. "No, he died a year ago last month. Claire, and I guess Marie too, hardly knew the man, to be honest. He was never a part of their lives."

"So when did Claire and Marie come back to the States?" Russell tipped his coffee cup to drink but realized the cup was empty.

I held out my hand. "I'll give you the rest." I poured it into his cup. "Marie joined a convent in France and then came over here to be with Claire. I think Claire came over in the early nineties sometime. I'm not sure of the date. She was an editor for French *Vogue* and they transferred her to the US."

"Where did they live?" he asked. "Ross and Anais, I mean. When they were living here?" His eyes were steady and interested.

"Ross Saunders worked in the mills in and around Philadelphia. So I'm assuming they lived somewhere in the city. I'll find out, if it's important."

"Hmmm. Listen. I have an idea. Let me feed you one good meal. A really good, heavy, solid meal, and you tell me everything you remember or know about your mother, your aunt, Anais, and your grandfather . . ."

"One condition." I put my cup into the sink. "Call Joanne and fire her as my bodyguard. And from now on, we do this together. And I'm moving back here for now. No babysitters."

"Not a good idea—"

"This is a deal breaker, Russell. I can take care of myself. I'm not living with Joanne forever while this house sits empty."

"When it comes to this, I'm not sure any of us can take care of ourselves. Look at me." He pointed to his swollen face.

"If someone wants to hurt me, they will, whether Joanne is with me or not. It may just put her in harm's way too."

He sighed. "Lock the doors and windows? Keep 911 on speed dial? Call me if you hear anything weird in the house? I mean it."

"*D'accord.* So, how heavy a meal?" I laughed.

CHAPTER 13

We were seated in the courtyard at the Mexican Food Factory. After pondering a dozen other restaurants in the area, we'd agreed on this one. The seating outside was nice, the food was decent, and they served drinks.

He pushed the basket of chips over to me. "Eat. Please."

I took a chip and nibbled at the corner. "What is it with you and my weight?"

He shrugged. "Talking to a woman about her weight is a no-no, but in your case I'll make an exception. You're thin. Anorexic?"

I hated that word. I shook my head. "Let's not start this dinner off with a diagnosis hanging in the air. Okay?"

He sat back in his chair. "So tell me what the deal was with you and your mother."

"The deal"—I leaned forward—"was that Claire, not to speak ill of the dead, was a bitch."

He smiled and shifted in his chair. "How so?"

I considered my words. "She could be very mean. Angry all the time."

"Abusive?"

The word stung. "Oh, I don't know . . . but there was the not-so-occasional smack in the face. And there was yelling, name calling. I didn't exist most of the time. As a kid I just found ways to entertain myself, stay out of her path."

"Sounds like it was hard."

I stared off into the bamboo planted around the courtyard. "We moved a lot, so I was kind of always alone, trying to adjust, off-kilter." I took another bite of the chip. "Just trying to keep my balance, you know?"

"Why'd you move so much?"

"A million reasons. She didn't like the community, the schools, the neighbors. It seemed like at least every year she was packing up."

"I'm surprised you managed to graduate high school."

"Ah, yes, well, there's tutors for that kind of thing. I spent my childhood playing catch-up."

"So how'd Claire get her money? It takes money to live. Not to mention move. Didn't she have to work?"

I thought about it. "She started off as a magazine editor years ago, but she never worked after she adopted me. Anais's family was loaded. I assume that Claire just got money from her."

"That's interesting in and of itself."

The waitress came with our drinks. "Claire had some issues with her sister, too. Neither of them is easygoing. Was easygoing, in the case of Claire." I cleared my throat. "Marie runs hot and cold and is a bit of a nut. Is this what you wanted to know?"

"I'm a captive audience. Tell me anything you want to."

"When I was little, I never felt Claire wanted me. She tried so hard to put on this perfect face for the world, you know, or for whatever school system I happened to be in at that moment. She'd always smile, say the right thing, hug me, or touch me when people were around, but it was very different when no one was looking."

He swallowed a yellow pill with his margarita. "Percocet. Pain."

"Great combo. I guess I'm driving you home."

His hair, which had been getting longer, curling in the back, had been shaved closer to his head after the accident. But he still had the little unshaven patch of facial hair right under his bottom lip.

"I always had this sense that we were different from everyone else. I had friends but I was never one of them, if you know what I mean."

"Different how?"

I shrugged. "Not the same. Maybe it was because she didn't want to get to know anyone. For us to be a part of anything." I dipped a chip in salsa and put it in my mouth. "She wouldn't come to the mother-daughter brunch at school. Or join the PTA fund-raisers. I'd bring home the info and she'd throw it away."

"Ever?" Russell asked.

"Hardly ever. We were always outsiders no matter where we went."

A breeze was blowing gently across the patio. Soft Mexican music mixed with the sound of the fountain a few feet away. The tequila was clearly making its way to my brain.

"So you grew up with that, just moving around, never getting to know anyone? How about Anais? She was a good grandmother?"

I laughed. "It's too bad you missed her. She was here after Claire died. Took the body back to France for burial. Yes, Anais was the best part of this adoption deal. For sure. Strong woman. Very strong. Quirky. Very French."

He leaned in, chewing an ice cube from his drink. "I imagine she was devastated at the loss. It's not easy to lose a child."

"I thought she might stay longer, actually. Spend time with me and Marie. But she finished her arrangements and left the next day." I tilted my head to the side. "She held herself together while she was here, though. Upset but composed. I don't think I saw her cry."

The waitress came and placed food in front of us. Russell had asked me if there was anything I didn't like on the menu. When I said no, he'd insisted on ordering for both of us. I wasn't hungry anyway, so I didn't mind. I'd gone to the bathroom while he placed the order. Now there were three plates in front of me. Guacamole salad, a mango-brie quesadilla, and grilled sea bass with red grits. "Russell, any one of these would have been fine."

He smiled. "Take some of it home. Anyway, getting back to your family."

"I was there, you know." I caught his eye. "That morning when Claire was dying."

He looked startled at my choice of words. "Really?"

"I found her on the floor in the hallway, near my bedroom door. Coming to me for help, I assume."

"Ava, that's awful. She was still alive?"

"Yes. She was. Her last words to me?" I smiled. "First she begged me for help. Then, while we were waiting for the ambulance, she prayed for my soul. Pleaded with me to be a better person."

His eyes narrowed slightly. "Really? What did she mean?"

I bit my lip. "Not sure. I'm surprised she didn't waste those breaths telling me I looked fat in my pants. She was always criticizing." It probably came out harsher than I intended, because Russell had a shocked look on his face.

He cleared his throat. "So, tell me about Claire's father, Ross."

"I'm afraid my information about him is sketchy. He wasn't a favorite topic of conversation in Claire's house. Though I did meet him a few times."

He leaned forward again. "Really?"

"Yeah. He and Claire had a few powwows. Not like family gatherings or anything. He'd meet her and they'd talk, but I wasn't privy to the conversation. Then he'd leave. Just go on his way. And he never acknowledged my presence. Funny, huh?"

"What was he like?"

"The meetings weren't casual get-togethers. He was abrupt, to the point. I stood off to the side. Both times Claire was—unsettled, I guess is the word, after we left."

"Hmmm. He was living in Philadelphia and would meet you wherever you were?"

"Yes. Once was in Pittsburgh. That was more planned, because Claire told me about it beforehand. The other time he just showed up when we were walking down the street in Philly."

"And that's it?" I nodded. He put the glass down. "Okay, there has to be someone who knows the whole Ross Saunders story. He's the key to this. I just have a feeling."

"Hmmm."

"After the double murder, I'm going to be looking into his death next. And you"—he pointed at me—"have access to a treasure trove. Claire's house. Dig. See if you can find any old letters or something in her stuff." His eyes were a bit unfocused. His words weren't slurred, but they were starting to melt together at the edges.

"Do you always drink this much?" I asked. "And pop painkillers at the same time? Because I really need you to have a clear head, Russell," I mimicked him. "No boozing. Clean up your act."

"Point taken. Bad, bad week. So bad . . ." Then he started laughing. "This is the most fun I've had in . . . never mind . . . Did anyone ever tell you you look like a cat?" He was chuckling.

"No, you're the first." It was amusing to see him like this.

"A skinny black cat with green eyes. One of those really slinky black cats. Cat woman." He reached out and tugged on the ends of my hair.

"Russell, give me your car keys."

CHAPTER 14

Joanne had insisted on coming over to make lunch, bringing two bags of groceries and a cheese grater with her. I'd opened the door still in my pajamas, despite the fact that it was almost one in the afternoon. I'd been drinking pots of coffee and sitting on the patio all morning, unable to bring myself to so much as comb my hair. Joanne just stared when I opened the door.

"Thank God I'm here." She stepped over some reaccumulating clutter on the floor and continued into the kitchen. "I'm going to make the best grilled cheese. Wanna help?"

"No, thanks, I'd only be in the way. I'm going into Claire's office, look around a little bit, if you need me." I started toward the stairs.

A hint of a smile crossed her face. "Hmmm, might want to stop by the bathroom and clean up a little while you're up there."

The morning that Claire died was so distorted in my mind. I'd stumbled from my room on my way to find desperately needed coffee, the remnants of the pint of gin I'd swallowed down the night before still flowing through my veins. I'd been out late, parked at Cooper River, sipping the gin from one bottle and then tonic from the other. My version of a mixed drink. I was angry at Claire for insisting I come back from Montreal after college. I'd made a reasonable life for myself in Canada—friends, freedom, and fun. It was easier to forget there, to pretend I'd had a normal, inconsequential childhood. I really didn't want to come back to her. I even appealed to Anais, who refused to get involved and refused to give me any money. She'd said, *"Se creuser la tête puis faire avec." Think hard and then deal with it.* The reality was that I'd been in Canada on a student visa, and getting a job and staying permanently were more complicated than I thought. By the time I got off the train in Philadelphia, I was frothing with resentment. So I dealt with it by being more bitter and angry at Claire than ever before.

Until the morning I saw her lying on the floor, in the hallway just outside her bedroom. She was dressed in her thin nightgown and robe, her hand pressed to her chest. She'd apparently been trying to reach my room when she'd collapsed. Phones in bedrooms, either landlines or cells, were tasteless and forbidden according to Claire, but in this case one might have saved her life. I had no idea how long she'd been lying there, but she was alive and asking for help when I leaned over her.

I got my cell phone and called 911. When the ambulance finally arrived, she was no longer talking and her lips had taken on a purply hue. They hooked her up to all kinds of tubes, the two EMTs speaking quickly in a medical language I didn't understand. I did understand, though, when they lifted her onto the gurney and took her out of the house, that it wasn't good. *Marie.* Marie needed to know what was happening. I called her and got her voicemail. I left a message and headed to the hospital, trying to follow the ambulance, though I could only hear the sirens in front of me.

When I reached the emergency room, Marie was there with her sister, as though transported on the wings of God. The two were huddled together. Claire was conscious and able to speak. I stood at the curtain and heard the words going back and forth in impossibly rapid French. It was so fast and the tone so hushed, I could only catch every third word. Then the words stopped altogether. Claire turned blue; codes were called and a nurse pushed me out into the waiting room. I never saw her alive again.

Now I stood at her polished walnut desk in front of the window, wondering where to begin. I drew back the curtain and looked outside. We hadn't lived here long enough for me to accumulate memories. I'd left for college only a year after moving in. I was surprised Claire had stayed here after I was safely tucked away at McGill in Montreal. Her life was her own and I'd assumed she would move on, as she'd always done. But she stayed in Haddonfield with her sister and put down some roots—for the first time I could remember.

I dropped the curtain and looked around. The office was organized. I'd combed through the desk already and found nothing of interest. Files, tax records, bills, receipts. I looked at the closet door. Claire always kept it locked; I was so used to the locked door that it blended into the wall. I hadn't come across the key. The thought had occurred to me that perhaps Marie had taken the key with her the day of Claire's death. She'd come back to the house and stayed with me that night while I lay in bed, unable to sleep, listening to the sounds of the floorboards creaking—Marie moving about. If she'd taken the key, there was a reason, and I doubted I'd ever get it back. I twisted the heavy marble handle. It turned, but a bolt lock held the door firmly in place.

Joanne appeared behind me. "Lunch is ready. Campbell's Chicken Noodle Soup and grilled cheese, mmm-mmm good . . . What are you doing?"

I kicked the door hard. "Trying to open this fucking door. But I can't find the key."

Joanne smiled. "I never heard you swear, Ava. I mean, other than in the courtroom. But it looks good on you. Can you say that in French?"

"J'essaie d'ouvrir cette putain de porte," I muttered. "*Merde*, Claire."

Joanne turned and headed down the hallway. "Keep it in English, it sounds much angrier. Come eat before it gets cold."

I moved the soup around in the bowl, occasionally licking the spoon so Joanne would think I was eating. I pondered the possibilities inside that closet. I felt like taking an axe to it. And I could—no one would stop me. I'd be doing as Russell asked—digging, or in this case smashing, into a potential treasure trove.

"I got some bad news yesterday. I didn't want to tell you, because I know you've got a lot going on." Joanne was spooning noodles into her mouth.

I stopped eating. "What? What bad news?"

"It's Russell."

"What? He's hurt again?" I felt a tingling in my hands and fingertips.

"Not like that. I should hurt him, though. He got engaged. To that little girlfriend of his over at Cooper." Joanne took a big bite of her sandwich. "It made me so mad."

"Ahhh. Not surprising. They've been together a long time." I managed to smile.

Joanne leaned so far toward me, I had to move my chair back a little. "You and I both know that's crap. You just had dinner with him and he does this? What the hell?"

I put my elbows up on the table and looked at her. "It wasn't a date; it was work. I don't even think he's attracted to me like that."

She took a bite of her sandwich. "Yeah, whatever. When is the last time you went on a real date?"

I thought about it. "Depends. What constitutes a real date? Like picking me up at my house, flowers? That kind of thing?" I grimaced. "My senior prom?"

"You forgot to count Luke Demaio. That was funny."

I tried to smile. Luke was a lawyer. Not even a nice lawyer. He was one of those slimy types, and he accosted me one day and asked if I wanted to meet him for happy hour at Tequilas in Philadelphia. I said yes only because he caught me when I was feeling lonely and sorry for myself. Bad idea. He talked too much and then tried to have sex with me in his car.

"Stop."

"No, because now that you let Russell get engaged, it's going to be that much harder to get rid of her." She tipped her bowl forward and drank the broth at the bottom.

"I let him? How did I let him?"

"You didn't give him the right signals or the time it needed. You pushed him away and you didn't have sex with him the other day."

I laughed. "Just imagine how awkward I'd be feeling at his wedding if I had. Because he would be marrying her anyway."

"Eat your sandwich. Skinny bones," Joanne muttered.

CHAPTER 15

Russell sat at his desk. He'd promised himself he was going to stop, but he couldn't. This case was the most fascinating thing that he'd come across in years, maybe ever.

After his dinner with Ava the other night, she'd driven him back to Claire's house. He'd been zonked on pain medication and a few margaritas. So stupid to let himself lose control in front of her. Especially since he wasn't so sure that the hit-and-run was just a random thing. He was losing his edge. But his head had been throbbing; he'd wanted a pain-free moment. The pill went down easy and the drinks easier. And everything that happened after that was blurred in an intoxicated stupor. She had been planning to drop him off at Juliette's, but he'd put up some sort of fuss in the car, so the evening had ended on her patio with her opening a bottle of Pinot Noir.

She knew exactly where the grapes had been grown in France. She told him over and over again in French. He tried to mimic her, but he couldn't get it right. She was talking and laughing, and the whole time he couldn't stop wondering about her mother, about where she'd come from. Though the wine was probably superb, he didn't remember a sip. He'd passed out and come to, the next morning, sprawled on the couch, shoes off, covered in a blanket. Ava had woken him with a cup of coffee so thick and dark he thought he was drinking bitter dirt. She was dressed already, had been outside.

"It's my I-got-plastered-on-downers-and-alcohol-and-didn't-go-home-last-night blend. Drink up."

He'd managed to get into a sitting position without throwing up. His head was pounding hard just beneath his eye sockets, but somehow the coffee helped. He was up and on his way home in half an hour, feeling sheepish. Ava was pleasant and teased him a bit, but the truth was, it was an idiot move. And what was worse, he couldn't remember exactly what had happened when they got back to her house. Not everything.

Days later he was still thinking about it. Ava occupied a corner of his brain and he couldn't force her out. He was mostly thinking about the investigation, but more than that. It was the way she looked, carried herself, moved. Her sense of humor. Also, he had to admit to himself, her vulnerability right now. Seeing her sitting in that diner, weeks ago, so sad, eyes moist, was too much. She needed him in a way Juliette hadn't in a very long time. He was going to figure this out for her.

"Are you still working?" Juliette came up behind him and put her arms around him gently. His neck was much better, still bandaged but not so painful. He looked at her hands. The diamond on her finger sparkled. She moved it a little under the light and giggled. "It's so beautiful, Russell." He smiled. It was an impulsive thing to do. He'd been pressured by his friends, by his parents, by his brothers, both of whom were already married.

But it was that night with Ava that had sealed it. She'd been talking away about grapes in France with that bottle of Pinot in her hand. He'd let her talk. He was just looking at her. She had on a dark-colored shirt and jeans. Her hair was down, falling onto her shoulders. He was watching her body move in her clothes, and he almost reached for her. It was the natural thing to do. But he'd caught himself. Sometime after that, his eyes had shut for the evening. He was hoping she hadn't dragged him to the couch but he couldn't be sure.

Things hadn't seemed so difficult a few years before. When he was younger, he did what he wanted. If this had happened back then, there'd be no question that he wouldn't have let himself fall asleep. He would have found a way to get her clothes off and worried about the fallout later. But maturity was supposed to be a good thing, wasn't it?

He left her house that morning and went to see his older brother. Jeff was married, with two children. He seemed happy, stable. Russell trusted his advice.

Russell sat in his brother's finished basement, feet up on the coffee table, spilling most of his guts, until his niece and nephew evicted them so they could watch Saturday-morning cartoons. He didn't tell Jeff the whole story. He didn't want his brother to get stabbed in the neck. But he told him enough.

"Russell, you're almost thirty-one years old. You're not a kid anymore. This isn't high school. Juliette loves you. You have a life with her. Everyone is just waiting for you to set the date." Russell had listened and nodded. "You're going to throw it all away, for what? For some girl you don't even know? Because she's pretty?"

"That's not it. She's more than pretty. But it's not even about her. Have you been listening to me?"

"I heard you."

"Maybe this has more to do with Juliette. Have you thought of that? Maybe I'm not sure of this marriage thing with her."

"This marriage thing?" Jeff looked at him. "You've been together for three and a half years. You know by now."

"So why do I keep thinking about this other girl? All the time. Why?"

"Let me tell you, wanting to have sex with other women isn't going to end just because you get married, so deal with it now. Don't do something stupid." Russell was quiet. "If you let this woman ruin this, I don't know . . . we're going to have a hard time accepting her. Is that what you want?"

"Jeff, that's not fair. This is my life." He was starting to feel defensive. "If I don't want to marry Juliette for whatever reason, because she's changed, or I've changed, or whatever, that's my decision." He stood. "You, of all people, should accept whatever I decide to do."

Jeff patted him on the back. "You'll do the right thing. You know you will."

He had bought the engagement ring the next day.

Juliette kissed his neck. He looked up at her. "I'll be there in a bit." She nodded and moved on, still looking at the ring in the light.

He opened the file and spread it out in front of him. He'd called in enough favors to get the whole Owens file. Reports, follow-up, pictures, notes. Every phone call the police had made five years ago was in there, every thought. Every detail available to try and figure out who had taken a Polaroid of the house, and why Ava's mother had it. He got up and closed his office door. He didn't want Juliette walking in on this. She'd seen worse in the OR, but that wasn't the point. He spread fifteen photographs across the desk and stared at them.

The first was of Loyal Owens. He lay on his side on the beige carpet. Half of his head looked like red mush. He'd been hit so many times his skull had caved in. He had been a large man. Tall and probably muscular in his younger days, some of his former self still visible through rolls of fat. His khaki pants and green shirt were stained red with blood.

Russell rocked slightly in his chair and studied the seven photographs of this man. Every angle added a bit to the story. He had tried to fend off his attacker. He'd died lying on his side, his hands splayed open, as if still fighting for his life. There was a grimace on his face, his lips parted, as if he'd died midsentence, the words caught in his throat.

The second set was of Destiny Owens. What part had she played? Destiny must have fallen forward, hit from behind. Then she'd been struck again on the back of her head. There were no other wounds present on her body. Her car keys lay only inches from her, apparently dropped when she fell. Her purse was next to her, the strap still on her shoulder. Never touched by the killer. The side of her face, covered in blood, was visible in the photographs. She wore no expression in death.

Russell pushed his chair back and stood up. He paced the room in circles. He had to look at the pictures again. He was missing something. The killer had probably been in the house, either waiting or surprised by their return. She enters through the kitchen, is hit in the head, falls, and is hit again. He, for whatever reason, enters the house through the front door. He hears the commotion in the kitchen? He starts to head in that direction when the killer comes out. A confrontation? How did the killer get a man of that size to the ground? Or did it happen the other way around? He was killed first, in the living room, and then she came in later? The autopsy had been inconclusive as to the timing. The killings were too close together.

He needed to get ahold of the physical evidence. In conversations with Ava, she had never mentioned the possibility that these two people might be her biological parents. Possibly because the only thing connecting her to them was that Claire had stored the photograph in with her baby things. That and the inscription on the photograph.

If he could, he would do DNA testing on the two victims and then test them against Ava's—see if there was any biological connection. But there was no way that was going to happen. This was all unofficial. Asking for testing would mean opening this thing up officially.

He stood and grabbed his coat. He needed to think, and he was better at thinking when he was moving. He would take a walk. He opened his drawer and pulled out his Ontario MK 3 knife. Then he loaded his Glock and slid it into his waistband. No one was going to surprise him this time.

As he crossed the lawn he made a mental list of everything he wanted to do. Get information on Ross Saunders, Marie Saunders, and Anais. Drive to Chestnut Hill to see the Owenses' house for himself. Talk to people in the area. Suddenly, he stopped.

Why hadn't he thought of this before? Running back into the house and locking the door behind him, he grabbed the phone and punched in a number.

"Charlie? Russell. I need a favor." Charlie Walker was a lieutenant in the Haddon Township Police Department.

"Name it."

"I'm looking for police records on a baby that was abandoned at the Holy Saviour Catholic Church in Westmont in January of nineteen ninety-three. Can you see if you can find out anything?"

"Nineteen ninety-three? January?"

"Female infant found in the annex just before Mass. January nineteen ninety-three. Call me tomorrow at my office if you find anything?"

"You got it. But I was here then, Russ, and it doesn't ring a bell. I'd remember a baby in a church."

"Well, if you find anything, hold it. Don't fax it. I'll pick it up. And please don't mention this to anyone."

"Gotcha."

He sat down heavily in his chair. It took everything he had in him not to rush over to Ava and talk to her about the case. To sit with her on her patio and hear her thoughts, hear her voice, which, even though she was raised in the United States, had the slightest hint of an accent. And to look into those strange, clear green eyes and see her smile back at him. He saw her in his mind, her hair pulled back, her crisp white blouse gaping slightly, the swell of her breast just visible.

"Russell, are you coming to bed?" Juliette stood before him. Her dark-blonde hair was tangled about her head.

"Yes," he mumbled.

CHAPTER 16

He sat at the back of the church so he wouldn't be noticed. Most of the people he'd known growing up in this neighborhood were long gone or dead, so the chances of being recognized were slim. The lights were dimmed; there seemed to be a hum to the quiet. He drifted back to the years he'd spent here as a kid, his life controlled by the church. His mother, before she died when he was eight, had been devout, sometimes in this church six days a week. And if he wasn't at early-morning Mass or Sunday Mass or involved in the Catholic Youth Organization or choir practice, he was in school, sitting half the day in this same pew with his uniform on, his head bowed, saying, "Hail Mary . . ."

The nuns at school had been cruel. He still had a scar on his index finger where his hand had been slammed in the desk. His knuckles had been slapped so many times with rulers they'd grown numb to it. His bottom bore no scars from the paddle, but many a night he'd been too sore to sit down. He was no different from any of the others. Loyal, who had been a particularly restless kid, always moving, was tied to his desk one day. Bill had had his chewing gum ripped from his mouth by bony nun's fingers, and then had his face slapped with the same hand. The humiliations they'd all suffered became part of who they were as adults. And though he was afraid of the priests' and the nuns' punishments, he was more afraid of his father. To go home and say he'd been disciplined at school would mean more beatings. Worse beatings at home. So he said nothing.

He'd had his confirmation in this church when he was eight years old. He, Loyal, Ross, and Bill screwing around in the back before the service started, nervous excitement. Father Jenson scolded them and boxed their ears till their faces were red, ringing with pain. They were sent to separate corners of the room, to face the wall and recite Hail Marys. Bill laughed from his corner and couldn't stop, causing a cavalcade of giggles from every corner. They were beaten with a strap, right before the service. He could still see Bill's red hair, laughing freckled face burning, tears collecting in the corners of his eyes. How—after years spent in the church, the daily Masses, Catholic school, the children's choir, altar-boy duties—after all of it, Bill could have gone on to become a priest was beyond him. He never could figure it out.

But it was that night after confirmation, that's when it all started. The four of them standing on the curb of Frankford and Allegheny. The streetlights had flicked on. It was dark, but none of them would be missed at home yet. In hushed voices they'd made their confessions. Then they'd started walking. All of them talking fast, over one another, interrupting and then repeating. It was the first time they'd spoken the truth they all knew, out loud. Loyal's face was caught somewhere between anger and fear. Bill's head was down, dejected. Ross, the stoic, pretending to be unaffected, was digging in his pockets for a loose cigarette he'd pilfered from his father's pack. They became permanently connected that night, their brotherhood of little boys. And before they scattered back to their homes, they'd made a pact.

Looking back, that night set the stage for everything that was to come. He would have done anything for any one of them. Fight, kill, die. How had things gone so wrong? It was like some larger force had been there with them that night under the streetlamp, cursing them to difficult lives and brutal deaths. Their pact—at the time it was just a venting of childhood what-ifs—took on a life of its own many years later and eventually destroyed them all.

Now the church was quiet. The Eucharist service wasn't starting for over two hours, but there was nowhere else he wanted to be. He felt a calmness and destruction within the walls of this building. Pulsing familiarity. And though it was sacrilege to pray for the strength to do something evil, to kill smoothly and cleanly, he was sure God understood the many variations of sin and would forgive him for finishing something that started when he was just a kid.

A soft voice came out of the darkness. "Excuse me, sir? Did you say you wanted to make confession?"

CHAPTER 17

Marie Lavoisier-Saunders sat in her spartan room at the Christ the King Convent. Her eyes rested on a spot on the wall that was bare—no religious relic, no picture, no decoration of any kind. The wall was eggshell white, clean of dirt, yet dulled and dingy from time. She was deep in disquieting thought.

The day her sister died had been miserable from daybreak. Pouring rain from the minute Marie opened her eyes. It was a Friday and there was only one Mass, at midday. She had to prepare herself physically and spiritually. She had been dressing when the telephone rang. The message from Ava was brief.

As she drove, she'd kissed her rosary and prayed that Claire was still conscious. The emergency-room cubicle was chaos when she got there, but her sister was alive, attached to monitors.

Marie had clutched Claire's hand. "What happened?" she whispered.

"Things are out of control, Marie. You need to call Maman. I'm afraid."

"What's out of control? Afraid of what?" When Marie looked up, Ava was there, standing by the cubicle, her eyes wide, riveted on the two of them. Marie pulled the curtain and put her head closer to hear her sister's last words.

The two thoughts that came to her when the doctor told them her sister was dead were, one, that now everything was on her shoulders, and two, that maybe Claire's death hadn't been an accident.

Marie opened her eyes. She was in the middle of the floor in her cell at the convent, a rosary in one hand. She had been rocking and swaying without even realizing it. Someone was pounding on the door.

She stood and went to open it, but it flew open before her hand even touched the knob. He stood in the doorway, dressed in dark colors, paunchy, short—a pathetic figure of a man.

"No," Marie said, voice quavering. She hadn't seen him in years, hadn't been completely sure where he'd been, though she'd always been certain he was circling nearby. Keeping a beady eye on things. His looks hadn't improved with age. She tried to shut the door on him but he pushed his way in.

"What do you want?" Tears welled in her eyes and she backed up to the wall. The last time she'd seen him he'd brutalized Claire, slamming her head against the hood of the car, demanding to know where Ava was.

He ignored her and walked the perimeter of the small room, his head down, hands clasped behind his back. He said nothing for more than a minute. Marie eyed the door and wondered if she could move fast enough to get past him.

His head snapped up, his glassy eyes met hers. "Claire kept me busy, I will say. Moving here. Moving there."

"Please, don't do this here."

He raised both arms and turned in a circle. "And where would be more fitting than here in the Catholic church, hmmm?"

Marie stared at the floor. "You saw her obituary?" she whispered. "I was so afraid of that."

"Her death led me to her. As funny as that sounds. And then Ava pops up like a baby bird leaving the nest. Going to Loyal's house." He spun to face her. "But you know that, right? And she's been talking to the wrong people. So why? Why now, Marie? What got her going?" He continued to pace, saying nothing for a minute. Then he stopped. "Whoever killed the others intends to kill me next, Marie. And then maybe you."

Marie jumped up—to confront him or escape, she didn't know. "Me? None of this has anything to do with me. This is about you and my father and what the four of you did." She pointed at him. "My father, dumping his sins on Claire—it destroyed her life."

"The minute your sister agreed and the minute you started protecting that child, it had everything to do with you. Do you think it's a coincidence that only you and I are left? Someone knows our secret. So you're going to help me find out who's been killing us off. Bill, Loyal, your father—and then we're going to get rid of Ava so there's no evidence left. Which should have been done twenty years ago."

Marie took a step back from him. "I was never completely on Claire's side in any of this. In protecting Ava. You know that."

"Interesting you say that, but I'm never quite sure with you . . ."

She blew air out of her mouth. "A few years ago we might be having a different conversation—with Claire and Ross still alive. But not now. Ava's becoming too much."

His eyes jumped to hers. "Why? What's she done? Tell me."

Marie shook her head. "I think she's . . . Never mind. Just know that I loved my father. When I heard from his own lips what he did, his reasons, I could never find it in my heart to turn my back on him completely. And I won't turn my back on his memory now."

He hesitated by the door, his face puffy, ugly. "Someone is out there watching and killing, Marie. You haven't gotten a photograph in the mail, have you? You know, of Claire's front door? I'm not convinced she had a heart attack."

His echo of her own suspicions made her hands shake. She said nothing.

"So, are we going to work together now? Let's do it or we'll both be gone."

She looked toward the cross on the wall. For years, she and Claire had sacrificed for others. Maybe it was time for self-preservation to come first. "What do you propose?"

He studied her for a second. "It's funny, we're both in agreement but for different reasons. You loved Ross. I hated him and hate him now for all this."

Marie's head was moving back and forth. "Well, he's dead. Someone else hated him too, apparently."

"Are you up for this, Marie? Getting rid of your niece? Because I can't have you backing out or double-crossing me. Or letting religion cloud your judgment at the last minute."

When she nodded, he said, "Good. I'll be in touch." With that, he left the room.

Marie stared after him, at the door, not moving from her spot. Everything she'd said to him was true. Ava had become a problem. Killing her, though, was another story. But Marie also knew that if she didn't cooperate, he'd just come back. And maybe kill her too.

"There has to be another way out. A third option." She turned to the cross. "God, please let me find it."

CHAPTER 18

I stood at the locked door in Claire's office, hammer in hand. No one else was in the house. I'd woken with the first sign of light—no Marie to suddenly "stop by," no Joanne to stand behind me, breathing on my neck, asking dozens of questions, all of which seemed time consuming and annoying.

The locksmith was due in a few hours to open the door. But I worried about a stranger seeing the contents before I had a chance to examine them myself. What was hidden behind this wooden barricade? Papers, documents, secrets, hidden pasts, jewels, photographs, dynamite, dead bodies? Each thought popped into my head and was discarded just as quickly. Too obvious, too stupid, too outlandish.

The door handle was one of the original fixtures of the house. Smooth, marble white. The lock had been installed in the walnut wood sometime much later. A pewter silver color, it sat directly underneath the handle. The hammer was useless. There was nothing to pound, and the lock was hard to get to. In frustration I dropped to my knees and slid the claws into the doorjamb and pulled.

"You're not going to get far with just a hammer." I dropped it and whipped around. Russell stood in the doorway. "You might need a crowbar."

He took a step into the room. "And you're obviously immune to Beethoven's fifth. I've been ringing the bell for ten minutes." He sat in the desk chair. "So . . . what's going on?" He motioned to the closet door. "A bit early for a break-in."

I stood and smoothed my jeans. "A bit early for a break-in, back atcha." I looked at my watch. "It's only 7:16. How'd you know I wasn't occupied up here? You know, doing something really private?"

He smiled. "You obviously were. Sorry for the interruption. That front door needs to be locked at all times. But you know that."

"What did you want?"

"I had to find you. And you didn't answer your cell."

I wiped my face with the back of my hand. "I couldn't sleep, and this closet has been rankling me. The locksmith is coming at nine thirty. I thought I might take one more crack at opening it before he shows. Want some coffee?" I left the room and went down the steps, not waiting for an answer.

Russell found me in the kitchen a few minutes later. He was wearing what I would call his uniform. Medium-blue button-down shirt and khakis. Dress-casual that he thought didn't scream *cop* to the general public.

"I need to talk to you, Ava."

I put the coffee beans into the grinder and pushed the button. "So talk," I shouted over the whirring of the blades.

"No, I need your full attention." He took my arm and nudged me toward the kitchen table. I shook off his hand and poured the grinds into the basket. I knew whatever he had to say wasn't going to be good news. I knew because he didn't tell me upstairs. He wanted to wait until the mood was right. And I was irritated at him—for reasons I didn't want to examine too closely. My heart was starting to flutter when I saw him, I was thinking about him when he wasn't around—not just worrying about his safety, but about what he was doing. None of that was good, no matter what Joanne thought.

He waited patiently at the table, just watching me. It took a full ten minutes for the coffee to brew, and he didn't move. He didn't try to make conversation with me. He just sat and waited and finally I ran out of distractions.

I put the coffee cup in front of him and took the chair across the table. I folded my arms and closed my eyes. "Go ahead, Russell. Shatter my world. What did you find out?"

He leaned toward me, as if proximity would soften the blow. "Charlie Walker, from the Haddon Township Police Department, searched all records from nineteen ninety-three. And ninety-one, ninety-two, ninety-four, too. There was never a baby abandoned at the Holy Saviour Catholic Church." He tapped his fingers on the table. "Or any other church in the area. At least, not one that was reported to the police. So, either it happened and it was kept quiet. Or . . ."

I opened my eyes. "Or what?"

"Or it never happened at all. It was a cover story—for you. No one else." His eyes were grave and unblinking.

I shook my head. "So they lied to me about everything. And it wasn't just Claire lying, but Marie and Anais too?"

He didn't move. "I don't think any of them lied to hurt you. Probably just the opposite."

"But what could be so bad that lying was necessary? Why make up some complex story? Why didn't Claire just pretend I was her real daughter?"

"Well, that's the question. I just don't know the answer. Yet."

I half smiled. "Glad to see you're not giving up on this. But it seems like the more you dig, the more questions pop up. Like who am I? If I'm not some girl abandoned at a church, who am I? Really?"

His hands wrapped around his mug. "You came into contact with this family somehow. Claire adopted you, maybe protected you at all costs. Did you ever happen to see any real adoption papers? Legal papers, growing up? Anything that would validate a part of their story?"

I shook my head. "No. And Claire told me very little."

"So it begs the question, how did she get a birth certificate, or anything, to register you for school?"

I shrugged. "I have no idea."

"More curious. You really are Jane Doe."

I stared at the bandages still adhered to the side of his head. His words made me furious. "I am not. I had a real mother. At some point I ended up with Claire. That's what you should be focused on. Who am I? Start there. Forget the murders for a minute."

He was startled at my anger and reached across to touch my hand. "I didn't mean—"

I shook my head and pulled my hand away. "Don't."

"Can I ask you just one question? What's your very first memory?"

My very first memory? Joanne had asked me the same thing. I closed my eyes. "I remember feeling more than remembering, if that makes sense. Darkness. The stained-glass windows. I was in a church. My mother was holding my hand."

"Claire?"

I shook my head no, and then yes. "I think so but I don't know. I need to be alone with this for a bit. Please? And like I said, if you start by finding out where I came from, that wouldn't be a bad thing."

He pushed up from his chair. "I don't want you to feel alone, Ava. You're not. I'll call you."

I heard his feet on the floor and the sounds of the front door opening and closing behind him. When I looked up, the room was empty. I took a breath and a half, trying to stifle this miserable feeling. I wanted Russell to find answers, didn't I? He said I wasn't alone, but I'd never been more alone in my life.

When I heard the locksmith leaning on the doorbell sometime later, I was still sitting at the kitchen table. The cup of coffee in front of me was cold and untouched.

◆ ◆ ◆

"Someone went to a lot of trouble to put this in. Are you sure you want it open?" He was bent at one knee, looking at the lock. "Last year I was hired to open a door just like this. Old woman had died. Family thought it might be filled with money or something. Wasn't." He gave me a fleeting look. "Dead cats and mothballs. She kept all her dead cats in this locked closet. Must have been a stench until they completely decomposed . . ."

"I'm very sure. And I doubt there are cats in there. Claire hated cats." I smiled.

"All the better reason to shove them in a closet."

"Oh, and please leave the locks in place. I don't want anyone to know that I've opened this door."

He gave me a curious glance. "Family drama," he muttered. "Give me twenty minutes, then. I'll try and leave it pristine. But the door will be open. I can't make keys to relock it."

I nodded and walked down the stairs and back into the kitchen. I busied myself by dumping the coffee and scrubbing the pot. The hot water and bubbles helped me think.

The thing that bothered me, that could bring tears to my eyes in an instant, was Anais. Claire and I had lived in many towns, many houses, while I was growing up, but Anais had only one. It was a constant, the North Star in my life, the place that felt like home. She was strong, consistent, disciplined, and that had given me the strength to endure the sudden uprootings, Claire's moods. I saw her for a month every summer and some scattered weeks during the year. But that time made all the difference. She taught me to read in English and French, to tie my shoes, to know how alkaline the soil was before planting a proper garden. I just could not reconcile that she'd conspired with the rest of them to keep the truth from me. Almost mocking my steadfast commitment to her. But maybe they'd lied to her too. Maybe she didn't know any more than I did. She and I needed to have a conversation as soon as possible.

"All done." The locksmith was in the doorway. "You were right, no cats."

"What's in there?"

"A lot of boxes. Nothing else." He held out a clipboard. "That's one fifty. Cash or credit."

The closet door was shut, and the only sign that the lock had been violated was bits of shredded wood on the floor. I entered the closet, partially closing the door behind me. A treasure trove. Maybe not gold, silver, or jewels. But heavily guarded information. My skin began to crawl. This was a large house that had had only two occupants for as long as I could remember. Claire had endless privacy. These boxes could have been in her room, under her bed, in that closet where I found the photograph, and I wouldn't have known. Why the locked door?

I surveyed the space. This closet was, like most of the others in the house, cut from other rooms. The original Victorian layout didn't allow for bathrooms or closets. At some point the rooms were redrawn. Cut to accommodate these modern conveniences. It was small, six feet square. High ceiling. I hit the light switch and then noticed the incandescent bulb in the fixture in the ceiling. It sizzled, and I thought the filament inside the bulb had burned out, but then it lit up. It made me wonder when Claire, or anyone, had last come in here. Then I saw a metal folding chair against the wall. There was lighting and seating. All that was missing was refreshments.

"Qu'avons-nous ici, Claire? Les secrets cachés du passé?"

The hidden secrets of the past. I unfolded the chair and took a seat, then pulled the nearest box to me. When I opened the flap and peered inside, it was filled with loose photographs. And I knew that the man who had stared into the camera was Ross Saunders.

CHAPTER 19

Russell stared out the window, the facts of the case zigzagging back and forth through his brain. So much information, so little information. His hands were tied, because he couldn't do anything to bring attention to his investigation. Getting information on the down low was harder and more exacting. It meant he had to go through numerous people, and those people had to be trusted. One leak and he could be called to account for what he was doing. If that happened, Ava would shut down. This whole thing would end. And he was too curious now to be that careless.

The key figure in this story was Claire, and Claire was an enigma. Born in Philadelphia at Pennsylvania Hospital, 1969. He was able to get that from a friend from the Division of Vital Records. Ross and Anais listed their address as 933 North Fourth Street in the Northern Liberties section of the city. Marie was born two years later. Same hospital. Same address. Anais jumped the US ship for an unknown reason and headed to France in 1974 with the two girls in tow. Poof. No records of the Saunders girls until Claire reappears in 1992. Twenty-three. Living in Brooklyn. Working as an editor for *Vogue* magazine.

Claire told Ava she'd been adopted as a baby. Found at a church in Westmont, New Jersey. That was the story. That would make Claire twenty-four when she adopted Ava. Odd for a young single woman to adopt a baby out of the blue—a baby abandoned almost a hundred miles from where she was living. And Claire's life in Brooklyn continued after the supposed adoption, as it always had—same apartment, same job. Until Ava was three. Then total disruption.

Claire's trackable life disappeared at that point because she didn't have any employment. Getting financial records would be hard, but it seemed that Claire, from that point forward, was funded completely by Anais. It was obvious that Claire and Ava were on the run. *From what?* He kept flashing to the image of the Owenses' house in Chestnut Hill. The double murder. The only thread of connection he could come up with was that Loyal Owens had been working in Pennsauken, New Jersey, in 1993. For a Camden County design company that manufactured cabinets and kitchen fittings, not even five miles from Westmont, where Ava was supposedly abandoned.

Deep in his gut, he started to think that pursuing a biological connection between Ava and the Owenses was the wrong track. There was another thread that connected the two, there had to be, and when he found it, it would be simple and obvious. It always was. He stared down at the name on his blotter. *Ross Saunders.* "It's you. I know it is. But how? And why?" He tapped his finger on the name several times. "Saunders and Owens," he said aloud.

"What's going on?" Juliette appeared at his office door. He hadn't even heard her come in.

Russell shook his head. "Just piecing together something for a case."

"Listen, don't forget we have a meeting with the wedding planner tomorrow at ten." She half turned away. "And I was sort of playing with the guest list and seating arrangements, even though it's a little early. I just can't help it. I have Joan and Jennifer sitting at different tables right now. But their daughters are in the same class at Saint Joan of Arc and want to sit—"

Russell's head snapped up. "What did you say?"

Juliette frowned. "What'd I say?"

He looked down at Ross's date of birth and then Loyal's. Born within four months of one another. "Same class at Saint Joan of Arc," he mumbled. Maybe the two men went to the same school. Grew up in the same neighborhood. He pushed back in his chair, hand on his chin. All he had on Loyal Owens was the autopsy and investigation reports. Very little background information. "So stupid." He didn't realize he'd said it out loud.

"Not really, Russell, the seating is everything if we want people to have a good time."

Russell stood up and brushed past her. "No, it's fine. I'll be there for your thing tomorrow morning. Gotta go." He kissed her cheek lightly.

"What—?" She didn't get to finish the sentence. He was down the steps and gone.

Twenty-five minutes later he was heading down Route 70 toward Ava's house. He needed to pass all this back and forth with her. Dig at her brain for lost or missing info. See if she'd found anything interesting in that closet. Maybe canvass Saunders's old neighborhood. And he really wanted to see her again.

CHAPTER 20

The neighborhood had changed so much over the past twenty years, it was difficult for him to remember what it had looked like before. He sat on the steps of what used to be a bar right off of Kensington and Allegheny. It was boarded up now, the windows covered with pieces of plywood, the door striped with yellow "Caution" tape. A big neon-pink sheet of paper was attached, screaming *Condemned.* He watched the people walking past—so much more diverse than when he'd lived here. It had been mostly Irish, Germans, and Poles, with some pockets of Jews and Hispanics. Now the community was gone, leaving drug addicts and transients in its wake. The families with the kids playing stickball in the streets had been replaced by filth and crime.

The Market–Frankford elevated train rattled above him, drowning out all sound for a few minutes. When he was growing up, that noise had blended so that he hardly noticed it. He could see the El train from his bedroom window, and the thunder of that train had lulled him to sleep. There used to be a string of businesses up and down Kensington Avenue, not far from where he was sitting. When he was a kid, before his mother got cancer and died, she would drag him along with her pull shopping cart to get groceries. The butcher shop was here. The small grocer. There was even a fresh-fish truck. Now it was all gone. Trash and empty dope bags littered the street, along with the occasional dirty needle or used condom. Filthy.

He stood up and started walking. He often wondered how things would be different if he could do it over again. If he woke up one morning and he was back in his apartment around the corner, with his father. If he'd never met his friends that night after confirmation but instead headed home to his corner bedroom, his comic books, and the sounds of Aunt Constance and his father watching TV and getting drunk downstairs.

He passed Saint Francis de Sales Church and stopped. His boots wouldn't move. He stared at the side door, memories spilling out so fast he couldn't catch them all. Only shadows of the past. Of Sister Alice whipping Loyal's knuckles with a ruler because she thought he was blowing his nose on his sleeve. When Bill told the nun that Jenny had no underwear on. He felt bad about that after, because he knew she had a crummy house—parents that didn't wash her clothes or feed her. But all the same, the nun lifted Jenny's skirt and whacked her bare bottom in front of everyone. He closed his eyes for a second. The bare bottom. He needed to keep moving. He saw a flash of Loyal. Loyal and Ross. Their bare asses as they pissed off the Tacony–Palmyra Bridge one sticky hot summer night after freshman year. Then Father Callahan in his robes—that soft, patronizing voice in his ear. He'd tried to push that man's face out of his mind for many years. Sometimes the eyes would come to him. Sometimes the mouth, but never his entire face. His body started to shake and he started to run.

The cold air both sobered and numbed him. He needed to get home. But the images followed him, of Ross and Loyal pissing into the night after they'd climbed the bridge. He wouldn't go with them. Were they laughing or crying? He couldn't tell. He heard the sounds from above and waited to see if their bodies would drop into the cold river. But the only things that fell were their streams of urine. Relief poured over him when he saw them climb down, alive and intact. But the redness in their eyes told him they'd both been crying.

He passed a liquor store and picked up a fifth of Jameson for old times' sake before boarding the El train at the Allegheny station. He was feeling old; the aches in his bones were slowing him down. He'd celebrated his sixty-seventh birthday the month before. Time was catching up with him. Sometimes, he would open his eyes in the morning and wonder if it was worth it, finding Ava. Getting rid of her. He was getting on, and even if things exploded now, how many more years did he have? How bad could it be? But it wasn't a logical thing. He had a drive. All or nothing. Loose ends drove him on. That and a deep hatred in his gut toward that whole family, but especially toward Ross.

The train jerked to a stop. He was at the end of the line. He trudged down the steps to the Frankford Transportation Center. He looked around, undecided if he should walk the seven blocks home or try and find a cab. It was getting dark outside. There were jostling crowds elbowing to get on the buses. He felt achy. Like he was getting sick. His throat felt tight and he was sure he had a fever. After ten minutes, he located a taxi and resigned himself to pay the five dollars plus tip for the luxury of not walking in the cold.

The little row home he was renting was dark. He stood outside after the cab had left, just watching. The neighbor, Mrs. Engles, had a light that went on automatically when it got dark. It was like a spotlight. Glaring, blinding, and horrible. It kept him awake some nights. His complaints were met with the sound of her screeching voice, so he gave up. Tonight was the only time he could remember it not going on. He glanced at her house, hoping nothing had happened to her. The sky was dense gray; the sun had gone down, just a sliver of color to the west, so it was only when he was right in front of his door that he noticed it was open just a crack.

He whipped his head around so fast he almost dropped his bottle of Jameson. The street was empty. Quiet. He pushed the door all the way open and stepped in slowly. The only sound he heard was the air going through his dry throat into his lungs. He forgot feeling feverish. Every nerve tingled electric through his body. He stood there for a full five minutes. Just listening. But there was no sound. Not even Mrs. Engles yelling at her dog, banging the walls, or slamming pots and pans. That would have been a symphony to his ears right now.

He flicked on the light. The room was small and dumpy. But it was the same as when he'd left it. He took a tour, room by room, hitting the lights, then checking the closets. Nothing was amiss. No one was here. Maybe he'd just forgotten to lock the door? He went to the kitchen and took out a highball glass, dropping two ice cubes into the bottom, then pouring in the whiskey till it reached the top. He rubbed his throat. It hurt so much the first gulp felt like a torch being shoved in his mouth, but the second wasn't bad. The third, just smooth whiskey. He wandered to the couch and flopped on it. Maybe he'd just sleep here tonight. He was too tired and too sick to go upstairs.

Just before his eyes fluttered shut, he saw the little Polaroid photograph of a front door, propped neatly against a picture frame.

CHAPTER 21

I sat on the floor and spread Claire's life around me. Boxes and boxes of photograph albums, loose pictures tied with rubber bands and string. Clothing, cut glass, mementos, artwork. Her father's life was in the closet too. Claire had acquired his things after he'd died. A multitude of boxes, photographs, scrapbooks, letters, his army uniforms.

I stared into his dark eyes. This was the first time I'd seen a good photograph of him as a younger man. Anais had kept a few pictures in an ancient blue album on a bookshelf in her living room. As a kid I would pull it out and pore over it. It was mostly the ones of her as a child in Vietnam that fascinated me. The beautiful dresses, the oriental flowers, the French architecture. She'd sit with me for hours telling stories about her parents, their house in Hanoi, the food, the balls, the travel. Halong Bay and Hong Kong seemed so exotic. By the time we'd gotten to the end of the book and the appearance of "the man with the black hair," as I'd always called him, Grand-Mère Anais's face would change, the corners of her mouth would go down, and she would inevitably shut the book on my fingers and say, *"Puis tout a changé. La fin." And then everything changed, the end.*

The ruin of French colonization in Southeast Asia and her meeting Ross Saunders had coincided, so that Anais couldn't separate them anymore. She viewed them both as the beginning of the destruction of her formerly grand lifestyle. *And then everything changed* summed it up for her.

But I had these photographs now and they were vivid. His face, his features, his smile, his awkward glances, stiff poses, it was all here, and I was really seeing him as a young man for the first time. Claire hadn't been completely estranged from her father. Like I'd explained to Russell, I'd met him a couple times. Briefly. And both of those occasions were odd. Odd in the sense that the two didn't seem to have any affection for one another, but their meetings were meaningful and intense—a half hour of words passing back and forth, and then they were both on their way.

I was around five during the first encounter. He'd never communicated with me, no birthday cards or acknowledgment of my existence, no greetings of any sort before that. Claire took me with her to a restaurant in Pittsburgh, explaining that we had to see a man, that it wouldn't take long. When I asked, "What man?" she said I'd never met him before. She never said he was my grandfather. The ride on the funicular stayed with me far longer than the meeting with the man with black hair. He was older, his hair now gray, so I never connected him to the man in Anais's book, not until much later. But even so, at first glance, I knew him. I'd met him before somewhere. And Claire was lying about it.

The second meeting was more recent. It was toward the end of my junior year of high school, when we were living in Willow Grove, a suburb outside of Philadelphia. Claire and I were walking down Chestnut Street on a particularly squally fall day. The tiny part of my face that wasn't covered in a scarf felt as if it were being sliced away by horizontal rain. I turned to Claire to say something and there he was, in front of us. Time had chiseled away at him, but I recognized him instantly. Claire looked startled, but composed herself quickly. He pulled her into a little pizza shop, very animated about something. I found a seat in the corner and played with the saltshaker, pretending I couldn't hear anything they were saying, until they abruptly got up and separated ways. Someone important to both of them had died. Claire's face had turned the color of the egg-white omelet she'd had for breakfast. We packed up and headed to Ann Arbor, Michigan, a month later. That might have been the last conversation Claire ever had with her father. I never saw them together again. He died just before my senior year of college, suddenly.

Now I was looking at him again. Even as a child he had deep-set, worried eyes. Catholic-school photos filled with small uniform-clad boys. The dark-haired boy turned into the dark-haired man. Tall, broad shouldered, more confident. Then handsomely dressed in his army uniform. Then a backdrop of lush Vietnam appeared. Beautiful beaches. A few were taken in the streets of Saigon, then a more formal one, Anais and him dressed up, going out for the evening. I picked up the photograph. Happy, naive Anais. Smiling. His arm was around her—young forbidden love. Anais didn't look like she was about to say *And then everything changed* in any of these pictures. There was no hint of the impending dangers of the American War looming that I could see. It was just a pretty, smiling young woman and her date, against an unbelievably beautiful backdrop.

At the bottom of the box was a stack of smaller photographs tied together with string. Polaroids. Though yellowed and worn with time, I knew they were the same size and shape as the photograph of the Owenses' house. Polaroids taken with the same grainy black-and-white film. I hesitated for a minute and then flipped through them. Photographs of trees. All of them.

I set them aside and pulled out another book. These photographs were of Ross's life. His parents holding him as an infant. I turned the page. Standing with his mother in front of a church in what I assumed was Philadelphia. Ross was around ten years old, in a suit. His mother wore a hat. Both were smiling. The next page was filled with scenes from the beach. The Jersey Shore. My mind was starting to wander and my stomach growled. I flipped the page. Staring back at me was a teenaged Ross. High school, maybe. The boy next to him, arm tossed over Ross's shoulder, I absolutely knew, was the man who had stopped to ask directions when I was in front of Loyal's house that day. I'd seen the man in the car for only a moment and a half, but there he was. The same probing eyes jumped out at me from fifty years earlier.

I stood up and paced, pulling my hair back from my face with my fists. I stopped and picked up the book again. *He was following me that day. He'd been tracking me.* I started to sweat. He stared into the camera, confident, cocky, so sure of himself, though even as a teenager he was ugly. Pug-like. The next photograph on the page was of four boys. All dressed in robes. Altar boys? Ross was there, along with Pug Man and two others. They were posed in front of the church, not smiling.

My cell phone was lying on the table. Cherbourg was six hours ahead—still early enough for Anais to be up. She was strictly a land-line woman. I'd tried to set her up with a cell phone a few years ago for emergencies. *Une urgence? Quelle urgence?* she'd sputtered. I finally gave up and left her muttering in angry French about Americans and their ridiculous ways. It was pointless to remind her the French had cell phones too.

I dialed her number and waited for the numerous clicks and the connection to her line. Her phone rang. And rang. No answering machine either. "Damn it, Grand-Maman Anais. This is an emergency. I need to ask you an important question." The sound of Beethoven overhead made me hang up the phone.

CHAPTER 22

He rubbed his eyes and sat up. He was so sure the Polaroid was of Claire's house, the front of her house, that someone had killed her and made it look like an accident. So when he stared down at the photograph, it took a few minutes to realize what he was looking at. It wasn't Claire's house at all. It was his own front door, partially open. Crappy, unfocused. The words *Two other woes are yet to come. Revelation 6:6* were printed underneath. While he had been on the stoop of the bar in his old neighborhood, reminiscing about the past, someone had been here, ready to kill him, ready to take a picture of his front door with their sick little camera. His hands started shaking and he thought he might vomit.

He dropped the photograph onto the table and whirled around. It was dark, quiet. Not even the glare from Mrs. Engles's bulb. Mrs. Engles? He went outside and peered next door. Absolute stillness. He tiptoed to her front window. If there was anything worth seeing inside, the grime smeared across the glass prevented it. He wanted to knock and make sure she was all right, or at least ask if she'd seen who'd broken into his house, but he was afraid. And the truth was, he really didn't want to know if she was all right. If he had to get out of here quick, he didn't need another body on his conscience.

He could feel a bit of jagged anger, the feeling that he wanted to punch someone, creeping over him—the alcohol was leaving his body, and the sobering reality was too much for him. He went back in, dropped some ice cubes into the glass, and filled it to the top with whiskey. Then he pulled out the other three Polaroids and set this one next to it. Four, all in a row, in order. Bill, Loyal, Ross, and now his. Why leave this picture now? Was it a threat? Why not just wait and kill him, as they had done the others? He wondered if there would be another Polaroid taken after he was actually killed. A two-for-one-special Polaroid deal. And then who would get the very last picture?

He read the writing printed on each one, thinking that maybe it told some story. Something he hadn't noticed before. Bill's said *The church does not exonerate all Sins.* It was written in dark ink. Black. Careful letters. The first *S* in *Sins* was capitalized, giving it more importance and meaning. He tapped his head. This first photo was meant to let the others know that Bill's death wasn't an accident—someone knew their secret. And what they'd done was unforgivable. Loyal's read *Destiny calls us, bound by Loyalty. All things that spring eternal can never be crushed.* Was this to let them know that the killer was aware Ava existed? He took a long gulp of whiskey. Ross's photograph said *Ave Maria, Joseph too.* There was no ambiguity in that one. They all knew who Joseph was. The killer was laying out the sequence of horrible events that had taken place that night. That message was only for him; the others had been killed off by that time.

But now this last picture. *Two other woes are yet to come.* Maybe what he'd said to Marie had been right. Maybe whoever was after him was after her too. He needed to get out of here, lie low for a bit. When it was safe, he'd finish things with Ava and disappear for good.

The Jameson had oozed back into his bloodstream, making him stumble trying to get up from the chair. He steadied himself before he hit the ground. Just then there was a knock on the door. He stared at it without moving. Maybe whoever had broken in before had circled back. If so, he was trapped. There was no other way out.

He lifted the edge of the curtain and peered onto his front patio. Without the glaring light, he could only see the thick outline of a woman standing at his front door, flashlight in hand.

He heaved a sigh of relief and flung the door open. Mrs. Engles was in her bathrobe, arms folded tight across her ample body.

"I'm glad you're in, Mr. Jones—" Her voice was heavy and raspy.

He shook his head. "That's not my name." It was the name of the previous tenant, and she insisted on calling him that no matter how many times he'd corrected her. "What's wrong?"

She flashed the light in his eyes. "I've been in my bed all night. Sick with the flu." She hacked a few times to make her point. "Came down to get a cup of tea and wait for my sister to bring me soup. And my light's out. Almost broke my neck."

"So what happened? To your light?"

"No idea. But I heard noise over here, thought you had company. Maybe you could change my bulb?"

He looked over his shoulder into the empty living room. "I don't have any company unless you count my Jameson."

He half expected her to ask who Jameson was. But she didn't. "It's a two-man job. Your friend left?"

He stepped back. "What friend? Someone was here?"

She moved the flashlight, shining it at his door. "I heard 'em. Thought it was Becky, so I looked out."

He rubbed his eyes. He wanted to smack her. "Who was it?"

"A woman. Tall, dark hair. Didn't hear nothing more, so I thought she went inside with you."

She took a step backward and he heard cracking under her shoe. "Glass," he said, pointing to the ground. The flashlight jerked up to the light fixture. The remnants of the shattered bulb shimmered in the light.

"Let me see that." He took the light from her hand and shined it around the small patio area. A rock, twice the size of a softball, lay near her doorway. "Your bulb didn't burn out. It was smashed."

Her face twisted up and she went into a coughing fit. "Well, that does it. Vandals around here now. I'm calling the police."

"This woman had dark hair? What was she wearing?"

She shook her head. "Black dress or a skirt, maybe. Something dark. That's all I saw, Mr. Jones. That and her going to your door."

"That's not my name." He shut the door in her face. He stood with his back to it for a few minutes, just breathing. *Marie.* It had to be. And she'd taken a picture of his front door.

First she'd agreed to help him, now she was threatening him with that camera. And how exactly did she have the camera? Unless she'd been the killer all along? The thought made him turn around and double lock his door.

CHAPTER 23

Russell was staring at me, an odd look on his face. The stack of Polaroids was in his hand. He'd flipped through them several times, looking for anything that might provide a clue as to who'd taken them. Or when.

"A frickin' oak tree? What are the odds the photograph you saw was taken with the same camera as these? They're both in black and white and both really grainy." He shook them. "Do they even make film for a camera that old?"

I shrugged. "That's a Google question. No camera or film in any of the boxes, though."

"The problem is that these pictures don't give any clue as to when they were taken. Fifties. Sixties. Or even later. Trees don't change over decades." He surveyed the mess in the room. "Do you remember an old Polaroid camera? From when you were little? At Claire's or Anais's?"

I stood up and started putting some of the albums back in the boxes. "Russell, there are a million Polaroid cameras in the world. Just because the photo of the Owenses' house happens to be a Polaroid—"

"And black and white? Both were this exact size?" He held up the little rectangular picture. "It's an odd coincidence—"

I smiled. "I think that's what a coincidence is. Odd happenings that coincide."

"The other thing?" He ignored me. "My niece has a new Polaroid—"

"Polaroid stopped making them. It's Fuji, I think, that's making the instant cameras now."

"Whatever. But they're all the rage now, apparently, and the photographs are different. Different size. More rectangular."

"All the rage?"

He ignored my teasing. "If these were taken with the same camera as the murder photo, it means that that photograph you found was taken by someone in your family, maybe. Someone who had access to the camera that took these. Claire? Anais? Marie?"

I snorted. "Yes, little Grand-Mère Anais with an ancient Polaroid camera around her wrist, murdering her way across the Eastern Seaboard with a box of old film in her back pocket."

"Joke all you want. Maybe she's like Madame Defarge in that Dickens novel, except instead of knitting she's taking pictures."

I threw a packet of envelopes at him. "I'm surprised you read *A Tale of Two Cities*."

He chuckled. "CliffsNotes. I hate Dickens."

"Getting back to what you were saying about my grandfather? And Loyal?"

Russell took his eyes off the pictures in his hand. "Yeah, I think they knew each other. It's the only thing that makes sense. Like they went to school together or something. They were born only months apart."

I smiled. Russell was so intent, so diligent and analytical, that I felt like I was presenting him with the answer to cold fusion when I put a picture of Ross Saunders and two other boys dressed in Catholic-school uniforms into his hand. "Voilà, Detective Bowers." I'd kept any images of the fourth, puggish-looking boy to myself.

His entire face exploded. Like a kid in front of the tree, Christmas morning. "This is it. This is it. This is the connection I've spent hours trying to put together. I knew it." He jumped up and hugged me. I felt his gun pressing into my hip bone. "Why'd you just let me sit here for the past half hour, Ava?" He let me go.

"It was a surprise for you. Interesting, huh? Schoolmates."

"Ross, Loyal, and who's the third boy?"

I peered at the face. "Claire would've known, maybe."

"Loyal and wife get killed. A photo is taken, and someone writes a message on it that references you. You were seventeen when the murders happened, right?" I nodded. "Where were you living then?"

"February of 2010, we'd just moved to Willow Grove, outside of Philly. Maybe two months earlier or something. Why?"

Russell was riveted on the Polaroids. "Hmmm. What was Saunders involved in?"

I scowled. "What makes you think this was my grandfather's fault? Your ideas are spiraling."

"That's how this works. Ideas come, some are good, some bad. See what sticks and makes sense. And we keep going till we get a lead."

"Well. I'd rather work by starting with the practical, like finding the school, getting the names—"

"The yearbook? Was there a yearbook in this stuff?" He turned and scanned the books and papers scattered across the floor. "And I wonder where that third boy is. It'd be great to talk to him."

I felt my heart twinge a little. Russell was seated on an ottoman, his knees pressed together, the photographs balanced in his lap. My mystery was swallowing him up. I could see it happening by inches. I studied his face, his eyes. It had been a while since I'd been attracted to anyone. Or let myself be attracted to anyone. I'd had a boyfriend, Paul, at McGill. A nice French Canadian boy who lived in Saint-Jérôme, not far from Montreal. He was funny and serious at the same time. Goal oriented, future oriented. We'd visit his parents or go to Lake Placid or Quebec City on the weekends. Sometimes, when it was freezing out, we'd just get food, stay in the dorm, and study all weekend. He'd call them *study-ins*. He was a year ahead of me, accepted into medical school at UCLA. And he had it all planned: that I'd apply to graduate school there the following year, we'd get an apartment together. But I couldn't do it.

This feeling of necessary isolation, of *When things get too familiar it's time to move on*, had been instilled in me by Claire. When the walls closed in, I had the instinct to bolt. Paul had been pulling the walls in around me. And no matter how hard I'd tried to ignore the suffocating feeling, in the end I'd bolted. Russell was different, though. He was already taken. Engaged. Joanne thought that would ruin things for me, but actually it only made it easier. I could connect but remain blissfully unconnected.

I leaned over him, brushing against his arm. "No, no yearbook. But if we can figure out what school it is, we can look it up, I'm sure. All that stuff has been loaded onto the Internet."

"Or"—he stood up—"we could go to the neighborhood where Ross grew up. Go to the schools and ask people? There can't be that many."

"You're not a sit-on-your-ass kind of guy, huh? More action? It's way too late to go to the schools tonight. I say we have a stay-in. Pour some wine, try and make some sense out of these pictures. Maybe find out what school that is. Whad'you think?"

"A stay-in?"

"Mm-hmm. Order in some Chinese. Or whatever. Pour some drinks and take these boxes apart, set all the pictures out to get a visual." I kicked some boxes to the side to make room in the middle of the floor. "Make a map of Ross Saunders's life right here." I motioned to the empty space. "Maybe something else'll pop up?"

He flipped the Polaroids again in his lap. "Where'd you say you found these? Maybe there's more."

My hands went to my hips. "The dining room, cabinet in the corner. I think there's a nice bottle of Pinot Noir in there. I just bought it. A California Pinot, but not bad. Go. I'll call for food. Chinese? Is that good?"

He pulled himself up from the chair. "Fine. Just an egg roll for me. Maybe some pork fried rice."

When I heard his feet hit the bottom step, I grabbed the photographs of Ross with the pug man—I'd purposely hidden them from Russell—and shoved them into my purse. Mr. I-Need-Directions was all mine. And I wasn't going to need a yearbook to identify him. I knew him already. But he'd been missing for so long, I had no idea where to start. I was going to flush him out to get some information. But I needed to do it alone.

CHAPTER 24

Marie scrubbed her hands in the basin and watched the bubbles and warm water swirl around her fingers, mesmerized. Then, as if someone had wound a key in her back, she dried her hands on the towel and ripped the wimple from her head, tossing it onto a chair. Her mind was hazy, her eyes moist. She'd been weepy and emotional all day. Thoughts of her family—what was left of it—had occupied her thoughts.

Ross and Claire were dead, both caught up in a whirlwind of other people's misdeeds. The difference was that Ross had forced other people to carry the burden. *An eye for an eye,* he'd said, trying to use the Bible to bolster his cause. The number of times he'd pleaded with his daughters the night he'd appeared on their doorstep, almost twenty years ago, couldn't be counted. It was that night that she understood why her mother had married him. That night, Ross Saunders was a whole person, a man who'd been fighting in one way or another his entire life, who would stand up to right or wrong when it mattered. Even if it destroyed everything around him. And it had.

She opened her eyes and blinked. Saw her father, covered in the blood oozing from the wound in his head. Having driven for hours from Philadelphia, he'd deposited himself on Claire's doorstep in Brooklyn, his eyes large and frightened.

"What happened? Were you mugged? Oh my God," she'd said.

But it was clear within minutes that wasn't the case. He had been the attacker and was now being chased. Claire had been unmoved. Unyielding. Panicked, she scanned the hallway to make sure no one was watching. She knew the implications of letting him in, yet in the end, in one swift pull on his arm, he was on the floor in the entryway of her apartment. Blood everywhere. Claire didn't dare turn on the lights to draw attention.

"Did you leave a trail to my door?" She opened the door again and inspected the carpeting leading to the elevator. "I can't have this."

"Please, Claire. I'll be dead or arrested if you don't help me. I don't have anywhere else to go." His voice was hushed, whispering. His entire body was trembling. "I've never asked you for a thing in my life."

"You've never given us a thing in our lives, you mean," Marie said.

But the two girls sat on the floor with him and listened to his story. Marie, having arrived in New York only a month before, had been particularly pained. His words maligned the very thing to which she'd given her life. And while he talked, the alcohol and sweat were lifting from his skin, even through the blood.

"Stop, Father, it isn't true. You're lying to protect yourself." Her voice reached near hysteria. "Stop now. Or I'll throw you back out into the hallway myself."

Claire put two fingers to her lips to quiet her sister, and it worked. Marie choked her tears into her lap, rocking back and forth.

"Go on," Claire commanded.

He did. He told them everything he could remember. The four friends. School. Confirmation. The night they made the pact when they were kids. How they'd met for drinks earlier that day for their thirtieth reunion. The stories started and then they all agreed, in an alcohol-adrenaline rage and fury: it was time to finish things the way they'd promised they would when they were kids.

He talked while lying on the floor, slumped to the side, holding his hand to his coat so as not to stain Claire's carpet.

"Not Father Bill. Not him too? Why?" Marie's head had tilted to the side; she felt her face twist in anguish. "That's not possible. He's a priest."

Ross had looked at her, his eyes only partially open. "I'm sorry. And they're after me now. Please. I know this is so much to ask. But I don't have a choice. I don't even care if I die. But—"

"No one is going to kill you."

Ross's breaths were heavy. "You have no idea, Marie. Do you think I drove this far for nothing? Begging you two for help?"

Claire had been pacing around their father, like a bird circling, ruminating on the implications of what he was asking. "Arrested is more likely. And you're drunk. This happened because you're a drunk. Drinking with those friends of yours. Like always. That's why Maman left you," she spit. "If she were here, what would she do?" She glanced at Marie. "We should call her. What time is it in Cherbourg?"

"Claire, no. No Anais," he begged.

"What am I supposed to do, then? If what you say is true, they'll be after us too. They may have followed you here, do you know that?" She'd turned her back and walked to the window, looking toward the brownstones across the street. "Anyone could have seen you. Why should we help? Why?"

His answer was simple. "Because you can. And no one else will."

"Everyone will be looking for you. Not just your friends," Marie stressed. "Eventually the police too. Come morning." She was still on the floor. She covered her face with her hands, protecting her from seeing him, his pleading eyes. "We can't cover up what you've done—"

"It's true. Marie is right. But I will let you stay for the night. For one night. Go to the car, be quick, and don't make any noise. I don't need any more trouble." Claire pointed to the door. In one second of weakness, she'd altered the course of their lives.

Marie pulled herself up. "I'll go. It'll be better." She'd removed her wimple, run her hand through her hair, and wrapped herself in Claire's long coat.

Claire cast her eyes downward to her father. "One night."

Marie now opened her eyes and took in each nuance of the wooden cross in front of her. That one night had turned into a lifetime. Of running, hiding, lying for a father they'd hardly known. It was the right thing to do, but how could Marie have fully realized the burden her sister would have to carry? How could she have known that that decision would ultimately break her?

But she was sure the killing had been over until *he* showed up at her convent door. The last one. Quiet, vicious, and still angry after twenty years. But now the last thread of this whole ordeal.

She just wanted to talk some more, figure out all the angles, make sure he hadn't come to the convent to test her, to get her together with Ava and then kill them both. But when she'd arrived at his house he wasn't home, and the relief and the blinding light from the neighbor's bulb had flooded over her at the same time.

Now she wiped the tears from her face and dried her hands on a towel. If he was going to force her hand, the only choice she had was to strike back quickly in a way that would frighten him and make him run away. She smiled and looked at her weapon. A Polaroid camera. The next move was his.

CHAPTER 25

Three bottles of Middle Sister Pinot Noir between us had plowed me under. Actually, I'd had way more than half of it myself. I'd swallowed the last bit in my glass and rolled over on the floor, opening my eyes sometime later, woozy, half-sick. I needed to throw up, but getting to the bathroom across the hall required moving. I swore under my breath. I was never going to drink again. Not like this. Not red wine on an empty stomach.

My Chinese food sat on the end table, barely touched. I'd taken a bite of beef with broccoli earlier, but it had been heavy, greasy in my mouth. Just the sight of the containers and faint smell of the salty soy sauce wafting out of them now made my stomach lurch. I managed to pull the metal wastebasket to me before my stomach exploded. It was all red liquid. I was afraid my choking would wake Russell, but he wasn't there. I was glad he'd missed one of my finer moments. It was then I felt cold against my nipple. I looked down. My breast had pushed against the metal can—not my breast in a bra and long-sleeved shirt, but my naked breast.

I flopped onto my back, realizing I had not just an exposed breast, but a completely naked body. What had happened? I remembered some of it through a sick haze. Joking around, laughing, maybe pushing the boundaries a bit with him. Rubbing his back when he'd been looking at those albums for hours. Encouraging him to lie on the floor with me and construct our chronological assessment of Ross's life. He hadn't resisted, that I remembered. *Shit.* I pulled the hair out of my face. Images of kissing him floated in front of me. We were lying down, the softness of lips against mine. Then there was laughing. And his hands on me. I couldn't pretend it was all just a drunken I-don't-remember-and-it's-not-my-fault incident. Because I did remember. Most of it, anyway. I didn't have a full grasp of the actual sex part, but everything leading up to it was crystallizing in my mind as the minutes passed. His arms around me, unbuttoning his shirt. *Shit again.*

I pulled myself up and staggered to the door. I needed Motrin and a tall glass of cold water. I walked past Russell curled up in my bed, lightly snoring. I pulled back the covers just a bit and peered at him. Naked. He'd twisted his body so I was looking at his rear end. I dropped the blanket. Maybe it didn't completely, completely happen. Maybe he'd stopped it. God, I hoped so.

Returning to the bathroom, I leaned my forehead against the cold tile, watching Russell's peaceful expression as he slept, resisting the urge to purge the contents of my stomach again. I opened the window to let air in. It calmed the pounding in my head and eased my stomach. I needed to get away from this mess I'd created. Run, that's what I did best.

I wiped my mouth on a towel and turned on the shower. I had to pull myself together. Get cleaned up and dressed. I needed to see Marie. Marie was the only one who could answer some questions about the photographs of Pug Man. I had to get to her before she started morning prayers.

Still half-wet, I threw on black jeans and a turtleneck and grabbed my purse. Russell was still snoring in my bed, his head at an odd angle off the pillow. I considered waking him but changed my mind. I didn't want to face a conversation about us rolling around the floor partially clothed. My nakedness, how he ended up here in my bed. I ran a hand across the back of his head, feeling his hair slide between my fingers. He moved with my touch. His eyes were closed, his lashes curling to his lids. I leaned down and pressed my lips against his. His mouth was warm and slack and smelled of Middle Sister Pinot Noir.

I pulled back and thought of Joanne. She'd be clinging to my sleeve, asking me for every detail of the night. We hadn't talked in over a week, and I missed her company. Maybe I'd clean the house and have a dinner party, like a normal person. Invite her and Russell, catch up. Tell her I needed help to curb the drinking. But I knew if I did, I'd never have a peaceful sip of wine again. I laughed at my own stupid thoughts. I'd never had a dinner party in my life and I wasn't a normal person.

The convent was dark when I arrived. I felt vomit rise in my throat a few times before I saw Marie's face in the glass. She pulled open the door.

"What's wrong, Ava?" She backed up to let me in. "You don't look well."

"Are you starting prayer soon?" I asked, moving past her into the foyer.

Marie's eyes flitted between me and her watch. "I can let them know I have an emergency if it's important." I nodded. "Go to my cell. I'll be there in a few minutes."

Her cell, as they called the rooms in the convent, did remind me of something a prisoner would live in. Around six feet by nine, with a twin bed shoved into the corner, the room was barren. A night table, small dresser, that was it. The art that decorated the space was dismal. Painfully religious. Depressing. Marie had a clear space in front of her wooden cross on which to prostrate herself. *What do you pray for, Marie?* Though she'd always been in my life, I hardly knew the woman.

I stood and started walking circles. I couldn't be sick here. The bathroom was down the hall, and illness might cause a huge commotion among the clergy. I couldn't risk it. I cracked Marie's window and breathed in the air, willing her to hurry. But she didn't come. I needed a cracker. Something. Surely nuns kept snacks, but after pulling open all the drawers, I found nothing but rosary beads. I walked the perimeter of the room several times and then pulled open her closet door, casually glancing inside. Nun's habits, a few slacks and sweaters. A winter coat. I moved a scarf on the top shelf and saw it. The side of a leather Polaroid camera case. *Oh, Marie.* I wrapped my hand around it to pull it down, surprised that it felt lighter than I remembered. I was just about to undo the clasp to see if it was empty when footsteps fell outside the door. It took two seconds and two steps to get back to the bed before the door opened.

"Ah. They gave me some time. That's good," she said, shutting the door behind her.

"Marie, I need your help. It's important for both of us."

"It sounds so serious. What happened?"

I pulled the photograph from my purse. "This man. I found this in Claire's drawer. I know Grandpa Ross." I pointed to him. "But this man?" My finger landed on Pug Man. "What's his name? Do you know where he is?"

Marie snatched the photograph from my hand. "Claire left this in her desk? Really?"

I nodded. "I need to find him."

"For what, exactly?"

"To talk to him," I answered vaguely. "That's all."

Marie startled me by clapping her hand across my mouth. I felt the rough bandage on her finger against my lips. "You don't know him, Ava. You don't. Do you hear me?" My stomach lurched; her skin smelled of antiseptic and I thought I might vomit against her fingers. I tried to pull her hand off my mouth but she held firm. "First the photograph of the house where people were murdered, and now this man. Why?" she hissed. "Why can't you leave things be? Stop digging into the past." I pulled at her pinky and bent it back until she released my face with a jerk.

I rubbed my jaw. "What is wrong with you, Marie?" I started to get up, but her hand went to my shoulder, holding me in place. "I was just asking a question, because there's no one else left to ask."

Her eyes kept me still. "Exactly. There is no one left to ask. Because they're all dead. Does that mean anything to you? Have you seen him recently? Has he come to you?"

I couldn't look at her face. I always had the feeling that Marie could read my thoughts. Know when I was lying. "No." I couldn't tell her he'd been following me that day. That he might have been in my house. "No. I don't think so. The picture was just familiar." I tried to get up but felt dizzy and dropped back down. "I know him from somewhere."

"Goodness. You really are ill." She moved her wastepaper basket over to me. "Don't throw up on my floor."

I shook my head. "I want to go now," I whispered.

"Listen to me, Ava." She took my chin, as if I were a child, so she could look directly in my eyes. "Things are getting complicated. You need to listen to me. Understand?" I nodded. She shook my chin a little with her hand. "No, listen. Do as I say. Think inside the box for once in your life. Now, I need to do something but I'll be right back." She went to the small desk in the corner and picked up her cell phone and a letter opener. I could only see a glimpse of it before it disappeared in the folds of her skirt. Long, silver. Sharp.

At that moment I felt panicky; things were out of control. I wanted to go home, see if Russell was up. Lie in my bed, drink water, figure this out on my own. "Marie?"

She turned back to me. "When you saw that picture, what was the first thing you thought?"

I searched for the words. "I didn't think, so much as feel."

"What did you feel, then?"

"Petrified. Confused. But mostly angry." She moved slowly toward me. "I remember things, Marie. Though it's hard to know what's true and what's not. It's all cloudy. But enough to know that I wasn't abandoned in a church as a baby. And maybe this man—"

She put her hand up. "Shut up, Ava." I saw her expression and closed my mouth, the syllables dying in my throat. She was hovering over me. "Never mention that again. To me, to him, or anyone else."

My head dropped between my knees. "Okay." I needed her to move out of my way. Then I was going to leave. I felt sweat dotting my hairline and the back of my neck. I wanted to hurl on her shoes. "Is he causing you some sort of problem now? Is that it? What's going on?"

"More than you know. I'll be back. You stay here." She was out the door.

I rubbed my face where she'd grabbed me. My eyes darted around the room, back and forth, always landing for a few seconds on the closet door. The camera. How long had Marie had it? If it was in the case, I wanted it. I tried to stand up, but the room tilted to the side and then began to seesaw around me. I fell back down, feeling the swaying beneath my lids.

I had no desire to stay here, to lie in this bed, with four pairs of Jesus's eyes upon me.

But I had no choice, I couldn't lift my head. And Marie had locked the door behind her. And so I really was in a prison.

CHAPTER 26

The sun streaming through the blinds woke him up. He tried to lift his head off the pillow, but it was heavy and his neck hurt like it had been stabbed with a knife. He rubbed it, looked around the room, and then eased himself back down. *Ava.* He lifted the covers and saw he was naked. He remembered Ava nude on the floor in the office. He hadn't seen a girl drink that much since college. And she was barely ninety pounds. But she'd come alive. Laughing. Unbuttoning his shirt. With no clothes on. Long dark hair, longer legs straddling him. Between the two of them they couldn't manage a zipper. He remembered only fragments after that. But he couldn't forget the expression in her green eyes. She'd been scared, vulnerable, needy. *Shit.* He'd never been sure what he wanted from her, but he never wanted this. Guilt and disappointment washed over him. *I had sex with her and I can't even remember it.*

He pushed the blankets off of him and stood up. His legs were heavy, and it took a while for the blood to start flowing. The bedroom was a mess, but Ava wasn't in it. "Ava?" A still-wet towel lay on the floor in the doorway to the bathroom. He leaned in to look. Nothing. Not even the steam remained. "She drinks a gallon of wine, gets up two hours later, and goes out?" His neck ached when he turned his head. "Where are you?" he whispered.

He stepped over the obstacles and went into the office across the hall. The closet door was open, papers spilled across the floor. Albums were everywhere. They hadn't done very good detective work last night. After the first three glasses of wine, he was just looking at the same blurry images. And listening to Ava talk. Then moving to the floor. He closed his eyes and saw her under him, her thin arms around his neck. *What the heck?* It was the in-between stuff that was fuzzy. Taking off her clothes—he drew a blank. Her body he remembered. The softness of her skin, her legs, her lips. Then nothing. His pants and shirt were balled up in the middle of the office floor. Hers were there too.

He dressed quickly and headed for the kitchen, thinking she was making the thick-as-sludge coffee she'd made the last time they'd gone out. He actually wanted a cup—but the kitchen was dark and empty. He moved some dishes out of the way and turned on the sink, splashing water onto his face. His stomach was heavy, his head swimming.

Ten minutes later he was sitting on her living-room couch, sipping a glass of cool water, wishing he'd not taken part in that third bottle of wine the night before. Red wine had never treated him well. He needed to give himself a minute to let his body settle, figure things out. Wait for Ava. She wouldn't have gone far, not without waking him, he reasoned. But as the minutes ticked by it was clear she'd maybe had a longer journey on her agenda this morning.

Her behavior was all over the place, drawing him in, distracting him, then pushing him away. Telling him only what she wanted him to know—that's what it felt like. He'd interrogated enough people to know that she was holding back three times what she revealed. And the more he saw her, the more he wanted to know what she was hiding, to draw her out. To figure out what was going on inside her head. It was consuming him. But she was a stinking mess. Her house was just a metaphor for her life.

He glanced around. The tidying she'd done before had long been untidied. Glasses, wine bottles. Clothes. He pinched the bridge of his nose and felt a jolt of pain shoot through his neck. "Mysterious," he said under his breath. "And the mystery right now is, where are you, Ava?"

It was in that second that he remembered his appointment with Juliette and the wedding planner. "God, no." He looked at his watch. It was ten thirty-five. "Oh no. No. No." He raced up the stairs and grabbed his shoes from under the desk. He stopped in his tracks and picked up the container of beef with broccoli and put a forkful in his mouth. The food made his stomach rumble. He took another bite and then noticed Ava's cell phone lying on the floor near the wastebasket. He picked it up. *So she gets up, showers, and leaves without her phone.* He clicked it on. Three texts and one voicemail. The texts were from Joanne. He was torn. Should he violate her privacy and listen to the voicemail? It was from a 215 Philadelphia number, left yesterday afternoon. His finger pressed "Listen" before he could think about it anymore. A male voice came on, thick with an eastern European accent.

"Ava, of course I remember Ross. Anything for his granddaughter. After three is good. Any day. I'll buy you a drink. Bring the picture, my memory is not so good anymore. I'll tell you everything I know."

Russell stared at the number. *Bring the picture?* What picture? To where? He found a pen on the desk and jotted the number onto the back of his hand.

He stared around the room. There was probably so much he'd missed in these boxes, important things, small things that were big, that would help piece things together, things about Ross, but he'd been too sloshed to really make headway. He had an inkling that Ava was playing with him a little bit, teasing out their investigation—to spend time with him? Or because she suspected he was on a path that would reveal something she didn't want to know about the family that raised her?

"I am going to figure this out despite you, Ava." He hesitated at the front door. "Do I leave it locked or unlocked? This is so typical of her." He left it unlocked and ran to the car in his stocking feet, shoes in one hand, the carton of Chinese food in the other.

CHAPTER 27

He parked his car on Hopkins Avenue and waited. Marie needed to come out soon. He was going to confront her about coming to the house with her camera, get her in his car, and drive. He'd put the child locks on in the back seat so she couldn't jump out. He had assembled rope, duct tape. He'd never kidnapped anyone before. She was more than twenty years younger, but he was counting on his maleness to make up for the difference in age. He turned up the heat to warm his hands. The cold air was creeping into the car, making him impatient.

He'd spent the night on his couch, tossing and turning. Marie's face had circled his brain until it hurt. Shadows jumped around him, causing him to roll on the creaky sofa until light came in through the front window. He realized the entire time he'd been trying to scare Marie into helping him kill Ava—telling her she might be next; it hadn't occurred to him that she'd been the one doing the killing. The nun? Killing Bill, then Loyal, and then her own father? It made no sense. But the camera didn't lie. And she had the camera.

He finally pushed himself up, showered, and shaved, taking freshly pressed trousers and a shirt from the bureau. *We might be poor but we're not slobs.* He thought of his father's words every time he dressed. This day, he'd decided, was to be the beginning of the end of the past.

Just sitting outside the church made his skin itch. He didn't want to look too hard at the doors to the chapel. His intention was to go to Ava's house, get that over with first, but when he'd gotten there, her car was gone; only a silver Jeep Cherokee was parked in the front. The cop's car. So he'd turned around and gone to the convent. Marie would be first.

His head was down when he noticed movement near the convent door. A thin woman dressed in black approaching. Dark hair. He knew her even before she turned so he could catch her face. Ava. She'd left the cop in her bed to come to a convent. Weird choice. Then Marie was there, in the window.

He lowered his head to the steering wheel. Anguish. A church. A convent. When would it end? He felt God playing a joke on him. He'd had to make terrible choices with worse outcomes his whole life, and every time there was a significant event, it was in a place of worship. And here it was again.

The two disappeared inside. That was it. He wasn't going in. This was a sign to leave well enough alone. Then a thought occurred to him; it was his thought, but it felt more like a guiding voice. *Go pray. Go into the chapel, kneel. Light a candle and pray.* He obeyed. Ten minutes later he saw why he was drawn here. Marie appeared in the chapel. Hurried and slightly flushed, she was speaking in a whispered voice to another nun. She gestured toward the outer buildings and then disappeared out the door. He slid out of the pew, genuflected, and crossed himself. And then followed her out the door.

She ran out of the chapel and across the yard. Now was his chance.

"Marie." He said it in a monotone voice. Not urgent. He didn't want her to run from him.

She whipped around, startled, and almost lost her footing. "What are you doing here?" she hissed.

He looked around to see who was nearby. Nobody. "When someone pays a visit, it's proper to repay the gesture. Don't you think?" He smiled.

"I'm not sure what you mean."

He reached out and took hold of her arm. "Oh, but you do. Why? Tell me why." He noticed the bandage covering her right hand. Had she cut it on his neighbor's light?

She tried to shake free, but he held fast. "Why what?"

"You left the photograph for me. Broke my light. Hurt your hand? And after we had such a nice agreement in place."

Marie studied him for a moment, her lips pursed. "If that's what you think."

"Is this a game?" He shook her arm to underline his words.

"You're the one playing." She broke free.

He looked at the ground. "The girl's worth nothing. Not your father's life, or your sister's. Has anyone but us searched for her over the years? In the past twenty years? Did they? Have you or Claire had knocks on the door, people saying, 'Give us back our little girl'?" Marie refused to respond. "The answer is no. I won't tell anyone about the photographs you sent. About Bill, Loyal, and Ross dying the way they did. If she's in there, bring her out. Don't make me wait any longer. This can be over, right now."

"Photographs *I* sent? You think I killed the others?" She half laughed, but it was hollow. "I didn't."

Her eyes darted toward the chapel, the convent, the woods. She looked crazed. "Ava came here to talk to me, I don't know about what yet, because I haven't had a minute to speak to her. But she looks ill."

"Then my timing is perfect. We're going to do this now."

He thought she was going to stall or make excuses, but she didn't. "Just meet me on the other side of Euclid in ten minutes. I'll get her there somehow," she responded.

He nodded. "Brown LeBaron. Don't screw me over. Or I'll come back for you both."

"Better idea. I'll follow you in her Honda." She must have seen the distrust on his face. "I'm not leaving her car here at the convent. And I don't feel like fighting to get her into the back of yours."

"If you disappear on me, this is going to get ugly."

She was already headed toward the convent door.

CHAPTER 28

Juliette had blown past him in a fit of anger. There were no words to calm her now. He'd really screwed up, in so many ways. The wedding planner had been there when he'd arrived home. Papers spread across the dining-room table. Venue options. Guest lists, a chart with tables and names filled in. Menus. Fifty menus. And ideas for cakes. This was the first meeting, but Juliette had applied herself since he'd given her the ring, concentrating on little else. And like she always said, when she put her mind to something, shit got done.

It was an awkward moment in front of a stranger. Mrs. Gleason felt the tension and was suddenly mute.

"I said ten. I was sure I said ten. Did you misunderstand? It wasn't clear?" Juliette underscored her anger by slapping the menus together in a pile. He knew her eyes were taking in his wrinkled clothes. Maybe her nose smelled the wine. "Took the opportunity to start the bachelor party early? That what happened?" She motioned to the number scrawled on his hand. "Maybe a hot stripper or—"

"I told you I'm on a case—"

"Mrs. Gleason, that's it for today, I think. I'll call you to reschedule," Juliette said, standing up.

"Well, I think we've covered some good options for today. It'll give you something to think about. I'll let myself out." And she was gone.

Juliette was only five minutes behind her. Her last words were clipped: "Case, my ass. Figure out what you really want, Russell. When you do, call me. But I'm not waiting forever." She slammed his door, opened it, and then slammed it again before leaving for good.

He dropped onto the sofa and rubbed his forehead. Juliette still had her own apartment, but since the engagement her belongings had crept in with her, filling every corner with her presence. He'd give her some time to calm down and then call her. Right now he needed aspirin and sleep.

He climbed the steps to the second floor and went into the bathroom, reaching for the medicine cabinet. Two things stopped him. The haggard reflection staring back at him and the phone number written across the back of his hand.

His eyes were sunken in. Underlined with dark-purple bags. His hair was a mess of curls smashed against his head. He was pale and exhausted. His neck twinged every time he moved his head, but he still lowered it to study the number. After grabbing the bottle of aspirin from the shelf, he headed to his office. *Let's see who called Ava.*

The number rang unanswered, no machine. He paused for a moment and dialed Ava's number. He glanced at the clock. She had to be back, it was almost eleven thirty. Where could she have gone? The phone rang until voicemail picked up. He wanted to circle back to her house, to see if by chance she'd passed out and didn't hear the phone, but he couldn't.

"Sleep. I'll call again later." He swallowed three aspirin, trudged to the bedroom, and fell onto the bed fully clothed.

He was awakened by the sound of his cell phone ringing beside him. He rubbed his eyes and felt crust rub off on his finger. "Christ, what time is it?" The clock glowed three thirty. He turned the phone over and looked at the number. Juliette. He threw the phone down again. He needed coffee and more aspirin before he could listen to what she had to say.

He sat up and looked at his phone. Five calls. Three from the office. They were calling to check in with him, see how he was, get a return-to-work date, no doubt. Two from Juliette. *Ava, where are you?* He dialed Ava's number and listened to it ring through to voicemail. *Damn it.* If she was sleeping, he was going to kill her himself.

He made coffee, swallowed some more aspirin, then dialed the number on his hand.

"W and K." The voice was female. Soft.

"I'm sorry, is this a business?" He pushed himself up to a full sitting position.

"Yes. W and K bar. Four thirty-five Poplar Street."

"Oh, I must have the wrong number. Sorry." He hung up and wrote the address next to the phone number on his hand. "And now, Ava, I'm coming to get you and we're going to pay a little visit to the bar together."

He showered, changed, and was headed to Haddonfield in less than fifteen minutes. There was something twisting in the back of his head. Instinct. Gut. A sense of dread.

Ava's house was dark. No silver Honda Accord in the driveway. He pulled up in front and sat there staring at it. He dialed her number again, but this time it went straight to voicemail. He shoved the phone into his pocket and started up her steps.

The door was unlocked when he turned the handle. He slid in and closed the door behind him. The room was in the same disarray as when he'd left. Russell wondered briefly if what he was doing would be considered breaking and entering, but climbed the steps to the office anyway and looked around. Her phone lay just where he'd left it. Out of charge now. She had never come back—or if she had, she'd left again without it.

He put the phone in his pocket and continued the tour. Everything was just as it had been: the wet towel was on the bed where he'd thrown it, even his empty glass was still on the counter in the kitchen.

His body started to tingle. *What happened to you? Where are you?* He'd asked these questions a million times on cases, with a professional distance. He could dissect things. Organize information. Make notes.

Get leads, when he wasn't personally involved. But this was different, and everything that had happened the night before was dancing in his brain. The wine, her sitting on the floor, laughing, drinking. Pretending to eat her Chinese food. Going through boxes. Laughing again. Kissing, her mouth on his. He shook the thoughts away. He couldn't replay that. But he knew she hadn't discussed plans for the next day, an appointment in the morning. Nothing. *Shit.*

He stood in the office. They both had intended to clean it up after they were finished. She'd wanted everything back in the closet, as if untouched. *Man, this is a mess.* He started in the corner, packing albums into boxes as fast as he could. He was sweating, starting to feel dizzy, the whole while pondering where Ava had gone. The bar he'd called? Was she there, drinking? A hair of the dog? Had she gone to her aunt's? Joanne's? Without her phone? Without telling him? *Missing person, forty-eight hours* kept playing in his mind. After forty-eight hours the leads grew cold. That was, if she really was missing and hadn't just taken off on her own to do some investigating without telling him. In that case, he really was going to be done with this whole mess.

His actions became more frenzied. The closet door open, he began throwing boxes in haphazardly. Five photographs of Ross and the boys sat on the desk. He needed those. That was his starting point.

He walked across the hall, taking in each nuance of the room, each fact, ticking it off in his head. She took her purse, left her phone. She took a shower. He glanced at his hand. The bar. Photos in hand, he raced down the steps to the front door.

As he opened it and stepped outside, he bumped full force into a woman. Tall and on the thin side, her hair was short, slightly wavy, and dark. Despite the miserably serious expression on her face, it was hard for him not to notice that she was strikingly pretty. High cheekbones, square jawline. Dramatic eyes. Full lips.

"Who are you?" she demanded. "And what are you doing in my sister's house?"

CHAPTER 29

He peeled the clothes from his body, his back and arms aching with every move, his muscles painful to the touch. The bathtub was small and old. Stained around the drain from rust, but he didn't care. He needed to soak. He lowered himself slowly into the hot water, steam rising to form fog in the small room. The one good feature of this crappy house was the water. It was always hot and there was plenty of it. The only thing that disturbed his soaks was when he heard Mrs. Engles through the wall, taking a bath at the same time. That was something he didn't ever want to think about too deeply.

He'd scrubbed his hands where he'd been cut, and washed the blood and dirt from his arms before getting into the bath, but he couldn't help but notice that the grime from his body was turning the water the color of weak tea. He didn't care. He rubbed the soap over his skin and then pulled his legs in so he could lie back, letting the scalding water fill the tub.

Ava had fought both of them to the end. That was unexpected. But Marie had cooperated like she said she would. Getting her into her car had been easy, apparently. And by the time she'd figured out Marie was following the old LeBaron, it was too late. Pale, thin, obviously ill, she'd trusted Marie to help her. To watch that trust fade away over the hours that followed was a beautiful thing to see and something he'd waited almost twenty years for. Even up until the very end, the very last second, she had questions. *Give me a name,* she'd said. As if it mattered now. *A name. That's all I want.* That's when he'd hit her. But she still didn't stop. *Where did I come from? Who am I? Give me a name. I know you know. You were there with Ross. I remember.*

At the mention of her father's name, Marie stepped in. Obviously torn, begging for it to stop and then finishing her off by wrapping her hands around the thin neck, choking the questions right out of her. Ava's body was limp, eyes rolled back in her head, lids partially open. He'd kicked her in the back a few times and once in the head, just to make sure she wasn't faking. *This would have been easier if we'd done it when she was three.* His parting words to Marie after they dumped her body and car in the Pine Barrens.

"Just keep your promise and leave town tomorrow. There's no reason for us to see each other ever again." Marie left without looking back.

He turned on more hot water now, letting it splash over his ankles, feeling the heat fill the tub. He closed his eyes and drifted off. The violence had made him sick, and he'd had to lean behind a tree to vomit without letting Marie see his weakness. The hitting, choking, and brutalizing the girl took him back to another time, when he wasn't the perpetrator, but the victim. And that was a place he never wanted to revisit.

Father Callahan's voice was in his ear. *When I was a child I used to speak like a child, think like a child, reason like a child; when I became a man I did away with childish things. Corinthians 13:11.* Not just a *memory* of the voice, but the voice. He flew to a sitting position; water splashed over the floor. *Do away with childish things. You're eleven now. Come here. Now. Stop acting like a baby. If you cry, I will tell your parents. If not, well, I'll take you to the movies. How does that sound?* He shuddered and covered his ears, shaking his head back and forth. The man was there now too, not just the voice. He was small in stature—as a boy he'd seen Father Callahan side by side with his own father and visually measured the priest at almost a foot shorter. Close-set eyes, always unfocused as if he wasn't sure what he was looking at. The voice, never loud. Calm. Condescending. Brutal. Manipulative. Confusing.

"Come here." Father Callahan reached for him. "Now, we talked about this crying before. I will always take care of you. You have a place here. You know that." Arms went around him, and for that moment he felt safe, loved, and protected.

He felt sad and strangely jealous that Ross had been Father Callahan's favorite. Ross was tall for his age, dark, handsome. Father Callahan was drawn to him. New baseball glove at the beginning of the season. Tickets to the movies, with popcorn and soda thrown in. Trips to see the Phillies play. Ice cream. A free pass. That's what Ross got. And Ross's parents loved Father Callahan right back. He was invited to dine with the family a few times a month. All the boys picked on Ross because of it. Dinner with Father Callahan. *What do you have to eat when he comes over? Wine and crackers?* They knew Callahan was grooming Ross for the priesthood. All the talk of seminary, education, training, made Ross's parents so proud. They just didn't know to what extent he was being groomed.

In front of the church it was shadowed and gloomy. He sat with Loyal in a small patch of grass at the front, looking at baseball cards. Ross was in the rectory with Father Callahan.

"When are they coming out? I wanna go home," Loyal complained.

He dug at the dirt with a stick, his eyes watching the door of the rectory. "Don't go yet. I don't want to go home."

Loyal sighed. "Five minutes and I'm out."

Just then Ross came tearing through the door, grabbed his bike, and pedaled toward Orthodox Street without saying a word. He and Loyal hopped on their bikes and followed Ross as far the Tacony–Palmyra bridge. Ross dumped his bicycle and started walking the footpath over the bridge and then climbed over the rails. Loyal climbed behind him out onto the metal planks, waving for him to come. But he was petrified of heights and couldn't slide over the rails without looking down. He began to fear Ross was going to jump. He'd been crying. He'd never seen him cry before. Bill and Loyal, yes. Never Ross. The earth tilted a little that night, slightly off course, and things would never be the same. *"I'm not going to Catholic seminary. I'm not. No matter what my parents say. I'm not doing any of this anymore. Father Callahan needs to stay away from me."* Red faced, tears streaming, Ross had stood up and walked farther out over the edge, Loyal behind him. The next sound was of laughter and their urine flowing.

He closed his eyes. That night he'd felt envious of Ross. Angry and jealous. Why Ross? Why not him? And Ross didn't even want the attention. Feeling special, in his world full of neglect, was something and not all bad. Being wanted, being told he was good and worthy, not only of Father Callahan's love but of God's love, was something too. There were days, back then, especially after his mother died, that that was all he had to hold on to. But deep inside, he knew a sickness had taken seed. And that seed would sprout in him, causing disgust, rage, and the worst kind of shame for the rest of his life.

The tub was growing cold. He pulled himself up and put on fresh clothes, bandaged his hand—not cut too bad. Then he'd sleep. He had time for a good sleep. He'd given notice on the apartment, so he had fifteen days to pack his things, make arrangements, and move out of Philadelphia for good. Move south and try to find some temporary work. Get on with his life. That was his plan. He knew he'd find peace somehow. Maybe he'd chased Ava for so long to get back at Ross. Ross had everything: looks, smarts, people that loved him. Parents that cared. For so long, the hate had taken up a little spot in the back of his brain. And then directed itself toward the girl with the dark hair. This time Ross hadn't won.

Ava was dead.

CHAPTER 30

The woman's face was frozen into a scowl, though the expression was softened by her large brown eyes. She wore dark pants and a gray sweater covered with a black trench coat, keys dangling from her fingers.

"Who are you?" she asked again.

Russell had never met her, but he knew this had to be Ava's aunt, Marie. Even in everyday clothes, she looked like a nun. "I was a guest of Ava's. She left early this morning and never came back. Have you seen her?" His eyes landed on the bright-red scratches on one hand and the bandage on the other.

"I was coming over to check the house. See how things were going over here. Where'd she go this morning?" she asked.

He crossed his arms, tucking the envelope of photographs behind him. He didn't want her questioning what he was taking from the house. "I'm not sure. She was gone when I woke up."

Her face twisted slightly. He wasn't sure if it was the thought of Ava waking up with a man, or just his presence that she found distasteful. "You must be Marie, Ava's mentioned you." He tried to smile. "Did you fall?" He pointed to her hands. The keys dangling from her fingers. "Those scratches look painful."

"Cleaning this morning in the church. Must have been the vents. Cleanliness is next to godliness, they say."

He knew he could stand on the porch and question her for an hour and all he was going to get were clichés and simple random, meaningless words strung together. He needed to get past her, to the bar. "I'll keep trying to call her"—though he felt her cell phone in his pocket pressing against his leg. "Maybe she'll turn up later on. Have a good day."

In one swift move, he darted down the steps and to his Jeep. He clicked the door open and was in the seat before Marie could even turn around. As he pulled away, he saw her on the bottom step, her hand raised, as if she needed to ask him one more question. Too late.

The sun was setting by the time he crossed into Philadelphia and was heading north on Fifth Street. Northern Liberties was one of those areas of the city that kept changing. Gentrification followed by abandonment and crime, then regentrification, had left many streets an uncertain mix. The W&K bar fit in perfectly. Poplar Street was busy, dotted with restaurants, hipsters, flourishing businesses, and lights. But this bar had a flat sign, barely lit. The outside reflected the abandonment-and-crime era, with the barred windows and door complete with a buzzer.

He pressed it and waited, wondering if the owner had a camera homed in on the patrons outside. He heard the click and pulled the heavy green metal door open. The room was dated, drab. An older, familiar crowd kept them in business, he realized as he scanned the back of seven gray heads at the bar. A man nearing seventy who was a dead ringer for Nikita Khrushchev stood behind the counter, leaning against the wall, talking to a patron.

Khrushchev's heavy eyebrows went up when he eyed Russell, but he said nothing until Russell leaned in. "What can I get for you?" The accent. It was the same as the message on Ava's phone.

"Anything on tap?"

Khrushchev shook his head.

"Then a bottle of Rolling Rock."

The thought of drinking anything made his stomach turn, but he had to order something. He sat at an empty seat at the other end of the bar and waited. Khrushchev made his way down to him slowly. His left leg was lame, leaving him to walk with an uneven stride.

"Russell." He held out his hand. The older man shook it hard and started to walk away. "How long have you been here? In this neighborhood?"

"Opened in seventy-two. Good year."

He took a sip from the bottle. "Changed some, huh?" Khrushchev nodded. No time for stupid small talk, he started to turn away again. "I'm a friend of Ava Saunders." Russell looked down. "I really hope you can help me. Have you seen her today?"

He turned and faced Russell, both palms on the bar. "I have not seen her today or any other day. I never met her."

"She's gone. Disappeared, and I know she told me she called you. I thought she might have come here in person. I've looked everywhere."

Khrushchev didn't move. "You a cop? You look like a cop."

Russell nodded. No sense lying. "I am. In New Jersey. And she's not in trouble or anything. She's my friend. She left early this morning and never came back."

"Maybe she went shopping? Ladies love to shop."

Russell shook his head. "No. She asked for my help with something involving her grandfather, Ross Saunders. We were going through photographs last night. She wouldn't just up and go shopping. Besides, she's not the shopping type."

He held out his hand to Russell. "Walter. I'm not sure I should believe you, but I do anyway. It's true I never met Ava in my life, but she did call. Yesterday."

"I heard your message back to her. She asked you to look at a photograph? That's why I'm here. You're the last person besides me that she talked to, I think."

Walter took a step back, his head tilted to the side. "She didn't talk to me. She talked to Katia." Katia had to be his wife. The K in W&K, he assumed. "Said Ross's daughter died. Now her, I met. When she was just a baby. Too bad."

"And . . ."

Walter didn't like having his story pushed along. "And that she was going through her mother's things. Found a picture of Ross and some friends. Wanted me to see it, to see if I knew where one of them was." Walter leaned back. "Told Katia to have me call her back. So I did."

"You knew Ross pretty well?"

Walter folded his arms in front of him. Russell knew this was a sign. People did it when he was pushing them too hard. Or they weren't comfortable with the interrogation. It meant *Back off.*

Walter hesitated. "He was a regular when he was working at Dubin Paper, down Delaware Ave. Lived on Fourth Street. Up a block or so. But he's dead now too."

He took a bigger sip of beer. "When did Ross die?"

"A year or so ago. He wasn't living in Philly no more. Moved out to Harrisburg." A customer at the other end of the bar called to him. Walter pushed up and limped away.

"Walter, how'd he die?" Russell asked when the old man was back within earshot.

Walter shrugged. "Fell and hit his head. Of all damned things. Survived Vietnam but killed by a bathtub." He looked at Russell's beer. "Is that it?"

"No. Look at these for me?" He pulled the photographs out of the envelope and lined them up on the bar. Then he saw Walter's face. "Oh, and a shot of Jack, please."

The old eyes scanned the images. "I knew them when they were older. Here they're just punk kids. That's Ross." A heavy index finger landed on one boy. "This one is Loyal." He picked up the photograph and held it closer to his eyes. "Little bastard. Always joking around." He glanced up at Russell. "He's dead too—killed in his house. Break-in or something. And this one"—he pointed to the third and last boy—"is Bill."

Russell had homed in on the photograph. "Bill?"

"Bill Connelly. Father Connelly." Walter laughed. "Never woulda known if he wasn't wearing his collar. Come to think of it, he's dead too."

Russell lifted the shot glass to his lips and swallowed the contents. "Let me have one more. How'd Bill die?"

Walter poured Jack Daniel's to the brim of the shot glass. "Died in the rectory, I heard. Not sure how. Natural causes. Was maybe five or six years ago." Russell drank the shot. His stomach had calmed down, but the whiskey had set his mind on fire. All of them were dead? Within a relatively short period of time. "But you're missing the fourth of the group. There was four of 'em all hung together."

"Who was the fourth? I didn't see any pictures of anyone else."

Walter shrugged. "I think that was the one Ava was interested in. Name was Jack. Jack Quinn. Quieter than those." He pointed to the picture. "And a little stupid—or maybe a lot smarter, depending on how you look at it. I always thought underneath all that quiet he was a vicious little prick."

"Is he dead too?"

"Never heard he was. Haven't seen him around here for a few years, and I have no clue where he's gotten to."

Russell stood up and gathered the pictures. "If Ava comes here, please, please tell her Russell is looking for her. And tell her I have her phone." He pulled it out of his pocket. "I'm worried about her." He took thirty dollars out of his pocket and put it on the bar.

"Don't need charity here." He pushed back ten. "This is good enough. And if you're around here, stop in, we like cops from New Jersey." He half winked at Russell. "Thursdays Katia makes dinner. Pretty good, too. Sausage and onions, maybe?"

Russell knew how the man stayed in business. This bar was some version of a pub in England. Once you were welcomed, you were welcome. He stumbled out on the street, noticing that it had come alive. Northern Liberties had reinvented itself again into a Millennial Central. The cool place for the bar-hopping sort. None of them were pressing the buzzer on the old W&K, though.

"Jack Quinn, I'm coming for you," he said as he slid behind the wheel of his Jeep.

CHAPTER 31

Marie pushed the door open and walked into the living room. "Good God" escaped her lips as she surveyed the destruction of what was once an airy, creative space. "Ava, you're going to hell," she whispered.

She took off her coat and threw it across the back of a chair. Now that her niece was dead, she'd come to remove any damaging evidence. To put things in order, close this chapter, if it ever really could be closed. Erase Ava's existence—something she desperately needed to do after the scene in the woods. But this was too much. Claire had purchased the house, the one and only house she'd ever been able to own in her life, mostly because of Ava, and Ava had nearly destroyed it within weeks. Garbage and detritus were everywhere.

Marie decided that minute that she had to clean all of it up, by herself, and that she had to do it quickly. It might take days and a dumpster, but she had no choice. She pulled herself up the stairs to Claire's room to find an old shirt to change into. Once inside her sister's world, she was mesmerized. It was untouched. Clean. Organized. The four-poster bed was neatly made, draped with a crinkled-silk mauve coverlet.

Claire had been gone well over a month, but Marie hadn't really grieved. There were times during prayer or Mass, or even just sipping tea in the kitchen, when she'd feel the tears on her cheeks and not even realize she was crying. It had all been so sudden, and the truth was that

Marie was still turning the reality of the situation over in her mind every day, seeing only bits and pieces at a time. The whole of it would be too enormous to handle at once.

The little Lavoisier-Saunders family had been small and was now even smaller. Marie's world was closing in, and the closer it came, the more she saw that it was a disgusting mess. Anais had insulated herself with distance and disinterest. Her emotions poured out when solicited, but in general, she'd occupied her time with the company of the Lavoisier clan and gardening. Nothing else. The loss of her daughter was no doubt devastating, but she kept her grief tightly bound to her chest.

And now Ava was gone too. She dropped onto Claire's bed and wondered if anyone else had lain there since her death. The sheets were cool and wrinkled, probably just the way her sister had left them. She lay flat on her back and sobbed, then rolled over, shoved her face in the pillow, and let loose a month's worth of anguish.

When she was finished, she knew she had an insurmountable task in front of her. Clean this house and sell it. Ask for a transfer back to France, nearer to Anais. The United States experience had been filled with terror, running, lying, murder, scandal, upset. At first the confusion, the adrenaline rush, had been addicting. After a few years it became exhausting and enraging. And in the end it had nearly driven her mad.

She pulled her sweater over her head and folded it on the back of the chair. Claire's closet was still full—Ava hadn't bothered to start sorting out these items, and Marie was glad of it. It almost seemed like her sister might come bounding in at any moment. She ran her finger over the garments hanging; nothing was appropriate. She sighed and went to the dresser. Perfume, hairbrushes littered the top. When she pulled out a drawer, she saw the book sticking out from under a folded shirt.

The pages were filled with tiny print, some English, some French. A mishmash of random thoughts. Marie felt her eyes moisten. She flipped the pages quickly, mesmerized by the writing, the ink, the time it took to make each entry. It seemed most of it was done with the same black pen, the letters looping and curling into one another. She stopped, wanting to see what was consuming her sister's mind in those months before her death. She ran a finger down the page and stopped.

Ava came in late last night. Just the way she was looking at me got me upset all over again. Angry to be here, to be reined in. She had that old Polaroid picture of the house in her hand, demanding information about Quinn I don't have. I should be doing more to protect myself but I can't. I'm just so tired and I don't feel any safer than I ever have but this time I don't know where the threat is coming from. From inside my own family? I need Maman.

Marie read the entry over again to be sure she got it right. Ava had known about the Polaroid of the Owens house *before* Claire died. She hadn't found it in a box like she'd claimed. The next entry started on another topic and never returned to Ava or the photograph.

Marie closed the book, struggling to understand the implications. Ava said she'd been digging in Claire's things after her death, found the picture and a baby outfit in a box in the storage area, been curious and gone to the house—never fully explaining how she'd located the house from just a little picture in the first place. The girl was on fire that day she'd returned from Chestnut Hill, weeks ago. Asking questions. But she'd apparently known about the photograph at least six months before that. Maybe she'd even been to that house before. Had Ava been testing her? To see what she knew? Was that possible?

Marie grabbed the book and read the last entry, written the night before her sister's death. *Aux grands maux les grands remèdes. Que faire?* Loosely translated, it meant *Desperate times call for desperate measures. What to do?*

Marie bit the bottom part of her lip, already red and raw. She often did this when upset, anxious. She'd been drawing blood for three days without realizing it.

"Menteur," she whispered. "Ava—you're a liar."

CHAPTER 32

Russell pulled up in front of the little yellow bungalow and took a breath. He had to think about his next move carefully. He hadn't been able to reach Ava all day. What if whoever had tried to run him over had done worse to her? If he reported her missing or started the rounds of hospital inquiries, he'd have to make the rest of this case official—turn over the information he had about the photo and its connection to a five-year-old double murder. Withholding important evidence in a murder investigation, hindering prosecution, obstruction of justice were just a few terms that might apply to his abject stupidity since getting involved in this debacle. Prosecution might be preferable to looking like a fool if they simply laughed him out of the station—he didn't even have the Polaroid of the house to hand over as evidence, and, he reminded himself, he'd never even seen it.

A sucker for pretty green eyes. That's what he was.

He didn't even open his car door when Joanne's eager face was at the window, peering in, her expression holding fear and excitement at the same time. "This is it," he muttered. "The pinnacle of my career. My trusty sidekick in a murder-and-missing-persons case."

She opened the Jeep door. "My God, you're late. Get in the house now. I made coffee."

He'd been pondering what to do when he picked up the phone the day before, not even sure which number he was calling—the Prosecutor's Office to report the whole ordeal or Joanne at the courthouse. There was only a two-digit difference between the numbers. He heard Joanne's voice at the other end and realized he'd made his decision without really making it.

Her house was situated in Haddon Township on Center Street. It was clean and simple on the outside, so he was surprised the inside was cluttered with bric-a-brac and pillows. Joanne had set up a space for them to talk, and Russell took his assigned seat as directed.

"So what do you need me to do? Anything?" she asked, pouring his coffee into a take-out cup. She smiled. "I came prepared with cups to go because I knew you'd be outta here two minutes after giving me my assignment."

"You're right. Ava's been gone a day and a half already. You know her better than anyone. Would she just take off like this, do you think? Without telling anyone?"

Joanne shrugged. "The one thing I do know about her is that she operates alone, deep inside that little head of hers. I've only gotten a peek inside that brain and then the door slams shut. So, I have no clue. Possibly."

"I've gotten myself into a bind now, so I have no choice but to either sacrifice my career or keep going." He sipped his coffee. "God help me, I'm going to keep going, work fast, and pray that she's not dead."

"Dead?" she said, alarmed. "Who would've killed her?"

"I'll tell you this, if I find her squirreled away somewhere, I'm going to kill her myself. Here's her phone." He put it on the table. "It's an iPhone 6. Can you charge it and go through everything? There's no passcode. Incoming and outgoing emails, phone calls, any activity at all. If you find anything, call me?" He put the lid on his coffee and stood up. "I put an unofficial alert out for her car, so if certain friends of mine see her plate number, they'll pull her over—"

"Or if it's abandoned." Joanne looked like she hadn't slept in days when she said that.

Russell nodded. "And I'm going to ask a friend to flag her passport, though I've pretty much used up any favors I had from people at the academy, the military. But if she tries to leave the country, I'll know."

Joanne was uncharacteristically mute. She just nodded and showed him out. Russell sat in his Jeep and reviewed the information he'd been able to gather on Jack Quinn. Sixty-seven years old. Last known address was some blocks from the final stop on the Market–Frankford elevated train. He pulled out and made a quick detour to Claire's house. He had half a hope that he'd see Ava's car parked in the driveway, but it was empty. He darted up her steps and rang the bell. He heard the faint sounds of Beethoven's fifth from within. He knocked and rang again, then slid his hand down to the knob and turned it. It moved and then stopped. Locked. Marie, who arguably knew Ava better than he did, hadn't been concerned—maybe she was more prone to taking off than he realized.

He headed to 95 North—the traffic was surprisingly light—and took the Bridge Street exit. He knew this area of the city well, lower working class, a bit run down, not great, but not exactly terrible either. Jack Quinn's apartment was only five minutes from the exit; he was in front of number ten Howell Street before he figured out what he was going to do when he got there.

It was the end unit, a two-story row home, on the minuscule side. He sat in his car and watched. There was no car parked in front, but that didn't mean anything. Maybe Mr. Quinn was carless at the moment. When he hadn't seen any movement for ten minutes, he got out and went to the front door and knocked lightly. No sound of stirring from within. He rapped again and then stuck a slip of metal between the door and jamb. The cheap lock popped open within a minute.

Russell hesitated. This was breaking and entering. If caught, he was going to pay the consequences. He had no reason or explanation for violating this man's privacy. Jack Quinn had done nothing but round out the numbers in a group of boys in Catholic school fifty years ago. But Russell's gut said there was much more to it.

Ava hadn't called Walter at the old W&K to look at pictures of Loyal and her grandfather or even Bill. She was gunning for Mr. Jack Quinn. His photos had been mysteriously absent from the albums she'd showed him, which meant she had removed them before he got there. She must have had a reason.

He opened the door wide enough to slide through and then shut it behind him. The room was worn and dated but impeccably clean, uncluttered. The few belongings Quinn had were piled neatly, as if he were getting ready to bolt. A creeping sensation came over Russell, as if something horrible were lurking close by. He imagined Ava's purse or clothes, or something even more gruesome, in the house. But from a quick search of both floors, he found nothing.

He walked to the desk. The dark wood was scarred from being violated with a sharp implement, but the surface was clean of papers. *Open the drawer.* He pulled on the handle of the middle drawer and stared. Four Polaroid images were lined up. Each of a different house. The one Ava had described to him was the second in the line. *Destiny calls us, bound by Loyalty. All things that spring eternal can never be crushed.* The hair on his arms stood on end. Four photographs meant four potential murders. Was Quinn a serial murderer? But the fourth was of Quinn's door. It didn't make any sense. He took the pictures and slid them into his breast pocket. He found a scrap of paper and scrawled a message across it and tossed it into the drawer. *I'm coming for you,* it said.

Whatever else you may be, Ava, you're not a liar.

CHAPTER 33

The Delaware River was choppy. Tiny whitecaps dotted the surface, along with the occasional beer can and fast-food wrapper. His footsteps fell heavy and quick as he crossed the Tacony–Palmyra Bridge to New Jersey.

He and the other three boys had spent many summer nights riding bikes across the bridge when they were kids, either to watch the drawbridge go up to let boats pass through or to find a dry spot in the marshy swamp at the other side and watch the sun setting over Philadelphia in the distance. They would pool their meager funds and buy a soda to share, listening to the frogs and crickets come out as it got darker. Sometimes they would try and start a small fire to keep warm. His fondest memories were of telling stories of mass murderers escaped from Holmesburg Prison. The stories got scarier and more graphic as the night went on. Bill's eyes would get wide; he was the easiest to spook and was always first on his feet, running back through the brush to the footpath to the bridge. And always the first to reach the Tacony side, breathless from pedaling, the redness in his face blotting out the ever-present freckles.

The four would part ways after the half-hour ride back to Frankford and Torresdale Avenues. Ross lived south, closer to Port Richmond, Loyal was four blocks north, and Bill was five blocks directly west.

They'd separate at the crossroads like four points on a compass splitting apart. Jack's route took him directly past Saint Francis de Sales and the rectory. If he saw the lights on, he'd stop to see if Father Callahan was awake.

The truth was, he didn't want to go home. His father was probably drunk. His aunt, Constance, would be stumbling around, pretending she hadn't been imbibing, though her wig was often tilted to the side or slipped down onto her forehead. The screeching and bickering between the two of them made his ears hurt. If he wasn't clubbed about the face, neck, and shoulders for being out past dark, or beaten soundly with a strap, he'd try to find something in the kitchen to eat before hiding in his room with the covers pulled up over his head. Those were the loneliest nights of all. The hours ticking by, unable to sleep because of the banging and yelling. His father crawling up the stairs on his hands and knees, his aunt passed out on the floor in the hallway. His stomach twisted at the thought.

Father Callahan had provided him human comfort that was rare. Attention, encouragement. The smells of the church, the warmth of the Father's arms around him, made him feel safe. It was a haven, exciting, confusing, devastating, and necessary all at once. With time he grew to understand their relationship and the tacit agreement that went along with it. And in that same amount of time, he became more upset at the fact that he had compromised everything for a man who really only tolerated his company because it was given and convenient. Father Callahan had never truly loved him. He gave his attention freely to Bill and Loyal as well. They were all interchangeable. Any of them would do. The only one who stood above them was Ross. And that was an ember of jealousy that would eventually burn out of control.

He finished crossing the bridge and found his way to Palmyra Cove, a nature park created in the marshes at the foot of the bridge. It was visited daily by hordes of schoolchildren piling from school buses or climbing from cars. Jack made his way to a bench and watched intently.

Wondering if any of the children were lonely. Or needed comfort, afraid to go home with the adult holding their hand. He would watch for hours. Never approaching, never causing a problem. He had impulses, but he never allowed himself to act on them. He'd witnessed the devastation that came from such things. Very up close. But just sitting here, whiling away the day, watching, made him feel like he was closing the circle. The spot where he'd sat with his friends to watch the sun set wasn't far. Sixty years had passed. They were all dead, but here the memories were still alive. And they weren't all bad.

By the time he'd made his way back home, darkness was setting in. He entered his house and locked the door behind him. Always happy to be in his little cocoon. Though by now he'd gotten rid of most of his belongings to lighten the load for the road. All that was left were the basics. He went to the kitchen and got a glass of tap water. He drank it straight down and then filled it again.

He flipped on the television and wandered to the desk. Every night he'd stare at the pictures, trying to figure out why they'd been taken, if Marie could have been behind all of it. The thoughts were stronger now after witnessing her vengeance with Ava. Maybe he should have killed Marie too.

But when he pulled open the drawer it was empty. He stared again. The paper was there, staring back at him. Blinking, almost. *I'm coming for you.* He stumbled backward and fell, clutching his chest. *Marie.* His breaths were heavy, his left arm tingling. He lay on his side with his face in the dark-green matted area rug, feeling like he was going to die.

CHAPTER 34

Marie dumped the box onto the floor and stared at the contents. Ava's school pictures fluttered to the floor. The little dress followed. She picked it up and turned it over. A hippo was embroidered on the back. Someone had sewn the dress by hand. Not *someone*. Her mother, probably, or grandmother. Her real mother. The stitches were neat, tight and exact. The sewing was flawless. If she hadn't known it was handmade, she might have mistaken it for a mass-produced dress sold at an upscale children's boutique.

Marie knew the dress was handmade, because she'd ripped the tag off herself. The little white one sewn to the top that had the girl's name on it. That topic was one that led to a huge falling-out. The two sisters didn't speak for over six months, and Anais had to intervene, though she agreed with Marie. *Change the girl's name.* Claire had resisted. *She knows her name, it'll only make things worse,* Claire had said. *She won't forget her name.* But Claire came around, and eventually she did forget, and Ava Hope she became.

The dress fabric was clean now. Marie had scrubbed the blood from it with her knuckles back then. Made it new again and let little Ava Hope wear it until it became a problem. She knew the hippo. She knew the hows, whats, wheres of the hippo, and would run her fingers over the doubled thread and cry for her mother. The crying was endless.

Screaming. Until Claire became so frantic she ripped the flesh on her own face with her fingernails. The neighbors heard the commotion and were starting to complain, to question. So Claire moved from Brooklyn to Revere, Massachusetts. And then to Clinton, New York. And the list went on. Until she wasn't running from questions, but running for her life.

Marie dropped the dress into the box. Did Ava remember any of it? She knew pieces, that was certain. And with enough pieces she'd be able to make a whole pie. The photograph and the little hippo dress were enough to make a whole buffet of pies. The worst fear of the past nineteen years was that the girl's memory would kill them all eventually. But Claire wouldn't throw the dress away. *No, it's the only thing left to her. Leave it in a box. What harm can it do?* Claire, a combination of warm heart and cold hands, face, language. The weirdest of mixes.

What will you do when she starts asking questions, when she challenges your baby-at-the-church story, Claire? It's going to happen one day. The golden question. No one had an answer, and when the day finally came and the questions burst forth like a volcano erupting, they'd never come up with a better plan than to deny all knowledge. But Ava was whip smart. Smacking her face didn't stop it. She wasn't going to let it go. Ever.

Marie went to the living room and opened the fireplace damper. The kindling was ready. She lit a match and saw the flame, heard the crackle. Ava was physically gone; now it was time to wipe her existence off the map. The album went first—the awkward elementary-school pictures, crinkling and dissolving in the flames. The little girl's face would be nothing but memory. Then middle school and high school. The collection was eclectic. Twenty different schools, maybe.

The hippo dress was harder. She held it in her hands. Part of her understood why Claire wanted to keep it. She turned it over and looked at the tiny remnants of the white thread that had held the tag. *Giada* had been written there with dark marking pen. Ava's name had been

Giada. The last remnants of the past. She held it over the fire for a minute, watching the flames dance around it, then dropped it. It landed hippo side out. Just then, the doorbell rang. *Merde.*

She pushed at the dress with the poker and then pulled herself up to open the door. "Yes?"

"Sister, can I bother you for a moment? It's important." Russell slid into the living room, then turned to face her, his feet planted.

Her hands fluttered out from her sides. "Is this an official visit? Officer—"

"Not exactly. Just looking for Ava. Is she here? I haven't talked to her in a few days."

Marie half turned around, as if startled. "Really? I thought she was out and about with friends. Or visiting—"

He looked over and saw the flames licking the brick around the fireplace. His face showed no expression whatsoever. "Is this a housewarming?" The dress was only beginning to succumb to the heat. The print of the dress, the hippo, were still plainly visible.

Marie tried to move subtly in front of it to block his view. "Ah, a joke, yes, a housewarming." She saw Russell's eyes glued to the mantel.

"The room certainly looks better. Getting rid of things?"

Marie held the flaps of her cardigan together with her fingers. "Ava's strength doesn't lie in housekeeping." Her mind was whirling. "Is there anything else you needed?" She noticed the light-brown color of his eyes, the intensity of the stare. His wheels were turning, she could tell.

"It smells like burning plastic. You're not putting plastic in the fireplace, are you? That's really dangerous—"

"No. No plastic. The fireplace hasn't been used in a while. You're just smelling disuse."

"No, burning plastic has a distinctive smell. Maybe plastic ties on the logs? Do you want me to check?" He stepped around her toward the fireplace.

Marie glanced back. The dress seemed shrouded by the protection of God. It appeared untouched by the heat and flame. "No, it's fine. I'm just burning some old things I wanted to get rid of."

"Part of the reason I'm here is that I've misplaced my wallet. I've taken my house and car apart and can't find it."

"I've not seen it." It came out clipped and sharp.

"Could you look in Ava's room? Maybe it fell under the bed?"

Marie shuddered at the man coming here and insinuating something that crass and then daring to ask her to search for his missing item. "I can do it for you but I don't have time now. I've got an appointment, so you'll have to leave."

He looked down, studying her shoes, then his head snapped back up. "My driver's license is in there. And my badge. Can't work without it. So, if you don't mind? I'll search her room, if you'd rather."

Marie moved to the steps, then looked down at the fire, torn. "No. I'll look. In her room? Anywhere else?"

"The office. We were in the office together. Maybe her bathroom? I took off my pants—"

"Fine." She darted up the steps to get away from him, before she could hear any more details.

She scanned Ava's room. She'd gone through most of her things already. The bed had been cleared. She dropped to her knees and looked under. Other than a few wayward cups that had rolled underneath, there was nothing. She crossed the hall and surveyed the office. Tidy, neat, and though she knew the closet had been violated, she wasn't searching through boxes to find a missing wallet.

She raced down the steps to find Russell sitting on an ottoman, staring into the flames, deep in thought.

"Nothing there. I'll leave a note for Ava to get in touch with you." Her hands were trembling again as she reached for the doorknob.

He stood up. "Thanks. Are you selling this place? Looks like you're packing up."

She half nodded. "With Claire gone, Ava and I decided it was for the best. She was supposed to help me pack, actually. Her job was the kitchen. But she's always been unpredictable, so I should have known not to count on her." She smiled, but her cheek muscles twitched. "Here one minute, off doing God knows what the next."

"Right." He walked through the open door and she shut it quickly behind him, flipping the locks into place.

She ran to the fireplace and prodded the logs with the poker. Fragments of blue threads from the hippo remained. The plastic buttons gave off a terrible smell. The rest had disintegrated in the heat. She kept poking at the embers, sparks flying up at her, landing on her hands and arms, until she gave up, dropping down onto the ottoman. Her face was red, not from the fire but from the tears that were streaming down her cheeks.

CHAPTER 35

Joanne stared down at the four photographs lined up on her dining-room table. "This scares me, Russell. I mean really scares me. Four murders?"

"Or maybe not. It doesn't all make sense. One is of Jack Quinn's door. Is he dead, do you think?" He took a bite of pizza and dropped it on his plate, then wiped his fingers on the napkin.

"Or maybe it was just a threat?"

"So the killer is still out there? Targeting Quinn next. Makes sense. But the fact that Quinn is still alive is a bit different."

"True. So tell me what happened, Russell. With Marie?"

He shook his head. "It was bad. She's burning things most people wouldn't burn. Like clothing."

Joanne's head dropped. "Ava's things? Getting rid of evidence? What?"

"A dress. Little dress. With a blue animal on the back. I saw that when I was coming in. And the place smelled of burnt plastic."

Joanne stood up. Her eyes were large. Her hands curled into fists. "That was the dress Ava showed me that was in the box with the photograph. It was a blue hippo—a sort of checked pattern, white and dark blue, maybe?"

He nodded. "Exactly. It was in the fireplace."

"Why get rid of her stuff?"

His chin was in his hand. "And the plastic? I don't know what it was. Maybe just the buttons on the dress. I was trying to see when

Marie ran upstairs, but the fire was too hot, with sparks everywhere. It looked like metal and plastic."

"Get a warrant, Russell. I'll get a judge to sign it. Search that house. I'm getting really afraid."

Russell's shoulders dropped in defeat. "I'd love to, but are you prepared for that?"

"For?"

"Being questioned? Asked why you withheld evidence in a murder investigation? When you knew what you know?"

Joanne crossed her arms. "It's not about me and protecting myself. I'll take what comes. But if she's burning Ava's things. Oh my God." She put her face in her hands. "This is awful. Ava's not coming back."

"It's not about me protecting myself either. Not completely. I can go tonight and give them all the evidence I have. Burning a dress is not illegal. We don't have anything else." He held her eyes with his. "Are you willing to do whatever, for nothing, and lose everything?"

She wiped her face. "Okay, so what now? What do we do?"

"Ava's not dead." He said it strong and clear.

"Then where is she?"

He shook his head. "I don't know, but I won't believe she's dead unless I see a body. She's not dead. And I'm continuing with this until the end."

Joanne stood up. "I went over her phone. She'd been trying to call France for days. Like twenty times she called that number. It doesn't look like anyone answered."

"Gotta be her grandmother. I wonder where she is?"

"I'll dial again. Maybe she was traveling."

Joanne picked up the phone and hit a button. The phone rang endlessly. She clicked the button and shrugged. "Not answering." She shook the phone at Russell. "That nun is behind this. That's what I think. Even if you don't have a warrant, you need to go back and really give it to her."

"Can you rephrase that?"

She half laughed. "Oh, you know what I mean. Don't perv on me. That's where you need to start."

Russell finished his pizza and took his plate to the sink. "Thanks for dinner." He turned and leaned against it. "Marie was nervous. Shaking like a death-row inmate. She could break."

"Leave it to a cop to use a death-row simile. What now?"

He shook his head. "Find Ava. And question Jack Quinn."

"What happened that someone wants to off all of 'em? Something they saw? Something they did?"

He was lost in thought. "Either one, maybe both. And it connects with Ava somehow. Where she came from." He held a finger up in the air. "Give me two minutes. I'm going to my car." He came back with manila envelopes under his arm. "Now I need your help." He dropped them on her table. "Reports from the Saunders and Connelly deaths. I need you to pore over them for me. Look for anything out of the ordinary. Anything I can grab on to. I need to find the commonality. The murderer left something behind. It's just nobody knew to look for it."

"While you do what, exactly?"

He stood up. "Find Ava. I can't handle all the angles at one time."

"How are you and your other little miss doing, by the way?"

Russell smiled. "Her name is Juliette. And we're doing. That's all I can say."

"Yeah? I say ditch her. Or when they ask if anyone objects to your union? I'm going to take over that ceremony."

He laughed. "You assume you're invited. Juliette doesn't have you on the list."

"Tell her it doesn't matter. I'll track you down."

He reached out and hugged her. "Thanks. I'll call you tomorrow."

"Come over. And bring either Ava in the flesh or that nun's head on a platter."

CHAPTER 36

He lay on his side, his face pressed into the matted green carpet. His breaths came slowly. His left arm no longer tingled. He could move but was afraid to. The desk chair was right in front of him. His eyes were less than five inches from the wood of the leg. He occupied his time by taking in every detail of the marred pine. The scrapes, the dings, the dirt. He'd cleaned the house in anticipation of leaving but didn't think to scrub the legs of the desk chair. When he got up, he'd tend to it. He wanted the place pristine. No one coming after him. Looking for him.

He also focused on the fact that someone had walked right where his head lay. Taken those photographs from the desk drawer and left the note. *I'm coming for you.* He thought with the Ava ordeal over, this part was done too. But of course it wasn't. By revealing himself to Marie he'd only made himself an easier target.

He rolled over on his back and took two deep breaths before pulling himself to a sitting position. He didn't have the luxury of staying another night. Not after two break-ins so close together.

He had a cousin in Torresdale. He'd go there for the night, get the rest of his money from the bank in the morning, and get a bus to South Carolina from the Greyhound station in Center City. He took the steps to the second floor carefully and lay down on his bed. The room was warm. He'd just changed the sheets. His eyes were heavy, his lids fluttering.

When he opened them he saw Father Callahan standing over him. His close-set eyes only inches from his. "Wake up, Jack."

He jumped and scuttled into the corner. "What are you doing here?" His heart was pounding, his breaths labored. "How'd you find me?"

"You know why I'm here. To talk about what happened. Years ago, with Ava."

He pressed against the wall, feeling a tingling in his left arm again. "You need to find Marie. Marie was the one who did it."

Father Callahan sat on the end of the bed. "You were the ringleader nineteen years ago. You destroyed nine lives. I counted. And now you're at it again. How many more will there be before you stop?"

"No. Loyal was the ringleader. And I didn't kill Bill, Loyal, and Ross. It wasn't me."

"Maybe not, but their lives were destroyed anyway, even before they died."

"I didn't kill Ava."

"So it was all Marie? Is that what you're saying? Don't lie."

"It was Marie this time."

"What does the Bible say about liars, Jack?"

He shook his head and said nothing.

"*A false witness shall not be unpunished, and he that speaketh lies shall perish.* Proverbs 19:9. We covered that in Sunday school, didn't we?" He stood up and smiled. "I'm sure we did. Were you not paying attention?" He began to pace. "You always were lazy, so I'll give you a pass on that one. Let's try it again. Did you kill Ava?"

Jack closed his eyes tight. Only the suggestion of light from the hallway came through his lids. "She's dead. But it was Marie. Not me. Marie. I was going to strangle her but she threw up on my hands when I was putting them on her, so I stopped." His voice had risen as if he were ten years old again, caught stealing a pencil from someone's desk. "Marie finished it. I swear."

"Did you give her body a decent Christian funeral? A funeral at all?" His tone now was calm. Monotone. Jack knew this so well. Father Callahan always got like this just before he erupted. Before he'd scream or threaten or hit. Or something much, much worse. His tone always dropped. Became placid, like he was in control. Like everything was going to be okay. It was all a facade. A lie. The slap came across his face. He felt the sharpness against his cheek like he had so many years ago.

"We put her body back in her car, in the back seat." Jack began to whimper. Almost a cry. "She wasn't breathing and she had no pulse."

The slap came again. Harder. "And what did Marie do with her? She was just a girl. Innocent, you know. She'd done nothing wrong. It was you four boys. What *you* did, that started this." He poked him in the chest. It burned.

"I know. But—"

"Where. Is. Her. Body?" The words were a harsh staccato line.

Jack was trembling. His left arm was no longer tingling. It was on fire straight up through his shoulder. His chest was heavy. Aching. "We drove her car to the Pine Barrens. A dirt road that cuts off of 72. We left her in the car." Spasms of pain shot through his chest. "Please help me."

Father Callahan watched. And then just shook his head. "No." It was a whisper in his ear. "Not yet."

He opened his eyes. "Father, please? I'm sorry for everything. I was angry at you. But please don't let me die."

But Father Callahan wasn't with him. Just a shadow of his ghost remained. Jack was still lying on the green carpet in the living room. He'd only imagined he'd moved upstairs. His heart was failing, he knew his life was seeping from his bones. Delirium was setting in. Before he shut his eyes he saw a figure step forward, the light at their back. The figure leaned close to his face.

"*A man burdened with bloodshed will flee into a pit; let no one help him.* Proverbs 28:17. Close your eyes now. You've done the work for me. It's time to die, Jack."

He felt the breath on his face. Was it real? He was drenched in sweat. His heart drummed and then fluttered. He recognized the voice, knew the person, the killer, the killer of Bill, Loyal, Ross. And he finally understood why it happened. He was seeing what all of them saw just before they died. But it was impossible. Wasn't it? He wanted to get up. To finally fight, but he didn't have the strength. He closed his eyes and obeyed.

CHAPTER 37

"Steve and Karen are coming over in about forty-five minutes, so, you know, if you want to shower, shave, change, fix yourself up?"

"Hmmm?" He'd been sitting for hours at his desk, just sorting details in his head. The blue outline of the hippo disintegrating in the flames. Evidence destroyed.

Juliette had costumed herself for this dinner party, he noted. Black cocktail dress—formfitting but not tight, upswept hair, her grandmother's diamond earrings, though she still held her stiletto pumps in her hand and chose to shuffle around in her Ugg slippers. It should have set off alarms for him to be on his best behavior. She'd hired a caterer, who had been banging pots in the kitchen for at least an hour, borrowed her mother's china for the table setting. Flower arrangements as a centerpiece.

"You've been in here all day, looking at those papers." She clapped her hands two times. "Chop-chop, let's get going. Get in the shower. Dr. Thomas is going to be here soon, and I want everything perfect."

Dr. Thomas was a prospective employer, that much he knew. A partner in a lucrative orthopedic practice at University of Pennsylvania, with offices all over South Jersey. But the fact that she was calling him Steve and his wife Karen meant that she didn't have too much to worry about.

"They've got an office in Chadds Ford. I'd love to live in Delaware County, wouldn't you? Get out of New Jersey?"

He took a breath and looked up from his papers. "I work in Camden, that's a bit of a hike. And no matter which office you see patients in? You're going to be taking call and operating in Philadelphia. You'll spend your life in a traffic jam."

Her mouth turned down. "Do what I ask, please, Russell. Get a shower, dress in the dark suit I bought for you, be nice—be charming, even. Don't talk about your cases or police work. Only if they ask." She started to turn around but then had more to say. "Oh, and if they do ask, highlight the Prosecutor's Office. The courts. The lawyers. 'Kay?"

"God, yes, Juliette. I'll talk about my in-chambers meeting with Judge Clark just the other day." He stood up. The comment was meant to be sarcastic.

"Is he a superior- or municipal-court judge? If he's superior, then that's okay."

She scooted down the steps, so he couldn't tell if she was being funny or obnoxiously pretentious. She'd forgiven him too quickly after the wedding-planner incident. He figured it meant either she'd found a way to speed-blast through her grudges or she was way too deep into the wedding plans and the idea of marriage to give up on him now. He was betting on the second, and it was giving him migraines.

He thought about Ava and how she might have reacted to this little dinner party, smiled at the thought of her messy house. He felt a slight punch in his gut. The more time that went by without finding her, the less certain he was that there was going to be a pleasant ending to the story. *Where are you? Talk to me.* He'd looked at the photographs all day, comparing the handwriting on each one, the color of the ink. He wasn't a handwriting expert, but they all looked to be written by the same person, maybe even with the same pen.

Joanne was still poring over the reports on the deaths of Bill Connelly and Ross Saunders, looking for anything that might stand out. He was counting on her. She was overbearing at times but had fabulous attention to detail, was used to reading mundane boring reports and condensing them, and had a personal interest. It was coincidence that he was thinking about her as he was getting out of the shower and that the phone number on his vibrating cell was Joanne's.

"Hey, listen. FYI. On a hunch I called the Cherbourg police and asked them to check on Anais. I was getting worried about her, ya know," she said just after he clicked the phone on. "Twenty calls, no answer?"

He dried his hair with the towel. "You called Cherbourg?"

"Uh-huh. And they called me back. The old lady's house is all locked up. She's not there. They looked. She must be traveling, which is a good thing. If she was dead, I don't know what I'd do."

"Wonder where she went."

"Don't know. But the only thing I've gotten so far out of this stuff is that Bill Connelly was deathly allergic to tree nuts. He had an EpiPen and everything."

Russell sat down on his bed. "So why didn't he use it?"

"Hmmm. They found the bag turned over, like he was searching for it but it wasn't there, apparently. But—"

"Are you kidding me? We have guests in fifteen minutes and you're sitting here naked, on the phone?" Juliette was in the doorway, fully dressed, stiletto heels making her slight form fill the doorway. "Now. Do you hear me?"

He heard the clip-clopping of her shoes going all the way down the steps. "But?" he prodded Joanne.

"Oooo, Russell, are you talking to me naked?"

He laughed. "Hurry up and finish, we have a swanky shindig going down here. I gotta get my suit on."

"Investigators found the EpiPen later. It'd rolled under the table."

"Interesting. Listen, I'd love to keep talking. Or even come over and read those reports, but right now I'm a monkey in a performing circus. I'll call you later."

"Fine. But I'd ditch that—"

"Bye, Joanne."

He hung up and had just managed to put all his attire on except for his suit jacket when the phone rang again. He looked at the number and grabbed it from the nightstand.

Doug's voice was in his ear. "Russell, you need to come here now. I found Ava's car."

Fifteen minutes later, Russell charged down the steps in jeans and a hoodie. Juliette stood in the doorway between the kitchen and the dining room. She leaned her back against the wall, her fists balled.

"No," she said between clenched teeth.

"They found a car in a missing-persons. It's my case. I gotta go."

"Have someone else do it. Not tonight, Russell."

He hesitated. "I really can't." He reached out to touch her hand, but she pulled it away and folded it under her arm. "This is my case and it's big. I'll be back as soon as possible."

"Don't bother, I don't want you back here."

The doorbell rang. "I kind of have to come back, it's my house," he said. "And you'll get what you want from these people, Juliette, whether I'm here or not. You always do." With that he opened the door.

He shook hands with Dr. Thomas as he passed him. "Sorry to miss the evening, I'm sure it's going to be great, but I'm a cop." He made sure he turned in just the right way so his gun was visible. "Just got a call. Prostitute roundup. Can't miss that." He leaned over and brushed his lips over Juliette's forehead before heading out the door.

CHAPTER 38

Marie stared out the window of her cell at the convent, her eyes wandering over the shapes of the tree branches, the door to the school across the street, the varying pattern of bricks that framed the windows, but her thoughts were fixated on the cop. He'd shown up just as she was burning the dress. He knew something. If he didn't before, he did now. She could tell by looking in his eyes. That vacant stare seemed practiced, but she saw the gears shifting behind his eyes. Old, too-familiar panic edged with paranoia was starting to take hold of her. Bouts of uncontrollable rage alternating with crippling depression would be next. She had no idea who she could trust. She needed family.

She heard a noise and whipped around to see Sister Regina there with a sandwich and a bottle of water. "You haven't taken a meal with us in days. And no dinner tonight? Are you all right, Marie?"

"You've no idea how not all right I am," she responded.

Regina set the plate and bottle on the side table and sat next to her. "Is there anything I can do?"

Marie looked at Regina's eager face. "I can't talk about it. But I do need to run an errand now. I won't be more than a few hours."

Regina nodded. "Do you need me to come with you? It's already dark."

Marie went to her closet and grabbed her coat. "No. I'm fine." Though the dark circles under her eyes and the marks on her face where she'd scratched herself in despair told a different truth. She grabbed the bottle of water and the sandwich. "Thanks, Regina. Do me a favor? Tell them I'm ill, not to be bothered. I'll be back soon," she added as she headed out the door.

The ride up Route 130 North to the Tacony–Palmyra Bridge was bumper to bumper. Marie was impatient and nervous. This part of New Jersey wasn't pleasant or pretty to her. It was one long industrial road filled with fast-food restaurants and gas stations, with stoplights placed every fifty yards. She chewed the corner of her sandwich, but the thick, dry bread stuck in her throat. She gulped the water to encourage it down.

Her thoughts were darting. She needed to go by Jack Quinn's to make sure he was really gone. She didn't trust that he'd left town like he'd promised he would. They'd parted ways after dumping Ava, with an agreement that she'd never see his miserable, ugly face again, but she feared he was still holed up in his house, maybe waiting for the right moment to kill her too.

She got to the exit for the bridge and turned right. The water of the Delaware River flowed beneath her—feeling the car move with the pressure of the wind made her yearn to get out, walk the overpass, just take in the lights of Philadelphia in the distance. She wanted to pull over, but there was no shoulder. *Not tonight,* she thought.

As she was rounding the corner onto the street where Jack lived, a figure darted into the road in front of her. She barely missed clipping them with her bumper, but they moved steadily without turning back. The hunched person, overwhelmed by a large black overcoat, streamed from view. *No, this cannot be.* Marie got out of her car, eyes glued to the vision that was disappearing. She knew the shape, the form, the coat instinctively. *Claire.*

Turning at the corner, the figure disappeared. Marie bent over for a second to catch her breath and then raced after her sister, screaming her name. But she was gone. *That did not just happen. It just couldn't be. I was there and she was dead. I'm going mad.* She reached inside her coat, searching for her cell phone, her hands shaky, but she'd left it at the convent.

Oh no, no, no. Her eyes flitted between the end of the street where the figure had disappeared and the row home in front of her. *Good God, no.* Number ten had a dim light coming from behind the curtains. She went to the door and hesitated only a moment before rapping against the wood. There was no answer. She knocked harder and then turned the handle. The room was warm; the glow of the desk lamp gave off a dim yellowish light that made the place look dingy, like a gas-station bathroom.

She saw his leg before she knew what she was looking at. It was straight, brown shoe still on his foot. She held her breath and walked around the couch. Quinn was stretched out, his other leg at an angle. His face was turned, half in the green carpet. His lips looked bluish. Marie studied him for a full minute, the reality coming to her in pieces. She'd prayed for this, for this man to go away. But his death now opened up more questions than it answered.

Forget what you saw. It wasn't real, she told herself as she stepped over Jack Quinn's body. After wiping her prints off the doorknob, she headed out into the night. *Get on a plane to France tomorrow. Get away from this place.*

She looked up at the night sky, the stars dulled by the glare of the outdoor light but still magnificent. Then her eyes caught something lifting and blowing in the breeze. She picked it up and knew it instantly. Black, thin, filmy. The peel-off layer from the back of Polaroid film.

She held it between her fingers, trying to make sense of it. Was this taken with the same camera? How was that possible? The camera had been in the closet at the convent. She'd put it there herself for safekeeping, away from prying eyes and fingers. Was it possible that she had come here and killed Quinn and didn't remember any of it? She'd never experienced blackouts before. Her symptoms were usually confusion, depression, despair, but she always remembered what she'd done—even if through a distant, blurry veil. But maybe the stress of the past months, of having to take Ava's life, had pushed her to a new level of insanity.

She whispered to God, the words finally coming, a prayer of five words, a short and simple *God, please help me, no.*

CHAPTER 39

Russell reached the access road off Route 72 in an hour and fifteen minutes. The Pine Barrens was a stretch of green and brown twisted pine trees and sugar sand that extended across seven counties in New Jersey. *Barren* was an apt description. The government had designated over a million acres of this dense forestation as a national reserve. Other than a few backwoods sort of folks who'd built cabins, choosing to escape humanity, it was undisturbed and desolate. The cutoff roads through the area were tricky and treacherous. Winding dirt paths took a person farther into nowhere. There were many stories of people lost on the back roads in the Pine Barrens, stranded for days or weeks. As a kid he'd trekked these woods at night with his parents on hyped-up Halloween search-for-the-Jersey-Devil excursions. But those were tourist events, complete with lanterns and a hot-dog cookout over the fire at the end.

This was different. The always-present source of illumination that came from streetlights, taken for granted, was sorely missed a mile into the barrens. *Dark* didn't describe it. When Russell's hand went to the gearshift, he couldn't see his fingers. The thin light from the dashboard was almost absorbed into an abyss and disappeared. Russell blew a stream of air from his mouth and felt it collect in front of him. It was so damned cold. And the darkness made it seem colder.

He checked his fuel gauge. One quarter of a tank. He hadn't thought to stop for gas, he'd been in such a hurry to get away from Juliette and her shit show of a party that he'd just jumped in the Jeep and taken off. It would be plenty, he was sure.

His stomach was twisting. *Ava's car.* Doug didn't say he'd found Ava's body and her car, just her car. What would she have been doing way out in the Pine Barrens? Or was her car deposited here? His tire hit a pit in the dirt road, and Russell bounced so hard his head hit the headliner. He kept moving, keeping track of his odometer. Doug had said approximately eight miles after the cutoff. It had to be coming up soon. His headlights were a beacon out here. He searched forward but saw nothing.

Where are you, Doug? His odometer read that he'd reached the eight-mile mark. Suddenly he was there and passed it. He caught the outline of something on the side of the road. A darkish mass that didn't fit in with the landscape of endless trees. No lights. He jammed on the brakes and screeched to a stop, then backed up.

"Jesus, Russell. I thought you'd never get here." Doug went around and opened his door.

He stepped out onto the dirt. "What the hell, Doug?" His head spun in both directions. "Where's your car? What're you doing out here alone?"

Doug smiled. "'Fraid of the dark? Buddy just left. Figured we could get her car out of here before they call it in again."

"I'm glad you trusted me enough to let him leave. If I didn't show up, you'd be screwed."

Doug moved to Ava's car and opened the door. "No doubts you'd get here eventually."

"So let's get going, then."

"Thing is, her battery is dead." He held up a finger. "But the key's in the ignition." He leaned against the car. "Let's see if we can jump it. You have cables?"

"Yeah."

"Somebody that lives in this backwoods paradise called it in. It's been here for days, they said. A friend at the state police called me as a favor 'cause I put out an unofficial APB on her car. But if this weirdo calls it in again, it's gonna be on the books. Which it really should be." Russell nodded, but Doug didn't see it in the dark. "Wanna talk about this? It's not too late to make this official."

"I should. But not tonight."

"If something happened to her, and I mean she just didn't purposely ditch her car back here, then this is bad, Russ. You know that. We need to start searching for a body. And if we find one, it's official anyway. I can't cover you for that."

"I know."

"Besides, you're destroying evidence. Forensics needs to go over this—"

"I know."

Doug rubbed his face with his hands. "You need to tell me this from the beginning. From the case that got you run over in the street in front of the courthouse to this girl." He waved his hand around. "What's going on with her, and why's she missing? This isn't nothing, Russ, and it's too deep for you alone."

"I'm not alone. Joanne's involved."

Doug pushed off the car and stood in front of his friend. His arms flew out to the sides. "Oh, you got Joanne helping you. Well, why didn't you tell me? Then it's all fine."

"Ava told Joanne before she even told me. I was stupid from the beginning and it's too late to be smart now. Help me jump the battery and we'll talk. Off the record."

The Honda Accord was idling smoothly. The gas tank read three-quarters full. Russell shined the flashlight into the car. Doug was right. He was destroying evidence. He'd wear gloves and do the best he could, but he needed to get the car out of here. His light caught a flash of something on the floor. He moved the light back and then reached for it. He pulled out a shot-sized vodka bottle.

"What is it?" Doug asked.

"Ava's last meal, I think."

He heard the crunching of Doug's feet on the pine needles, moving away from him. He came back a few minutes later with a larger light from Russell's Jeep. "Turn the car off. We're doing a quick body search now."

"In the dark?"

Doug pulled on gloves. "You take this side of the road, I'll take the other. They wouldn't have dragged the body far. You have your cell phone on you?"

Russell nodded and pulled it out. But there were no bars. "Doesn't work."

"Shit. Stay within shouting distance, then. Meet back at the cars in half an hour."

Russell watched Doug disappear into the trees. He shined his own light ahead and hesitated. He'd been in many situations that scared the crap out of him. This wasn't even in the top twenty. But there was something worse about going off the road into the Pine Barrens in the dead of night in search of a body, with nothing but one thin stream of light to guide him. He moved ahead, trying to keep the cars in view. He knew if he got disoriented or lost in here, that was it. He'd have to count on Doug to find him.

Animals scurried by his feet, rough pine branches blocked his path. His light was cast downward, looking for a disturbance of earth, clothing or items, anything out of place. He wasn't even ten minutes into the search when he heard his friend's screams. "Russ! Here. Got something."

CHAPTER 40

Joanne had been hunched over her kitchen table for hours, dissecting the reports Russell had given her. She clicked on her phone and checked the time.

"Ten o'clock. God." She pushed back her chair and stood up to stretch. She'd called Russell five times, but they went to voicemail. A little doubt landed in the back of her brain and occasionally moved forward, capturing her attention, causing a stir of panic in her gut. If Russell disappeared, that was it, she was heading straight to the Prosecutor's Office and telling them everything.

She sat down again and opened the report for the fortieth time. Bill's and Ross's deaths had both been ruled accidental. But with a more critical eye looking for abnormalities, the window of possibility cracked open enough to allow foul play to enter. Someone could have given Bill a dose of tree nuts and hidden his EpiPen, then threw it back under the table after he was dead. And Ross—he'd fallen in the bathroom, like so many others of a certain age—a random terrible thing. But Ross was found naked, on his left side, on the floor, his head only inches from the tub. A large contusion on the right side of his temple. The report ruled it as accidental, assuming Ross didn't die immediately from his injury and had moved, crawled or repositioned himself before death. But what if he hadn't? What if he'd died upon impact with an object?

Hit on his right side and then fell down to the left with the blow? That would make more sense.

The deaths of Loyal Owens and his wife stood out from the others—not made to look like an accident. A deviation in the cause of death for a serial killer was extremely unusual. They'd assumed the killer had been lying in wait and was caught off guard, forced to kill in a brutal way. But maybe they were wrong. What if it hadn't been the same killer? Maybe it was a copycat—someone who knew of Bill's death and the photograph and took the opportunity to get rid of Loyal. *But who? And why? And they would need to use the same camera. Or one identical. Think, Joanne, think.*

She had hung a whiteboard on the wall near her chair and would write ideas down as they came to her. This one was added below nine others that had occurred to her while reading. She was never a linear thinker—her thoughts jumped around, so she'd start separate columns for different subject matter as the thoughts came. One was titled *Ava.* She tried to remember everything she knew about her friend and then divided it into sections—*know for a fact, know secondhand, unconfirmed.* She was shocked at how little was on the board in those columns. The girl was a wisp of smoke in the wind. Yet the two had spent substantial time together. How was that possible?

She was about to reach for her phone to call Russell again when she saw car lights in front of her house. She peered from behind the curtains to see Ava's Honda pull up and stop. She rubbed her eyes, not sure it was true, and then flew out the front door.

She backed up when she saw Russell's Jeep pull up behind it. Doug and Russell both opened their doors at the same time and stepped out onto the curb.

"Where's Ava? What's going on?" she demanded.

"We found her car in the Pine Barrens," Doug offered.

Joanne backed up farther. Her hands went to her face and she felt tears appear on her cheeks. "Where is she, Russell?"

"Let's go in."

They followed her into her house and she made coffee. Russell examined her whiteboard notes. "This is good work, Joanne. It puts it all together for us."

Joanne came back and handed them both coffee mugs. Then she picked up the silver letter opener and pieces of duct tape Doug had found in the woods. "This seals it. We need to report this now. Get prints on this. See if there's DNA on this tape."

"I have a better idea. Let's assume there is DNA on the tape. Let's assume it was on her wrists. Somehow in a tussle the letter opener was dropped. Or she had it and used it to cut the tape," Doug said. "And we just move forward with that premise."

"We'll go back there in daylight and look for other things left behind and/or a body. When we can actually see what we're doing," Russell added. "We don't report it until we have a body."

"What if she's not dead, guys? What if she got away and is lost in the woods and's been there all this time?" Joanne asked.

"We'll find her."

Doug was looking at each Polaroid, picking it up, absorbing it, and then putting it back down. "This is interesting and amazing."

"So in the meantime, what are you going to do with Ava's car?" Joanne asked.

Russell smiled. "I'm going to park it in her driveway, leave the key in the ignition. And watch for fireworks."

"Oh my God, that's brilliant. See what that crazy nun does? Then follow her?" Joanne added.

"And you and me," he said to Doug, "are going back to Jack Quinn's. Maybe actually question him without him knowing he's not being officially questioned?"

Doug nodded. "This is all going to end with a dead body, a full investigation, our dismissal, and maybe charges for all of us. But at least I'll have a friend while I'm sitting in Camden County Jail."

Russell eyed him. "They'd send us out of county, don't you think?" He patted his back. "Come. We need to drop off Ava's car and make sure no one sees us, then I'll take you home."

"So what's next for me? What do I do?" Joanne asked.

Russell studied her for a second, thinking. "Tomorrow is Saturday. Wanna stake out Ava's house tomorrow, early in the morning? As early as you can get there. See if anyone shows up? Just for a few hours until I get back from Quinn's?"

"Me? Really?" She jumped up and hugged him. "Thank you. I thought I was going to be on desk duty forever." She started making a list of stakeout supplies as they were leaving the house.

CHAPTER 41

Marie thought the world might be coming to an end. Signs of the apocalypse and all. The long night had been spent sleepless, with thoughts of her sister running through her head. She closed her eyes and imagined Claire. Her face, her whole being. Five seven, thin, wider shoulders than hips. The black moleskin coat she'd bought on a cold day in Switzerland, way too big for her slight form, but she loved it. She said it was like wearing a blanket. Lushly lined in silk, it had a large hood edged in fox fur. A no-no, she'd told her sister, but Claire didn't care. With the belt tied just right, she could carry it off. And she did, until the weather changed and she was back in her Hermès double-faced cashmere overcoat.

Claire had a distinct walk. A walk with a twist that was always there. Marie teased her, telling her she was swishing to make the most of her small hips, but the truth was, she'd done it for as long as she'd been walking. It was something nobody could know or imitate even when they tried. The person she'd almost hit last night had that exact coat on. It was nearly one of a kind in the United States. And they fled down the street away from her with that same Claire signature walk. Or did they? Did she just see the coat and imagine the rest? It was dark. Claire was dead. Marie had approved the apple-green Versace dress before they'd closed the casket and Anais had taken her away for good. This wasn't possible.

She stood and paced the small area of her cell. There was only one explanation. She was going mad again. The stress of losing her sister, taking care of Ava, the emergence of the photograph, and Jack Quinn had pushed her brain to the sizzling point. That was all there was to it. She picked up the phone again and dialed her mother's number. But the old woman didn't answer. Her mother had been gone way too long and hadn't mentioned traveling, but Anais was unpredictable and spontaneous. She hung up the phone and stared at the receiver.

Then it dawned on her. The black coat. She could run to Claire's and see if it was in the closet. It was always in the front closet, wrapped in a garment bag during the summer, hanging free in the winter. She'd passed away before the really cold weather had set in, and Ava had done little or nothing to sort out Claire's belongings.

She wrapped herself in her jacket, slid her hands into her gloves, and donned her hat. Venturing out in the cold was the last thing she felt like doing, but she couldn't get the thought of that stupid coat out of her mind. She slid behind the wheel of her old Hyundai and started the engine—it ran rough until it warmed up, rattling loud enough to bring faces to the windows of the convent. She pulled out of the parking lot and headed to her sister's.

She saw it as she turned onto the street. Her heart pounded; her palms, even in the cold, began to grow damp. Her throat closed. *Ava's car.* It was in the driveway, like it belonged there. How was this possible? Marie pulled over two houses up and parked. She walked up the block, looking at the silver mirage, not sure if it was real or another delusion. Her fingers felt the solidness of the metal door. Frigid. She then touched her fingers with her other hand. There was a collection of pine needles stuffed down around the wiper blades, and some broken needles were embedded in the treads of the tires.

She peered inside and then opened the door. The car was empty, the keys hung in the ignition. Marie straightened and looked up and down the street. Nothing was out of the ordinary. The car had been left deep in the Pine Barrens, where they'd unloaded Ava's body. She pulled the keys from the ignition and popped the trunk. Empty.

Someone knew what they'd done and had brought the car back.

She raced up the steps to the house and unlocked the door. The house was cold and quiet. She'd turned the thermostat down to sixty to save money. The sound echoed against the walls when she shut the door.

"Ava?" she yelled. Her voice bounded off the walls, making it sound hollow. Marie's voice was met with silence.

She raced from room to room, but the house was empty, as she knew it would be. Finally she flopped onto the couch and stared into the fireplace. Thin blue threads from the burned dress remained. How long was she going to have to cover up for this thing? Then, as if her memory had suddenly jostled her brain awake, she remembered why she'd come here in the first place. Claire's coat in the closet. She took tentative steps to the door; her hand hesitated on the doorknob. She wanted to know but she was petrified to find out.

A sharp intake of breath and then she yanked the closet door open. Claire's coats lined the rod, some in plastic garment bags, some without. She went through them one by one, unzipping bags, pulling out items to examine them. And finally, there it was. One white bag remained. She knew this was it. Her hands were tingling. Her breaths fast and shallow. She unzipped the bag and stared at its emptiness.

Her hands flew through the closet again, pulling out all of the coats. Marie ran up the steps to Claire's closet in her bedroom and pulled open the walk-in. After a half hour of rifling, she came up empty.

Her sister's coat was inexplicably gone, and Ava's car had mysteriously appeared. Marie tore from the room, down the steps, and out the front door. There was too much at stake to leave it alone now.

CHAPTER 42

Joanne parked her car half a block down on the opposite side of the street, positioning herself within good viewing distance of the house. Her thoughts were like mice in a maze, traveling down one path until they hit a dead end, then scrambling and going the other way. Her whiteboard was in her mind, all the facts scattered across it. The year *1996*, crucial, written in the middle.

She'd surmised that maybe Ava had been found or was kidnapped and acquired by Claire in that year. Before then, Claire's life had been simple and ordinary. Then she abruptly left her job. The little girl would have been three. Or maybe just four. Certainly old enough to remember something. Joanne was hounded by that question: Did her friend remember anything about her life before then, and if so, why did she live in silence?

Kidnapping would account for Claire moving around, having no employment, so she couldn't be traced. But why would a single twenty-seven-year-old woman want to kidnap a baby when she had her entire life in front of her and could presumably marry and have children of her own? Unless she couldn't? Joanne shook her head. *No, wrong track.* Claire's life was too orderly and logical for her to do something like that.

But people and the things they did continued to shock her over the course of her work in the courts. Women and men killing their own children so as not to lose a boyfriend or girlfriend, who usually turned out to be a drug-addicted loser; a father slitting his six-year-old daughter's throat during an argument with the child's mother. A woman biting off her infant son's penis because the father was oppressive. And the list went on and on. A twenty-seven-year-old kidnapping a baby wasn't even a blip on the crime screen, really, in the scope of human atrocities.

Of two things she was certain. One, Marie was behaving suspiciously, and two, Ava remembered something—and whatever those memories were, they had shaped her into a weird, ethereal creature who, at her core, was unreachable.

Joanne checked her watch. It was almost noon, and she was freezing. She'd imagined a stakeout as exciting, adventurous, but it was really just sitting in a cold car doing nothing. Her Dunkin' Donuts coffee was half-gone, and her egg-white flatbread sandwich was but a few crumbs on her jacket sleeve. She'd been here for over three hours and she wanted to get home, make lunch, and stare at her whiteboard.

The mailman came along the block, moving slowly from house to house. He was just part of the neighborhood scenery, like the cars or people walking their dogs, until he stopped at Claire's house. He slipped an envelope into the box and went on his way. Joanne saw it but didn't think anything of it for a few minutes. Then curiosity crept in and stayed long enough that she got out of the car, pulled the envelope from the box, and went back to her car. It was legal-sized, addressed to *Occupant*, computer printed. No return address. *Maybe nothing, maybe something.*

When her finger hit the hard edge inside the envelope, her heart started to race. She pulled out a Polaroid, rectangular with white edges. Exactly like the others that were sitting on her kitchen table, black and white, of the front of a house. *And now I am done* was printed underneath. Her skin was prickling, and all she could do was drop the picture onto the seat and dial Russell's number. He answered on the second ring.

"Guess what?" she said before he could say anything.

"Jack Quinn is dead," he answered. "We just left his house. Maybe natural causes." He heard her breathing heavy through the phone. "I was going to call you, 'cause we're ten minutes from the Pine Barrens, service gets splotchy."

"Russell, I've been sitting here for hours. The postman just dropped off a letter. Guess what it is?"

She heard Doug's voice in the background. "Jesus," Russell said. "Not another picture of the front of a house? Quinn's? So it wasn't natural causes. Who was it addressed to?"

"*Occupant*, but obviously meant for Marie or Ava."

"What's the inscription say?"

"*And now I am done.* So I guess the killing is over and that's good, but I'm freaking out. There's a weirdo murderer on the loose."

The line started to get crackly. "Listen, Joanne, don't worry. You're not in any danger. Watch out for the nun. Keep your phone on and sit tight. I'll call you when I can." He hung up.

Joanne sat staring at the house, the fear gnawing at the edges of her composure. Tingles started in her hands and worked their way up her arms. Did he say the killing was finished? Meaning Ava was really dead? Her heart dropped when the full implication washed over her. The weirdo murderer had killed her friend.

She felt tears start in the corners of her eyes. When she looked up, the tall, dark-haired nun, bundled in her drab gray coat and little cream-colored knit cap, was making her way slowly toward Claire's house. Joanne noticed she'd parked two houses back and chosen to walk the distance, though there was a spot right out front. *That's right, Marie, approach slowly. There might be an irate woman in that car, pissed off because you ditched her Honda in the boonies.* Marie reached out her hand to Ava's car, like a man abandoned in the desert might reach to touch the illusion of a palm frond. *She thinks she's seeing things.* Joanne watched her complete her inspection of the car and then tear into the house.

Now we're getting somewhere. Joanne got out of her car and approached the house cautiously. She wasn't sure if Marie would remember her, and was counting on hiding in those folds of anonymity if they came face to face. She peered in the side window, which only afforded a limited view of part of the living room and the entryway. Marie was sitting on the ottoman, staring into the fireplace. Then she seemed consumed with the front closet and coats. Before Joanne could even make a guess as to what was happening, she heard the front door open. Marie was running like she was being hunted. By the time Marie reached her car, Joanne was ready to pull out behind her at a safe distance.

Joanne knew where they were headed fifteen minutes after leaving Haddonfield. *Bingo.* Pine Barrens. She glanced out the window. It was a sunless gray winter day; the sky was the color of pewter, bordering on rain or wet snow. *Damn it,* Joanne thought. No gloves, and not the warmest coat, and she was wearing her brand-new boots. Not waterproof winter boots either. She thought *stakeout* meant sitting in her car, warm and dry, drinking coffee and observing, not traipsing through the woods after a psycho-nun.

She reached out to her phone and rang Russell's number. It went right to voicemail.

Russell, you'd better be there waiting for me. That's all I can say.

CHAPTER 43

"I can't frickin' believe the man's dead. Did we just leave a murder scene? Is that what we did?" Doug asked.

"I don't know, but I'm not staying around to call it in." Russell glanced at his friend. "Do you want to?"

"Man, come on. Another picture shows up? We can't—"

"The last one said, *Two other woes are yet to come.* Two other woes. Then Ava goes missing and Quinn dies. Now they're done." Russell turned onto the access road into the Pine Barrens.

"Start tracking here for eight miles," Doug said. "Interesting the nun was left out of this now-you're-dead loop. Wonder why."

Russell glanced at him. "Think she's the killer? Of all of them? But why? And the envelope was mailed to Claire's house. Makes no sense. No one would get it but Marie."

"So best guess, what's this Polaroid killer all about?"

"Four boys all grew up together. All four dead. Each had a photograph taken after death. How they all ended up with Quinn is a mystery. But he gets them all. But he's not killed. Not yet. I thought he might have been the one doing it. Killing them all over something that happened way back when. That was my best guess."

"Not. Now he ends up killed and another picture shows up."

"Square one."

"I'm gonna ask. I don't have a choice. What was going on with you and Ava?"

Russell slowed the car. "I got dragged into this—"

"I didn't ask about the case. I asked about you and Ava. What gives?"

"You mean, did she give?" He stopped the car. "This is eight miles. We were parked right here yesterday."

Doug put on his hat and gloves and grabbed his flashlight. "Did she? 'Cause you're all wrapped up in this. Like it's personal."

Russell opened the car door. "I wish I could remember."

Doug hit his arm. "Whoa, wait. You don't remember? Remember what?"

"We were together the night before she disappeared, drinking wine and looking at pictures. The girl can put it away. I remember some of it, but I don't know what happened. I woke up in her bed, no clothes on, and she was gone."

"You're leaving out a few steps there. What happened before you couldn't remember?" Russell shook his head. "So all things are go with Juliette?"

They started to walk into the woods. "Didn't you get your save-the-date card yet? It should be coming any day now."

Doug pulled his arm and stopped him. "Most of the guys we know are divorced or screwing around. You know how it is. Don't start off this way. Don't get married if you don't want to."

Russell was concentrating on the ground in front of him. "Nothing with Ava, if she's alive, is going anywhere. She's a mess."

Doug started walking and pointed his flashlight at Russell. "That's two separate conversations, man. Ava might be a mess, but she's a hot mess. Looks like a freak, maybe. Two totally different women. You ask me?"

"I didn't."

"Too late. With Juliette, she's gonna pull you, set the pace. That's not all bad. Tuck you into the back seat with the child locks on. You might have a nice view of life along the way. But Ava." He smiled. "Just from the little I've seen at the courthouse, that would be like a roller coaster. And maybe you'd be holding her down in the seat so she didn't jump off. Both are good."

Russell flashed to a fuzzy image of Ava naked in his lap. "I can't tell Juliette what I can't remember. And instead of talking to her about it, I keep pissing her off." The sky was getting darker. Russell felt a heavy drop on his head. "Great."

"'Cause you think she might make the decision for you. But hate to tell you, she won't. So figure it out."

Russell shined his light at the ground and kept walking. "There's nothing to figure out. We might've spent the last ten minutes talking about a dead girl."

"First rule, never arrive at an assumption without all the facts. Though it's a shitty day to be collecting facts." The raindrops had turned to sleet and they were pelted by bits that made their way through the trees.

"So, this was where you found the letter opener and tape." Russell shined his light down and pulled out the three sticks he'd shoved into the ground near a tree to mark the spot. "If she cut herself loose, then she probably would have kept going, away from them, away from the road."

"And if she were dead, why'd they bother cutting her hands loose at all? Why not just bury her near here? It's off the road enough." Doug looked around, hands on his hips.

"Let's keep looking. There's more out here, I can feel it. Let's stay on this side of the road. Yell if you find anything." Doug nodded and they went their separate ways.

The sleet was getting heavier and thicker by the minute. Enough was dropping through the trees that every few seconds he'd feel a freezing ping on his neck. Russell stopped and leaned against a tree. Sometimes he'd talk to dead victims or missing people, have a conversation with them, as if they could answer, as if it could help him get into their heads. More than once it had given him a new direction in a case or a new perspective. He took a breath.

"What happened to you, Ava? After you left me. Where did you go? Where are you now?" He inhaled the cold, wet air and waited for an answer. Nothing came. "Did you run away because of me? Did you have a meeting with someone that morning? A meeting that maybe didn't go well? Who brought you out here?" He listened to the plinking of ice hitting branches. Everything was cold and quiet.

He'd never admit it to anyone he worked with, but he always felt like he could tell if someone was dead, just feel it in his bones once he got to know enough about them. He'd know if their spirit wasn't around anymore. It made no sense. He wasn't New Age or spiritual. It was just a feeling, a gut instinct that guided him. Though he knew he'd never hear the end of the ribbing if he whispered that to anyone—it might even end his career.

He was completely still, waiting to get a feel for Ava, but nothing came. He started walking again, then stopped and listened. Quiet. The sky was streaked with deeply shadowed clouds. The sleet was still falling. The trees all looked identical. He shouted Doug's name as loud as he could and then leaned against another tree. He heard moisture hitting the leaves above, and the scurry of a squirrel climbing a tree. He breathed deeply, smelling fresh and rotted pine in the same breath, but the sound of Doug's voice was nowhere in the air. He shouted again until he realized it might be better to head back while there was still light.

These woods were different from most in that there were no markings, no differentiation in foliage or growth. It was all pine. One after another, and sandy soil. He had no way of marking his path other than to shove three sticks upright every fifty feet as he went. He tried to use the light to gauge his direction, but it was useless. No sun, only clouds and rain.

He stopped to take a break, calling out again. When he looked up he noticed a dark spot in the dirt about ten feet from him. At first he thought it was a patch of earth that was wetter than the rest, but as he got closer he realized it was a strap. He reached for it, lifting it with his fingertips. A black leather purse emerged from the dirt. The main compartment was empty. There were two zippered inner compartments. He opened one and found a receipt and a pack of gum. The receipt was from Total Wine & More. A case of Pinot Noir had been purchased two weeks before. Middle Sister—a California wine and, coincidentally, the same wine they'd been drinking the night before Ava had disappeared. And she'd had plenty of bottles.

He heard a noise and swung around. Doug was coming at him full force through the trees.

"Russell, man. Oh my God. I heard your voice but couldn't find you." He looked at the bag. "What is it?"

"A purse. Empty. No wallet or keys. Just a receipt for booze. I think it's Ava's."

Doug heard his words but his eyes were focused fifty feet away, over Russell's shoulder. At a mound of dirt and pine needles that rose from the ground in the shape of a body.

CHAPTER 44

She tried to dodge heavy traffic by heading through Chatsworth to reconnect with Route 72, but it was taking longer than she expected. Marie jammed on the brakes and almost slammed into the white car in front of her. *Damn it!* The coat was gone. Ava's car appeared. How'd it get back? She'd left Ava's lifeless body in the car. Who'd been watching her in the Pine Barrens while she and Quinn took care of Ava? She could've asked Claire's neighbors, seen if they might have been taking out the trash and spied whoever deposited the car back in her driveway, but there wasn't time. She looked in her rearview mirror, paranoid that someone was following her.

Freezing rain pelted her windshield; she turned on her wipers. Everything with Quinn and Ava had happened so fast, it wasn't organized or clean. And she'd been thinking faster than Quinn, trying to minimize his involvement—he was so vicious and angry. And now he was dead too. She put her hand in her pocket and felt the Polaroid film seal she'd found. Another photograph had been taken outside his door. It didn't matter if he'd had a heart attack, choked to death on a sandwich, or been murdered. Someone had been there with him when he was dying. The thought made her stomach twist.

She turned onto Main Street and pulled into the general store. She needed coffee and some Advil. Her head was pounding, and she felt she might be sick in her car. Claire's diary was in the back of her mind. Always lurking, even when she wasn't thinking about it. If Ava had known about the Owenses' house six months before, why'd she pretend she'd just found the photo after Claire died? What was she doing during those six months? Claire's diary was all she had to go on. And the going was slow. Claire's abrupt switching of languages, alternating style, big and loopy, small and slanted, hindered things. Most of it was cryptic, indirect. The most cryptic of all was the last entry, written the night before she died. *Desperate times call for desperate measures. What to do?*

Marie tried to think about those last months with Claire. The two sisters had become distant, but not because of an argument or disagreement. Her sister was simply spending most of her time alone, retreating from the world. Marie had gone to the house one morning and had to let herself in. Claire was huddled under her covers, complaining of vague physical symptoms. Nausea. Body aches. Headaches and chest pain.

"Please," Marie had pleaded. "Get up. I'll take you to the doctor."

Claire's face looked sunken. Her spirit defeated. "No, *sors d'ici*." Then she'd turned away. Not a *please go*, but more a *get the heck out of here*.

At the time, Marie thought Claire was stressed, or had contracted a lingering virus. It didn't occur to her that her sister might be struggling with something other than an illness—or the never-ending danger Ava's presence brought into their lives. Something even more terrible. Because she had no other choice, Marie had retreated to her life at the convent. And Claire became more distant and quiet. And Ava? What of Ava?

Ava got a job interning at the court as a translator, in the middle of this. Marie had mapped it out. Ava applied at the courthouse four days after Claire's entry about Ava having the photograph. She started the job the next month, digging her heels further into Camden County.

Making ties. Hanging out with lawyers and police detectives, like she had no intention of letting anything end.

Marie stood in line at the general store and ordered a small coffee, black, and took a bottle of Advil from the rack.

She stared into the clerk's eyes. "Oh, and I need a flashlight." The clerk nodded. "And maybe a good knife."

"We definitely have them. This way." He led her to a section of the store where camping goods were displayed.

Marie took a long time searching the half-aisle inventory of the small store. She chose a medium-sized flashlight and a pack of D batteries. The knives were all very expensive, made for hunting and fishing, sharp and thick enough to slit a deer clean through from tail to gullet. She ran her finger over the tip. Perfect.

She paid for the coffee, Advil, flashlight, and knife. And then ran her thumb over the thick stack of twenties in her wallet. Her rainy-day fund. At last count it was nearly $850. She should have stashed more when she'd had the chance, but this was enough to get her away, pay for a hotel and some meals. But not enough for an ultimate escape. She didn't want to use a credit card or pull large sums of money from her account unless she had to.

She was concentrating so deeply that she almost didn't notice the short woman with streaked brown hair and a green bubble coat, wearing three-inch-heeled Cole Haan boots, staring at her from the other side of the aisle. When the two women locked eyes, Marie felt a wave of familiarity wash over her. Then she felt paranoia sliding in behind it. Where did she know this woman from? But when she looked up again, the woman was gone.

Marie paid for her items, stowed her seven dollars' change in her wallet, and went out to her car. She threw the items in her trunk and pulled out of the store, made a left onto Route 532, and headed not straight toward the access road to the Barrens, but back toward Route 72.

She saw the accident just in time. A tractor trailer had slid off the small road, through the guardrail, and hit a tree. Police lights were everywhere. In a split second Marie skirted around the accident, the lights, the officers, and sped to the junction of 72, well aware that it was getting dark and the rain was forming slick ice patches on the road.

She never looked back to see the little red Toyota Corolla stopped just before the accident by the frantic hand of a police officer. Nor did she see the woman in the driver's seat slam the steering wheel with her fist.

CHAPTER 45

Joanne stripped off her clothes and pulled on her flannel pajama pants and matching top. She went to her desk with a big cup of coffee and planted herself squarely in front of her files. It had taken an hour and a half to make it back home—the roads were a mess, the traffic horrific, and Marie was long gone. She'd failed in her mission to follow the nun, and she knew Russell would be disappointed. But she wasn't trekking through the woods to tell him the news. She realized her time would be better spent researching, poring over the information she had. There was something here, she was fairly certain, if she could find it.

She had Ava's phone, the whiteboard, and all the notes she and Russell had compiled. Nineteen ninety-six. Claire was in Brooklyn at that time. Ross Saunders had been living in Philadelphia, near Fishtown. Marie was in France, in the convent, or had just moved to the States. Anais was in Cherbourg. She glanced at the four boys' names. What did that year mean to them? She pulled out Ross's records. Born 1949. Post–World War II Philadelphia. He would have been forty-seven or forty-eight years old in '96. She took a sip of coffee. *What would these boys have in common when they were forty-eight years old?*

She flipped pages rapidly and then sat back in her chair. School was what they'd always had in common. School. The Kensington–Frankford neighborhood. Childhood. School. At forty-eight they'd maybe be going to their reunion. A big one. Thirty years. She looked at the information Russell had on Claire. Brooklyn, same job until August of 1996. Then she started moving, and moving a lot. The summer of '96. She jabbed her pen onto paper and then wrote a note at the bottom of the whiteboard.

She randomly Googled *summer of '96* but nothing came up that was of any interest. Then she Googled *summer of '96 Philadelphia.* Again, nothing of interest. "I need newspapers," she whispered. Then she Googled *Saint Francis de Sales Church.*

The page was filled with current photographs of the parish priest, Father James Ryan, and pictures of activities, congregants. She looked at the clock. It was almost eight. She dialed Russell's number and it went to voicemail. Tomorrow morning, she thought, she was going to go to that church. But right now, she had to focus on what was in front of her. Ava's phone.

The girl hadn't put a password lock on it, which was weird, but it was a good thing. She'd combed through it before at Russell's request, looking for information. Mostly concentrating on incoming and outgoing calls. Maybe there was something more. She turned it on and watched the usual apple light up the screen. Joanne got up and poured herself another cup of coffee. The phone dinged, indicating some activity—a text or phone call. She raced back to the table. One missed call and a voice message from a local number were displayed.

She clicked the button and heard a female voice come on. A breathy "*Nous avons besoin de parler.* Oh shit." And then it clicked off. Joanne played it back a few times, listening to the voice and tone. Was it familiar? She held her finger over the "Call Back" button and took a breath. It rang and went to voicemail. She hung up and called back again, expecting it to go to voicemail again, but instead someone answered.

"Who is this?" Joanne whispered after seconds of dead air. Then she heard a click in her ear.

It had to be Anais. It had to be—the woman had disappeared from Cherbourg. Maybe she was in the United States and had picked up a burner phone. Or Marie. Was it Marie? She tried to place the nun's voice in her head, but came up blank. Or maybe another family member she didn't know.

Joanne sat at her computer and punched in the reverse-phone-number website. She carefully plugged in the digits. The phone number came back as a cell phone registered in Haddonfield, New Jersey. In order to get more information she needed to pay ninety-five cents. It definitely wasn't a burner.

Joanne fumbled with her wallet, finding the right credit card. She paid the money for one month's unlimited access to the website and then waited. It seemed to take forever. A *Loading* sign appeared on her computer screen. Just then her own phone rang.

"Joanne." Russell's voice. "You're home?"

"Yes." Her eyes were on her computer screen. The name popped up on the screen. *Claire Lavoisier.* It was registered to the address of the house in Haddonfield.

"We'll be there soon. We're on 72, but traffic is bad."

"I know. But get back here, now. I mean right now. I have something to tell you."

"Yeah, us too. Hey, lock your doors and hang tight. We'll see you in an hour." He clicked off. She hung up and stared at that name. This wasn't possible. Someone had to be using Claire's phone. *What the hell is going on?*

Then it dawned on her that Ava's phone was on. Someone could pinpoint exactly where that cell phone was, as long as it was on. She went to the table and with trembling fingers shut it off.

An hour later, when she heard a bang on her front door, she was so scared she had to peek through the curtain and see Russell's familiar face before she'd unhook the chain.

CHAPTER 46

Marie took the turnoff from Route 72 onto Bay Avenue and crawled through the back roads near Manahawkin. She slowed near an old hotel, pulled in behind the building, and parked. A faded gray sign hanging from two hooks swayed in the wind. This was her best hope—little more than a fisherman's hole-up for bad weather. *Bayside Inn.* It was closer to the bay than the ocean, that was true, though it wasn't anywhere near water.

The smell hit her when she opened the door—it was intimately connected in her brain with danger, and she felt her heart start to flutter. Mold with a hint of Lysol underneath and years of grime in between. She registered under the name of Joan McAllister, a name she and Claire both agreed they would use when staying here, paid cash, and went to the front room with peeling striped wallpaper and a sagging bed. She'd asked for this specific room, 203, as always. Then she checked her watch and waited.

This inn had been a go-to hiding spot for Claire on and off over the past twenty years. Completely out of the way, cheap, and relatively safe, and there were stores less than a mile away for all needs. A nothing spot where no one asked questions and, even better, no one cared. Claire had stumbled on this hotel, driving south on the Garden State Parkway. A missed turn and, confused, she'd ended up on Bay Avenue.

Initially, she'd run into the hotel to get directions back to the parkway, but while standing in the entryway, she'd realized this could be it. A safe haven. Marie had chuckled when she'd first seen her choice. Her sister with her Birkin bag and Louboutin heels hiding in this dank crawl space. But she found Claire was quite adaptable when her life was at stake. In those cases, jeans, a drab cardigan, hair in a top knot, and an old fishing shack served her well.

The sisters had an agreement. If Claire disappeared and wasn't answering her phone, it meant she was in trouble or people were asking too many questions—something was wrong. If her sister vanished, Marie was to come here first. On the seven or so occasions that this had happened, she'd found her sister here with Ava in room 203. But now Claire wasn't just missing—she and Ava were both gone and there was no finding either of them hunkered behind this flimsy plywood door. But on an inkling, a last hope, Marie had come anyway.

She sat on the bed and felt the springs give underneath her. A terrible, filthy thing. She pulled back the covers to inspect the mattress for signs of bed bugs. Bringing those creatures back to the convent would be very bad. The mattress was yellowed from time, but there was nothing else untoward under the sheets. Marie's breath came fast. Coming here was a bad idea. This place was nothing more than a cesspool of bad memories.

Quinn's face invaded her thoughts. His ugly eyes, staring, always coming when least expected; he was the only one of the four that had refused to let things go. It had become more vengeance than self-preservation for him to find Ava, she was sure. But the sisters could never understand why. Quinn was no more or less guilty than the others in what happened. Connelly, the priest, had probably prayed his fears away, and Loyal had secreted himself away within the folds of the middle class, the memories and guilt only allowed to invade the outer fringes of his waking thoughts.

The sky had been clear, the morning of the worst confrontation with Quinn. The almost royal blue had been uninterrupted by clouds. She and her sister talked of taking the three-hour drive from Willow Grove to the Jersey Shore later in the day. Marie hadn't seen a beach in over a year and had been looking forward to it, but it never happened. Instead Quinn happened, the emergency room happened. He'd been lying in wait, following them as they went, letting them drive for over an hour and a half, through Philadelphia and into New Jersey, all while he watched from a distance.

Marie rubbed her head and went to the grimy window. The sun was starting to go down. The streets were empty; the rain and cold had washed people indoors. She watched drops of rain slide down the outside of the windowpane and turned away. The memories came flooding back. Quinn accosting them in the parking lot. The sky had turned from dreamy blue to angry gray, the rain just sprinkling the sidewalk when they got out of the car to grab a coffee at a diner. Claire was saying something about the weather. "Not much of a beach day now" or something like that, and he was there. His bitter, twisted face, the tiny livid eyes coming alive beneath folds of skin.

He'd latched onto Claire's hair, demanding Ava. Ava was nearly fourteen by then, almost grown up, but she wasn't with them. Ava was with her grandmother in Cherbourg. With each refusal to tell him Ava's whereabouts, he'd pulled harder, twisting and slamming Claire's head into the hood of the car. Blood spilled down the side of her face from where her eyebrow split open against the hot metal. Marie stood by, motionless, feeling that concrete had grown around her feet. She had no voice. She heard the thump of her sister's head, her screams, saw the dripping blood, but she couldn't do anything. He only ran away like a rabid dog sprayed with a hose when someone had yelled to them from across the parking lot.

The conversation with Anais that night wasn't pleasant. *Enough. I'll send Ava back, you take her to the police and tell them everything.* Claire had refused, and the arguing between them became loud and repetitive. In the end Anais wouldn't help them. *I will give you only enough to pay your bills, but that's it. I won't let you come here, I won't clean up Ross's mess if you continue to protect him. What is wrong with you?* Then she'd slammed the phone down in their ears. Marie always wondered how much of it Ava had heard on the other end.

Marie now dialed Anais's number in Cherbourg and listened to it ring. *Maman, this time I really need you.* But Anais didn't answer. She clicked the phone off and watched the light that came through the dirty window dim until it was gone.

She put her coat over the stained pillow and rested her head for just a minute, letting her mind drift. She and Claire were girls at the beach in Oostende, Belgium. The breeze blew across their damp skin, making them shiver. Anais was in her beach chair, blue hat on her head, sipping water and reading a magazine. The sun was glorious. The two girls wore matching blue bathing suits, dancing in the frigid waves as they approached. Laughing. Splashing each other. A tapping sound intruded into her dream. The ice cream vendor was knocking his scoop against the cart. The girls were in line for a cone, holding Belgian francs firmly in their little hands. Claire ordered chocolate for both of them. The tapping came again as the man put the dipper into the container of water and then hit it against the cart to shake the excess off.

The sound came again, louder. Marie opened her eyes to find herself in a fetal position on the bed. The tapping sound was coming from the door.

CHAPTER 47

Both men were soaking wet and covered in dirt. Joanne hesitated at the door, not letting them in.

"Look, there's a hose around the side of the house. It's cold, I know, but do you mind? Or I'll boil some water and put it in a basin out there for you. 'Cause you're both crummy dirty."

Russell glanced down at his clothing. "We have so much to tell you, are you serious?"

"God, then strip for me. Leave all your dirty clothes here on the porch. I'll get you stuff to wash up."

They obliged and sat on her sofa in just boxers and T-shirts while she prepared a basin with hot water for them to wash themselves. "Ava's purse, I'm pretty sure. Total Wine & More is totally Ava," Joanne said. "So to recap, you got frickin' lost in the Pine Barrens, found Ava's purse, and then a grave—but it was just filled with deer parts?"

"Here it is." Russell threw the purse down on the table. "I don't remember it, but I wouldn't. Do you?"

She put the basin on the table and handed them each a bar of soap, a washcloth, and a towel. "Wash in the basin with soap. Then dry with the towel. And don't make a mess."

"The purse is a higher-end Dooney & Bourke, if that helps," Doug volunteered.

Joanne sat down and pressed her fingertips against her temples. "She had a black purse, but I can't say one hundred percent it's hers."

Russell dipped the washcloth into the steaming water. "There wasn't anything else in the immediate area. And we wanted to get out of there. If she's dead—"

Joanne stood up. "Don't say that. Don't."

"We had to leave. It was completely dark, but there was no body, Joanne. Not right there. So there's hope," Doug offered.

Russell ran the cloth over his face. "Exactly. But I'm wondering about the contents of the purse. Why dump it?"

"Maybe she just grabbed her wallet and ran," Joanne jumped in.

Both men looked at her. "Really? Someone's after you and you're running, so you stop to take your wallet and leave your purse?" Russell asked. "Why?"

Joanne started to pace and then grabbed her hair in her fists. "Too much. We got Ava gone. We got someone with Claire's phone calling this one, talking in French. We got the weird nun that got away. We got Polaroids. We got four dead men. And we got no clues." She stopped and turned, going in the other direction. "Something connects all of this, you know? Something terrible. Ava wouldn't just leave."

"So the phone call—play the message for us," Doug asked.

She placed the phone onto the table and turned it on. The apple appeared and then the standard black screen filled with icons followed. Joanne found the message and pressed "Play." *"Nous avons besoin de parler,"* "Oh shit," and then nothing. She played it three more times, looking at Russell and Doug expectantly.

"When I called back, someone answered, then hung up. I shouldn't have said anything to her, and I'm sorry. I was freaking."

Russell had finished washing and was drying with the towel. "Call back again."

"Really?"

She pressed the "Call Back" button and held her breath. The phone rang. It was still on. It went to voicemail. She tried again with the same result.

"The phone is still on and charged. Let's leave a message," Russell said.

"Seriously? What message are we leaving? 'Weird French woman, why are you calling Ava's phone? Where is she? Do you own an old Polaroid camera?'" Joanne said.

Doug laughed. "How about, 'We need you to call back. We have important information about Ava'? If she called, she's looking for her too."

"And who's making this call? Me? I'm calling this psycho? Which then means the phone needs to stay on to get a call back. I'm not having this phone traced to my house." She jabbed at Russell with her finger. "Or next you'll be finding my purse buried in the Pine Barrens. Which, by the way, I bought at Target on sale."

They both laughed. "I can take the phone," Russell offered. "It doesn't matter who answers it when she calls back."

"So you leave the message." She pushed the phone to him.

He picked it up and called. The phone rang again. This time it didn't go to voicemail. Russell heard the line pick up. He was startled but he jumped in quickly. "Hello, you don't know me. I'm a friend of Ava's and I'm looking for her. Do you know where she might be?" He said it quickly. There was silence, but the line didn't click off. "She left her phone. That's why I have it. Do you know her?" Russell heard small breaths at the other end of the line. "Anything you know would be helpful." He heard noise in the background that sounded like a public area, commotion, a racket. Then the line went dead.

"Shit." Russell hung up. "They wouldn't say a word. But I'm going to call and leave a message anyway. Maybe they'll call back when they're ready."

Joanne reached out and turned the phone off. "No. They have nothing on us but the sounds of our voices. No names, no addresses.

Nothing. Let's not jump into this. Whoever that is? They didn't want to talk. And they're not going to change their mind tomorrow."

"French-speaking female means Marie or Anais. I vote Anais. She's closed up her house, not answering her phone. She must be in the US," Doug said. "Either way, it seems they don't know where Ava is."

"Or it's Claire," Joanne volunteered.

Both men looked at her. "So, she didn't die? Or she brushed off the dirt, climbed out of her grave, and now she's looking for Ava?" Russell asked.

Joanne studied the edge of the table, refusing to look either of them in the eye. "I have this creepy feeling." She held up a hand to quiet them. "So let's keep that way on the back option burner. Okay? And not throw it away yet."

Russell smiled. "So, either Claire, Marie, or Anais has no idea where she is."

"So what now?" Doug asked.

"Tomorrow I'm going to Mass in Philly at Saint Francis de Sales. I want to see if there's anything interesting there—ask old parishioners if they remember the boys or know them," Joanne said.

Russell stood up. "Sounds good. I'm exhausted and filthy. I'm going home. Let's talk again tomorrow."

Joanne blocked his path. "No way you're leaving me here alone. After that phone call. Ava's purse in the dirt. Uh-uh. No. And the phone was on for a little while—anyone could have traced it right here. No."

Doug moved past her. "My wife is waiting for me. I'm out." He pulled on his dirty clothes. "Be careful, both of you. Call me with details."

Russell ended up making himself comfortable in Joanne's son's room, since he was visiting his father. He fell asleep looking at his phone, wondering if he should call Juliette and explain everything or forget it and defend himself in the morning. He chose the latter.

CHAPTER 48

Marie's senses awoke with the noise, one by one. The sound came to her ears, but it was dim, not recognizable. Then the smells of the Belgian salt air in her dream transformed into dampness with the underpinnings of mold that held up the hotel walls. Her eyes opened and she saw the shadows of the window curtain, the dingy picture of a boat on the water that hung on the opposite wall. She rolled over and pushed herself to a sitting position. The soft tapping came again. Marie was jolted awake in a second. She ran her hand through her hair, her heart beginning to thump against her rib cage, her skin prickling. She clicked on the light and looked at her watch. Three twenty-five in the morning.

She put her feet to the floor, realizing that she'd fallen asleep fully clothed, with her sneakers on. She felt gritty, dirty, and brushed at her clothes as if that would unwrinkle them. After tiptoeing to the door and peering through the peephole, she caught a glimpse of a hand pulling away. But she knew that hand. She unhooked the chain and opened the door, pulling the ghost in, snapping the door shut behind her.

"I cannot believe this," she whispered. "How are you here?"

She was dressed in jeans and a long-sleeved blue shirt. Her hair was pulled back tight, leaving her face all angles and cheekbones; the dark moleskin coat, the hood edged in fox fur, hung on her body. She'd seen this specter fleeing from Quinn's.

Marie crossed herself. "Did you crawl from the grave?" She covered her face, afraid to look up. "How is this possible?"

"Thought you were rid of me when you buried me, Sister?" She entered and stood in the middle of the room.

Marie walked over and sat down on the edge of the bed. "I'm losing my mind. I'm losing my mind—sitting here waiting for a ghost." She rocked back and forth. "And here she is." She gestured to the woman.

"Yes, and I need to stay that way. A ghost. I've been roaming around these backwater, backwoods, run-down places for what feels like forever. I can't do it anymore."

Marie kept her head down, rocking slightly. "Oh dear God, what's going on?"

She sat next to Marie on the bed and pulled out a cigarette pack. "I was passing by and saw your car. Perfect timing, I'd say. I need your help." She put a cigarette to her lips and lit it.

"I was there, at Quinn's apartment. I saw his body. But then I saw your body once too, so maybe that means nothing." Marie pulled her coat to her and rummaged through the pockets. "And I found this." She showed her the peel-off layer from the film. "Outside on his front patio."

"Huh. Someone took another photograph. After he died." She took the film and rubbed it between her fingers.

"You took the photograph," Marie answered. "I saw you there—"

"Are you sure? Or is this one of your imaginings that you're famous for?"

Marie said nothing. Her head trembled slightly. "You're trying to make me think I'm crazy. But I know what I saw."

She stood and pulled a pint bottle of whiskey from her coat pocket. "You carry film in your pockets. I carry drink. Is there a glass in this place?"

"Look in the bathroom," Marie responded.

"Never mind." She unscrewed the cap and lifted the bottle to her mouth, taking a long swig. "So, do you have any cash?" Marie pulled the bottle from her hand and put it to her own mouth and swallowed. The woman chuckled. "Drinking now, are we, Marie?"

Marie felt the whiskey burn down her throat, then handed the bottle back. "Right to the point. Are you leaving the country? Was that the plan? Anais will never have you there. She won't help you, you know."

"No, you don't know that."

"Anais has turned a blind eye to the past for how many years? Demanding we settle this mess on our own. Why do you think she'd open her arms now?"

The woman drew on the cigarette and then blew the smoke in a thin stream out the window. "She wasn't mad at us really, she was just angry at Ross." Marie studied her, waiting for more, but there were minutes of silence before she spoke again. "So angry at him for what he did to this family when he was alive, and then even angrier at us after he died. There's no pleasing her."

"Ross didn't have to die in all this." Marie pulled her sweater tighter around herself. "He could have been spared."

She shrugged. "Someone didn't agree with that and killed him anyway."

"You mean you didn't agree and you killed him anyway. And created this shit storm for the rest of us!" Marie realized she was screaming but she couldn't stop herself. She'd been waiting to say this for a long time.

"Watch yourself, Marie. That camera is still out there somewhere, and I'm sure there's more film too. It's just a matter of finding your door."

Marie grabbed the bottle back and took a swig. "Is that a threat? Are you threatening me?"

"I'm not looking to fight. We're in this together, remember?"

Marie shook her head. "Self-preservation has always been your number-one concern." She took the cigarette and drew the smoke into her lungs. It burned more than the whiskey, and she coughed before handing it back. "Surviving your untimely death and staging a comeback—ingenious. But you're not going to stick me with this mess, I'm telling you now." In the dim lighting the ghost's face was drawn, the skin under her eyes bruised with dark circles. Like something was eating away at her soul.

She lay back on the bed and blew smoke toward the ceiling. "I wouldn't dream of it, Marie."

Marie glanced over at her. "So who got the photograph of Quinn's door?"

She sat up. "You, of course. You're all that's left."

Marie's eyes widened. "And what would the message on this last photograph say? Not that you would know for sure. But guess." She held the sarcastic tone in her voice.

The woman snorted. Then she tipped the bottle and swallowed as much as her mouth would hold. She screwed the cap back on and put the bottle in her pocket. "Don't give any of this too much thought, Marie. The squirrels are taking over your brain again. Money?"

Marie nodded. "But first, a few questions."

The woman nodded. "Go. But be quick."

"The diary. I found it in the dresser."

"What about it?" The cigarette was hanging from the corner of her lips for a moment before she pulled on it and then took it from her mouth. "Just ask your question, for God's sake."

"The photograph of Loyal's house. Was in the box with the hippo dress—"

She stood. "That photograph was in with Ross's things when he died. It's been floating around the house since then."

"So what have these past six months been about? I don't understand. I don't understand any of it."

She took a few steps to the middle of the room. "All I can say is Ava's dead, and though I think it was pretty nasty and gruesome, not the way I would have worked it out, it might just really be for the best. You'll see."

Marie's heart felt heavy. "It was awful and you know it. How we got to this point I'll never understand."

"You asked about these past six months? They've been about truth. It's time for it all to come out. All of them—Connelly, Owens, Quinn, and Ross—started something that destroyed my life." She shook her head violently. "Now enough questions. Cash? Please, Marie?"

Marie flipped open her wallet and started counting. "Is two hundred enough to hold you? I only have seven and I need the rest for myself."

"I need everything you have." She dropped her cigarette on the floor, stamping it into the carpet with her heel. "In fact, if you could get more, like a few thousand more, that would be good."

Marie held the stack of bills in her hand. "What're you doing with it? Tell me."

She looked at her watch. "I know a guy who's willing to do anything for cash, and I need his help." She reached for the money but Marie held on to it. "Seven hundred might do for a deposit, but I need more, and I can't exactly access my own bank accounts, can I?"

"Seven-hundred-dollar deposit for what? Thousands for what? What could possibly cost that much? What is it you need done?"

Her face twisted in frustration. "God damn it, Marie." She ripped the money from her hand. "You don't need to know." She took a phone out of her pocket. "I'm keeping it turned off, but I'll turn it on every day from noon until twelve thirty. Call me. Or leave a message and I'll get back to you. Then we'll plan a place to meet. You need to get more money. I'm counting on it." She stuffed the phone back in her coat. "Watch your back. It's dangerous out there." She opened the door and left.

Marie sat staring after her, not sure if the lingering smoke was part of a dream. When she woke up later with the heaviness of whiskey in her stomach and nicotine in her lungs, she still wasn't sure if the whole thing had been a vision.

CHAPTER 49

Joanne stared at the whiteboard, transfixed. She poured another cup of coffee and checked her computer: 5:32 a.m. She'd been up for an hour, at least, unable to really drift off; she'd had these facts, names, dates twirling around in her head. She'd checked in on Russell, asleep in her son's room, twisted in the Jedi sheets. The Lego Death Star only inches from his head, his hand on the empty jacket of the Black Ops 2 video game. She'd watched him for a minute, realizing that, though they weren't that far apart in age, she had no romantic feelings toward him. He was more like her son plus twenty years. The fact that he had actually stayed with her after he'd seen the petrified look in her eye was something she'd never forget.

She considered showering and changing so he didn't see her in her worn flannel pajamas, hair pulled back from her face, no makeup, again. But after a moment's contemplation she was back at her desk, running through the facts. The main connection between everything in this mess was the church. The four boys, Loyal, Jack, Bill, and Ross, all went to the same church. The school was an extension of the church—same clergy. She put her chin in her hand and stared, ideas coming and going.

She started her computer and waited for her screen to load. "Let me see," she muttered. After Googling *1996* in various phrases connected with Philadelphia, she sat back in thought. "Okay, how about this?" She entered *Saint Francis de Sales*. The same homepage came up. Then she Googled *Saint Francis de Sales school*. A second page appeared, filled with children in Catholic-school uniforms laughing, surrounded by adoring clergy.

In the search field for the website, she entered *class of 1966*. The site used a third-party search engine, and a list of search results popped up.

Joanne stopped and examined each one. Most were connected to class members of the year 1966, with links to mentions of them on other websites. She went down them one by one, getting impatient and bored. She didn't care if John O'Carroll was recognized by the Pennsylvania Bar Association or if Michael Dugan got his contractor's license revoked. All of these people were in that same class at Saint Francis de Sales, but not relevant to what she was looking for. She kept going down the page until she saw Bill Connelly's name pop up. *Here we go.*

She clicked on it and was redirected to his obituary. She saw his face and full cassock robe, and read the account of his death, anaphylactic shock from allergy. Joanne printed it and moved down the list. The next was Loyal Owens. There were five entries for him. *Of course. Because he was obviously murdered.* She spent a few minutes reading each article about the murder of the couple, investigations, theories, updates. She printed his obituary and put it to the side.

The next was Ross Saunders—just one link to his obituary. She printed that one and added it to her pile. Her eyes scanned down the page, taking in all the information; most she already knew. When she reached the bottom she noticed a section for comments. Thirty-five people had added commentary underneath the article.

Joanne pushed back and got up, pouring more coffee into her cup. She stretched and rubbed her neck. *Let's see what people had to say about Ross Saunders's death.* Most were classmates who'd added an *RIP*, or *Thoughts and prayers are with the family*. But as people had continued to add comments, it became more of a conversation—people adding or responding to what someone else had said.

—Sorry to hear about Ross. Peace to family members. Remember him at the prom with Mary Ellen Jones?

—Ha, yes. The chaperones? Sister Margaret and Father Callahan? Callahan had him pegged for the seminary—followed him around all prom night making sure he didn't even get a kiss. Creepy guy. How shocked were any of you when Callahan was caught with a woman? I mean, maybe caught too late, but the woman part? Come on.

—Don't speak ill of the dead. No idle gossip on here.

—How can this class not gossip about it? It's all we do gossip about. Father Joseph Callahan's reputation ruined posthumously. Better late than never.

Joanne printed the comments and copied the web address. Then she started over with a new Google search. *Father Joseph Callahan. Saint Francis de Sales Catholic Church.* When she clicked on the first search result, her screen was filled with images. She stared for minutes, scrolling down. Reading as much as she could quickly. The priest with the close-set eyes, smiling, next to the scandalous headline. She stared at the date. July 17, 1996.

She flew out of her seat so fast her chair fell to the floor, crashing into the radiator. The noise roused Russell, who appeared at the bedroom door, his hair smashed to the side of his head.

"What's going on? What time is it? Are you going to that church you were talking about?"

Joanne looked up at him. "Oh, yeah. I went to church and look what I found." She pointed to the computer screen.

Russell read the article, stopping every second to look at Joanne or comment. "This is it, Joanne, maybe pinpoints the original sin in the whole entire mess."

"Certainly the genesis," she retorted. She printed the article and put it in the middle of the table.

Priest and Lover Murdered During Tryst in Chapel at Saint Francis de Sales Church.

Russell perused the article again. "Joseph Callahan? Joseph?" He picked up a Polaroid and read the inscription. "Ave Maria. Joseph too?" He looked at Joanne. "They were referring to the priest when they wrote this inscription?"

Joanne took the picture from him, feeling pieces falling into place. When she turned to talk to Russell he was already headed to the front door. "Let me go home, shower, change. I need to think on this and I need to move when I think." He pulled on his dirty clothes. "I'll be back. Oh." He turned. "I'll take Ava's phone." She handed it to him. "And thank you, so much."

"For?"

"Not making me go to that church with you. I was dreading it. Bye." He shut the door.

She stared after him and then down at the article. "Halle-frickin'-lujah."

CHAPTER 50

Marie sat on the windowsill, staring down at the empty streets below. A mechanic shop across the way was dark. Boat parts were scattered all along the side of the building. Some were up off the ground, some lay torn apart as if disemboweled by animals. The odors of the stale room were getting to her. She opened the window, letting the wet, cold air blow through the room, but the smell of cigarette smoke lingered in her nostrils. The dampness had seeped into her bones, and no matter how hard she rubbed at her arms, it wasn't leaving.

The world was closing in, getting smaller by the second. She had convinced herself that the whole episode the night before had been a nightmare. A vivid, explosive, unbelievable nightmare. Just a conjuring of her imagination. Believing she'd dreamed it up made her breaths become more even, her heart rate slow, but at the same time her mind was spinning into a whole different dimension of panic. Was she starting to lose it again?

The two years that Anais had put her away in that dark, secluded hospital didn't seem that long ago, the memories lending themselves to constant fear. And what had she done to deserve it? Moodiness? That was what teenagers were made of—moods and attitude. Was it the drinking? The weekend she ran away to Paris with Giselle and ended up in a strip club in the fifteenth arrondissement? Anais was more embarrassed about having to enter the police station to collect her than she was about the incident itself. Or maybe it was the sex with her boyfriend. Or more like the multiple sex partners.

Marie knew all those things had played into her mother's decision to put her away, but they weren't the straw that broke the camel's back or the icing on an inedible cake. In the end it was the cutting that pushed Anais to sign the commitment papers. Marie's legs were clean now, only thin white lines nearly invisible against her pale skin, but at one time they'd been carved up with a razor blade and dotted with cigarette burns—all her own doing.

She could almost smell the antiseptic of the room with the white tiled walls where she'd been confined years ago. The paper gowns. The loss of privacy, being forced into restraints. Her body wasn't her own. People could come and go, touching her, moving her, dehumanizing her. But what was worse was the fear of total loss of control, of not knowing what was real, what to believe. Her senses had betrayed her. She was petrified of going back to that place inside her head again. Of needing to cut to release the pain.

She grabbed her phone and called Claire's number. That ghost she'd conjured had pulled that unmistakable maroon flip phone out of her pocket, Marie remembered. The call went to voicemail. Then a voice came to her. *Wait until noon.* She looked at her watch. It was only 8:17. At that moment she saw the cigarette butt ground into the carpet. She crawled on her hands and knees and picked it up slowly, as if her world depended on it. This was real. The ghost had smashed it with her heel. And Marie didn't smoke, hadn't smoked regularly in twenty years. But when her eyes lifted up she saw a pack of cigarettes on the table. Marlboro Lights. That had always been her brand. Loose change lay scattered across the table next to it. Was it possible she bought it and didn't remember?

Marie grabbed her purse and tipped it onto the bed. A wallet, change, glasses, pocket New Testament. A pack of gum. And a crumpled receipt from the general store in Chatsworth. The knife, the Advil, the coffee were on there. No cigarettes. She picked up the pack gently—like it might disappear in her fingers—and opened it. Five cigarettes missing. She put her hand to her chest. Her lungs had felt heavy, her mouth filled with the feel and smell of nicotine, when she'd woken up.

She smacked her cheeks with both hands. *Hold it together, Marie. There is another way.* Marie grabbed her purse and keys. The words of her psychiatrist from thirty years ago were ringing in her ears. *If you're not sure if what is happening is real, then reality-check it. It's okay. Question the details. Delusions are always lacking in detail.* "Oh, Doctor Rasmussen, this delusion had plenty of detail," she muttered as she rushed through the lobby to the dingy glass door and out into the street.

Marie jumped in her car and headed down the road. The snippets of conversations she could remember from the night before were on a play-rewind-replay loop, circling her brain. *Seven hundred might do for a deposit, but I need more, and I can't exactly access my own bank accounts, can I?* What could possibly cost that much money? A hit man? But who was left to kill? And if she wanted someone dead, why wouldn't she just do it herself? Unless the person was unreachable or too close. But who? Marie closed her eyes. She and Anais were the only two left. *Watch yourself, Marie. That camera is still out there somewhere, and I'm sure there's more film too. It's just a matter of finding your door.*

Why would she suddenly want to kill her or Anais? Marie's mind ticked off the possibilities. Money, maybe. Anais hadn't been generous with her gifts recently. Just the opposite. Every cent calculated and then transferred. Money given for necessities, with a little padding for a few luxuries, but nothing more. By killing Anais, certainly the funds would flow, but at what cost?

She fumbled for the cigarette pack on the seat next to her, put one to her lips, and lit a match. She drew deeply and then blew the smoke out of the cracked window. If this dead woman had crawled back from the grave, dragging something very dark with her, Marie needed to stay alert, play the game. There was nothing to do but go back to the convent and gather some things, withdraw money from the bank—maybe all of it. If this wasn't just a symptom of a major psychiatric setback, the truth would reveal itself.

Watch your back. It's dangerous out there. "It is indeed," she muttered.

CHAPTER 51

The service had ended, and other than the chorus of flickering candles at the front of the church, it was dark and eerily quiet. Joanne sat in the first pew and watched the glimmers of light bounce off the crucifix hanging behind the candle display. She was mesmerized. There was a quiet calm to all of this that she'd never experienced. Her father was a nonchurchgoing Catholic and her mother was Jewish. Synagogue on an occasional holiday or not at all. She wasn't used to the soft hush of quietude in religious halls.

The priest came into the chapel; she didn't see him, only heard the gentle rustling of his robes as he moved closer.

"Sister Christine said you wanted a word?" His voice was soft, patient.

Joanne stood up and turned to face him. "Oh, yes, Father Ryan. I do."

"I have a meeting with the youth organization, but I can spare a minute. What can I do for you?"

She looked down at the polished wooden floor, trying to think of how to say it without causing offense. "My friend, Ava . . . Well, no, let me start over. I'm very much trying to sort out some business for a friend, and the more I search, the less I find, but the one thing I do know is that it all leads back here."

His head tilted. “Here at the church? How so? I don’t understand.”

“My friend? Her grandfather went to church here as a boy.” She caught his eye and knew what she was seeing. His guard was rising. “He’s passed away now, but there are so many questions.”

“About his faith?”

She smiled. “No, I think his faith was fine. I think her questions are more concerning Father Callahan.”

The priest’s head dropped so she was looking at the bald patch in his thinning brown hair. “I don’t believe I’m at liberty to engage in any discussion about that. He’s been gone for almost twenty years.” His head snapped up. “What possible questions could I answer?”

Joanne clasped her hands together. “Maybe we could begin with exactly what happened to him? It haunted her grandfather. And maybe even killed him.”

“You’ve come to the wrong place if you’re looking for gossip. This parish suffered terribly, and I’m not interested in rehashing.” He took a step back. “Good day.”

“I’m so sorry if that’s what you thought I was doing. It’s not. I don’t want to gossip and rehash. I want to find my friend, who’s been missing for over a week. Which, believe it or not, is connected to Father Callahan’s death somehow. Sorry to have wasted your time.” Joanne picked up her purse and started to head out. Inside she was fuming. More fueled by her embarrassment than anything else.

“What happened to your friend?” His voice came as she was walking away.

Joanne turned around, her purse held tightly in both hands. “She disappeared last Saturday. She was looking into the death of her grandfather and his friends. The one thread connecting it all was this church. And I think, Father Ryan”—she took a step closer to him and lowered her voice—“I don’t want to start trouble, but I just need to understand. If I can figure it all out, maybe I can find her.”

He listened without speaking and hesitated for half a minute. "Come to my office? We can talk there." He turned and started walking, assuming she would follow him.

He led her through main areas where a few congregants milled about in choir robes. Somewhere deep down she felt she'd violated something by being here. Or that she was opening a door and peeking inside at something better left unseen.

He came to an office and waited for her to enter in front of him. The room was functional—desk, chair behind it, dark-gray couch, a few guest chairs. She sat on the edge of the couch and waited. He shut the door and then took a seat behind the desk.

He held his hands as if praying, his fingertips touching. "So you understand, we—this church—don't talk about these past events. The canon lawyers have barred everyone from discussing this matter with anyone outside of the order."

"It was almost twenty years ago. I'm not interested in suing or publicizing or anything. I just want to find Ava." She sat back on the couch and crossed her legs. She knew getting him into this office to continue the discussion was major. She wasn't giving up now.

He mirrored her and leaned back in his chair, his hands relaxing. "What did you want to know? And I have to ask, how could this priest's death possibly relate to your friend's disappearance?"

"Not sure yet. But she was very interested in her grandfather's death. And the death of his three friends. One of them was a priest—"

"Really? A priest here?"

Joanne shook her head. "No. And his death was ruled accidental, but it's suspicious." She had Father Ryan's full attention now. "Then it was Loyal—"

"Is that a name?"

"Yes. It's a name. Loyal Owens. And he was murdered in his house. Bludgeoned to death. Then it was her grandfather, Ross. And then—" She stopped herself from mentioning Jack. She hadn't seen anything in the papers about his death. It was possible he was still lying on his living-room floor, decomposing.

"And then?"

"She started trying to figure out how or why they all might be killed. The one thing they had in common was church. And the priest at the time was Callahan."

"That's an error in thinking. They lived in the same neighborhood, maybe their parents knew one another, did they play sports together, have the same coach? The list goes on and on."

"But the one commonality they all had that was unifying and horrible was Callahan's death."

"What are you saying?" He shifted in his chair. "How can you know that?"

"It's the only thing that makes sense."

Father Ryan smiled. "This is all speculative. Maybes and perhapses. I'm not sure they're connected at all. But I will give you a few facts, since you've held my interest this long. Father Callahan is a touchy subject. Not a model priest. It's perhaps lucky for the diocese that he passed away when he did." Joanne was concentrating on every word. "There had been rumors of indiscretions. Now"—his voice rose—"nothing was substantiated, so I don't feel at ease openly discussing this."

"Please. You'll never see me again. I promise."

"Are you Catholic, Mrs.—"

"Watkins. And it's *Ms.* And no. My father was, but he got out . . . Oh, sorry, I mean he didn't attend services. And my mother was Jewish. So no."

"Hmmm, so this is all just scandalous to you. You have no investment in the church."

Joanne stood up in frustration. "I'm not looking to denigrate the church. I like the church. Or the idea of it, anyway. I'm just trying to tie up loose ends and figure this all out."

He motioned for her to sit down and then looked at his watch. "I've only a minute, but here it is. Father Callahan was rumored to like the company of children, boys specifically. The whispers were getting louder within the diocese, and they were considering transferring him, from what I know. But he was killed the night of July sixteenth, nineteen ninety-six, right here in the chapel. And of all things, he was with a woman. The worst of indiscretions. And, quite frankly, shocking to all that knew him."

"Worse than with kids?"

He leaned forward. "Of course not. But to be caught without clothes, you know, and to be in the chapel itself? Not in the rectory or one of the halls?" His eyes showed weariness. "It was blasphemous. And it's taken years to try and put this congregation back together."

"They were naked? Who was the woman?"

"That's the odd thing. Unknown. Never identified. Her picture was widely distributed at the time. No one responded. Early twenties. Caucasian. She wasn't a member of the congregation."

"Seriously? How is that possible, that she was never identified? She had to have family, someone."

There was a soft rap on the door and it opened. A boy of about sixteen stood there in robes. "Father, I'm sorry to disturb you, but the youth organization is waiting for you."

Father Ryan raised his palm. "Thank you, Peter, I'll be right there." The door closed. "The Internet was just in its infancy at the time, but I believe the case is still open with the police. The only images they had of her were death photographs and an artist's rendition. Not inspiring likenesses, I'm sure." He stood up. "I'm afraid that's all I know. Please?" He motioned for her to follow him out the door.

"Where could I see those photographs, do you think?"

He strode down the hallway, forcing her to make painfully quick steps in her heels to keep up with him. "The Philadelphia police, I presume, which is perhaps where you should have started before you came here." He stopped short. "Now, I hope you will keep your promise to me?"

"Which is?"

"That you will keep your mouth shut and I will never see you again," he responded and then hurried away.

She left the church and rushed to her car, only to find all four of her hubcaps missing and large scratches near the lock mechanism, as if someone had attempted to break in. "Fabulous. Just fabulous. Thank you, Philadelphia."

CHAPTER 52

Russell opened his eyes to see Juliette standing over him. "I come bearing gifts." She placed a mug of coffee on the coaster. "Late night?"

He rolled over and felt a bolt of pain shoot through his lower back. He'd come in earlier, dropped onto the couch in exhaustion, and dozed off. "Terrible night."

She tightened the belt on her thick blue robe and sat on the couch near his feet. Her hair was pulled up off her neck; some pieces fell forward in little curls around her face. It looked all I-just-got-out-of-bed messy, but he knew it was actually artfully constructed with hair spray and bobby pins. He'd seen her spend thirty minutes in the bathroom mirror just to hang around on a lazy Sunday morning.

"Your boss left a message for you on the machine. He wanted to know a firm day for your return to work. I'm guessing he tried your cell first." She took the end of her belt and studied it. "So maybe you should tell me all about this supposed case you've been working on. All the time you've spent running around. Not coming home." She gave him a closed-mouth smile but her eyes were ice. "Because at this point I really think I need to know."

He turned and put his feet on the floor. "Look, I've been helping a friend—"

"Really, Russell? That's cool. In fact, so cool that I think you should invite your friend over for dinner tonight. Or maybe we can all meet out. You choose the restaurant."

He imagined Joanne and Juliette sitting across from one another at a dinner table. He couldn't help but suppress a smile. "Not a good idea. I'm going to get a shower." He stood up and started for the stairs when the doorbell rang. He opened the door to see Joanne there, bundled in her dark-green bubble coat, her face eager and anxious.

"Really sorry to barge, Russell, but I need to talk to you right now." He saw Juliette craning her neck to see past him, to get a look at the female that was standing on their doorstep.

"Not good timing." He said it low, hoping she'd take a hint, but she was oblivious. She pushed past him into the living room.

The two women stood facing each other. Juliette was five inches taller and thirty pounds lighter, but she still let her eyes dance over the woman, sizing her up, desperate to figure out the connection between her and Russell. Finally she decided she was the victor in all categories and relaxed. "Be nice, Russell, invite your guest in for coffee." She smiled at Joanne. "Please?" She motioned for Joanne to have a seat.

Russell shot Juliette a look and then obligingly sat. "What's up?"

"I went to the church this morning and talked to Father Ryan. I had this hunch. There's more than was in the paper, Russell. Wait'll you hear."

"You went to Philly this morning?"

"Mm-hmm. Father Callahan was killed that night right in the chapel with a woman, like the paper said. The two of them were found naked, or sorta naked, together. But"—she half turned in her seat—"he seemed by all rumors to prefer the company of little boys. So it's odd, huh?"

"The priest told you that?"

"Yeah, but there's more. The woman was never identified. Early twenties. Caucasian. That's it. And in that paper we saw, there was no picture of her, right? No name, no picture."

"Interesting."

"Father Ryan said the only photograph was an autopsy picture and maybe an artist's drawing of her. So I was thinking you could get a friend in Philly to send you those pictures. And anything on her person when she died."

"Wait here." He jumped up and went into the kitchen with his cell phone.

Juliette was still standing in the living room where she'd been, pulling the belt on her robe even tighter, if that was possible. There was a sea of silence between them, neither woman saying a word for minutes.

"So, how do you know Russell?" she asked.

"I work at the courthouse. He's—"

Russell came back with his laptop and flipped it open. "I made a call. John's going to send me what he has. Lucky he was in the office. It might be a while." He looked at their faces and then back at his computer. "Juliette, can you do me a favor? Get me another cup of coffee?"

Juliette looked caught between telling him to screw off and doing as he asked. In the end she chose the latter. She grabbed his mug and disappeared from the room.

When the last glimpse of her blue robe vanished around the corner, Joanne leaned over to him. "She's really pissed I'm here. Let's go to my house? I'm so uncomfortable." She was still wrapped in her green bubble coat, and no one had offered her any of the promised coffee.

"So the priest is killed with a woman? But he likes little boys? That's more than odd, I'd say. How'd he know her, I wonder. She wasn't a congregant. Maybe a nun from another parish? From a convent in another country?"

"Maybe he likes little boys, little girls, young women, or whatever moves and is vulnerable. Maybe he was a scumbag predator. We've seen enough of them in jail, Russell."

Russell nodded. "True. But those sorts usually end up on the radar. Especially if he's targeting adults too. We need to know more about him—wait, here's the report. That was fast." His fingers flew over the keys. The attachments came up. He clicked on one and made it bigger.

The two huddled closer, staring at the screen. "Oh my God," Joanne whispered. She glanced up at him, but he was staring at the crime-scene photographs. She turned her head. "This is so wrong. He was wearing his collar." The bodies were both on their sides, facing one another. The priest was naked from the waist up. His shirt and collar were visible to the side. His pants were unzipped, open, but not down. The woman was naked. Her clothes were cast in a ball, the sleeve of a shirt draped over one of her legs. Everything was covered in blood.

Juliette came back in and circled around to look at the screen. Her face was scrunched in concentration. "They're doing so much more with DNA now, it's surprising they haven't figured out who she was," Juliette offered. She placed the mug next to Russell and sat down at the table.

"It fell off the grid, maybe. I'm sure they've checked it against missing persons, but we're talking twenty years now," Russell said. "She has a nondescript face." He pointed at the artist's drawing. Long medium-brown hair. Brown eyes. He clicked on another attachment and then printed it. "A list of items found at the scene. Come." He walked to the printer and pulled the pages. "Let's go over them." He picked up his coffee cup. "Did you want some?"

"I have a great coffeepot at my house, Russell. I think I'll take a copy of that report and go there."

"Please?" He handed her the list.

Her curiosity won, and she was immersed in the report within seconds. "Woman killed by blunt-force trauma to her head—no purse. Nothing. Multiple prints at the scene—matched the whole congregation, practically."

"I want to go to Claire's house." His voice brought her back into focus.

"You mean you want to break in?" Joanne asked.

"It might not be that complicated. Maybe the back door is open?"

"Isn't that still against the law, Russell?" Juliette asked.

Russell shrugged. "No worse than not reporting bodies or missing persons."

"Why? What's there?" Joanne lowered her papers and stared at him. "What's worth breaking in for?"

"A candlestick."

Joanne dropped her papers onto the table. "Is this Clue or something? The dirty perv priest was killed in the chapel with a candlestick? What?"

He smiled. "That's exactly it. The priest was punched and kicked to death, but the woman was hit with something."

"So why do you think it was with a candlestick?"

"Because I saw one that I think looks a lot like this one"—he pointed to the crime-scene photo with a candlestick visible in the background. "It was in the boxes of Claire's and Ross's things in the closet."

"But don't you think the church or the police would have noticed it missing?"

"We haven't finished reading the reports. Maybe they did," he said.

"But why wouldn't they get rid of it? Clean it, give it to Goodwill? Take a nice drive out of the city, throw it in a dumpster?"

"Reason unknown. Somehow it ended up with Claire. Maybe she kept it as blackmail or to keep someone in line? Guessing here. Not even sure it's a match."

"This is kind of exciting. Can I come?" At that moment Juliette was filled with childlike enthusiasm.

Joanne and Russell looked at one another. "Three breaking into a house might be a bit much. But maybe we can tackle this separately. Juliette, concentrate on ways to identify the woman. Make a list, from medical to outlandish. Joanne, see if you can find a camera shop or an expert on film and photography. Take those Polaroids and get a date on the camera used. And the kind of film too. I'll go to the house. I know where the candlestick is," Russell said.

"Who made you boss?" Joanne blurted. Juliette smiled.

"I've always been boss, since you and Ava dragged me into this." He started walking her to the door. He opened it and waited for her to walk through.

She whipped around to face him. "Fine, Russell. I'll go track down the camera and film. Call me later." She heaved her purse back up onto her shoulder and marched down the walkway to her car.

Juliette came up behind him and put her arms around his waist. "I wish you'd introduced us earlier, Russell. I really like her."

CHAPTER 53

Marie arrived at the convent and parked across the street. She checked her watch—6:35 p.m. Dinner and prayer. The conclusions she'd come to during the two-hour drive in slow-crawling traffic from the Bayside Inn were that, number one, she needed to get her things together, leave the church, and lie low for a while. Hide out and wait. The family complications were becoming overwhelming. Then she wouldn't be available to supply money, get rid of dead bodies, or involve herself in issues that weren't her concern. And two, she needed to find Anais.

Marie snuck quietly into her room and shut the door behind her. Once inside, she rushed to the closet, yanked an overnight bag from the top shelf, and stripped down to her underthings, her pants crumpling around her ankles. *No more dowdy clothes for me.* She pulled on the jeans and white turtleneck that she'd taken from Claire's closet weeks ago. They weren't a perfect fit, but close enough. She slid small hoop earrings into her ears and gloss across her lips. She didn't own any foundation, mascara, or blush, but she'd remedy that soon.

She slipped on a brown leather jacket, expensive yet casual, and then a pair of tall boots, more borrows from Claire. When they were girls, people often thought they were twins—they were the same height, same basic shape, had the same hair color, with faces that bore only slight differences. Marie's eyes were larger, the color tinged with green, while Claire's were smaller and darker. And Marie had a mole near her temple. But the younger girl made the confusion worse by stealing her sister's clothes and her sense of style. That all changed when Marie joined the convent at twenty-two. They were never confused with each other again.

She stared into the only mirror she had—one that sat on her dresser, just large enough to see her face in. Her hair was still a rich coffee-bean brown with no hint of gray, thick and wavy, the ends resting just at her chin. She ran a comb through it and tucked strands behind her ears. She'd hidden her features behind her religion for too long.

Seeing the angles of her jawline, the high cheekbones, the enormous eyes, the straight nose, she realized she'd barely paid attention to her looks for over twenty years. Tiny lines had formed at the corners of her eyes. She pulled at them with her fingers. "I've given the best years of my life to a psychiatric hospital and then a church," she muttered. "Pull it together, old girl."

She picked up the mirror and ran it down her body, catching glimpses as she went, trying to assess the whole. "Claire would just kill me if she saw me wearing this getup." Then her face flattened at the irony of that statement. She fished through her drawers and pulled out the hunting knife she'd bought at the country store in Chatsworth and stuffed it into her plain black purse. "It's the one thing I forgot to steal from my sister. A nice purse."

She glanced into the closet one last time and pushed aside the scarves and gloves. The old tan Polaroid case was where she'd left it. She reached for it, hesitating. It was empty, she knew. The biggest mistake—letting the camera out of her sight—would come back to haunt her. It was only a matter of time.

She thought back to when she and Claire were children, just moved to France with their mother. No notice, no discussion. They'd just packed and left. Everything in France was different and new. Even the language. The two girls were sad, crying, asking constantly when they could go home. Marie thought she'd never see her father again. Claire discovered the old camera in the closet and fell in love with it. The heaviness of it, the bellowed pop-out lens. Anais gave them boxes of roll film and sent them on their way.

It took some practice to use, as it was manual and the shutter speed had to be adjusted in between takes. Antiquated was what it was. Anais had offered to buy them a newer camera that produced color prints, but they'd refused. The two girls loved that old relic. It'd occupied them for months—she and Claire running around snapping pictures of each other while Anais sat in her chair, sipping wine or reading magazines.

When Claire returned to the States, Anais sent the camera to her as a gift. The roll film was no longer manufactured and was difficult to find, so Anais had taken the camera to a little hobby shop in town and found someone who could alter it to accept the new instant film. It was a sentimental joke. But the alterations to the camera rendered it even more difficult to use, and the resulting prints were of terrible quality, grainy and monochrome. It didn't matter to Claire. She'd loved it. *If you're homesick, take some pictures,* Anais's note had said. Who would have guessed that heavy metal box would be connected to a string of murders decades later?

Where was the camera now? Marie felt some measure of panic rising inside her. She dropped the box of film into her bag and slipped out of the building without anyone noticing, glancing back only once at the place she'd called home for the past five years.

CHAPTER 54

The house was dark, with a vacant, abandoned feel. The small things that screamed *occupied* were absent. There was no decoration on the porch, no welcome mat. A fall wreath still hung from the front door, faded and beaten from the winter cold and wind. No porch light snapped on to illuminate the path. The mailbox was stuffed to the brim. The postage-sized front lawn was strewn with debris, leaves, and sticks, and the bushes were growing odd horns, desperately in need of being trimmed. Joanne stared at it. If anyone wanted to pick a house to rob, this would be a good bet, except for the silver Honda Accord parked neatly in the driveway.

Joanne had fumed for hours after leaving Russell's house. Everything had been set for her and Russell to break in and look for the candlestick. It was going to be fun, exciting. But then his little miss with the upswept hair had to horn in and ruin it. Joanne had gone home, pacing and ruminating until the sun went down, and then decided in a moment fraught with impulse that she'd do it herself. She knew the layout of the house, and she had a better excuse if she got caught. Ava was missing. Her car was in the driveway and Joanne was afraid she was inside, hurt or worse. So she broke in. She knew the cops would not only buy it but help her search the house if it came to that.

She'd pulled on dark sweat leggings and a black hoodie, perfect cat-burglar wear, she thought, and headed to the house alone as the sun was dipping in the sky. She figured she'd have time to search the boxes, get home, make some calls about the camera, and then present everything to Russell while she was cursing him for sidelining her in the first place. But when she got to the house and was faced with the prospect of actually breaking a window or crawling on her hands and knees, she got a case of the second thoughts.

The front door was locked, and after testing the front windows, she'd determined she couldn't open them either. The path along the side of the house ended at a wooden gate. She pressed the latch lock and squeezed her eyes tight. It clicked open. She breathed a sigh of relief. *One step at a time, Joanne.* She looked at the patio and remembered sitting there with Ava, drinking coffee or wine. Laughing. Over the summer, when the humidity made it hard to breathe, they'd bought packages of premade frozen margaritas and a kiddy pool and spent a Saturday afternoon sitting in it, dipping their feet and drinking. The yard was still the same, but those comfortable, normal days seemed forever ago.

The drape was only partially drawn across the sliding-glass doors, so she could see the dining room, part of the kitchen. It was sort of the same as she remembered. Not cleaned out, but minus Ava's clutter, it shouted *Staged for an open house*. She pondered her options. There was a back door into the garage. She could try that and then hope the door to the house was open. Or, as a last option, she could force the basement window, the width of which was slightly smaller than her waist. It didn't occur to her that the sliding-glass doors might be open until she pulled on one and it slid on its casters. *Very sloppy, Marie.*

She locked the door behind her and surveyed the room. The house had been peeled down to the basics. Her mind was urging her to get to the closet, search the boxes for anything resembling a candlestick, and get the heck out. But she couldn't. She'd spent time in this house with Ava and needed to see something of her presence. A trace. A small empty vodka bottle in the corner; the ever-present hair bands she'd wrap around her wrist and use to pull her hair off her face when she was tired of it; her sunglasses, large, that covered half her face for a reason. When she wore them, red bleary eyes always emerged from underneath. Joanne couldn't leave without a memento.

She walked into the kitchen and ran a hand over the granite countertops. At first glance the room was empty, just waiting for new tenants, but Joanne noticed something was off. A coffee cup was in the sink, the remnants of the drink still in the bottom. She pulled open the refrigerator. A quart of milk, half-empty. A sandwich from Wawa half-eaten, the rest saved for a later meal. On the windowsill was an ashtray with two smoked-to-the-filter Marlboro Lights, as if perched there so someone could crack the window to blow the smoke into the outside air. The real-estate woman, maybe? Joanne picked up a butt and then dropped it. *Disgusting.*

She scanned the living room and then took the stairs and went immediately to Ava's bedroom. The door was open. The bed was made and covered in a pale-blue duvet. The floor was cleaned of clutter; the stack of boxes, never unpacked when Ava'd arrived back from college, was gone. *She's wiped away all traces of you.* Joanne ran her hand over the bed and pulled open the closet. Ava's clothes hung from plastic hangers. Neat, obviously sorted through. Enough was here to convince anyone Marie thought she was coming back—just staying with friends for a week.

The dark Hermès blazer Ava wore to the courthouse—a gift from Claire, she'd said—that Joanne was convinced would fit a ten-year-old was there. Expensive looking even from across the room, the dulled gold buttons, the attention to fit and detail. Ava would throw it on over black trousers for work, or ripped jeans in the evening. The ultimate I-have-money luxury item. She ran her fingers over the fabric. Wool? Or a wool-cashmere blend? It was soft and gorgeous.

Joanne slung it over her arm and peered into Claire's bedroom. The duvet had been pulled up hastily, the pillows haphazard. A towel was hanging on the knob of the bathroom door. Joanne reached out and then hesitated, her fingers afraid to touch it. When she clasped it, it was damp. She stared, trying to put the pieces together. A real-estate woman might make coffee or bring a sandwich to an open house, and maybe even smoke in the kitchen, but there's no way she'd be showering. She pushed the bathroom door open and looked inside. There were drops of water still clinging to the shower door.

Just then she heard a noise. A scraping coming from downstairs. She froze, her whole body listening. *Damn it, it could be Russell.* Then she heard it again. Louder. She slunk to the wall and waited. It was a rattling, like someone was pulling at the windows. Then nothing. She tried to slow her breaths. Then the unmistakable sound of a door opening somewhere in the house.

The office. She needed to get to the office. She yanked off her boots and slid across the hallway. When she pulled the closet door open, she saw it was filled with boxes. She shoved them to the side and sat with her back to the wall. Her head dropped to her knees and she breathed. She still had the blazer, now balled up in her lap.

Her fingers ran over the buttons, tracing the *H* repeatedly. Joanne wasn't letting it go. Not until she saw her friend wearing it again. Not until she could stand next to her at the Victor Club and see her throw back vodka on the rocks or shots of tequila with the blazer draped over the back of a chair.

A close-by noise jolted her. Joanne squeezed the fabric in her fist. Someone was in the hallway. She heard the scuffle of feet, then saw the flicker of light. Whoever it was thought better of it and left the lights off. More shuffling of feet.

It's not Russell. He'd never do that and draw attention to the house.

Joanne's heart began to pick up its pace. She'd been wrong. So wrong. The thing to fear most in coming here was not that she might get caught by the police and possibly arrested. It was this—being trapped with no one to rescue her.

She heard movement close by, maybe just in the doorway of the office. Soft rustling. Then a whispering voice. The door to the closet was open a crack, the office was shadowed, but from Joanne's vantage point she could see the back of a woman, tallish, wearing a bulky coat. The woman moved, seeming to take in the room, then muttering the word *merde*. Then a rattling of French words in a low tone.

Joanne knew enough French from hanging by Ava's side to know that *merde* meant *shit*. The muttering got closer, and Joanne sensed she'd moved nearer to the closet. Joanne peered through the crack to see her back as she turned. Thin face, hair cut just to her shoulders. The hood was bunched up so her full profile was hidden.

Oh my God. Oh my God. It's Claire.

Joanne started to push herself up, to crawl from the space in a panic, and then stopped. She dropped back down and put her head into the coat, rocking back and forth. This woman was alive, walking around, calling people on her cell phone, despite the fact that she'd been buried weeks ago. How was this possible?

When her heart slowed down and the sweat left her skin, she realized she was sitting in a closet with a potential murder weapon. She shuddered. The boxes nearby were open, stacked on top of each other. Her fingers reached in one and felt just papers. Papers on top of papers. She turned to the side and pulled at a flap. A small table lamp, an ornate ashtray, some coasters, knickknacks. And then there it was. A collection of three candlesticks. She pulled at one and heard the crash of items falling around it back into the box. Joanne sat still and waited. She counted to sixty. There were no footsteps. She examined the shapes of the candlesticks with her fingers. Two matched, one was odd. Gold, from what she could tell in the light. Heavy. Square. She wrapped the candlestick in the jacket. It was making her skin crawl. The images of the crime scene. The blood. The bodies. That this sharp end might have punctured the woman's skull.

Her mind jumped to Russell. She realized that he might show up and have no idea anyone else was in the house. She had to warn him about this. She immediately went to check her pockets for her phone, then remembered she was wearing leggings.

Her phone was in her glove box three streets over.

CHAPTER 55

Ava's hair was brushing against his arm. She moved slightly and the strands trailed along his skin.

"What are you doing?" he asked.

She held the glass to her lips and drained the contents. "I'm looking with you. Don't you want my help?" Her mouth was near his ear, he felt the breaths hit his ear and smelled the wine at the same time. He glanced up, seeing she was biting her top lip as she read over his shoulder.

He smiled. "I need your help. But maybe you should start over there." He pointed. "You're distracting me."

"Am I?" She leaned down so her chin rested on his shoulder. He picked up his own glass and realized it was empty. It had been full only ten minutes before. "Do you need a refill?" she asked, taking it from him, letting her fingers touch his for a moment.

He knew what she was doing but he couldn't understand why. The timing was weird and it seemed forced, even through the three glasses of wine he'd consumed. He wasn't against a woman taking the lead, but it was almost like she was putting on a performance.

She set his glass back in front of him. It was filled right to the rim. "Drink. It's going to be a long night." Then she sat on the edge of the desk, covering some of the photographs he'd been looking at.

He picked up the glass, trying to keep the wine from spilling over the edge. The redness dripped all over everything, the desk, papers, his hands. She licked the wine from his skin and leaned in to kiss him.

He moved back. "Ava?"

"I like you, Russell." Her words were slurring, melting together. "And there might not be another time."

He put his hands on her shoulders to keep her from moving. "Why wouldn't there be another time?"

She leaned so that her mouth was inches from his. "It's almost all over. You just don't know it." Then her lips were on his and he forgot what she'd said. The buzz in his brain was pulling things in and out of focus. He felt her move so that she was in his lap, the lightness of her body against his. "You're smart. And you'll get there," she whispered. "I know you will."

"Get where?" He was lost in the moment.

"To the end of this," she said. She unbuttoned her shirt. "And when you do? It'll be shocking."

His hands were on her waist, the bones against his fingers. "What's shocking?" He was swimming; he needed more wine. He started to reach for the glass and she stopped him. "Let me." She picked it up and moved it to his mouth, tipping it slightly against his lips. "Tell me when." His mouth was full and he touched the glass, pushing it back and swallowing.

"Enough." He wiped his mouth with his fingers.

"The truth is shocking." She kissed him briefly. "And the truth will set all of us free." Then she laughed. "Well, maybe not all of us. It'll bury some of us." She stared at him, her eyes taking on a tenderness he'd never seen in her before. "But know that I like you, Russell. I really like you. It's why I let Joanne choose you. Now I might be sorry." She stood up and began unzipping her pants.

"Whad'you mean?" His lips were having trouble forming the words. "Choose me for what?"

She was stripped of her clothes, intoxicated and vulnerable, yet he felt she was completely in control and always had been. She straddled him, pressing into him. "It might have been different with us. With you, maybe." She kissed him. "But now it can't be. Just tonight—"

She was beautiful. He thought briefly of Juliette. Then he didn't. He ran his hands over her body. "Why just tonight?"

"Because if I die, and I might, remember this—Loyal's house is just the beginning. It's where we needed to start. Follow the trail from there to Frankford and—"

"What?" He was startled and pulled his hands back.

She pressed her index finger against his lips. "Shh. Listen. To Saint Francis de Sales. Find out the woman's name. It'll lead you in a circle back to Claire and Marie. Find the truth. For me?"

Russell buried his face in her hair. It smelled of lavender and Pinot Noir. "Claire's dead," he muttered. "And you think you're going to die? I won't let that happen."

"There's a French expression, *sentir le sapin*. That's how I feel." She rubbed her hand along his neck and then started unbuttoning his shirt. "And yes, Claire's dead," she whispered in his ear. "Or is she?"

Russell bolted up. He was sweating, his heart pounding. He looked around. His living room was filled with fading late-afternoon light. He heard the grandfather clock chiming five thirty. He rubbed his head, disoriented. Had that really happened? Was it a dream? It was so vivid. He could still smell her. Russell lifted his fingers to his nose, disoriented, thinking lavender and wine would fill his nostrils.

What had she said? That they needed to start at Loyal's? And follow the trail back to Claire. And find out the woman's name. He'd dreamed it. All of it, he was sure.

Juliette came into the room, dressed in jeans and a sweater. "You up, sleepy boy? I went to the store, got steaks for dinner—"

He stood up. "Hold off on the steaks, Jules." He headed for the steps, taking them two at a time. "I need to get to the house."

"Now?"

He stopped midway. "You don't know Joanne. She's probably there now, breaking a window. I can't believe I slept so long."

Juliette smiled, which took Russell by surprise. "Funny. Someone needs to give you a run for your money. Go. Text me on your way home and I'll start dinner." She turned to go back to the kitchen when she stopped. "Don't get caught, Russell. The banks are closed. It'll be hard getting your bail money tonight."

He laughed. "Right. Leave me overnight. It might be good for me."

He kissed her cheek on the way out. "Thanks for understanding." She simply nodded. "And think about a way to identify the woman who was killed with the priest? That would be great."

Even when he was driving to Haddonfield, he still felt as if he were in the dream. He could see her face. It was real, but like most dreams, it was fading. Crumbling around the edges. How could she know she was going to die? What was the expression she used? *Sentir le sapin.* He practiced the syllables over in his head so he wouldn't forget, though he knew it was nonsense his brain had concocted to sound French. And why did she question whether Claire was really dead or not? It was all surreal and impossible. *God, Ava, are* you *really dead? And what did you get me into?*

CHAPTER 56

Marie sat at the bar at the Liberté. The lights were dimmed, and a jazz ensemble played softly in the background. She sipped her martini and stared into the mirror across from her. She was unrecognizable. She'd stopped at Macy's and had her makeup done, purchasing all the items they'd used to make her eyes jump out of her face, her cheekbones contoured, her lips lightly blushed. Four men had already tried to sit near her, buy her a drink, but she wanted to be alone.

After pondering her options, she'd driven her rusty Hyundai to Philadelphia, parked it at a meter with no intention of ever retrieving it, booked a room at the Sofitel hotel, so very French, and waited.

She thought about an afternoon seventeen years before. Five-year-old Ava had given up her crying fits, only occasionally babbling gibberish in her native tongue, only now and then screaming *Mamma*, and only once in a blue moon mentioning the events of that night two years before, the details ever fading, changing in the little girl's mind.

The day had been hot at only nine o'clock in the morning in Bakersfield, California. The sun, searing. Claire had rented a two-bedroom ground-floor apartment in a complex that looked to be filled with unnoticing transients. The air conditioning was only able to pull some of the heaviness from the air. Ava had been whiny and miserable since the sun came up. Crying, sweat collecting on her forehead and rolling down her round cheeks. Claire had tried everything. Cups of cold water, VHS tapes of her favorite shows, toys, dress up. None of it worked.

In desperation she'd filled a shallow wading pool in the front yard with cold water and put Ava in to soak while she made some phone calls. The child stomped and splashed, filled plastic cups with water and poured them out. All was well until a neighbor passed by and stopped to chat with the child, the questions innocuous—*Are you having fun? What's your name? How old are you?* Claire was deep in conversation, not concerned about what was happening, until the neighbor hung around, the conversation with the girl taking too long for simple questioning. Claire moved toward them, the phone still against her ear, to hear Ava saying in a loud, clear voice, "My mother is dead. She's with the angels." When Claire approached, Ava looked up into her face and pointed at her. "She helped take her to the angels."

Claire snapped the phone shut, picked the girl up from the water, and smiled at the neighbor. But the older woman wasn't budging.

"What does she mean by that? She said her mother was killed? And that you helped?" The woman tilted her head to the side, waiting.

"She has an imagination" was all that Claire could manage. "She must have been watching something on television." The lies, the subterfuge, were still unpracticed. This life was new to Claire.

"Are you her mother?" she asked.

"Of course I am. I'm Joan, by the way," she lied. Her heart was pounding, but she kept the frozen smile firmly in place.

Ava shook her head. "No. She's not *Mamma*." The pronunciation of that word unmistakably Italian.

"Why would a child say such a thing?"

Claire's hands began to tremble. "Like I said, television. We need to go now." Claire turned abruptly and started to walk toward her front door.

"Wait, you said your name was Joan. What's your last name?" she asked, and Claire shut the front door in her face. Claire and the little girl evacuated the apartment at two in the morning. Their belongings shoved into boxes. Their taillights disappearing down the road and out of California forever.

Family was family. And Marie had been there for it all, helping to pack meager items into cardboard boxes and shove them into the back of the Volvo station wagon—in the snow in North Dakota; in the rain in Edmonds, Washington; in the stifling heat and humidity of Fort Myers, Florida. She'd been torn from convents in the middle of the night, claiming family emergency, the invention of excuses testing her creativity. She'd kept track of Claire, finding her at the Bayside Inn when she disappeared altogether. Marie had been her assistant, confidant, and bank when funds were short. To think this was what it had come to was heartbreaking.

She had no clue where she was going from here. But she didn't have long to figure it out. She only knew for sure that she was done with the convent. And that her sister's house was now off limits. She was ready to reinvent herself and move on.

Marie sipped the last drops from her glass and tapped the side of it again. Another one would make three. Her head was starting to buzz. The bartender came and took the glass away, quickly replacing it with a fresh one. Someone sat down on a stool a few away from hers. She sensed his presence before she even turned her head to get a look. He was youngish, maybe early thirties. Dirty-blond hair. He wore a black hoodie with a red hood and red sneakers to match. He glanced at her twice and she noticed his eyes were gray with little speckles of blue. The third time, he held her gaze and smiled.

CHAPTER 57

Russell pulled up in front of the house and turned off his engine. How he hated this. The thought of risking his career again to break into a house to try and find a murder weapon from twenty years ago was ludicrous. Why was he putting so much at risk for this woman? The reasons why had apparently jumped onto a hamster wheel and were racing through his brain constantly, to no avail. The answer was elusive.

Ava was elusive. The first time he'd caught sight of her, months before in the courthouse, winding through the halls, her thin body dressed completely in black, he was curious. Curious in a generic way—the culture of the place, a relatively small, incestuous environment, dictated that newbies, particularly women, be vetted, interrogated, sized up, and then pigeonholed. He'd sidled up to her at the snack bar, where she was getting black coffee, no sugar, and made an attempt at small talk.

"Are you new here?" Not original. "I'm Russell. I work over at the Prosecutor's Office."

She turned and smiled. Her eyes warming toward him, taking him in. "Ah, a lawyer? How very nice." Her accent was American but it wasn't. She took her coffee to a table and sat down as if he didn't exist.

He followed her only because she'd blown him off. The women who worked in the courthouse were usually friendly, accommodating, flirtatious, or at least tolerant. It helped pass the time. He sat down and saw the flicker of irritation cross her face and then quickly disappear. "I'm not a lawyer. Detective," he said. "At the Prosecutor's Office."

She peered at him, the corners of her lips tilted upward. "Not a good one, or you'd know I want to be alone." Then she'd laughed as if she'd been joking and held out her hand. "Ava. And I only have a few minutes and I have to be back in court—translator." She stood and gathered her things. "Bye, Detective Russell."

And so it began. Conversations in the halls, an occasional lunch outside. He noticed her. There was something smart and edgy that drew him in. She was funny and detached. Interesting but not interested. He found himself looking for her now and then, and was always thrilled when he happened upon her by accident. He didn't imagine anything would come of it. It was innocent until that day he'd met her in the diner.

And so he'd jumped stupidly at the chance to help; though he'd played impatient and irritated to Ava and Joanne, inside he wasn't really. Inside he'd been aroused both intellectually and emotionally. Sitting with her, going out to eat with her, poring over photographs, hadn't lessened his inclinations. Neither had her naked body in his lap. Even then, he thought he'd at least made an attempt at resisting, though he couldn't be sure. Now his heart was dragged down with the possibility that she might be dead. But he couldn't say the words out loud, not when he was by himself, and certainly not if he was within five hundred feet of Joanne.

He stared at the house. Dark. And took out his cell phone. He pulled up Google Translate and phonetically typed in the phrase that was circling his brain. *Sentir.* How do you spell that? After two tries he hit on it. *Sentir*—to feel. Could he have known that, or did he make up the syllables in his dream? The last part of what he remembered Ava saying was going to be more difficult. Her French was rapid and the endings confusing to the English speaker. He kept plugging in variations but was getting nowhere. *Feel what, Ava?* He thought the word started with *sap*, so he put that in and kept altering the ending, hoping that something would hit. Then it did. The translator took his *sapain* and made *sapin*—fir. He looked at it and pressed the audio. The voice came on, pronouncing the word exactly as Ava had. Feel the fir? Like a fir tree? He knew he'd just been dreaming and tossed the phone onto the empty seat next to him.

He reached for the door handle to start the process of breaking into the house when he caught movement out of the corner of his eye. A woman, moving fast down the path by the side of the house and then almost running when she hit the street. He knew her immediately. Joanne. He'd been right, she'd come to the house without him. She'd gone home defiant and angry and had come here and broken in somehow. He half smiled, admiring her bravery. He backed up and tried to circle around, needing to maneuver the car each time so that he was facing the other way. By the time he'd finished, Joanne was gone, turned the corner. Poof.

He started to pull out in a rush, eager to follow her, to get to her house to see what she'd found, when he saw a flash of light inside the house, in a second-story window. He stopped and stared. Someone had turned on the light for just a second. A flick of the switch. Unmistakable. Who? Marie? He stepped out of the car and started for the door. If Marie was there, it wasn't a big deal. He could make a million excuses for showing up. He strode purposefully up the walkway and then stopped. He saw it again—this time downstairs. A quick burst, like a match being lit, then the soft glow of maybe a candle. The sheer white curtains in the downstairs windows weren't protecting any secrets. Why would someone light candles when the lights worked? Ambiance? Or hiding?

The glow moved and then was gone. Russell stood motionless on the sidewalk, aware that he would draw the attention of anyone passing by. He took the stone steps quickly and rang the bell, stuffed his hands in his pockets, and waited. He could hear the bell, and was half-certain he heard shuffling noises from behind the door, but it didn't open. He tried again, standing very still, listening, trying to watch through the glass panels on the side of the door. Nothing.

The cold was seeping into his bones; the mist coming from his mouth warmed the end of his nose. Whoever was in there wasn't interested in company tonight. His eyes landed on the mailbox, the flap partially closed, bursting with white envelopes, flyers, and junk mail. He reached out and opened the box—add tampering with mail to his list of transgressions, it didn't matter at this point. He stuffed the mail under his jacket and headed down the steps. Joanne's house was ten minutes away and undoubtedly warm.

He shut the car door and pulled the mail from his jacket. Credit-card offers for Claire, a host of real-estate cards, even more home-improvement advertisements, and one lone envelope addressed to *Occupant*, address typed, no return address, postmarked Philadelphia. Russell sucked in his breath. This was exactly what Joanne had described when she was here before. And that envelope had contained a Polaroid of Jack Quinn's house. *No, no more death. Please.*

He slid his finger along the seal and ripped it open. His worst fear was realized when a picture fell out. It wasn't the front of a house. It wasn't a house at all. It was a body.

Russell dropped the Polaroid onto his lap and peeled out onto the street.

CHAPTER 58

Joanne was panting and sweating, and couldn't breathe. Years ago she'd suffered from asthma attacks but hadn't had any in so long she'd gotten rid of her inhalers. She was leaning over the kitchen sink, the wheezing audible and getting worse. The harder she pulled at the air, trying to get it into her lungs, the more panicked she became. She was getting dizzy, seeing the walls start to spin, when she felt a hand on her back.

"Slow it down, Joanne." His voice was low and calm.

She bent her head lower. "Asth—" was all she could manage before a paper bag was pushed up against her face.

"Breathe into the bag."

She shook her head. He thought she was having a panic attack. She wasn't. But he held the bag against her mouth, giving her no choice. And after a few minutes her breathing slowed until she could push off the sink and make her way to the couch. She held the bag against her face herself and continued to breathe.

"Are you okay now?" he asked. Joanne shook her head. He flicked the picture up and down against his leg. "You need to stay with me, Jo. I hate to say this, but I can't do this alone. I need you."

She pulled the bag from her mouth. "Doug," she said.

"No, I need both you and Doug. For different things." He got up and went into the kitchen, poured cold water into a glass, and brought it to her. His eyes kept landing on the candlestick sitting on the coffee table. "We need to go over what we have—"

"What's the point, Russell? Ava's dead." Her hand gestured to the photograph. "And someone took a picture of her body for proof. And you don't seem all that upset."

He glared at her. "You don't think I'm upset? I am. But the only thing I can do about it is move forward. There's a killer still on the loose. Still killing, I'd say. Marie may be the next target, but I can't be sure. Maybe it's over."

Joanne threw the paper bag down onto the couch next to her. "The other photograph said *Now I am done*. It's over. Quinn and Ava are dead. Done."

"Why would someone send photographs to Claire's house? If they were intended for Marie, why not send them to the convent? It makes no sense. Claire's dead—"

Joanne stood up. "She's not. I saw her. I saw her like I'm seeing you. She's living in that damn house. Making coffee, eating a sandwich, taking a shower. Go see!" She jabbed her finger at him. "I only got out when she went into the bathroom and shut the door. I was scared for my life."

"Sit down or I'm gonna bag you again." She obeyed. "Claire being alive is impossible. She had a funeral. A viewing too?" He eyed her sideways, waiting for an answer.

"No. A memorial service. The grandmother took the body back to France for burial."

He dropped his head and rubbed at his hair, deep in thought. "If she faked her death, the question is how. And, of course, why." He looked up. "And did Ava know?"

"She didn't. I saw her face after Claire died. So where do you want to go from here, Russell?"

Russell glanced at the phone, the candlestick, and the cigarette pack. "Why'd you steal her jacket? She wore this a lot." He ran his hand over it.

Joanne nodded. "I didn't mean to take it, but it was in my hand."

He picked up the candlestick by the top. "We need to compare this to the one in the crime-scene photos. Won't be exactly a scientific match, but—"

"We know she's in the house, so we need to get her out. Somehow. Get the gas company to say there's a leak. Set it on fire, I don't know." She stood up and started to pace. "Or maybe we could just go and break in. Confront her? What'd we have to lose?"

"And—"

"Then figure out the identity of the woman who was killed with Father Callahan." She looked at Russell. "We could use help with that."

"Tell me what you saw again. When you were in the closet? In detail."

"Someone came up the steps. They muttered *'merde'—shit* in French—then words I didn't know. I saw her turn—saw the side of her face. It was Claire. I know what she looks like."

"No lights, right? So you were seeing this in the dark?"

She nodded. "It was dark and she had on a big coat. Shortish dark hair."

"And you're sure it wasn't Marie? The two look alike, even in the light."

"I don't think so." She was shaking her head violently. "Don't try and confuse me."

"But the two are the same height, from pictures I've seen. Same basic shape. Both have dark hair. And Marie's been crawling all over that place. Burning things. I just think maybe you were mistaken."

"No . . ." Her eyes landed on the photograph. It was taken from a short distance away; Ava was on her back, her head turned slightly toward the camera. Eyes partially open in a dead stare. Blood covered her neck and part of her face. Her arm was extended outward, enough of the hand visible that you could see defense wounds on the palm. Even in black-and-white grainy film. The picture was taken at almost ground level—pine needles surrounded the body.

"I think it was Marie. In any case, we need to call that number, see who answers, keep an eye on that house. Eventually she has to leave." He stood up. "I had this dream about Ava. It was so real."

Joanne's eyes went from the photograph to Russell. "What was it about?"

"The night before she disappeared. She was sitting in my lap. Saying weird things. Like, 'You're almost there. We had to start at Loyal's house. Then go to Saint Francis de Sales. It'll lead you back to Claire and Marie.' Then she said she was going to die."

"God." She put her hand across her mouth.

"She used this French phrase that I must have made up, because it makes no sense. *Sentir le sapin*, I think. I looked it up. It means *to feel the fir*, like a fir tree. The whole dream was so real I didn't know if it was a memory."

Joanne was listening intently. "Really?"

"But it must have been just my mind, making up crazy things."

Joanne's eyes were moist. "What if it wasn't? What if she knew—"

"Ava also said she let you choose me. Like she orchestrated it. Is that possible?" Joanne had turned on her phone and was engrossed with the screen. "What're you doing?"

"Just looking," she answered. In less than a minute her head snapped up. "*Sentir le sapin* is an idiom. Literally it means *feel the fir*, because they used fir trees to make coffins. It means *not long for this world*, or *one foot in the grave*. Russell?"

"I didn't make it up," he whispered. "She dragged us into this on purpose. Then the rest of it has to be true too."

Joanne felt like her lungs were going to collapse again, so she sat very still. "What now?"

Russell picked up the photo from the table and started walking toward the door. "The dead woman with the priest is the key." He put his hand on the doorknob and turned to look at her. "And everything leads back to the Lavoisier sisters. I'm going to find Doug."

CHAPTER 59

She thought he knew her—the way he kept staring at her. A member of the church, maybe? A friend of Claire's? He was two bar stools away, but his eyes followed her, either by directly looking at her or by watching her reflection in the mirror. He had a round, youngish face, blue eyes. Nondescript hair that was neither brown nor blond, buzzed short to his head. Marie had finished her third drink and realized maybe too late that everything was getting fuzzy. But it felt so good after the tension that came with hypervigilance and heightened anxiety.

"Do I know you?" She stood up but held the back of the stool to steady herself.

He smiled. "I should know you, I think. You're very beautiful."

Marie snorted and started to walk toward the entrance. Just another man in search of something she was never going to give him. But something about this one was odd. He was obvious, bold, and his dress too casual for this hotel. Not the usual clientele. She turned and walked out of the bar, her purse slung over her shoulder. Her head was steering toward the front desk. *Refuse to leave. Find safety,* she was telling herself. But her wobbly legs instead took her right out into the lobby, to the elevator banks.

He was behind her. His long legs keeping stride with hers, though he gave off airs that they weren't together, that he was just headed in the same direction. Until they were standing side by side. He was only an inch taller, looking directly into her eyes.

"I'd push the button and get on if I were you. Now."

Her gaze was straight ahead. "And if I don't?"

"Why do that? This doesn't have to be difficult."

Marie's head whipped around to face him. "What?"

He pushed the button and the elevator opened. "That's what I call service. Come on." He stepped inside.

She hesitated. Her mind was trying to sort out the facts. She took a tentative step forward, then abruptly turned and ran, her body off-kilter in boots with three-inch heels. She pushed open the hotel door and tore outside into the darkness. Sansom Street was narrow and alleylike, not a great place for making an exit, but she hadn't been paying attention. Marie knew if this man got her alone, he was going to kill her.

She'd gone and done it—hired a hit man with her seven hundred dollars.

Marie needed safety, an open restaurant, a place with people. The street was dotted with shops and stores, all closed up for the night. She was sweating, the alcohol slowing her movements and increasing her panic. Then there it was, the Dandelion, a restaurant on the corner with the lights still on.

She pulled the heavy glass door open and rushed past the bar to the bathrooms in the back. The stall shut and locked, she put her back to the wall and tried to breathe. How did he find her? Follow her? Was it that easy? She had to get her car and get out of here. But everything was in her hotel room at the Sofitel. Everything. She'd reserved for three nights to give herself time and space to think, not expecting this. Leaving all her things was out of the question. She had clothing, cash, and personal items. And then really essential items that couldn't be left behind.

She heard movement in the stall next to hers—she stood completely still, waiting for the sounds of normal use, which didn't come.

She clutched her purse tighter, knowing she had her car keys and wallet with her; for now that was enough to get away. But why have her killed? Marie had intended to give her the money she needed, had done everything she'd asked. They hadn't really argued at the Bayside, had they? Even if they had, was this what it had come to? She rubbed her face and tried to clear her thoughts. The alcohol was making her dizzy.

Again she heard a noise in the next stall. How fast did she need to move to lose him? She tried to visualize where she'd deposited the car, which direction to go when she got out to the front door. Tears of frustration gathered in the corners of her eyes. She counted to five, flung open the bathroom door, and raced toward the entrance. Too late or not late enough. He was standing there, outside the restaurant entrance, a look of bored impatience on his face. He hooked his arm around hers when she charged out, and started walking back toward the hotel, pulling her along with him.

"That was fifteen minutes of my life I'll never get back, lady. Not a wise choice," he hissed in her ear.

"What do you want with me?" Marie stopped full tilt in the middle of the sidewalk, resisting against his pull. "I'll scream right now."

"A chat, Marie. I thought we'd have a chat in your room, that's it. It's actually important."

"Talk here." She moved over closer to the buildings, looking for some way out. But everything around her was dark, damp, and empty. "She sent you here? You've followed me?"

He dropped his head and pulled up the hood on his sweatshirt. "She said her name is Claire, so I'll go with that." He reached out and pulled up her hood too, obscuring her face from any passersby. "And yes, I followed you."

Marie pulled her arm from his grasp. "Why? Why would she want me dead when I'm the only person who can help her now?"

He shrugged. "Don't get so dramatic. We're just talking . . ."

Marie tried to keep her face neutral, but her brain was darting from fact to fact. If this man had been sent to kill her, Claire had probably told him too much. Hired him to erase the last pieces of this story. "Go back to her. Tell her I have access to more money. Whatever she needs. Tell her I'll help her," she blurted. "I can get more money from Anais if that's what she needs. I know I can."

Marie knew she was going to die, either right on the sidewalk or maybe in her hotel room if he could get her back there. Either one, her life was over. Her mind started flashing back to how she'd spent her time. To her childhood in France. To Anais and Claire, when things were so much simpler. To her father, how little she'd known him and how she'd wanted to.

To the dead woman, naked and pale, found with the priest. The night Ross showed up in Brooklyn, bloody. Telling his story. The woman's purse in his car.

"Why take her purse, Papa?" she'd asked through clenched teeth and trembling lips.

"I had it in my hand when I ran. I don't know," he'd answered. "Identifying her will be harder. Next to impossible." Marie had backed up, afraid. "I didn't do this thing to her, baby. You have to believe me."

Marie shook her head. "No." A simple word that meant *No, I won't help you cover this up. No, I won't take her purse. Or the murder weapon. No, I don't believe anything you say.*

In the end it became yes. *Yes, I will cover this up, hide the murder weapon, destroy evidence, lie, and run for the rest of my life. Yes.* But the purse was the worst of it. Passport, identification, immigration papers. A wallet containing fifteen US dollars and change. A hairbrush. A lipstick. The remnants of an entire life story fit neatly into one black cross-body bag.

For the longest time, Marie had spread the contents of that purse out and stared at them, marveling at fate. How random events could end a life. The ordinary Maybelline Coffee Kiss lipstick the woman had probably used that morning, like she did every morning, not knowing that swipe of color would be the last. She'd gone about her routine that day, taking the bus from social services to food banks to shelters, trying to put together a life for herself that would never happen. She should have left religion out of that equation. She would still be alive.

"How much money are we talking about?" he asked.

She knew she'd made a mistake in mentioning that. Now he was going to rob her and then kill her. Her back was against the brick wall, her body braced for whatever he was going to do to her. He leaned toward her, his face too close, his hand pinning one arm. Too close. She couldn't breathe. Air went into her lungs and didn't come out.

She felt her sharp knife plunging deep into his stomach area before she'd even thought it through. She pulled him to her and cupped his face with one hand so that a couple walking by thought they were lovers. Her other held the handle of the blade. She pulled it out quickly, his body folding into hers. His eyes, open, held an expression of surprise.

She whispered in his ear. "Shh. Go call Claire. She'll patch you up. Tell her I'll do the same to her if she doesn't leave me alone. Can you remember that?"

He held the brick wall with one hand to brace himself. His eyes clouding over. "You're too stupid to know what you just did, you crazy bitch."

CHAPTER 60

"You know the deal, Russell. I told you when we were out in the Pine Barrens." Doug leaned forward in his chair. They were seated in his living room, the afternoon sun dipping down into the western sky, casting weird shadows across his carpet.

Russell tapped at the photograph. "This isn't a body. It's a picture of a body."

Doug stood up and began a slow pace in front of the sofa. He didn't speak for several minutes. "Same difference. This is too much," he said finally. "What we need to be doing is figuring out how much to report, how to report it so it makes sense, and what parts we can keep to ourselves."

"There's no way to be selective. If we turn in the photograph, where'd we get it? How long did we know she was missing? How about her car?"

"Nobody knows about the car. It wasn't official," he pointed out.

"Doug, they're gonna run it for prints. Are mine all over it? And we took evidence from the back seat. Then there's the letter opener and the tape we found in the woods. What do we do about that?"

"If she's dead, her body's going to turn up. Eventually. And then they'll put all this together anyway. So let's sort it out first. We go in and tell the truth, no lies to remember. Just lies of omission."

"And Joanne?"

Doug stopped pacing and looked at him. "She's not in this. She can't keep anything straight."

Russell's mind was spinning all the angles around. "I did wear gloves when I drove her car back. But what about all the other photographs?" He knew Doug was right. They should have turned this in a long time ago.

"They're not relevant," Doug said. Russell's head snapped up. "Not really. We only need to turn in—"

"It's a string. We pull one end, the whole thing follows. And why is it okay to turn in Ava's picture and not the others?"

Doug sat back down in his chair. He was getting fidgety, running his hands up and down his pant leg. "Because those other bodies aren't going to suddenly float down the Delaware River or come to the muddy surface of the soil with the spring thaw. This is self-preservation only."

"Okay. Okay. Let's run this through. We say I opened the mailbox because Ava'd been missing for more than a week. I was worried. Her aunt didn't seem concerned. It was wrong, blah blah blah, but the picture was in the envelope."

"Her car was there, in the driveway. Unlocked. Keys in the ignition. You went in the car"—he motioned to Russell—"before you realized anything had happened to her. She had a habit of doing this disappearing thing, so her aunt said. Makes sense."

"The letter opener and the tape we keep to ourselves," Russell said. "What about the candlestick?"

"If they start with Ava's disappearance and probable death, they may never connect it to the priest. So the candlestick is irrelevant."

"But Ava's death *will* lead to Marie. And that's where they need to focus. She's all the evidence they need." Russell stood up and took a deep breath. "If this goes wrong, Doug—"

"It's not going to. We're going to sit here, all day if we have to, and get everything pounded out. But tell me about the house. Joanne said she saw Claire? Like actually saw her?"

He nodded. "Yeah. But I think it was Marie. The two looked a lot alike. Now why the nun's sitting in a dark house, no clue."

Doug ran a hand through his hair. "You should've put a tail on her a long time ago."

"You mean I should have tailed her myself. There was no one else."

Doug looked at his friend. "I'm really sorry about Ava. I know you liked her."

Russell nodded. He felt a pang somewhere deep inside him when he let his mind sit still long enough to realize she was really dead. From the picture, it looked like she was attacked but put up a fight. And the death took place somewhere in the Pine Barrens. While he was asleep in her bed, his liver working overtime to get rid of the Pinot Noir from his system, she was being driven to the woods and slaughtered like an animal, the killer only hesitating long enough to snap a picture. Was Marie calculating enough to do that? And more curious, why would she? He shivered and his pocket started rattling. It took a few seconds for him to realize it was his phone.

"Guess what?" she said.

"What, Joanne?"

"That blazer wasn't Ava's. I kept looking at it and it seemed too big. Then I pulled out a picture of us at Gail's retirement party—when we went to the Victor Club? Ava was wearing her jacket. Except hers was single breasted. This one is almost identical but it's double breasted."

"So?" He was getting impatient. Not in the mood for trivial details.

"So the jacket I have has to belong to Claire. It was hanging right in that front closet. I saw it and assumed it was Ava's. But it wasn't. They just look the same."

"And?"

"And, Mister Moody, I'm-Too-Busy-for-This, Claire's jacket had something in the pocket."

"What?"

"A pawn ticket. Philadelphia. 'Joe's Pawnshop—We Buy Gold.' Eleventh and South."

"Why would Claire have pawned anything? She had money." He was thinking out loud more than asking a question.

"How better to hide something temporarily? I'm heading over there to see what it is before you talk me out of it. Bye."

He ended the call and looked at Doug. "So as we're thinking about turning in the evidence for one piece of the puzzle, all the other pieces keep growing in number."

After two and a half hours of brainstorming, interrogating each other, stopping and starting, backtracking, and fixing details, they landed on the perfect blend of outright truth and outright omission.

Doug patted Russell's back. "Are we ready? Calm, steady, just like we practiced. We've got this."

CHAPTER 61

Marie stood with her back to the wall. She was having trouble breathing. She'd just left the man on the street to die. He'd still been standing, holding on to the brick to keep himself in place, when she'd rushed away. Maybe he'd crumpled onto the sidewalk. Maybe he was at the hospital now and the police were checking the surveillance cameras for the killer. Maybe.

She'd come back to the hotel, locked the door, and chained it. It was a beautiful suite, luxurious, flowers filling the vases on the nightstand. Thick bedding, a Jacuzzi bathtub, and separate tiled shower area. Nothing bad could possibly happen in a space like this. She could just stay and order room service until her money ran out. How long would that be?

She replayed what had happened over in her mind. What exactly had happened? He'd attacked her. He'd chased her and pulled her down the street back to the hotel with the intention of killing her because he was paid to do it. She had convinced herself she was crazy. That she was paranoid, connecting things that weren't real. And here it was. *Enough of a reality check, Dr. Rasmussen?* This insane woman was now turning on her family. No other reason. Enough.

Though no matter how many times she said the word *enough*, it didn't register. It was never going to be enough. She wasn't the one who started the war. The words said back there in the Bayside Inn were coming true. *It's dangerous out there.* Indeed. Marie began to pace. What now? Where was she? What did she want?

She stopped and closed her eyes, thinking of how the knife sliced his clothes but hesitated at the skin, resisting going through, stretching the skin that was protecting his organs, almost like God was giving her a chance to back out and run away. But she ignored it and pushed harder and felt the pop of the metal piercing his flesh.

What was worse, stabbing someone or choking the air from their lungs? She'd done both now. Ava'd been cut but Marie hadn't done it. She'd watched, horrified, unsure whether to attack Quinn or help him. She'd watched Ava's face, twisting in pain but defiant till the end. Then Marie jumped in and wrapped her hands around the girl's throat and watched her eyeballs roll back in her head. Saw her fight, felt her clawing at her hands, a spirit inside of her that didn't want to give up. Struggling against a darkness that was inevitable.

Marie released the air from her own lungs, let it stream from her mouth slowly now. She'd left the convent with her bags days ago, but religion had left her soul that day in the woods with Ava. And it wasn't coming back. That day had brought nightmares and flashbacks and a repeated pondering of events from nineteen years before. Her thoughts went to the dead woman with the priest, even when she willed them not to. Wandering into the church that night, unaware. And though Marie hadn't seen it happen, the images were in her mind as if she had. She'd certainly seen the aftermath.

She'd seen the pictures of the woman. Dark hair. Hazel eyes. Fair skin. A look in her eye that said life had been unkind, but there might be hope. The photograph on her passport even showed a smile curling her lips just a bit upward, as if there was still something to be happy about. She'd arrived in Philadelphia not even four days before she was killed. Wandering about the city with nowhere to go. Until she'd stumbled upon the shelter of the church.

Marie put her hands to her ears, trying to block out the memories of that night. The terrible fight between her and Claire after their father had abruptly arrived covered in blood, asking the impossible from the two of them.

She'd agreed to go to the car that night in Brooklyn so Ross wouldn't attract any more attention. She'd fetched the murder weapon and his bloody coat wrapped in a plastic bag, and more, a bundle that she carried against her shoulder. She'd returned to find Claire in a rage. She'd agreed to all of this—Ross, on the floor, covered in blood, had broken her down—but now she was in a panic, had folded herself into a big armchair, consoling herself with tears. She blamed Marie for feeling pity for the man, for the softness that always played in her eyes.

"You're a fool, Marie," she'd spat, her eyes rimmed with red, her breath filled with wine. "You've destroyed us both."

Marie set the plastic bag on the floor. "Can you think of anyone but yourself, Claire?"

"People are dead. And more will die, Sister." Claire had jumped from her chair, semi-intoxicated, wobbly, and uncontrolled. "They will. You got us into this mess and you will pay with your own life. Mark my words." She stormed to her bedroom and slammed the door.

The noise made the hefty bundle in her arms squirm. She placed the child on the couch and covered her with a blanket. The girl who was not yet Ava opened her eyes, confused and disoriented from sleep. "Mamma?"

Marie placed a cool hand on the child's forehead. "Shh. Go to sleep." She couldn't help but notice the girl's dress and arms were sprayed with blood. How could Claire just turn away from this?

Promises made so many years ago had finally come home to roost. Marie walked into the bathroom and stripped off her clothes, turned on the shower, and watched how the steam filled the room. Then she stepped under the hot torrent, all the while considering her options. If someone attacked her, they were going to be surprised to find no softness in Marie's eyes anymore, just hard, calculating self-preservation. And the knife she'd hold would absolutely be capable of piercing skin, flesh, and bone.

CHAPTER 62

The pawnshop was on the corner of Eleventh and South, another area of the city that had changed over the years. It was becoming more commercial, connecting more with the end of South Street closer to the Delaware River. The outside of the shop had little appeal to draw customers in. A large white *We Buy Gold* sign filled the grimy window. A neon *Open* light was in the upper corner. The glass door had the shop hours, the rules and regulations. This business survived by drawing the needy, not the browsers. It was small, crammed with all kinds of odds and ends people had either parted with for a quick bit of cash or surrendered by lack of payment.

Joanne had learned the rules of the pawn business in one frenzied weekend in Vegas with her brother. Every item that was pawned was registered; the owner had to present identification and was fingerprinted. Sometimes even photographed. The ticket she held was for an item pawned a week and two days ago—not enough time for a payment to be due. But in order for Joanne to retrieve the item, the original owner—whoever had dropped the item off—would have to sign the ticket over to her. But she had absolutely no idea who that was, even if she wanted to try and attempt a forgery.

Joanne put on what she thought was her best, most innocent smile and pulled open the glass door. The man behind the counter was older, balding, and not interested. He squinted up at her and dropped his head back down, though she was standing in front of him.

She pulled out the ticket and placed it on the counter. "I wanted to know how much I owe on this." She said it with authority though her palms were sweating, her hands trembling, so she shoved them in her coat pocket.

He took the ticket and then pulled out a ledger book. No computers here. "You just left it. Not a whole lotta interest. Three twenty-seven even'll do it."

Joanne tried to hold back the surprised look on her face. "You'll take credit cards?"

He nodded and disappeared in the back of the store. A few minutes later he came out with a cardboard box, about eight by eight square, and dropped it onto the counter. "Boss was hoping you wouldn't come for it. He could sell it easy, maybe not here—not the right clientele—but the right collector? Worth a bundle."

"Can I see it?" She started to reach for the box.

"Money. Then it's all yours. And I need your ID."

"Fine." She reached into her wallet and handed him her credit card.

He took it without realizing she hadn't given him her driver's license. He opened the box and pulled out a Polaroid camera in a plastic bag. A very early 1950s model. And three boxes of film. "The camera is not so rare. You can still find them. But not modified like this. To take modern Polaroid or Fuji film. Vintage made modern. How long have you had this?"

"Lord, I don't know. I'm a pack rat. Tons of stuff in my attic. Belongs to my grandmother. I dropped it off for her as a favor."

"Not unless you dyed your hair and gained some poundage since then." He realized he'd been insensitive. "Sorry." He pulled the photograph from an envelope that was shoved in an accordion file. "We take pictures when we take an item."

Joanne stared into the mugshot-style photograph of a thin woman, dark hair cut to just below her ears, part of her bangs swept across her face. Eyes cast downward. The picture was dark and blurred. It was hard to make out the features. Claire? "Okay, it's my cousin. She was short of cash when she turned this in, and I wanted to do her a favor—pick it up as a surprise." Her eyes were riveted on the date in the corner. The camera had been pawned two days after Ava disappeared.

His face creased. "Can't do it. You know that. Unless you can get her to sign over the ticket to you." He pointed to the box printed on the bottom right-hand corner of the ticket. "Bring it back signed, with the money, and it's all yours."

"Her whole name on the ticket is Claire Lavoisier-Saunders. Would I know that if she wasn't related? She went to France. Won't be back for at least three weeks. Help me out here."

"I don't care if her name is b-o-b Bob. It's not happening. It'll be more than three twenty-seven when she gets back. Call for the total. You still got plenty of time on this."

"Fine. Do me a favor. Don't open the camera or play with it, and especially not the silver button that takes the picture." She pointed at it through the plastic bag. "It's very fragile and it broke before. Just keep it safe and I'll be back."

"Right." He shoved the camera and film back in the box. "Remember interest is accruing."

She heard the bell of the door closing behind her as she left the shop. Claire was alive. And she was here. Or had been here—just over a week ago. She was involved in this debacle. And took the murderer's camera to the pawnshop. How? Why?

Her mind was spinning but her stomach was churning. Only seven blocks down was Copa. The best quick margaritas and Mexican food in the area. She started to walk in the direction of the restaurant—seeking comfort in food and drink was always good. She stuffed the pawn ticket back into the slot in her wallet.

She scurried down the street, dialing Russell's number. It went to voicemail. "Damn you, Russell, this is important. Call me back. Urgent-urgent."

◆ ◆ ◆

Russell heard the phone vibrate in his pocket but couldn't answer it. He was seated in the interrogation room at the Prosecutor's Office—this time on the other side of the table. "So, let's go over this again, Russell. Detective Bowers. You chose not to file a missing-persons report on Ms. Saunders, though she's been missing for weeks, until you intercepted this photograph?"

CHAPTER 63

Marie had splurged and ordered a salad, broiled shrimp, a cheese spread, and a magnum of champagne. She'd finished showering and wrapped herself in a large white robe. She desperately wanted a drink—something much stronger than champagne—but she was petrified to leave the room. If the stabbed man wasn't dead, he might be waiting, and if he was dead, the police would certainly be circling like wild turkeys looking for prey. This cache could last her all day.

She had the food spread in front of her on the bed and was picking at the salad, the champagne half-finished, when there was a rap at her door. She jumped, pulled the robe around her, and backed against the wall, almost afraid to take a breath. The knock came again, louder. She tiptoed and peered through the peephole. One man stood there. She didn't know him. His head was down; he had a thick shock of brown hair. Definitely not the man who'd met the end of her knife.

"Either you need to open the door or I'll be waiting in the lobby for you when you eventually leave the room, Ms. Saunders. I know you're in there."

She looked through at him again. He looked like nobody. Not a criminal and not really a cop, but it was hard to tell these days. Maybe someone from the hotel? With a question about her reservation? He did say he would be in the lobby. But why wouldn't they just call the room? She hesitated only a second before whipping the door open. He wasn't from the hotel.

He escorted her back inside and shut the door. "I'm Detective Johnson from the Philadelphia Police Department. I have some questions for you, Ms. Saunders. Do you mind doing this here? Or would you rather get dressed and come downtown? Either one is fine, I didn't mean to intrude."

She sat down on the wing chair and crossed her legs. "Am I obligated to answer questions, Detective? Without an attorney? Have I done something wrong?"

He smiled and she felt awkward, sitting in nothing but a robe. She took a long swallow of champagne. "You don't have to answer anything if you don't want to. But it's odd, because you don't even know what I want to ask."

She swung her legs a bit to the side. Her insides were on fire with nerves, and she was only hoping it didn't show on her face. "I've been here for two days. Just left the convent after more than twenty years, and I needed to sort myself out." She sipped at her champagne and poured more in her glass. "What is it that you wanted?" She knew it was about the man she'd stabbed. There'd be no other reason for the police to be here. She formulated a quick plan. If the questions got sticky, she'd just end it, tell them she'd meet them at the station, and then disappear.

He sat down across from her. "Your niece. Ava Saunders? When is the last time you saw her?"

Marie bit down on her lip so hard it drew blood. She wasn't expecting this, and the nerves inside of her exploded. Her brain was clicking through the options. How much did they know? How could she answer and not trip over herself? "Several weeks, I'd say. I don't live with her."

He opened a notebook. "You lived at Christ the King." She nodded. "And Ava was staying at her mother's house in Haddonfield?" Marie nodded. "But you've been preparing the house for sale?"

She nodded again. "It was always the plan after my sister died, that the house would be put up for sale. So, yes."

"And where was Ava going to live?"

She shrugged. "She's finished college, has a job. I assume she's either going to stay in the area and get an apartment or go to France. My mother is working on arrangements for her there." *Keep everything in present tense.*

"And it hasn't concerned you that she's been gone for weeks? No word. No work. Not answering her phone?"

Marie shrugged. "She took some time off from work after her mother, my sister, died. It didn't concern me that she wasn't at work. And we weren't so close that we spoke every day. I didn't even know she wasn't answering her phone."

He looked down. "Yes. Claire Lavoisier-Saunders." He looked up. "She died two months ago—"

"One month, two weeks, and four days, to be exact."

"Yes. And she was Ava's mother? Biological or adoptive?"

Marie stood up. "What exactly is this about, Detective? Ava missing? I don't know where she is. She might've gone to France. Did you call my mother, Anais Lavoisier? Maybe she went to Canada to see friends? She went to school in Montreal."

He stood. "We don't believe she's left the country."

She shrugged. "Then I don't believe I have any other suggestions. She'll turn up. She always does."

"Meaning she disappears often?"

She tried to smile but gritted her teeth instead. "Like a bird in flight. Here, there. Where will she land next?"

He shifted his weight but didn't move to the door as she wanted. "You didn't like her? Any particular reason?"

Marie edged away from him. "I didn't not like her, Detective. She's family, just always a little unsettled."

He didn't budge. "So you haven't talked to her? No one called you to see if you'd seen her?"

Marie's mind flitted to Russell, the day he came to the house. "As a matter of fact, her friend Russell, a detective, I think in Camden, came by the house when I was there sorting through things. He asked about her. I told him the same thing."

"Was her car there? When he came by the house?"

Marie was startled. *The car.* She shrugged. "I don't remember, honestly."

"But he was asking for her? So if her car was there, you'd have known, I'm sure?"

Marie shrugged. "I might have, but I don't remember."

"At some point it was returned. The car."

Marie leaned over and opened the door. "Then I guess you know more than I do. I don't mean to cut this short, but I have things to do."

"Just two more questions," he said. She held the door and didn't respond. "One, why has someone been calling Ava's phone from Claire Saunders's cell phone? It wasn't disconnected after her death?"

"I guess it wasn't. And two?"

"Do you have any idea who might've taken this picture?" He held out the photograph of Ava for Marie to see.

She let go of the door and stumbled back onto the bed. "Oh my God. She's dead? Ava's dead?" She held out her hand to see the picture.

"So let's start this questioning all over again. I need to know what Ava was involved in before she disappeared, when you last saw her—the truth this time. And if you've had any occasion to visit the Pine Barrens recently." Marie didn't respond but leaned over and grabbed her glass, swallowing the rest of her drink. She was stuck. She couldn't answer any of these questions. He knew too much. "Oh, and one more thing. Was your sister cremated? Or was her body interred?"

She glared up at him. “My mother took her body to France for burial. And I think I’d like to end this now and contact my attorney. I’ll be in touch.”

“This isn’t actually a Philadelphia problem. It only came on our desk because you’re here. When Haddonfield PD went looking for you, a Sister Regina Collins at Christ the King said you might be here, in this hotel.”

Regina. Marie had told her she was coming to the Sofitel to rest. From now on she’d have to keep her plans to herself.

“So do me a favor and contact an attorney in New Jersey. And then stay there. They’d prefer you find a place in Camden County, actually. Your sister’s house? Or the convent, maybe?” He handed her a card. “That’s Detective Hughes from Camden that’s going to be overseeing the case. Have your lawyer call him in the next couple days. But don’t wait too long, or I’m sure they’ll put out a warrant.” He opened the door and was gone.

She heard it snap shut behind him, but her head was down. Her fate was either death at the hands of family or imprisonment for the murder of her niece. Which was worse? She rushed into the bathroom and threw up the contents of her meager lunch.

CHAPTER 64

Russell was lying on the couch, staring at the ceiling. He hadn't moved in over an hour. He was looking at the way the light hit the plaster, making it seem like the paint was peeling. It wasn't. He'd checked twice. Juliette came in and sat down at the end of the sofa, putting his feet in her lap.

"There's nothing I can say to make this better, Russ. But it's not as bad as it could have been. You know that, right?"

He didn't move his eyes. "I could have gotten fired. I could have gotten Doug fired, so you're right."

She tapped his feet. "How's Doug?"

He gave a half shrug. "As well as I'd expect. He doesn't blame me, exactly."

"Look. Let's go out. Go to dinner. You pick, but I feel like Mexican. Mexican Food Factory? Margaritas."

He felt sick to his stomach at the name of the restaurant where he'd gone with Ava just weeks ago. "Not hungry."

She stood up. "Fine. Let's have drinks here. I can make martinis. And I know we have beer—"

"Beer and food isn't going to change the fact that I've been suspended for ninety days. I have a permanent letter in my file—*obstructing justice*, it says. But worse than that—Doug does too."

"You knew this might happen when you turned this in. You got off kind of easy, I'd say." She hesitated. "I do need to ask you why you did all this, Russell."

"Which part?"

"What was it with you and this girl? Ava? Were you with her? Cheating? What?"

"Pile it on, Juliette. My plate isn't full enough." He couldn't even look at her. He knew she was right. He'd almost thrown away everything, his career, Juliette, for this woman he knew nothing about.

"You obviously don't need dinner or drinks with me, you've got this whole pity party going on alone. For the record, I think you were. And I think that's a big part of what you're feeling. Guilty. And this moment might not be the time to talk about it. But at some point, we have to."

"Wrong. Wrong and wrong. I feel guilty about Doug. I feel guilty about Joanne. And I feel terrible that Ava was killed and that she knew she would be . . ."

Juliette stopped. "What do you mean she knew she would be?"

He rubbed his face. "She told me she knew she was going to die."

Juliette sat down again, her head tilted to the side. "She thought someone was after her?"

He shrugged. "Not sure. She didn't seem scared. More like it was an inevitability, like time was running out. But she was drunk."

"Okay, wait. Stop. Tell me everything from the beginning."

He closed his eyes and tried to remember everything she said. Juliette was quiet, taking it all in.

"So she handpicked you to go running after the mystery, like a dog?" Her voice had risen. "And you did?"

"I guess I did. It had everything. Old serial murders. Photographs. An abandoned child. A dead woman—"

"You mean Claire? Or Ava?"

He sat up. "Both, really. Or neither. I could use those drinks now."

Juliette got up. "I'll grab some beers. This is interesting. There's an answer in all of this that we're missing. We need to go over it again." She disappeared into the kitchen.

Russell smiled. He should have clued Juliette in a long time ago. Her mind was a razor's edge.

A few minutes later she came out with two bottles and an opener. She popped the caps off and handed one to him. "So again, what did she want you for? To legitimately look into things for her or to uncover information she already knew? To lead you where she wanted you to go?"

Russell was thinking. "Maybe both? She seemed to be looking for something."

"What? What was she looking for, Russell? Think."

He put his head down so far it was almost in his lap. "To know why Claire had the Owens picture."

"Did she ever wonder if they were her parents?"

He stopped to think, all the conversations playing through his mind. "I wanted to get DNA but couldn't. Because it wasn't official. But I don't remember her pushing it. Or really asking."

"So that wasn't a question for her. Because she probably knew they weren't. So what was she asking about?"

He sat upright. "Jack Quinn had been stalking her—broke into her house. Took the picture. She was concerned about that."

"What else?"

"When I told her she wasn't abandoned in the church as a baby, she told me to find out who she really was."

They looked at each other. "In the very center of this is the woman that died with the priest. The big unknown. Is that it? Maybe?" Juliette offered. "I'm just throwing things out here."

"We need to find out who she was. Her name. And maybe that's what Ava wanted from me from the very beginning. To find her name. And to flush out Quinn?"

"Because the woman was her mother? With no name. Murdered and left naked?"

His cell phone rang. He put the phone to his ear and heard Joanne's loud voice at the other end. "I will give you two guesses as to what was pawned. And who pawned it," she said. "Never mind guesses. It's the camera and Claire—I told you she was alive. I couldn't get it, but I saw it."

Russell looked at Juliette. "Can you get to my house now? I turned the case in to the Prosecutor's Office this afternoon."

"No you didn't, Russell! Why, when we were so close?"

"Doug."

He heard the sound of her car door opening. "I'm on my way. But you better have food and drinks waiting. I'm giving up Copa because of your nonsense. Doug's an idiot."

CHAPTER 65

By the time Marie found her car where she'd parked it, she was trembling, soaked through to her undergarments. Rain pounded the sidewalk and street, and the sweet leather coat she'd borrowed from Claire was destroyed. After the policeman had left her hotel room, she couldn't eat another bite of the enormous spread. She wanted to sit and pick at the salad, order some more champagne, and think. But every second hung in the air, filled with fear of another invasion. Every noise made her jump. Her stomach was sick and she'd vomited several times before she could bring herself to get dressed.

Go back to New Jersey, he'd said. Get a lawyer. Check in with the Camden County Prosecutor's Office before they came looking for her. She reached for her phone and dialed Claire's number again. It went to voicemail. She held the phone in her hand. She was completely and utterly alone in the world for the first time ever.

"This is your fault. I've got the police crawling all over the death in the woods. I got a stabbed man who's God knows where, who, by the way, you sent after me, that they'll connect to me sooner or later"—she shook the phone, yelling at it, though no one was on the other end—"and you started all of this. All of it!" She threw the phone into the seat next to her; it hit the door and bounced onto the floor. "I knew I shouldn't trust you. You're going to stick me with this, just like I thought. And everyone says I'm paranoid!"

After crossing the Ben Franklin Bridge into New Jersey, she was on autopilot and ended up in front of Claire's house without thinking. The Victorian was dark. Ava's silver Honda Accord was still in the driveway; a few stray pine needles still clung to the wiper blades. *Get yourself together, Marie. Go in, dry off, relax. Call a lawyer in the morning.* She took two deep breaths and fished the house keys out of her bag.

The rain had settled to a steady drizzle but she was already drenched, her dark hair plastered to her head; the water had soaked through her leather boots and oozed between her toes with every stride. She'd just stepped through the door and turned on the light when she saw the black-and-white car pull up in front of the house.

"Shit," she muttered. "They told me I had a few days." She dropped her purse onto the floor and waited. Her chest was heavy, she couldn't handle more questioning now.

Two plainclothes officers headed toward her. One was tall with brown hair, and for a minute she thought it was Russell, but as he got closer she saw she was wrong. The other, shorter and darker, both in hair and skin, approached slowly. Though they saw her standing on the porch waiting for them, they were going to do this in their own time.

"Ms. Lavoisier-Saunders?" the shorter of the two said.

"It's just Saunders, actually. The Philadelphia police said I had time for this interview. I need to contact my lawyer. So . . ."

They looked at each other and then back at her. "Is that your car?" They pointed to the silver Honda.

She took a step back toward the door. "How could you know I was coming here, anyway? I didn't even know. Like I said, I'd like to contact my lawyer. Can I come in tomorrow? Just tell me where to go."

"I think there's some confusion, Ms. Saunders. We got a call on this Honda Accord, that it was involved in an accident tonight. Registration led us here. What matter are you referring to?" The tall one was taking the lead.

"I was just in Philadelphia talking to—it doesn't matter. The car belongs to my niece, Ava Saunders. But no one's been driving it."

He walked over and put his hand on the hood. "It's warm." Then he went to the driver's-side window and peered inside.

She was starting to panic. "Look. You don't have my permission to look in that car. I need you to leave now." Marie was trying to stand her ground, hands on her hips, but she was ready to sob, and the officers seemed to hear it in her voice.

"Ma'am. There's something dark smeared on the passenger's-side seat. From here it looks like blood." The two officers climbed the steps to the porch, where she was standing. "Are you okay?" They seemed to be scanning her from head to foot, looking for an injury. "Something happened with this car. The fender bender at Haddon and Cuthbert that was called in is the least of it. So you come in and talk, or I call this in and we take you to the station." She started to open her mouth but he put his hand up. "And yes, if you want, call your lawyer—that might be a good idea."

Marie pushed the front door open and motioned them inside. Though she felt dizzy and was desperately trying to put the pieces together, none of them fit. No one had the keys to that car. The night it showed up in the driveway, she had taken the keys from the ignition—the ones that had belonged to Ava—and put them in her purse. Claire was the only one with the spare set. In one quick survey, she saw the bottle of whiskey on the dining-room table. She couldn't tell, but was pretty sure it hadn't been there before, and also pretty sure it was empty. The clean, ready-for-show house had been dirtied by someone.

The shorter officer took a seat on the sofa and started. "Haddon Township Police, by the way. I'm Officer Jeffers, this is Officer Diorio. We got a call about an accident at the northeast corner of Haddon and Cuthbert—you know, near the Wawa. No major damage to the other car. But the silver Honda Accord, with those plates, took off."

Marie peeled off the leather jacket and hung it on the doorknob of the closet. She pushed wet strands of hair from her face. "I need a towel. Excuse me for a minute."

She started up the stairs and stopped. A bloody handprint on the wall—the bottom of a handprint, anyway—smeared, as if someone was using it to brace themselves going up the steps. And a few more spots farther up toward the landing. She turned slightly and looked behind her. Drops of blood were spattered on the floor near the front door. She froze in place and turned around. "Never mind. I don't need a towel. This won't take long."

But the officers saw it too. Jeffers put a hand out. "Don't move. When's the last time you were here?" he asked. "In this house?"

Marie shook her head. The tears were starting, and as much as she wanted to stop them, she couldn't. She had no answer for any of this. "I don't know," she whispered. "A week, maybe. I was in Philadelphia, at the Sofitel. The Philadelphia police were there questioning me about something else. They can vouch for me."

"We're going to look around. Make sure no one is hurt. Okay? You stay here." Diorio climbed the steps slowly.

Marie was frozen in place. There was something terrible upstairs. Another dead body. She knew it. And there was absolutely nothing she could do but stand here with the short cop and wait for what was coming. Though her mind kept playing over and over: *Claire, please do not let this happen. Claire, please do not let this happen.*

"Jeffers," the cop finally called down, "call for an ambulance and backup. Possible homicide. There's a white male up here on the bathroom floor. Looks like he was stabbed in the abdomen. Blood is congealing. Might have been dead for a while."

Marie just closed her eyes. "White male. Stabbed," she whispered. She dropped onto the couch. *Probably wearing a black hoodie with a red hood. Red sneakers*—the man she'd stabbed earlier had been magically transported to the upstairs bathroom. *Fuck.* She almost said it out loud, but she didn't. From this moment forward she was keeping her mouth shut. This was all a setup.

CHAPTER 66

Marie picked up her phone and dialed the number, but it went to voicemail. The entire front yard was filled with cars now. An ambulance was parked behind the Honda Accord. She'd been sitting on the couch for over an hour, still in damp clothes. The police had allowed her to use the bathroom twice. And she'd made coffee. But the rest of the time she'd been confined to one spot on the sofa so as not to contaminate evidence.

She started to push the buttons on her phone again when the officer glanced at her. "Who are you calling?"

"I need to call my lawyer. I have that right," she said. He stood three feet away, directing traffic to the second floor.

"You need one, I'll say that. Go ahead, but stay right here on the couch where I can see you. Or I'll cuff you."

She dialed the number, fully expecting it to go to voicemail again. She moved the phone slightly from her ear when she heard a voice. "Hello?"

"Where are you?" Marie hissed. "I'm at the house. With a dead body and a house crawling with cops. What did you do? Where the fuck are you?"

"I actually saw them pull up. As I was leaving. I watched from down the block. Sorry, Sister. I didn't plan it this way, but you stabbed my forgery man."

Marie leaned forward and put her hand to her head. "Forgery man?" she whispered, glancing over her shoulder at the officer. "You sent him to kill me."

She heard a laugh on the other end of the phone. "You're out of your mind. He was getting me a fake passport, driver's license, birth certificate, so I could leave the country. Not cheap, you know. I sent him to you to see if you needed one too and so you could give him the rest of the money. But did that happen? No. You stabbed him. And"—she hesitated—"I'm beginning to think you've gotten crazier. Like I-need-to-go-back-to-the-loony-bin crazy, or just more aggressive. Really aggressive." Marie heard the distinctive sound of her pulling on a cigarette. "You cut him up and left him on the street, Marie. To die."

"So you brought him here?" She looked up to see paramedics bringing the forgery man down on a gurney. His face was a shade of pale gray that only death knows.

"He called me. I wanted to save him, actually. To save you and me. To patch him up and fix this nightmare you created. Where else could I take him but my house? Think about it."

Marie stood up, and the officer came closer to her and motioned for her to sit back down. "So you had an accident on the way here, hit someone with a dying man in the car, just took off, and parked the car in this driveway anyway? And then just left him here?"

"Are you recording this?"

"No," Marie whispered. They were putting him in a body bag. The zipper starting at his feet, going up to his abdomen, where he'd been stabbed, all the way up over his face, erasing a life.

"Swear to God?" And then a chuckle.

"This isn't funny. It's not the time to be making stupid jokes."

"The situation got out of hand, is what happened. I had him all bandaged up, lying on the bathroom floor, but he recovered a little too much and he was pissed you stabbed him. I don't think he was going to let it go. So I killed him for you. Finished what you started. You see now? There was no other choice."

"Where are you? Where's Anais?" Marie demanded.

"She's meeting me in Paris tomorrow morning, if I can actually get out of this shit town. I'm in a hotel, waiting for my passport to be delivered."

Marie saw the forensics team in their white suits going in and out of the front door. "So . . . he forged enough for you to get a passport? And you're leaving to fly to Paris. Meeting Maman? And me—what am I doing?"

There was a hesitation. "He got me a driver's license before you killed him, so it was hard, but yeah, I got enough to get a passport. You're on your own."

Marie leaned forward, rocking slightly on the edge of the sofa. Forensics went by, talking about hair and fibers, partial prints. "You won't make it out of the country. They're combing the upstairs bathroom now. You left some hair and fingerprints, I think. So they'll know you're not dead."

There was nothing on the other end of the phone for some seconds. "Did I? Or were they your hairs from your brush? Guess we'll have to see."

She dropped her head to her hand. "Why are you doing this to me?"

Her voice was angry. "You left me in an impossible position, Marie. I spent months putting all this together, to finally make things right and get out. I finally got Anais to agree to help me, and that wasn't easy."

"I don't believe that," Marie spat. She glanced up. The officers had their backs turned, not paying any attention. "Not after Ross. She won't let you do this to me."

There was a sigh. "Look, I really am sorry, but if they blame you, they won't come looking for me. I'll handle Anais. Bye, Sister."

Marie knew she'd been led right into a trap. "The whole world was better off when you were dead. Why'd you come back, anyway?" She didn't wait for an answer before clicking off the line.

She watched from her perch on the couch. People coming and going, whispering. The body was gone to the morgue. The white-suits were finishing up. She saw two officers approach her and knew time was up. She barely flinched when they put the cuffs on.

CHAPTER 67

It was the shoes. Black leather flats. Slip-ons. Leather sole. Nondescript, for the most part, except they weren't. Russell'd gone through the police reports at least seven times, reviewing the Jane Doe's meager belongings, and he kept returning to the shoes. Maritan was the brand. Manufactured by a small company in Verona, Italy. The detective had followed through at the time of her death, calling the company, talking to the owner. They'd only been in business a year, and their sales were primarily local. Exports were minimal. And in 1996, no online store.

Where would she have gotten the shoes from? He pushed back in his chair. During the initial investigation they'd put the artist's rendition of her face up everywhere and not one person responded. Well—that wasn't true, but not one response led to anything. No one knew her. How she ended up in the church with those shoes on was a mystery.

"Makes no sense," Juliette said. "A woman doesn't walk around with nothing. No purse? Even if she were new to the area, she'd have something. A passport, a comb. Whoever killed her probably took it."

"What advantages do we have now that Detective Bishop didn't have when he investigated this in ninety-six?" Russell asked. He was thinking out loud.

Joanne sat up suddenly. "Marie knows her name, I bet ya anything."

"More Internet connectivity. Better data banks and much more sophisticated DNA testing," Juliette answered Russell's question.

"The world is much more connected than it was twenty years ago. So let's suppose this woman just got here, in this country, maybe a few days before. From Italy—"

"Why—" Joanne started.

"It's the only thing that makes sense. Her shoes. It's her shoes. So, at the time they contacted Maritan. They sent photographs of the woman, but nothing came of it. But maybe if we post her picture on every website we can think of—Italian websites, missing persons in Italy. We ask for help from the police there. Maybe we'll get a hit. I can't believe she has no family at all . . ."

Juliette leaned on the back of his chair. "Bad timing for turning this in. Or you'd have had a free pass to see Marie in jail before she makes bail. And I'm assuming she will, because rich people don't sit there long."

He put his chin in his hands. "I had no choice. Doug was going to turn it in anyway. But you're right. Getting her in jail, angry and vulnerable and ready to talk, would have been great."

"Figure out a way to get in there and see her. You're smart." She put a hand on his shoulder and shook it. "And let's get posting. But I suggest we use the artist's rendition. The actual dead photo is creepy."

"Yeah, I'm stinking mad at you and Doug for turning this in. I found the camera." Joanne jabbed at her chest. "Me. Not you. I should have never called to tell you about it."

His eyes flickered irritation. "Even if you'd managed to get that camera out of the pawnshop, we have no way of running prints and matching it to a data bank without drawing attention. At least now I'm partially looped in and John'll call me if they get anything. Are you working tomorrow?" he asked.

Her eyes widened. "Yeeess," she said slowly. "Why? What are you thinking?"

"Can you go to the jail? Interview Marie? Talk to her?"

"I don't have any reason to go into the jail. None. We call if Judge Simmons needs anything over there."

Russell took her by her arms. "We left your name out of all of this. I can't go. Only you. Make up a reason."

She shook free. "You don't think they're going to find it odd that I'm all up on Marie after what happened with you? Give them credit for two brain cells." She rubbed her arm where he'd grabbed her. "How about Juliette? They don't know her at the jail. She can say she's a lawyer. She's pretty, they won't question her too much."

Juliette raised a hand without turning around. "I'm on call tonight. Then I have a meeting in the morning. Besides, I'm not a good liar."

"Russell, the jail doesn't know you're on suspension. Just go in, act like everything is normal, and it will be," Joanne offered.

He scowled. "If I got caught, I'd have my badge pulled. Period."

"I guess we could find a real lawyer to do it," Joanne said. "I know plenty. If they get questioned, it's no big deal. They can say they wanted to handle her case pro bono. It happens all the time." She hesitated. "Just give me a list of questions they need to ask."

Russell felt his phone vibrate and moved into the dining room to talk. "Okay, thanks, John. I appreciate it. No. I owe you. Bye." He walked back into the living room. "Marie's prints are all over the camera. The print on the button that snaps the picture belongs to Marie. There's three other sets of partial prints on there, but they don't have a match."

"So Marie was the last one to touch it. Maybe she took that last photograph of Ava?" Joanne said.

"We can't be certain. Maybe Marie took the camera out to photograph something else afterward. Not knowing?" Juliette offered.

Joanne shook her head. "Photograph what? The camera was pawned two days after Ava disappeared."

He grabbed his coat. "Well, we're going to the jail before Marie disappears. Juliette, post that drawing wherever you think you might get a hit. And thank you."

Joanne glanced at her watch. "Offices are closed, so the usual crowd is gone. I'm going with you. If you're putting your job on the line, so am I. Done. Let's go."

◆ ◆ ◆

People were lined up outside the correctional facility, waiting to go in for visits. Joanne pushed the white buzzer on the front door and waited. Russell was behind her. Her hands were stuffed in her pockets, her head down. She'd pulled her hair back tight from her face and removed all traces of makeup and jewelry, then changed into a black shirt and pants. No sequins, no designs. Nothing to remember.

Officer Parker opened the door. "Hey, Russell, what's going on?" He moved to let them into the cramped entryway. "Who're you here to see?"

"Marie Saunders. She didn't bail, did she?" he asked.

"Hell no. See the news vans on your way in? Lawyers and cops have been here all day. Which one is she?" He pointed at Joanne.

Russell forced himself to smile. "She wants to be both, actually. A newbie following me. Saunders up in Two North?"

Parker nodded. "On close watch, suicide gown. High profile." He pointed to Joanne again. "Might be easier for her to get in to see her, so they don't have to get her dressed and all."

He opened the door so the two could go through to the lobby. Russell didn't recognize the officer at the front desk.

"Badges?" he asked.

"Crap, I left it in the car, but I'm with the Prosecutor's Office. And she's a paralegal, here to take notes for me."

The officer nodded. "I've seen you"—he indicated Russell—"in here before. Just give me your identification, then." They both obeyed. "And sign the book."

Just then, Russell's phone began to ring. He turned and pulled it from his pocket. He spoke for several minutes. "Go on up, Joanne. I need to take this—it's Juliette. She has an idea. I'll meet you upstairs. Second floor. Ask the center officer."

Joanne took the visitor's pass handed to her and went through the slider doors. She glanced back and caught Russell's eager, frustrated expression before the door slammed shut behind her.

Joanne was seated in a locked room within the women's unit, empty except for a few tables and two chairs. The walls were cream colored, dingy, and marred with the occasional dent. The results of some altercations could be seen in the various holes and cracks in the plaster. Marie finally appeared, her dark hair greasy, lank, plastered to her head; dark circles spread beneath her eyes. She was wearing a bulky, sleeveless quilted gown, held together with Velcro, and white sneakers—nothing else. She tried to balance on the plastic chair across from Joanne while keeping her legs closed to preserve her last bit of dignity. Joanne couldn't help but notice that even in this state, Marie had an imperious air—back straight, placid expression.

"Marie, I'm Joanne. I worked with Ava over at the courthouse."

Marie scanned her up and down.

"Ava's been missing for well over a week now. We've been looking for her—me and Detective Bowers. You're the last person that saw her alive. I know that for a fact. You might've even taken that death photo of her—your prints were all over the camera." Marie's expression didn't change, but her eyes widened. "And I really need to know what happened."

"And you think I'd tell you, if I knew?" Marie shifted in her chair.

"You've run out of friends. And your family has apparently turned on you. Have they even gotten you a lawyer?"

Marie was staring at a spot behind Joanne and seemed to be in a trance. "My mother doesn't know I'm here."

"But your sister does?" Joanne threw it out there, watching Marie's face carefully. Her expression barely moved. "She's alive? I'm pretty sure I saw her." Marie said nothing. "Help me a little and I'll call your mother. I'll do whatever you want."

Marie leaned closer to Joanne, and she couldn't help but notice the body odor, the breath. "I don't think you're going to be able to reach Anais. I've been trying for the past couple of weeks."

"So you're fine taking the fall for all of this. The dead man in Claire's house, Ava's death, then there's the string of Polaroid murders. Should I go on? You're looking at life, no parole." There was silence from the other end of the table. "They're not getting you a lawyer—Anais and Claire. So best of luck with a public defender." Joanne started to stand.

Marie became slightly agitated, shifting in the chair. "Look. I need you to go to the airport before it's too late."

"For what? Where at the airport?"

"I'd start with the international terminal, because she's headed for Paris."

"Claire?"

Marie kept her head down so Joanne couldn't read her expression. "She's meeting Anais there tomorrow morning, so I assume it's an overnight flight."

Joanne waved her hand at her. "Back up. I need to ask you some questions."

Marie folded her arms across her chest, holding the smock closed. She seemed to be thinking. "I'll give you a few minutes, but only because she deserves whatever she gets."

Ten minutes later Joanne raced down the hallway to the elevator bank, expecting that when she reached the lobby Russell would still be waiting there for her, but the lobby was empty. She spun in a circle, looking, and headed for the doorway.

"Ms. Watkins? We need your visitor's badge," the officer said.

She threw it on the counter and took her driver's license.

"Did you have a phone? Don't forget it in the lockers."

Joanne raced to the booth—the locker key was shoved into the pass-through. Her mind was racing, her fingers fumbling to get the lock open. "Shit," she muttered.

She grabbed her phone, tossed the key back into the slot, and ran for the door. "Russell, where are you?"

Once outside, she turned on her phone and watched the apple appear on-screen. "Come on. Come on." She scanned the sidewalk while she waited for her phone to load. No sign of Russell. She dialed.

"Russell, where are you? Doesn't matter. Get your ass to the airport," she said.

"I'm in my car now," he responded. "I came back to get a bottle of water while I waited for you. Come on."

"I'm not coming with you. To the airport. I can't."

"Yes you are. I'll pull onto Federal Street—"

"No, Russell. I'll Uber it home. Just listen to me for two minutes and you'll understand." She spilled her conversation with Marie and ended the call with "Hurry up. I'll see you at my house. Keep your phone on."

CHAPTER 68

The times before all this happened, before all the photographs, the murders, before Ava disappeared, seemed so long ago. The normalcy of having a beer at happy hour at the Victor and then stopping by Cooper on his way home to see Juliette seemed hazy and distant. He felt like Dorothy swooped up by a cyclone and plopped down in Oz.

He tried to remember what his relationship with Ava was like before. When he just knew her first name. She'd walk the halls with a folder under her arm, or wait for the elevator, head down, tapping a pen against her thigh. She never seemed to belong, but he couldn't say why. *Taciturn, cold, distant*, those were the words used to describe her, but she wasn't any of those things to him. She was more like a set of blinds with slats that would open or close abruptly and apparently for no reason. She'd brighten, the green eyes laughing, and it was normal. But then those slats would twist shut, cutting her off from everyone. Bright and dismal, sweet and sour—whatever the description, it left her an enigma, ethereal.

A child of abuse or trauma? he wondered. Maybe mildly physically abused by Claire, a slap there, a pinch here, but then emotionally abused on top of it. Had her life been torment, growing up? All that moving from town to town, never fitting in? Never having one person to count on? Except Anais. She'd spoken so beautifully about her grandmother. One day they'd shared a bench outside at lunch and talked about Cherbourg. He'd listened and watched her face. It genuinely lit up. Her grandmother was that light that kept her moving forward, and Claire had been abject darkness that trapped her in silence.

Claire. Smart. Chic. Capable. Why had she never married? She was attractive, from what he'd seen. She was also educated and independent. Her life seemed odd the way it had played out. Ava had called her a bitch, and he was sure that was true. But was she a bitch to everyone? To Marie too? He had no information to go on. The little Ava had told him suggested the sisters got along, or at least cooperated with one another to a certain point. A complicated family, filled with lies, secrets, sabotage, and mental illness.

He slid into a short-term parking spot and jumped out of his car. When he entered the terminal at the Philadelphia International Airport, most of the people were collecting near the British Airways kiosk. No one stood out. He wandered from one end to the other, casting an eye over the queues. His heart was jumping; he knew his time was dwindling. Qatar Airways had only two people waiting to check in for a flight to God knows where. He had no choice but to buy a ticket to get through security, so he fished through his wallet for a credit card.

"Hong Kong is our next flight out," the woman said. "You have a little under an hour, so you need to hurry. Flexible fare, two thousand three hundred forty dollars." She took his credit card. "But do you need flexible if you're here? I mean, it's costing you almost a thousand dollars more."

"Yes, flexible. I might change my mind in the next hour."

"A man who isn't sure what he wants but travels light getting there?" She was mildly flirting with him. When she saw his confused expression she added, "No luggage?"

"No. No luggage." His eyes weren't on her. He hadn't stopped looking through the lines for a familiar face.

He knew, once he'd passed security, to look in British Airways, Lufthansa, or Delta gates. Marie had said she'd be headed to Paris. But for all he knew, she might detour to Milwaukee first to throw everyone off. And he knew that international flights also departed from other terminals. The futility of it made him almost stop in his tracks and give up.

He flopped down in a chair at an empty gate. His eyes were glued to the people as they passed. *She's here somewhere. Keep walking.* He was so absorbed in his task he almost didn't hear his name being called over the loudspeaker. His flight to Hong Kong had boarded and he wasn't on it. *Crap.* It just announced his presence—and if she were smart, she'd recognize it and hide. Could this get any worse? He pushed himself up when he saw the bar across the aisle. A small nothing bar with a large counter and a few tables in the back. A win-win. If she wasn't there, he could get a drink, keep an eye on passersby, and figure out step two hundred.

He ordered a Sam Adams and took a seat at the counter, turned slightly toward the entrance so he could watch people come and go. He was reaching for his phone to call Joanne when he saw a woman with dark hair seated at a table, almost out of sight. When she turned slightly he saw her face.

The waiter was at her table. "Another whiskey neat, please, and a glass of water," she said.

"Water for me too, please." Russell slid into the seat next to her. "Going somewhere so soon? And without Marie?"

She smoothed her hair and tucked a piece behind her ear. She tried to contain her shock but didn't succeed. "What?" Her face burned red.

"Surprised I found you?"

The waiter brought their drinks and walked away. "You're a detective," she commented. "I should have figured you would put it together." She glanced around. "But you're alone? No entourage to arrest me?"

He wrapped his hand around the beer bottle and ignored her question. "Tell me why you did all this. I need to hear it from you."

"Which part do you want to hear? Why the chase? Why the killing? Why am I not dead?" The loudspeaker announced his name again. *Last call for flight to Hong Kong.* She smiled. "That's you? Hong Kong. Go."

"I'll pass. You were saying?"

"The woman murdered with the priest. She was a person. Just like you or me. Murdered for no reason." She motioned around her. "The fact that she was alone, no family, no one came for her body, makes it worse. Killed and stripped naked, humiliated—"

"And I assume this happened to her because she stumbled in on the killing of the priest?"

"I assume you're right. But maybe she had a child with her. And maybe those four men were going to kill the child too—because she was a witness." She turned to him. "Maybe they tried to kill her but one of them grabbed her—"

Russell tilted his head to the side. "That's why you were on the run? They were looking for the child?"

"Quinn was, anyway. The rest, maybe not so much." They were both quiet for a few seconds. "Do you know where the woman's body is?" He shook his head. "In an unmarked grave, in a cemetery near Port Richmond, here in Philadelphia."

"So why not make her name known, if that's what you wanted? Expose Connelly, Owens, Saunders, and Quinn. Give her a headstone. Bring flowers. Why all this?"

She snorted. "That's a great idea. And maybe I did go to Connelly just to talk, you know, sort it out. Get her name. I thought about going to Ross first, but he would have created a stir—calling family members. You know."

He sipped his water, his beer almost untouched. "And?"

"And maybe even though Connelly was a priest—and I thought the most compassionate of all of them—he wasn't much for repentance. No apologies. No remorse. No information. More worried about his own skin. He even threatened me." She turned to him, her face lit with rage as if it were happening all over again. "And maybe it set something off inside me. I'm a daughter of hypocrisy and secrets. So I settled it the way I knew how." She left the rest unspoken. "Have you found her name?" Her eyes were large and hopeful.

He shook his head. "Not yet. I have a few leads—"

"That you will eventually find it means everything, even if I'm not around to see it. Her family will come for her, take her back where she belongs."

Russell looked at her. This was all she'd wanted. Something that most people take for granted. A name. Trying to put right something she had nothing to do with twenty years ago. And no one would help her. And that set her off on a quest for information that led to at least six deaths. "Did Marie know what you'd done? Did Anais? Did—"

She tipped her head back and swallowed her whiskey in one gulp. "I have"—she checked her watch—"two hours and twenty minutes till my flight leaves. Every story has multiple sides. Let me tell you mine, because it's a doozy. And if, after that, you want to arrest me, I won't resist."

He felt her eyes on him, but he couldn't lift his head. The vein in his neck was throbbing, and it was everything he could do to control his anger. "You only have two hours. Start talking, Ava."

CHAPTER 69

The plane touched ground at Charles de Gaulle, the wheels skidding to a stop across the tarmac. I peered out the window for any sign of *policiers* but only saw multiple aircraft and airport personnel working in the dismal morning gray. Anais was there somewhere, in one of those buildings, waiting for me. If I could make it through customs, and Paris, my chances of escape would be certain. I took a breath. Three more steps to freedom.

Russell's questioning had been methodical, predictable. And thorough—with a layer of anger and betrayal on top. I'd chosen him well that day I saw him standing at the elevator banks on the second floor of the courthouse. He'd been motionless and preoccupied when I spotted him, but I saw the seriousness in his posture and the softness around his eyes. I'd scanned him up and down until he caught my eye and then I smiled. Bingo. It only took three days for him to approach me again when I was getting coffee.

Getting an able body—somebody capable of getting the investigative ball rolling, to ultimately put a name to my mother—that's what I'd wanted. That's what I'd been searching for. Years of not knowing who I was, who she was, with just threads of memory to guide me. The killing, the blood, the turmoil were vague in my mind. I'd begged

Claire and Marie for the truth, but they'd never budged, insisting they knew nothing.

I needed someone who was sympathetic to me, who would see me as a lost soul, someone who would do this for me off the record, compromising their own career in the process. That was key. A compromised career gave me leverage for blackmail.

After I returned home from college, I'd scoured Claire's house for information, possible only because she was sick. But all I'd found was the photograph of the house. The photograph I'd sent to Ross nearly five years earlier. What did it mean that Claire had separated it from his things and slid it in with my dress? Had she suspected the lengths I'd gone to for the truth? If she had, it had only made her hold on to what she knew more stubbornly, right up until the end.

But I'd still made use of the photo. The inscription that referenced me was irresistible, filled with coincidence, intrigue. I knew Russell would go for it with a little push from Joanne. The meeting at the diner—mustering hurt and tears. He went for it. Deep. Maybe too deep in those weeks following. I had to play my role carefully.

The customs line was long and thick with commotion and conversation, my ears assaulted by at least five different languages. My mind flipped back and forth, making sense of fragments of English, then French, then English again, Spanish, bits of some eastern European language. The rest of the sounds floated past me untranslated. I gripped my passport in my hand, my fingers aching. It was good, official, issued by the US government, but I wasn't sure if it had been flagged since I'd boarded my nonstop flight from Philadelphia. Russell's face, or, more specifically, the flickers in his eyes as I'd told my story, worried me.

After our talk he'd walked me to the gate, his hands in his pockets, and stood near me as they called for boarding. He didn't touch me or hug me. He kept distance between us. I wondered why he felt the need to see me get on the plane. I suspected that it had more to do with wanting to be rid of me than wishing me off with blessings. Had he chosen to accept my explanations? Maybe only because the alternative was so obviously career devastating. I would never know. His actions and demeanor never betrayed his thoughts.

As I moved forward in the line toward French Immigration now, I was aware of officers standing in available corners, hypervigilant; the airport crackled with the tension of the possibility of untoward events. I smiled. I was the untoward event. The line crawled forward and I kept checking my watch. Anais was meeting me on the bottom level, near ground transportation. From there we were headed on a train leaving for Barcelona. Then we'd board a cruise ship that would be at sea for seventeen days, hitting ports in Spain, France, then Italy, Croatia, Montenegro, and Greece. She'd mapped it out—with multiple ports of call, I could jump off anywhere along the journey, though the Balkans were an obvious choice, and catch a flight to Vietnam. It had all been well planned, so why was I so nervous?

"Venez ici." The man was waving his arm to me and I stepped forward to the counter. He opened my passport and scanned the documents, his head down, concentrating. I shifted my weight, almost afraid to breathe. His eyes flitted upward to meet mine. *"Où êtes-vous née?"* he asked. *Where were you born?* Why was he asking when it was clearly printed on my passport?

I hesitated. *United States.* The forgery man had given me what he thought was a well-known French name. His idea of a little joke. How should I answer? *"États-Unis,"* I mumbled.

"Marie Curie?" he asked. I was afraid he'd question it, as it was so blatantly stupid. I merely nodded. How long would I be in France and where was I going to be staying, he asked in French. "Do you need me to speak English?" he continued after several moments of silence.

"Non, ce n'est pas nécessaire. Je vais à Barcelone en passant par la France. C'est un voyage spontané, donc je n'ai pas de dates exactes," I blurted. He smiled. His shoulders relaxed. He seemed surprised and pleased that I didn't need him to translate into English. I'd explained

I was traveling to Barcelona but the dates I would be in France were not exact.

He stamped my passport, waved me through, and motioned for the person behind me to move forward. One hurdle completed. I walked faster to retrieve my luggage and get out of the airport. Anais's gray head was there, in the crowd, her carefully arranged curls around her face. Her dark coat and outrageously expensive purse flung casually over her shoulder. She smiled wide when she saw me.

"You made it. Where's Marie?" She kept looking behind me as if her remaining daughter would magically appear.

"Grand-Maman, that's another story. I will explain as we go. Let's get a taxi." I started to turn away.

The old woman gripped my arm. I felt her iron fingers pressing into my flesh through three layers of clothing. "I just had this feeling something was wrong. What happened to her?"

"She was detained, sorry to say, but that'll all be cleared up soon, I'm sure." I couldn't tell her I'd set Marie up. Not yet.

CHAPTER 70

Joanne stared at Ava's death photo. It looked so real, but she had to have taken it herself. The eyes were vacant, but then maybe that's because there was nothing in her soul to begin with. The longer she stared the angrier she became. *She lied to us. Used us.* Marie's face had been completely vacant of expression too, Joanne had noticed, during their brief jail conversation. Her voice didn't betray any emotional connection to the fact she was confined in a six-by-six cell, while sitting straight-backed on the plastic chair.

Joanne stood up and started to pace. Russell was at the airport—he would catch her; he had to. She imagined his reaction, how surprised and angry he'd be that it hadn't been Claire after all—just dear, sweet, conniving Ava. Her mind flashed to memories of Ava and Joanne's son sitting side by side at the kitchen table, building something with Legos. How could any of this be true?

She was steeling herself for Russell's devastation, her anxiety increasing as the seconds ticked by. Moments later she heard the familiar sound of his car engine pulling up in front of her house. She sat and put her hands in her lap, her head down. She heard the door open and then shut, footsteps across the hardwood floor.

When she didn't hear any words for almost a minute, she looked up. Russell was standing in front of her, hair tangled, eyes wild, hands in his pockets.

"I guess you finally found her, huh? Where is she?" She looked past him, almost thinking she might see Ava lingering in the doorway in handcuffs.

"In the air somewhere over the Atlantic. Joanne—"

She was on her feet. "No. No. You were too late? You missed her? How?"

"The plane was lifting off the tarmac by the time I got through security." He dropped a paper on the coffee table. "I had to stand in line for half an hour to buy a ticket so I could try and catch her at the gate."

She picked the paper up. "Returnable, I hope?"

"Yeah, returnable."

"Are you effing kidding me? She's gone? Call now and have her detained when she lands. Where's she landing?"

"Direct to Cuba."

Joanne was quiet for a few moments. "Cuba? Seriously? Land of Fidel and the Bay of Pigs?"

Russell shrugged. "Quick direct flight. Impossible to track her from there. No extradition or cooperation to be had."

Joanne grabbed the dead-Ava picture from the coffee table and crumpled it in her fist. "Shit."

His face flushed.

"You know what I think?" She watched him carefully. "I think there was no direct flight to Cuba. I think you saw her, talked to her. I think you made a choice to let her go." She grabbed her phone. "I'm going to call the airport to just see what flights were going out—"

"Stop." Russell walked to where she stood and took the phone from her hand.

Her eyes shot daggers at him. "You know, it never occurred to me that at some point you'd turn on me. What happened? Did Ava eat your soul while waiting for her flight?"

Russell shook his head. "No, she ate my brain." He dropped down onto the sofa next to her. "And the whiskey didn't help either."

"I think you have about thirty seconds to start talking before I throw you out of my house."

He half turned toward her. "From the beginning, this didn't make any sense. Something was off. I couldn't get to it exactly, but it was there."

"Yeah, Ava was bullshitting us the whole time. That's what was off. Then she ran off, leaving us to believe she was dead and that Claire was alive."

"Yes, she did have us running in circles. But why'd she drag us into this in the first place?"

Joanne stood up and rubbed the fronts of her thighs. "I need coffee. You want some?"

He nodded and readily accepted the mug filled to the brim, taking a large sip before he spoke again. "Ava isn't random or careless or stupid. She wanted a cop involved, and you were a conduit to a cop." Joanne felt her face crumple at those words. Russell reached out and touched her arm. "I mean, that's not all you meant to her. Just in terms of this case."

"So why'd she need a cop? If she took all the pictures, and did all the killing—and I'm assuming she did—wouldn't that be risky?"

"Not if she was planning on disappearing anyway. And not if she thought she could control the cop."

"Control you? She's not that dumb."

He propped his chin up with his hands. "Maybe not so dumb, she did a pretty good job of it. But I think this all served a larger purpose. Getting me to find out her mother's name. That's what this has all been about. That's what everything was about."

Joanne said nothing. Her mind was whirling the pieces of the puzzle around, trying to make them fit. Then she stood up and put the cup on the coffee table. "So Claire knew she was killing people?"

His fingers were steepled, the tips just touching. "I think she figured it out when Ross died. That's why she made her come home from Montreal. To keep an eye on her. Make her stop."

Joanne put her head down and laced her fingers over the top of it. "Makes no sense. Why pretend she was Claire?"

Russell stood up. "That's the funny part. I'm not sure it was intentional, at least at first. She said she grabbed the big coat because it was like a blanket. Warm. The only phone she had was Claire's that she found in the desk drawer in the office. I'd taken hers by that point. She called her own phone, thinking Marie had it. But you called back. And then I called her."

"So why'd she go out to the Owenses' house that day, acting like she had no idea what happened there? I don't get it."

He shrugged. "To get the ball rolling with us, to play the legitimately confused victim, to draw Quinn out. You pick."

"That fucking bitch."

He had no answer. "You asked me how I could let her go? I begged her not to get on that plane, but not for the reasons you think. Either way—stay or go—she's doomed. I let her go to save you. Both of us, really."

Joanne's eyebrows shot up. "How's that?"

"If I detained her, she was going to take us down with her—all the withheld information, interference in a criminal investigation, obstruction of justice. We would have been arrested, and you might have been sitting right next to her in the county jail."

"So how do you figure she's doomed by traipsing off to Europe or wherever? First class, I assume."

"One, because Marie will have a high-powered attorney making bail as soon as her mother knows she's in jail. Seven hundred and fifty thousand cash. And trust me, Marie's going after Ava as soon as she gets a chance. And two, because Ava's walking into a trap she made for herself. Anais will never accept that she's killed six people, including her grandfather, just to get her mother's name. There's no way out for her."

CHAPTER 71

The water was rough; the Mediterranean Sea rocked the long boat until my already-twisting stomach felt ready to empty itself. I was a bundle of nerves, looking over the itinerary every ten minutes, trying to decide where to jump ship. It would be almost seventeen days until we hit the Balkans. Kotor, Montenegro, might be my last stop, but enduring seventeen days on this ship was going to be difficult.

Anais had been quiet since the airport. She hadn't asked me about Marie or about why I'd needed to flee the States so suddenly. Her silence was like a storm in the distance—I could see dark clouds gathering but could only watch and wait. She had some plan, I was sure, and the whats and hows were putting me on edge—paranoid. The only thing I knew for certain was that I needed her to willingly hand over the bank account she'd set up for me and the money she'd put in it—that was key, if I was going to get away from this situation and figure out where my new life would begin.

I heard the door open but didn't turn around to see her come in. I was too busy taking in the clear crescent moon from our balcony deck chair. She slid into the seat next to me, the jangle of her bracelets hitting the armrest. She swung her feet up. I smelled a hint of liquor on her before she even opened her mouth.

"So, tomorrow we hit Toulon. Do you know where you might be getting off this ship?" Anais asked.

I gave a slight shrug. "Not France. So you're stuck with me for a few more days."

"Two days in France, then three stops in Italy. Take your pick." Her lips curled upward. "You've been so quiet since we've been on board. You didn't want to eat in the dining room? Or have drinks with me?"

"I'm not hungry, Grand-Maman." I tried not to look at her.

"You don't look well. Those dark circles under your eyes are taking over your face. And maybe they should." She turned her head and a glint of light hit her diamond earrings, scattering a prism across the balcony. This woman had been my heart and soul at one time. My grandmother, mother, protector, teacher. "Why is that? Guilt? Guilt has a funny way of chewing up the soul. Are you feeling guilty, Ava?"

Was I? Nervous, impatient, angry, on edge—all those fit better.

"Where's Marie?" Anais asked. "I've been patient but I really need to know—right now. I haven't been able to reach her."

Here we go. "She stabbed my forgery man. She's in jail."

Anais shot upright, glaring at me. "In jail? For murder? And you waited a day and a half to tell me?" She started to stand. "I need to get her out of there."

"It wasn't my fault, Grand-Maman. The police grabbed her right before I left Philadelphia."

Whenever Anais was angry, her French became more rapid and clipped. I could barely catch the meaning of her next words. "She couldn't reach me by phone so she mailed a letter last Thursday to the house. I got it before I met you at the airport, when I went home to pack a few things."

"What's it say?" I felt my pulse rise. Marie was sitting in a filthy jail cell three thousand miles away and she was still messing with me. "Did she tell you she and Quinn choked me in the woods? Working together,

I might add. That she left me for dead? Did she tell you that in her little letter? Or did she leave that out?"

"She said Quinn came to her and forced her hand. That it was because of her that you're still alive."

"Pffft" was all I could manage.

"She said she tried, Ava. She tried to help you after they left you in the woods—leaving you a knife to cut the tape, your purse. And your car. Not to mention the precious camera you tried to steal from her closet."

"She wasn't doing me a favor by leaving the camera. She hit me with it when she saw I had it. And it was a letter opener she dropped next to me, not a knife. My purse was soaked and ruined, but yes, there was cash in it. I lay in those woods, bruised and beaten, tied up for two days before I could get myself out. No food or water. Animals running around me. She had no clue if I was dead or alive, so now she did me a favor?"

"She didn't let Quinn kill you, so yes—"

"She just let him cut me, kick me in the head—"

She whipped around to face me. "I'm not saying it was right, but Marie's always held on to some romantic image of her father and what he did years ago, so it doesn't surprise me it came to this, but I doubt she wanted you dead." She waved her hand at me. "You survived."

"Really? I survived?"

"So tell me why you're pretending to be dead to everyone, Ava? Why this plan to take a cruise and disembark? It's a little dramatic."

I stared out the window. "If I'm dead, they won't come looking for me, so maybe Marie did do me a favor there after all, leaving the camera with me. It all worked out."

"Who's looking for you? All four men are dead—including your grandfather."

I looked at her sharply. What had Marie told her? "You haven't given me any details of where the money is," I said. "What bank. Where do I go when I land in Hanoi?"

"We have many days still to talk about that."

The old woman stood up and went into the cabin. I heard her lift the phone and place an order. When she came back she seemed charged and determined. "You look like you haven't had a bite in days—I ordered you a little something. And then I want to hear your side of what happened."

I thought for a fleeting moment about how easy it would be to jump from the boat and swim toward the lights. The air was warm, thick, and salty, and I wondered if the Mediterranean Sea was the same. How far were those lights?

"Marie said some things in the letter," she said, "and I haven't been able to sleep since. This family is in shambles. When you first came to us—"

"Please don't—"

"I begged my daughters to turn their father in to the police. To turn you in to social services. And I made some decisions—decisions to not let all of you live with me, not give them money to buy their way out of this—so I'm to blame, in a way, for some of this."

What she was saying was true, and I didn't know how to respond. At any point along the way Anais could have ended this by letting us all come to France. Quinn never would have followed.

"I thought they'd give in at some point," she continued. "I was beyond angry at Ross for pulling my daughters into the middle of his mess with that disgusting little priest. But time passed—"

"Grand-Maman—"

"And now Claire's dead. Ross is dead. You, for all intents and purposes, are dead too. So what did all this get me?"

"What did Marie say in her letter? Can I see it?"

Anais's face turned a shade of red and then blanched. "She said Polaroids were taken after Ross and his friends died. That not only were they all murdered, but someone used that stupid camera I sent to Claire to take pictures afterward." Her head was down, her fingers kneading her forehead. "Ava, why?"

"She blamed me?"

"I've been sick about it, and I can't find an answer."

"No—"

"If you'd used any other camera I never would have known. But that camera I had altered only takes black-and-white. Terrible black-and-white pictures, at that."

There was a knock on the door. I got up and opened it, returning moments later with a tray of cheeses, two glasses, and a carafe of white wine. I poured one for Anais and then filled my glass to the brim.

"There's no other camera like it. Finding that little man in Cherbourg that tinkered with cameras, having him alter it, was a joke for Claire. A sentimental joke."

"I went to Bill Connelly. I did. I only wanted to know my mother's name so I could try and track down my family. But not only wouldn't he tell me, he threatened me. Another shitty priest. He threatened me, Grand-Maman. He called me names."

"So you killed him? My God, Ava."

I folded my arms as if I wanted to fold up into a ball and disappear. "It wasn't like that."

"It was exactly like that. And the Owenses? The man who was butchered with the hammer? Ava? You did that?"

"The one butchered with a hammer was the one who decided to stage the affair scene in the church after my mother was dead. He undressed her and put her next to that disgusting man. I overheard more than any of you realized, understood more, remembered more. It took me years to piece it all together. But they all deserved what they got."

She looked a sickly gray. "What's the matter with you? I raised you, almost. In the summers. This isn't possible. Ross saved you that night." She tried to stand up, but her legs were wobbly and she stumbled and fell back down into her seat.

"After he helped orphan me. And yet even when I begged him, when he knew what I'd done to the others, he still refused to tell me my mother's name. Why?"

She took a long drink and then held the glass in her lap. When she looked at me there were tears in her eyes. "And Claire?"

The wine burned going down my throat. The moments before Claire died, when she was in the emergency room, she'd been whispering to Marie. I couldn't hear it, but Claire had been looking at me. That minute between the two sisters kept me up at night.

She got up and staggered into the bedroom. I wasn't sure if it was the alcohol or if she needed to get away from me as fast as she could. I reached for the carafe and refilled my glass. Then I followed her. She was holding a letter—Marie's letter?—tightly between her fingers.

"I took Claire's body back to France not just to bury her but to have a real autopsy done. A thorough autopsy. And you know what they found?"

"What?" I felt my heart sink. I couldn't lose the love of this woman. I had to make her understand.

"An elevated potassium level that maybe is consistent with a heart attack. But Claire was a relatively young woman in good shape. It didn't add up. They also found some needle marks, very faint. Six of them on her upper right arm. One very fresh, like she was given a needle that very morning she died."

"You think I elevated her potassium or something? Stuck her with needles? Anais," I begged. "I was back and forth to the doctor's with her before she died. They were giving her B12 shots. You have to believe me. I didn't do this."

She leaned toward me, her face only inches from mine. "I think you'd been poisoning Claire for months. After you got back from college. That's why Claire was sick for so long, complaining of those headaches, tired all the time. But when pills didn't work, you escalated to injecting her. Six times?"

"No, no, no, no." I whipped my head back and forth and the tears fell, rolling down onto my cheeks. "Grand-Maman . . ." I couldn't have her believe this. I'd admit to everything else I'd done, but not this.

"At first I wasn't sure if it was Marie or you. I needed to stay away from both of you until I figured it out. But then I realized it had to be you—because she knew what you'd done? She'd threatened to turn you in? That's what I think. You destroy everything you touch."

I recoiled from her words. "You're wrong. I've admitted to the rest of it. But I didn't do this to her." I tried to put my hand on her, but she shoved me away.

"The truth, Ava."

"The truth is all I've ever asked for. So you try it, for a change. Tell me my mother's name."

There was sorrow in her eyes, genuine sorrow, but disgust too. "Is that where we are now? Will you kill me too? To get that woman's name? Am I your final victim?" I wanted to say something, but couldn't. "What difference did it make what her name was once you became one of us? We should have let those men kill you. You're more of a monster than they ever were." Anais pushed off the chair and went back out onto the deck. "You can go, stay. Get off at the next port, it doesn't matter. I will call the police. You'll take Marie's place in that filthy cell."

"I need you to understand." I felt the wine churning my stomach and thought I might throw up. I tried to hug her but she put out her hand. "Ross was an accident. I wanted to talk to him but he was too angry. And—"

"All you had to do was take what Claire gave you. Make a life for yourself." She wheezed and grabbed her chest.

"He called me a stupid little girl."

"I want you off this ship in the morning. There is a flash drive in my purse with the bank-account details. Take it, but I don't want to see you again."

"Grand-Maman, I'm the same person I always was." I searched for a memory. "Remember when you took me on the trip with you to Avignon? And you let me swim—" I grabbed her against her will and held her. She smelled of perfume, Chanel, like she always did. "Please don't hate me, Grand-Maman. I'm sorry."

"Hate you? I never want to look at you again."

The spray from those sputtered words sprinkled along my arm. I glanced up. This was over. No more waiting for Montenegro. The lights in the distance hadn't moved. It had to be land. One of the towns that dotted the Riviera. Marseille, maybe—though they were dim and probably much farther away than they looked.

I went back into the cabin and fished through her bag, then returned to the deck. "You're the only person I ever loved, Grand-Maman. Remember that."

I thought briefly of Russell and Joanne, and in that moment I felt twinges of sadness for what I'd put them through. Joanne had been simple, helpful, accepting. It had caught me off guard and drawn me in at the same time. And Russell had believed in me. He'd trusted me up until the end. And even in those last moments at the airport, he'd chosen to let me go. Given the right circumstances, he would have loved me. He did love me. If I showed up at their doorsteps now, they'd let me in, let me tell my story and maybe even forgive me. There weren't many people like that in the world.

In one quick motion, I climbed the deck railing. I knew the water would swallow me up and I wasn't going to live. But I wasn't living anyway. I'd traded my life for revenge—vindication for the mother who had sewn my clothes, who'd dragged me into a church seeking shelter.

I heard the splash and felt the water consume me, but it took a few moments to realize what I'd done. The drop was farther than I'd expected, and the sea slapping against my arms and legs made it hard to move at first. The water wasn't warm and salty at all. It was cold and heavy, weighing me down.

The boat pulled away quickly, leaving me completely in the dark. I saw Anais peering over the railing at me, stunned and confused, before she disappeared into the night. She'd always underestimated my resourcefulness.

I turned on my back and kicked wildly, heading toward the lights in the distance, feeling freedom or death was just within reach. One or the other was fine. Or maybe the truth was that to me, they were the same thing.

EPILOGUE

He rolled over at the sound of his phone and glanced at Juliette. She was deep within the covers, not stirring at the loud trill. Almost thirty-six hours on call had rendered her unconscious.

"What's up, Doug?" He got up and went into the bathroom, whispering as he moved.

"Are you sleeping? At five o'clock at night?"

"Just lying down with Juliette for a minute—"

"Listen, I thought you might be interested in this. Marie applied to leave the county and the country, special circumstances."

"What circumstances?"

"Her mother died. Two days ago, and I think the judge may let her go to manage things and attend the funeral. She only has two more months on parole and she's been a model inmate and parolee."

Russell put his back to the wall. "What happened to Anais?"

"Not one hundred percent sure but I think complications from a stroke. She'd been in the hospital for a couple weeks."

"Is that confirmed? No foul play?" His heart was starting to jump in his chest.

He heard Doug chuckle. "It's confirmed as much as it's going to be. Leave it alone, Russ, it all worked out. You and I still have a job, Marie had to sit in that filthy jail for months—"

"Not long enough."

"Listen, I just wanted to tell you Anais died and Marie's probably going to be allowed to leave the country. I didn't call to go over the Ava thing again. She killed six people. I'm sorry she jumped—"

"She jumped off a cruise ship to get away from something—God only knows what was going on. And I knew when I let her go at the airport she was going to die. I knew she was walking into a trap."

Doug sighed. "Don't say that out loud ever again—that you let her go. Again, she killed six people—maybe more."

Russell was thinking, saying nothing for a few moments. "She did. But—"

"No, no, no. I gotta go. I'll keep you posted. And rethink that Vietnam honeymoon thing. There's plenty of other places you two can go. You're not going to find her there. She's dead."

"I'm not looking for her."

"You're always looking for her. The over-the-water-hut thing is nice but they have them in Fiji too. Or Bora-Bora. They found Ava's body, Russell. Six months is long enough. Let it go. Say hi to Juliette. See ya."

He heard the line click off and stuffed the phone in his pocket. "They found the remains of *a* body. Not *her* body," he mumbled. "Off the coast of Turkey. How the hell could her body have ended up there?"

He went to his office and turned on the light. His notes were in the top drawer, handy at all times. He spread them out in front of him and scanned them, though he knew every detail by heart. Yes, it was the remnants of a female body that washed up on the shore near Foca, Turkey, four months after Ava jumped. A pretty far distance for a body to travel on the open sea, given she'd jumped ship off the coast of France.

A body that was little more than a skeleton—no hair or teeth. Initial DNA was inconclusive. They were awaiting results of more up-to-date short-chain DNA testing but weren't optimistic about getting results. Officials had tentatively identified it as Ava's remains due to threads of clothing still clinging to the bones—the black jeans and silver top matched what she was wearing when she jumped from the ship. The recovered body also had a healed fracture to the left femur that matched an injury Ava had sustained when she'd fallen off a swing at the age of ten.

He stared out the window, watching a squirrel climb the branches of an oak in the backyard. That was Ava, a squirrel. Nimble, crafty, shape shifting, always on the move, difficult to catch. Even his memories of her were elusive, fragments of their night together drifting to him in dreams. Her haunting green eyes, frightened, vulnerable, needy. *Sentir le sapin.*

He stood up at the sound of that voice in his head and put the file in his desk, slamming the drawer shut. Enough was enough. His wedding was weeks away. This chapter was over, and even if it wasn't, it was going to have to be. He couldn't start a new life looking over his shoulder.

He padded down the steps to the kitchen. Make coffee, figure out food for tonight if Juliette woke up and was hungry. Finish the application for Rutgers Law—a new challenge—and then start looking over the details of a new case they'd thrown in his lap the minute his suspension ended. He felt his phone vibrate against his leg and knew before he even looked at it that it was Joanne texting. Doug had called her, no doubt, and now she was all stirred up.

You need to come over here right now. Drop what you're doing. He took a breath and grabbed his car keys. Her house was dark when he pulled in up front, and his knocking on the door went to pounding and then to banging before he saw the edge of the curtain lift.

Joanne pulled him in and locked the door behind her. "Keep the lights off." She grabbed his arm, dragging him to the living room. "There." She pointed to the coffee table. "Get it out of here."

The Polaroid had been pulled out of a plain white envelope, no return address, mailed from New York, NY. He picked it up by the edge and studied it. He didn't know the door in the photograph but he imagined it was Anais's. The film was in color this time, the shape and size the same as any current Polaroid. A dark-green door, cottagey, with climbing roses and ivy visible around it. Underneath, written in dark ink: *Dans chaque fin, il y a un début. Ce n'est pas fini.* And then two dates next to it, the first of which Russell knew without checking would match the day Anais died. The second was three and a half weeks away. His wedding date.

"I already looked it up. It means, *In each end, there's a beginning. It's not over,*" she blurted. "And we can't say anything about this or it'll draw her here—one day I'll see some sort of bright camera flash going off through the front window, and then they'll find me dead from food poisoning or something."

Not only was Ava alive, she was toying with them, mountain lion and mouse. It would never end. Were he and Joanne safe? Would Ava show up at his wedding and sit in the back? Would he find her standing in front of his house one day? They'd found her mother's name months ago. He was convinced it was the right person. Ava had an uncle, aunt, plenty of cousins, and a grandmother who all lived near Brescia, Italy. Only miles from the store where her mother had purchased those shoes.

Her mother, only nineteen years old, had run away from home with her boyfriend and her two-year-old daughter. Nobody had heard from her after that. How she'd ended up in the United States, in Philadelphia, was a mystery. So was the boyfriend. He never came back to the area again and the family had assumed they were together. They positively identified her and even told a story about the day she'd bought the shoes. She'd gone shopping in Verona and visited her sister, who was working as a seamstress in a shop there. She spotted the shoes in a small storefront and begged her sister to lend her the money. Little did her sister know that she'd be murdered wearing those very shoes less than a year later.

"She said it's not over. What's not over? The killing? Her need to find out her real name? Why'd she put your wedding date on that picture? Is she coming? She's close by, Russell, I can feel it . . ." Joanne was breathing fast, her fists clenched at her sides.

Russell thought of Juliette curled up in her covers, alone and vulnerable, unaware of any of this. Easy prey. He jumped up and ran out the door. *In each end, there's a beginning? No, Ava, don't do it. Not again.*

ACKNOWLEDGMENTS

Many thanks to my children, Eva Elizabeth and Ian, who sacrificed numerous nights of my company so that I could put this story to paper. The evenings I spent with a computer in my lap, saying, "Just one more chapter," or "The edits are almost done," were ultimately for you. I want to make you proud.

To Caitlin Alexander, who has edited two of my books and counting. You took this book in shambles and created something coherent and readable, all the while making it seem simple. I could not have done any of this without you.

To Liz Pearsons, the acquisitions editor, who saw enough merit in my work and had enough faith in this story to sign not just one book, but a sequel as well. I am forever grateful to you.

Thanks to Kjersti Egerdahl, who pulled *The Book of James* from obscurity and started me on this path with Thomas & Mercer. I really saw myself as a writer for the first time because of you.

Many thanks to Shelley Brancato, who has always been my first editor, my first audience, and has given me her time, not to mention reams of paper—and her honesty, though not always what I wanted to hear, has made me a better writer.

To Dr. Peter Brancato, who has been hearing about this story for years, and always took the time to ask how my writing was progressing, who took brief snippets of time from telepsychiatry to give me plot ideas and advice.

And many thanks to Ellen Akins, the other Ellen, my mentor and editor, who started this book with me in the MFA program at Fairleigh Dickinson University. Your guidance allowed me to learn the ropes of the editing process and prepare myself for what was to come. I consider you one of the most gifted writers and I was honored to be a student.

To Yolanda Hughes, for endless encouragement and life coaching on the fly. The hours I've spent with you at the Camden County Jail, manning the mental-health office, will always bring a smile to my face. I appreciate you for your honesty in all things, and for always having my back.

Lisa Field, thank you for always giving me your ear, no matter what the topic, and for reading and saving the multiple copies of my work.

Thanks to the people on the Polaroid camera forum for providing more information than I could absorb about the history of instant cameras and film—makes, models, and picture size. I found a new love for Polaroids and even bought a 1950s Land Camera and ancient film because I am convinced I will produce one good picture.

And lastly, gratitude goes to Dr. Jim Varrell for allowing me to remain in his employ knowing full well that many hours at work were spent doing edits on this book.

ABOUT THE AUTHOR

Photo © 2017 June Day Photography

Ellen J. Green was born and raised in Upstate New York. She moved to Philadelphia to attend Temple University, where she earned her degrees in psychology. She has worked in a maximum security correctional facility in the psychiatric ward for fifteen years. She also holds an MFA degree in creative writing from Fairleigh Dickinson University. The author of *The Book of James*, Ms. Green lives in southern New Jersey with her two children.